FROM CHRISTMAS TO ETERNITY

BY
CAROLINE ANDERSON

HER LITTLE SPANISH SECRET

BY
LAURA IDING

Caroline Anderson has the mind of a butterfly. She's been a nurse, a secretary, a teacher, run her own soft furnishing business and now she's settled on writing. She says, 'I was looking for that elusive something. I finally realised it was variety, and now I have it in abundance. Every book brings new horizons and new friends, and in between books I have learned to be a juggler. My teacher husband John and I have two beautiful and talented daughters, Sarah and Hannah, umpteen pets, and several acres of Suffolk that nature tries to reclaim every time we turn our backs!' Caroline also writes for the Mills & Boon® Cherish™ series.

Laura Iding loved reading as a child, and when she ran out of books she readily made up her own, completing a little detective miniseries when she was twelve. But, despite her aspirations for being an author, her parents insisted she look into a 'real' career. So the summer after she turned thirteen she volunteered as a Candy Striper, and fell in love with nursing. Now, after twenty years of experience in trauma/critical care, she's thrilled to combine her career and her hobby into one—writing Medical Romances™ for Mills & Boon. Laura lives in the northern part of the United States, and spends all her spare time with her two teenage kids (help!)— a daughter and a son—and her husband. Enjoy!

FROM CHRISTMAS TO ETERNITY

BY
CAROLINE ANDERSON

Grateful thanks to Dr Jonathan Messenger for his help with the neurological issues, to James Woledge for pointing me in his direction, and to my editor, Sheila Hodgson, who over the years has tolerated with good grace my terminal inability to deliver on time. Thank you, all.

First published in Great Britain 2012
by Mills & Boon, an imprint of Harlequin (UK) Limited.
Harlequin (UK) Limited, Eton House, 18-24 Paradise Road,
Richmond, Surrey TW9 1SR

© Caroline Anderson 2012

ISBN: 978 0 263 89212 3

Printed and bound in Spain
by Blackprint CPI, Barcelona

Dear Reader

This is my 90th book, so I wanted it to be special—a little bit different. I've never shied away from tricky issues, and I love to read stories about relationships that have been dragged back from the brink, but this one proved challenging to write for many reasons.

It's so easy to take each other for granted, just to assume you're all going in the same direction, but what if you're not? And what if, just when you tackle that issue, something far, far bigger intrudes and puts everything into perspective?

This is the story of Andy and Lucy Gallagher: a couple with three children, a marriage in meltdown and a potentially life-changing disease that strikes when they're at their lowest ebb. Andy survives, but will he ever be the same? And can their love cope with the changes that follow?

I hope you find their journey as thought-provoking, moving and emotional to read about as I found it to write, and that you come out at the end believing, as I do, that love can conquer everything life throws at it if you want it to. And that, for me, is the key to the universe.

Love

Caroline

Praise for
Caroline Anderson:

'From one of category romance's most accomplished voices comes a beautifully told, intensely emotional and wonderfully uplifting tale of second chances, new beginnings, hope, triumph and everlasting love. Caroline Anderson's THE WEDDING OF THE YEAR is an engrossing, enthralling and highly enjoyable tale that will move you to tears and keep you riveted from the first page until the very last sentence. Moving, heartbreaking and absolutely fantastic, with THE WEDDING OF THE YEAR Caroline Anderson is at her mesmerising best!'
—*www.cataromance.com* on
ST PIRAN'S: THE WEDDING OF THE YEAR

'Photojournalist Maisie Douglas and businessman Robert Mackenzie have been more or less amicably divorced for almost two decades, but the upcoming marriage of their daughter, Jenni, stirs up old emotions on both sides. Very young when she married him, Maisie—pregnant and disowned by her family—was miserable living in Scotland with Rob's judgmental parents, and left after little more than a year. Maisie hasn't found another partner and neither has Rob. Can they find a way to trust each other again, after all this time? This lovely reunion romance is rich with emotion and humour, and all of the characters are exquisitely rendered.'
—*RT Book Reviews* on MOTHER OF THE BRIDE

CHAPTER ONE

'Hi, this is the Gallaghers' phone, leave a message and we'll get back to you.'

Andy glanced at the clock and frowned. Six o'clock? When did that happen? And of course she wasn't answering, she'd be feeding and bathing the children. Just as well, perhaps. He knew she'd go off the deep end but there was nothing he could do about it. No doubt she'd add it to the ever-growing list of his failings, he thought tiredly, and scrubbed a hand through his hair.

'Luce, don't bother to cook for me, the locum's bailed so I'm covering the late shift. I'll grab something here and I'll see you at midnight.'

He slid the phone back into his pocket and shut his eyes for a moment.

He didn't need this. He had an assignment to finish writing by tomorrow for a course he'd stupidly undertaken, but they were a doctor down and it was Friday night. And Friday night in A&E was best friends with hell on earth, so there was no way he could leave it to a junior doctor.

For the hundredth time he wished he hadn't taken on the course. Why had he thought it was a good idea? Goodness knows, except it would give him another skill that would benefit his patients—assuming he was still alive by the end of it and Lucy hadn't killed him.

He heard the doors swish open, and knew it was kicking off already.

'Right, what have we got?' he asked, turning towards the trolley that was being wheeled in.

'Twenty-year-old male driver of a stolen car versus brick wall.' The paramedic rattled off the stats while Andy did a quick visual check.

Not good. Hoping it wasn't an omen for the coming night, he gave a short sigh and started work. Again.

'Noooooooo! Oh, Andy, no, you can't do this to me!' Lucy wailed, and sat down with a plop on the bottom step.

A little bottom wriggled onto the step beside her, Emily's hip nudging hers as she cuddled in close. 'What's wrong, Mummy? Has Daddy been naughty?'

She gritted her teeth. Only her staunch belief in presenting a united front stopped her from throwing him to the wolves, but she was so tempted. He absolutely deserved it this time.

'Not naughty, exactly. He's forgotten he's babysitting you while I go out, and he's working another shift.'

'Well, he can't,' Em said with the straightforward logic of the very young. 'Not if he promised. That's what he tells us. "You can't break a promise." So he has to do it. Ring him and tell him.'

If only it were that easy. She stared at Em, her hair scraped into messy bunches that sprouted from her head at different heights. She'd tied them in ribbons and Lucy knew it would take an age to get the knots out, but she didn't care. Just looking at her little daughter made her heart squeeze with love.

'Go on, Mummy. Ring him.'

Could it be that straightforward?

Maybe.

She called him back, and it went straight to voice-mail. No surprises there, then. She sucked in a breath and left a blunt message.

'Andy, you promised to babysit tonight. I've got book club at seven thirty. You'll have to get someone else to cover.'

She hung up, and smiled down at Emily. 'There.'

'See?' Em said, grinning back. 'Now he'll *have* to come home.'

Lucy had her doubts. Where work was concerned, everything—everybody—else came second. She fed the children, ran the bath and dunked Lottie in it, then left the girls playing in the water while she gave the baby her night-time feed, and still he hadn't called.

She wasn't surprised. Not by that. What surprised her was that even now he still had the power to disappoint her...

It took an hour to assess and stabilise the driver, and just five seconds to check his phone and realise he was in nearly as much trouble as the young man was.

He phoned Lucy again, and she answered on the first ring.

'Luce, I'm sorry—'

'Never mind being sorry. Just get home quickly.'

'I can't. I told you. I'm needed to cover the department.'

'No. *Somebody's* needed to cover the department. It doesn't have to be you.'

'It does if I'm the only senior person available. Just get another babysitter. It can't be that hard.'

'At this short notice? You're kidding. Why can't you get another doctor? It can't be that hard,' she parroted back at him.

He sighed and rammed his hand through his hair again, ready to tear it out. 'I think a babysitter might be a little easier to find than an ED consultant,' he said crisply, nodding at the SHO who was waving frantically at him. 'Sorry, got to go. I'll see you later.'

Lucy put the phone down and looked into her baby's startlingly blue eyes. 'Oh, Lottie, what are we going to do with him?' she asked with a slightly shaky sigh.

The baby giggled and reached up a chubby fist to grab her hair.

'Don't you laugh at me,' she said, prising the sticky little fingers off and smiling despite herself. 'You're supposed to be asleep, young lady, and your daddy's supposed to be at home and I'm supposed to be going out to my book club. But that doesn't matter, does it? It doesn't matter what I want to do, because I'm at the bottom of the heap, somewhere underneath Stanley.'

The young black Lab, sitting by her leg doing a pass-able imitation of a starving rescue case, wagged his tail hopefully when he heard his name.

No wonder! Guilt washed over her, and she swallowed down the suddenly threatening tears.

'Sorry, boy,' she crooned, scratching his ears. 'I'm a rotten mum. Five minutes, I promise.'

She settled the yawning baby in her cot, fed the poor forgotten dog and then headed upstairs again to herd

Emily and Megan out of the bath and into bed. She'd try ringing round a few friends. There must be *some-one* who wasn't doing anything this evening who owed her a favour.

Apparently not.

So she phoned and apologised to Judith, and then changed into her pyjamas and settled down in front of the television with a glass of wine, a bar of chocolate and a book.

She might not be going out tonight, but she was blowed if she was working. Stuff the ironing. Stuff the washing up. Stuff all of it. As far as she was concerned, she was out, and it would all still be there in the morning.

Angry, defiant and underneath it all feeling a little sad for everything they'd lost, she rested her head back against the snuggly chenille sofa cushion and let out a long, unsteady sigh.

They'd had a good marriage once; a really good marriage.

It seemed like a lifetime ago...

The house was in darkness.

Well, of course it was. Even if she'd managed to get a babysitter, she'd have been back long ago. He pressed the remote control and the garage door slid open and slid shut again behind him as he switched off the engine and let himself into the house through the connecting door.

There was a bottle of wine on the side, a third of it gone, and the remains of a chocolate wrapper. The kitchen was a mess, the dishwasher hanging open, half loaded, the plates licked clean by Stanley.

The dog ambled out of his bed and came wagging

up, smiling his ridiculous smile of greeting, and Andy bent down and rubbed his head.

'Hello, old son. Am I sleeping with you tonight?' he asked softly, and Stanley thumped his tail against the cupboard doors, as if the idea was a good one.

Not for the future of their marriage, Andy thought with a sigh, and eyed the bottle of wine.

It was after midnight. Quite a lot after. And he still had to finish the assignment. God, he was tired. Too tired to do it, too wired to sleep.

He took a glass out of the cupboard, sloshed some wine into it and headed for the study. There was a relevant paper he'd been reading, but he'd given up on it. He'd just read it through again, see if it was any less impenetrable now than it had been last night.

Not much, he realised a while later. He was too tired to concentrate, and the grammar was so convoluted it didn't make sense, no matter how many times he read it.

He needed to go to bed—but that meant facing Lucy, and the last thing he needed tonight was to have his head ripped off. Even if it was deserved. Dammit, there was a note on his phone, and it was in his diary. How could he have overlooked it?

And would it have made any difference, in the end? There'd been no one to cover the shift when the locum booked for it had rung in sick, and he'd had to twist his own registrar's arm to get him to come in at midnight and take over.

He let out a heavy sigh, gave the dog a biscuit in his bed and headed up the stairs with all the enthusiasm of a French nobleman heading for the guillotine.

* * *

She'd heard the crunch of gravel under tyres, heard the garage door slide open and closed, heard the murmur of his voice as he talked to the dog. And then silence.

He'd gone into the study, she realised, peering out of the bedroom window and seeing the spill of light across the drive.

Why hadn't he come to bed?

Guilt?

Indifference?

It could have been either, because he surely wasn't *still* working. She felt the crushing weight of sadness overwhelm her. She didn't know him any more. It was like living with a stranger. He hardly spoke, all his utterances monosyllabic, and the dry wit which had been his trademark seemed to have been wiped away since Lottie's birth.

And she couldn't do it any more.

She heard the stairs creak, and turned on her side away from him. She heard the bathroom door close, water running, the click of the light switch as he came out then felt the mattress dip slightly.

'Luce?'

His voice came softly to her in the darkness, deep and gruff, the word slightly slurred with tiredness.

She bit her lip. She wasn't going to do this, wasn't going to let him try and win her round. She knew what would happen if she spoke. He'd apologise, nuzzle her neck, kiss her, and then her traitorous body would forgive him everything and the moment would be lost, swept under the carpet as usual.

Well, not this time. This time they were going to talk about it.

Tomorrow. Without fail.

He lay beside her in the silence of the night, listening to the quiet, slightly uneven sound of her breathing.

She wasn't asleep. He knew that, but he wasn't going to push it. He was too tired to be reasonable, and they'd end up having an almighty row and flaying each other to shreds.

Except they hadn't even done that recently.

They hadn't done anything much together recently, and he couldn't remember the last time he'd made love to her.

Weeks ago?

Months?

No. Surely not months.

He was too tired to work it out, but the hollow ache of regret in his chest was preventing him from sleeping, and he lay there, staring at the ghostly white moonlight filtering round the edge of the curtains, until exhaustion won and he finally fell asleep.

'Did he come home?'

'Not until very, very late,' she told Emily. 'Here, eat your toast. Megan's had hers.'

She painstakingly spread butter onto the toast, then stuck the buttery knife into the chocolate spread and smeared it on the toast, precisely edge to edge, her tongue sticking slightly out of the side of her mouth in concentration. When it was all done to her satisfaction, she looked up and said, 'So didn't you go at all? Even later?'

'No. It doesn't matter.'

'Yes, it does, Mummy. He broke a promise!'

She blinked away the tears and hugged her daughter. Their daughter. So like her father—the floppy dark hair, the slate blue eyes, the tilt of her lips—everything. Megan with her light brown curls and clear green eyes was the image of her mother, but Emily and Lottie were little clones of Andy, and just looking at them broke her heart.

Em was so straightforward, so honest and kind and loving, everything she'd fallen for in Andy. But now…

'Where is he? Is he still sleeping?'

'I think so. He came to bed very late, so I left him. What do you want to do today?'

'Something with Daddy.'

'Can we feed the ducks?' Megan asked, glancing up from the dog's bed where she was curled up with Stanley gently pulling his ears up into points. The patient dog loved Megan, and tolerated almost anything. 'Stanley likes to feed the ducks.'

'Only because you give him the bread,' she said drily. 'Yes, we can feed the ducks.'

'I'll go and wake Daddy up,' Emily said, jumping down off her chair and sprinting for the stairs.

'Em, no! Leave him to sleep—'

But it was too late. She heard voices on the landing, and realised Andy must already be up. The stairs creaked, and her heart began to thump a little harder, the impending confrontation that had been eating at her all night rearing its ugly head over the breakfast table.

'Daddy, you have to say sorry to Mummy because you broke a promise,' Em said, towing him into the kitchen, and Lucy looked up and met his stony gaze and her heart sank.

'I had no choice. Didn't Mummy explain that to you? She should have done. I can't leave people to die, Em, promise or not. That's my biggest promise, and it has to come first.'

'Then you shouldn't have promised Mummy.'

'I would have thought our marriage vows were your biggest promise,' Lucy said softly, and he felt a knife twist in his heart.

'Don't go there, Luce. That isn't fair.'

'Isn't it?'

His glance flicked over the children warningly, and she nodded. 'Girls, go and get washed and dressed.'

'Are we feeding the ducks?'

'Yes,' Lucy said, and they pelted for the door.

'I want to carry the bread—'

'No, you give it all to Stanley—'

'*Are* we feeding the ducks?' he asked when their thundering footsteps had receded, and she shrugged.

'I don't know. I am, and they are. Are you going to deign to join us?'

'Luce, that's bloody unfair—

'No, it's not. You're bloody unfair. And don't swear in front of Lottie.'

He clamped his teeth together on the retort and turned to the kettle.

'For heaven's sake, Lucy, you're being totally unreasonable. I didn't have a choice, I let you know, I apologised—'

'So that's all right, is it? You apologised, so it makes it all OK? What about our marriage vows, Andy? Don't they mean anything to you any more? Don't I mean anything? Don't we? Us, you and me, and the children we've had together? Because right now it doesn't feel like it. It feels like we no longer have a marriage.'

He turned and stared at her as if she was mad. 'Of

course we do,' he said, his voice slightly impatient as if her faculties were impaired. 'It's just a rough time. We're ridiculously understaffed at work till James gets back, and I'm trying to get this assignment done, but it doesn't mean there's anything wrong with our marriage.'

'Doesn't it? Just sleeping here for a few hours a night doesn't qualify as marriage, Andy. Being here, wanting to be here—that's a marriage, not taking every shift that's going and filling your life with one academic exercise after another just so you can avoid us!'

'Now you're really being ridiculous! I don't have time for this—'

'No, of course you don't, that would involve talking to me, having a conversation! And we all know you won't do that!'

He stalked off, shut the study door firmly and left her there fuming, the subject once again brushed aside.

He watched them go, listened to the girls' excited chatter, the dog whining until the door was opened, then trotting beside Lucy and the buggy while the girls dashed ahead, pausing obediently on the edge of the pavement.

They went out of the gate and turned right, and Lucy glanced back over her shoulder. She couldn't see him, he was standing at the back of the study with Emily's words ringing in his ears, but he could read the disappointment and condemnation in her eyes.

He'd been about to go out into the hall, to say he'd go with them, but then he'd heard Em ask if he was coming.

'No,' Lucy had replied. 'He's too busy.'

'He's *always* too busy,' Emily had said, her voice sad and resigned, and he'd felt it slice right through him.

He should have gone out into the hall there and then and said he was joining them. It wasn't too late even now, he could pull his boots on and catch up, they wouldn't have got far.

But he didn't. He really, really had to finish this assignment today, so he watched them out of sight, and then he went into the kitchen, put some toast in, switched the kettle on again and made a pot of coffee. His hand shook slightly as he poured the water onto the grounds, and he set the kettle down abruptly.

Stress. It must be stress. And no wonder.

He tipped his head back and let out a long, shaky sigh. God, he'd got some work to do to make up for this. Em's voice echoed in his head. *Daddy, you broke a promise.* After all he'd said to them, everything he believed in, and he'd let them down. Lucy should have explained to them, but frankly it didn't sound as if she herself understood.

Well, she ought to. She was a doctor, too, a GP—or she had been until they'd had Lottie. She was still on maternity leave, debating going back again part time as she had before, just a couple of sessions a week.

He didn't want her to go back, thought the children needed her more than they needed the money, and it was yet another bone of contention. They seemed to be falling over them all the time, these bones.

The skeleton of their marriage?

He pressed the plunger and poured the coffee, buttered his toast with Emily's knife and then pulled a face at the streak of chocolate spread smeared in with the butter. He drowned it out with bitter marmalade, and sat staring out at the bedraggled and windswept garden.

He couldn't remember when they'd last been out there doing anything together. June, maybe, when Lottie was three months old? He'd mowed the lawn from time to time, but they hadn't cut the perennials down yet for the winter, or trimmed back the evergreens, or cleared the summer pots and tubs. Lucy had been preoccupied with Lottie, and he'd been too busy to do anything other than go to work, come home to eat and then shut himself in the study until he was too tired to work any longer. If he'd made it into the sitting room so he could be with Lucy, he'd had the laptop so he could carry on working until he fell into bed.

He must have been mad taking on the course, but it was nearly done now, this one last assignment the finish of it. That, and the exam he had to sit in a fortnight. Lord knows when he'd find time to revise for that. Lucy was taking the kids away to her parents for half term to give him some time to concentrate, but he knew it wouldn't be enough, not if he was at work all day. And there was still this blasted assignment to knock on the head.

Refilling his mug, he took his coffee back into the study, shut the door and had another go at making sense of that overly wordy and meaningless paper.

Or maybe he should just ignore it and press on without referring to it. Then he could finish the assignment off this morning, and tonight he could take Lucy out and try and make it up to her.

Good idea.

* * *

'Don't cook for us, I'm taking you out for dinner.'

Lucy looked at him as if he was mad. 'Have you got a babysitter?'

'Not yet.'

'Well, good luck with that. Anyway, I don't want to go out for dinner.'

He stared at her, stunned. He'd bust a gut finishing off the assignment so he could spare the time, and now this? 'Why ever not? You like going out for dinner.'

'Not when we're hardly speaking! It's not my idea of fun to sit opposite you while you're lost in thought on some stupid assignment or other for a course you've taken on without consulting me—'

'Well, what *do* you want to do?'

'I don't want to *do* anything! I want you to *talk* to me! I want you to share decisions, not just steam ahead and do your own thing and leave us all behind! I want you to put the kids to bed, read them a story, give me a hug, bring me a cup of tea. I don't need extravagant gestures, Andy, I just need *you* back.'

He sighed shortly, ramming his hand through his hair. 'I haven't gone anywhere, Lucy. I'm doing this for all of us.'

'Are you? Well, it doesn't feel like it. It feels like you're just shutting us out, as if we don't matter as much as your blasted career—'

'That's unfair.'

'No, it isn't! You're unfair. Neglecting your children is unfair. When did you last put Lottie to bed?'

He swallowed hard and turned away. 'Luce, it's been chaos—'

'Don't give me excuses!'

'It's not an excuse, it's a reason,' he said tautly.

'Anyway, I'm around tomorrow. We'll do something then, all of us.'

'Are you sure? You aren't going to find something else to do?'

'No! I'm here. All day. I promise.'

'And I'm supposed to believe that?'

'Oh, for God's sake, I haven't got time for this. I've got work to do—'

'Of course you have. You always have work to do, and it's always more important than us. I don't know what the hell's wrong with you.'

This time she was the one who walked off. She shouldered past him, went into the utility room, shut the door firmly and started to tackle the ironing while Lottie was napping.

His phone rang just before eleven that night, while he was printing off the hated assignment. HR? Really?

Really.

'Oh, you're kidding, Steve! Not again.'

'Sorry, Andy. There isn't anyone else. James isn't back in the country until tomorrow, or I'd ask him. It's just one of those things. I'll sort a new locum first thing on Monday, I promise.'

He gave a heavy sigh and surrendered. 'All right— but this is the last time, Steve. And you owe me, with bells on.'

He hung up, and sat there for a while wondering how on earth he was going to tell Lucy. She'd skin him alive.

And deservedly so.

He swore softly but succinctly under his breath, stacked the papers together, clipped them into a binder and put the assignment into an envelope without even glancing at it. It was too late to worry. It had to be there on Monday, and it was already too late to post it. He'd email it, but the hard copy would have to be couriered.

He'd do that on Monday morning, but now he was working all day tomorrow there was no time for any meaningful read-through before he sent it on its way. He'd only find some howler and, frankly, at this moment in time it seemed insignificant compared to telling Lucy that yet again he wasn't going to be there for any quality time with her and the kids.

It was *not* a conversation he was looking forward to.

She was asleep by the time he went upstairs, and he got into bed beside her and contemplated pulling her into his arms and making love to her.

Probably not a good idea. He didn't have the energy to do her justice and he had to be at work in seven hours. Cursing Steve and the sick locum and life in general, he shut his eyes, covered them with his arm and crashed into sleep.

The alarm on his phone woke him long before he was ready for it, and he silenced it and got straight out of bed before he could fall asleep again. Hell, he was tired. He stumbled into the bathroom, turned on the shower and got in without waiting for it to heat up.

The cold shocked him awake, and he soaped himself fast, towelled his body briskly and then ran the razor over his jaw. His hand was trembling again, he noticed, and he nicked himself.

Damn. It was the last thing he needed. He dried his face, leaving a bright streak of blood on the towel, and pressed a scrap of tissue over the cut to stem the bleeding while he cleaned his teeth.

He went back into the bedroom, leaving the bathroom door open so he could see to get his clothes out without putting on the bedroom light. He didn't want to disturb Lucy—because he was hoping to sneak out without waking her? Probably, but it was too late for that, apparently.

'Andy?' she murmured, her voice soft with sleep. 'Are you OK?'

Was he? Frankly, he had no idea. He pulled clothes out of the cupboard and started putting them on, and she propped herself up on one elbow and stared at him.

'What are you doing, Andy? It's Sunday morning. We don't need to get up yet.'

'I have to work. Steve rang last night, and I promised to do another shift—'

'No! Why?' She shoved herself up in the bed, dishevelled and sleepy and so beautiful she made his heart ache, her eyes filled with recrimination and disappointment. 'Andy, you *promised* me! Why on earth did you agree? We don't need the money, but we need *you*. The kids need you. *I* need you.'

'And the hospital needs me—'

'So put it first. Again. As always. Go on, go ahead—if that's more important to you than us.'

'Of course it's not more important!'

'Then don't *go*!'

'I *have* to! There's nobody to cover the department.'

'So they'll have to shut it.'

'They can't. They can't close the ED, Lucy, you're being totally unreasonable.'

'Well, you know what you can do, then. Go, by all means, but don't bother coming home tonight, or any other night, because I can't do this any more.'

He stared at her, slightly stunned. 'Is that an ulti-matum?'

'Sounds like it to me.'

'Oh, Lucy, for heaven's sake, that's ridiculous! You can't make me choose!'

'I don't need to. Strikes me you already have. You come home after the children are asleep, you leave be-fore they're up—and when you're here in the evening, you're shut in your study or sitting behind your laptop screen totally ignoring me! What exactly do you think you're bringing to this relationship?'

'The money?' he said sarcastically, and her face drained of colour.

'You arrogant bastard,' she spat softly. 'We don't need your money, and we certainly don't need your at-titude. I can go back to work for more days. I'm going back anyway next month for three sessions a week. They've asked me to, and I've said yes, and Lottie's going to nursery. I'll just do more hours, more sessions. They want as much time as I can give them, so I'll give them more, if that's what it takes.'

He stared at her, shocked. 'When did they ask you? You didn't tell me.'

'When exactly was I supposed to tell you?' she asked, her voice tinged with bitterness and disappoint-ment. 'You're never here.'

'That's not true. I was here all day yesterday—'

'Shut in your study doing something more impor-tant!'

'Don't be silly. This is important. You should have told me. You don't need to go back to work.'

'Yes, I do! I need to because if I don't, I never get to have a sensible conversation with another adult, because you certainly aren't around! You have no idea what it's like talking to a seven month old baby all day, every day, with no relief from it except for the conversation of her seven and five year old sisters! I love her to bits, I love them all to bits, but I'm not just a mother, I'm a doctor, I'm a woman, and those parts of me need recognition. And they're sure as hell not getting them from you!'

He sucked in his breath, stung by the bitterness in her voice. 'Luce, that's not fair. I'm doing it for us—'

'No, you're not! You're doing it for you, for your precious ego that demands you never say no, always play the hero, always step up to the plate and never let your patients down. But you're a husband and a father as well as a doctor, and you're just sweeping all that under the mat. Well, newsflash, Gallagher, I'm not going to be swept under the mat any more. I don't need the scraps of you left over from your "real" life, and nor do your children. We can manage without you. We do most of the time anyway. I doubt we'll even notice the difference.'

He felt sick. 'You don't mean that. Where will you live?'

'Here?' she shrugged. 'I can take over the mortgage.'

'What, on a part-time salary? Dream on, Lucy.'

'So we'll move. It doesn't matter. All that matters is that we're happy, and we're not at the moment, so go. Go to your precious hospital if you really must, but you have to realise that if you do, you won't have a marriage to come back to, not even a lousy one.'

He stared at her, at the distress and anger and challenge in her eyes, and, for the briefest moment, he hesitated. Then, because he really had no choice, he turned on his heel and walked out of their bedroom and down the stairs.

She'd cool off. He'd give her time to think about it, time to consider all they'd be losing, and after he finished work, he'd come home and apologise, bring her some flowers and chocolates and a bottle of wine. Maybe a takeaway so she didn't have to cook.

And he'd make love to her, long and slow, and she'd forgive him.

Two more weeks, he told himself grimly. Just two more weeks until the course was finished and the exam was over, and then they could sort this out.

They'd be fine. It was just a rocky patch, everyone had them. They'd deal with it.

He scooped up his keys, shrugged on his jacket and left.

CHAPTER TWO

HE'D gone. Turned on his heel and walked out.

She'd heard the utility room door close, the garage door slide up, the car start. Slightly open-mouthed with shock, she'd sat there in their bed, the quilt fisted in her hands, and listened to the shreds of their marriage disappearing off the drive in a slew of gravel.

The silence that followed was deafening.

She couldn't believe he'd gone. She'd thought—

What? That he'd stay? That he'd phone the hospital and tell them he couldn't go in, his wife had thrown a strop and threatened to kick him out? Hardly. It wasn't Andy's style. If he didn't talk to her, he sure as eggs didn't talk to anyone else.

And he'd told Steve he'd do it, so it was set in stone. It seemed that everything except them was set in stone.

She felt a sob rising in her throat, but she crushed it ruthlessly. This wasn't the time for tears. She had the children to think about. Later, maybe, after they were in bed again, she'd cry. For now, she could hear Lottie chatting in her cot, and she pushed the covers aside and swung her legs over the edge of the bed, heading for her baby on autopilot.

She'd pack him some clothes—just enough to tide

him over, give him time to think about things—and drop them off at work. Maybe that would shock him to his senses, because something surely had to.

She walked into Lottie's room, into the sunshine of her smile, and felt grief slam into her chest. What had their baby done to deserve this?

'Hello, my precious,' she crooned softly. 'Oh, you're so gorgeous—come here.' She scooped the beaming baby up against her heart and hugged her tight. Delicious, darling child, she thought, aching for what was to come. The fallout from this didn't bear thinking about.

But Lottie didn't know and she didn't care. She was beginning to whine now, pulling at Lucy's top, and she took her back to bed and fed her.

She was still breastfeeding her night and morning, but she might not be able to keep it going, she realised with a sick feeling in the pit of her stomach, not if she had to get the girls ready for school and out of the door in time to get to work. She stared down, watching her daughter suckle, treasuring every second of this fleeting, precious moment.

The baby flung her little arm out, turning her head at a sound from the window, endlessly curious and distracted now her thirst was slaked, and Lucy sat her up in the middle of the bed and handed her a toy to play with while she packed a bag for Andy.

It seemed so wrong—so unnecessary! Why couldn't he see? Why couldn't he give them the time they surely deserved?

Damn. She swallowed the tears down, threw his razor and deodorant and toothbrush into a washbag, tucked it into the holdall and zipped it up. There. Done. She'd drop it in later, on their way out somewhere.

The zoo?

No. It was cold and rainy. Maybe she'd take them swimming to the leisure centre, to take their minds off Andy's absence.

Oh, help. She'd have to tell the girls something— but what?

That he was working? So busy working he didn't have time to come home, so he was going to stay at the hospital?

That was a good point. She had no idea where he'd stay, and she told herself she didn't care, but he might need to wear something at night. She unzipped the bag again, put in the emergency pyjamas which never saw the light of day and a clean dressing gown and the slippers his aunt had sent him for Christmas last year, and tugged the zip closed with a sinking feeling.

Christmas. It was only a little over two months away.

Would he be there with them for Christmas? What if he never came to his senses?

What if they simply didn't matter that much to him?

She choked down the sob and scooped Lottie up, carrying her and the holdall downstairs and putting her in the high chair with some toys while she put the bag into her car. He'd need his laptop, she realised, and went into his study to get it. She wasn't giving him an excuse to come back here tonight and try to win her round. They'd been married ten years now and she knew how his mind worked. No. He had to take this seriously.

There was a large brown envelope lying on the lid of his laptop, the address written in his bold, slashing script. His assignment, she realised. She frowned at it.

His writing was untidier than usual—because he was so tired? Probably. His fault, she told herself, crushing the little flicker of sympathy.

She put the envelope into the case with the computer, threw in the power lead and his flash drive, then remembered his mobile phone charger, as well, and took the case out to the garage.

By the time she got back into the kitchen, the girls were coming down the stairs, giggling and chasing each other into the kitchen.

Oh, lord, how to tell them?

'Morning, darlings.'

'Morning!' Emily reached up as she bent down and kissed her, then went and sat at the table, legs swinging. 'Mummy, what are we doing today?'

Megan's arms were round her hips hugging her, and she stroked her hair automatically and tried to smile at her daughters. 'I don't know. What would you like to do?'

'Can we feed the ducks with Daddy?' Megan asked, tipping her head back, her eyes pleading.

She hauled in a breath, her smile faltering. 'No, sorry, he's had to go to work.'

'But he said he wasn't working today!' Emily said, looking appalled. 'He *promised* us!'

'I know. He didn't want to go but they didn't have anyone else. And he can't let people suffer.'

The words had a hollow ring of truth, but she brushed them aside. He *could* have said no. They would have found someone, or if necessary closed the unit. Or he could at least have talked to her about it, instead of presenting it as a *fait accompli*.

'Actually, he's going to be so busy he's going to stay

at the hospital for a few nights,' she said, the lie sticking in her throat. 'So, anyway, I thought maybe we could go swimming after breakfast. What do you think? And then maybe we can get pizza for lunch.'

Their replies sounded fairly enthusiastic, but there was something missing, some extra sparkle and fizz, another dimension that should have been there.

Andy. Their father, her husband, the man who broke promises.

Don't go there!

'Right. Who wants what for breakfast?'

It was tedious and chaotic and half the people didn't need to be there.

Realistically, they could have got anyone to cover him, he thought grimly as he worked his way through the sprains and strains and fractures that yesterday's sporting fixtures had left in their wake. It was all basic stuff, the sort of thing that any half-decent doctor could deal with, and the thought made him angry.

'Right, you'll need to come to the Fracture Clinic to-morrow morning between eight and nine for assessment and a proper cast. Here's a prescription for pain relief.'

He scrawled his signature on the bottom, handed it over and walked out, shaking his head and rolling it on his neck. It ached, and he couldn't think clearly. He was so, so tired. Maybe Lucy was right. Maybe he should have just said no, and they would have had to close the unit. That might have made them sit up and take notice and get a bit better organised.

In the meantime, he needed a coffee. A strong one.

'Oh, Mr Gallagher, your wife dropped your case and

laptop off. They're behind here,' the receptionist said as he passed her.

He stared at her for a shocked half-second, then nodded. 'Yes—of course. Sorry, miles away. Could you stick them in my office?'

'Sure.' She eyed him thoughtfully. 'Mr Gallagher, are you OK?'

'I'm fine, Jane. I'm just tired,' he muttered, and then went behind reception. 'Actually I'll take them myself,' he said, and hoisting the bag and laptop case up, he headed for his office.

He could feel her eyes boring into him all the way, hear the speculation starting. Damn Lucy! Damn her for making it all so much worse than it had to be.

He shut the door, dumped the bags on the floor behind his desk and slammed his fist down on it.

How *dare* she! How dare she bring his things in like that and make a public spectacle of their dirty laundry?

He pulled his phone out of his pocket and speed-dialled her number. It went straight to answerphone. Screening his call?

'I've just been accosted by a curious receptionist who handed me an overnight bag,' he said shortly. 'What the hell do you think you're playing at? Call me!'

He cut the connection and threw the phone down on the desk in disgust.

She'd meant it. She'd really, really meant it.

He felt numb, and slightly sick. And homeless? Where was he going to stay?

Stupid. He should just go home, have it out with her, make a few promises—*and keep them*, his conscience prodded—and deal with it. Except he was angry— angry with Steve for asking him to cover again, angry with the whole locum situation, angry with Lucy for not being reasonable, but most of all angry with himself for letting it all get out of hand by not saying no. Not to mention taking on the course, which was the just the last straw on the back of this failing camel that was their marriage.

And it wasn't going to get any better until the course was over, until he'd sat the exam and could put the whole damn thing to bed. Then he could go back to Lucy and talk about this.

And in the meantime, they could have a cooling off period. Lucy could calm down a bit, so could he, and he could shut himself away somewhere and work so he had the slightest chance of passing the course, to make the whole thing worthwhile.

It was half term next week and Lucy had already arranged to take the children to her parents so he could revise in peace. So he'd check into a hotel, get the exam out of the way and then they could all get back to normal.

But first, they needed to agree on what they were telling the children, because the last thing he wanted was them thinking that their marriage was coming to an end when it wasn't—or at least, not if he had anything to say about it.

He pulled the telephone directory out of his drawer, looked up the number of a decent hotel chain which had a motel nearby and booked himself a room.

And then he went back to work, asked one of the nurses to bring him back a coffee when she came back from her break and took the next set of notes out of the rack.

* * *

The receptionist gave him a wide berth for the rest of the day.

He wasn't surprised. Gossip travelled like wildfire through hospitals, and even though there was nothing to know, really, he could sense the speculation.

He hated it. Hated that they were talking about him behind his back, hated that when he walked out at the end of the day carrying his bag and laptop case, he could feel eyes following him.

You're imagining it, he told himself, throwing the cases in the car and slamming the boot, still furious with Lucy. The motel was just a couple of minutes away, on the road into town, and he checked in and went straight to his room.

Clean, functional, with a kingsize bed, a sofa, a desk with a work light and a bathroom with a decent power shower, it was the generic hotel room. Everything he needed, but soulless and empty, because the only thing he really needed was his family.

His throat felt tight, and he swallowed hard and dumped the bags on the bed. She still hadn't called him. Why not? It was six o'clock. She'd be dealing with the children.

Fine. He'd go over to the indifferent restaurant, get himself something to eat and then come back here and work, otherwise this whole damn fiasco would be pointless.

She stared at the phone, her lip caught between her teeth, and psyched herself up to call him.

He was right. She shouldn't have dumped his stuff in reception. She'd been steaming mad with him, but she could as easily have put it in the boot of his car and sent him a text.

She owed him an apology for that, and he was right, they needed to talk about the children, to arrange a time for him to see them so they didn't feel cut off from him. That was the last thing she wanted.

Sucking in a deep breath, she dialled his number, and he answered on the first ring.

'This better be good, Lucy.'

'I'm sorry,' she said, before he could get another word in. 'I didn't think. I was just cross. Andy, we need to talk.'

'Yes, we do. You don't just kick me out like a damn cat and then publicly humiliate me in front of the entire department. You owe me more than that, whatever beef you might have with me. And you owe the kids more. They're at school with other staff members' children, and you know what hospitals are like, so what story are we coming up with so they don't end up being screwed over by this nonsense?'

'It isn't nonsense, Andy. Our marriage is foundering, and you have to start taking that seriously.'

'Oh, I take it seriously. Very seriously. I also take my job seriously, but the kids come first, even if it doesn't seem like it, and right now, I'm being pulled in so many directions I can't be reasonable about this. Of all the times to pick—'

'It's because of this time!' she interrupted. 'Precisely *because* of what's been going on! And that blasted course—'

'I don't want the children thinking there's a rift in our marriage, not until we've tried and failed to work it out, and I don't want that to happen under any circumstances, but I can't deal with this now. I'll do what you say, I'll keep out of the way, get this exam over and the course finished, and then we'll talk, but play fair and cut me some slack, Luce, because I'm so tired I'm at breaking point.'

His voice cracked, and she swallowed a sob. She nearly told him to come home, but what he said made sense.

'OK. We'll do that. I've told the children you're so busy at the hospital that you're going to stay there for a few days. We'll stick with that. I'm away with them next week anyway, so you can work undisturbed. And then after the exam, we'll talk about this. OK?'

He gave a ragged sigh. 'OK. I'll come round tomorrow night and see them for a few minutes.'

Her heart hitched, but she had no choice, and he was right. 'OK. Want supper?'

'No. And don't tell them, just in case I get held up. I don't want to break any more promises to anyone, so it's easier if I don't make them.'

Her eyes filled, and she nodded. 'All right. Well—get here if you can.'

'I will. And—oh, nothing. Doesn't matter. I'll see you tomorrow.'

The phone went dead, and she stared at it. What had he been going to say?

I love you?

Unlikely. He hadn't said it for ages. A year, maybe? She couldn't remember, it was so long ago.

She pressed her hand to her mouth, but the sob wouldn't stay down, so she buried her face in a cushion to stifle the sound and wept for the man she loved and might have lost...

* * *

He finished on time on Monday, by a miracle, so he could get home in time to see the children. He needed some things from the study and a few more clothes, as well, and he wanted to see the children so much it made him ache inside. They hadn't asked for any of this, and he didn't see why they should suffer.

Lucy's car was still on the drive, and he pulled up beside it and headed for the front door. As he slid his key into the keyhole he wondered fleetingly if she would have changed the locks.

No. The key turned, the door swung quietly open and Stanley was there to greet him, tail lashing, tongue lolling in delight.

'Hello, boy,' he said gruffly, and then Emily was in the hall, looking pleased to see him but a bit wary, and it nearly broke his heart.

'Mummy said you weren't coming home this week,' she said, hanging back a little. 'She said you were too busy and you were going to stay at the hospital.'

Oh, Em. He ushered her back into the kitchen where Lucy was wiping supper off Lottie's face and hair and arms.

'Well, they finally got a locum so I finished early,' he said truthfully, 'so I thought I'd come and see you all for a few minutes and pick up some stuff. And I'm really sorry about yesterday.'

'Are you staying here tonight now, then?' Megan asked innocently, and he glanced up and met Lucy's guarded but feisty eyes and smiled grimly.

'No, darling, I'm sorry, I've got to go back to work. So, what did you guys do yesterday?' he asked, suddenly desperately sorry that he'd missed it. 'Did you have fun?'

'Mummy took us swimming, and Florence was there,' Megan said, 'and we all went swimming together.'

'Florence?' he asked.

'Ben Walker's daughter. She's in Megan's class,' Lucy filled in, and he nodded. He knew Ben. He was an obstetrician, and he'd met little Florence when she'd dislocated her elbow a couple of years ago. He'd married his registrar, Daisy, and they'd had a baby since. They were a nice family. Happy. Stable. Unlike them...

'And Daisy was there, and Thomas, and Daisy's going to have a new baby soon!' Emily said. 'And then we went for pizza, because Florence's Daddy was at the hospital, too, and Mummy and Daisy are going for coffee tomorrow after we go to school. And it's not fair, 'cos they'll have cake, and I want cake,' she added mournfully.

He found himself smiling, despite the ache lodged solidly behind his sternum. 'Sounds like you had a good day,' he said, but Megan was hugging his legs and tugging at him for attention.

'Please can you read us a story?' she asked, her pleading eyes shredding him.

He shook his head, wishing he could but there just wasn't time, not if he was going to get any work done. 'No. Sorry. I have to sort some things out and then get back, but I will one night soon.'

Her face fell, tearing another strip off his heart, and she gazed sadly up at him. 'When, Daddy?'

Always questions. Questions that demanded answers that nearly always seemed to be promises destined to be broken.

'Soon,' he said again, knowing it was meaning-less but unwilling to make another promise that fate could so easily break, and he hugged her, pressing a kiss to her toffee-coloured curls and letting go. Emily trailed him into the study and stood watching while he searched for a memory stick with some information on it he needed, and in the background he could hear Lottie crying tiredly and Megan crooning to her while Lucy cleared up the kitchen.

'Why can't you stay here and work?' Em asked, squiggling one toe on the floor, her leg swinging from side to side rhythmically as she watched him. 'You always do.'

'It's not that sort of work,' he lied, and felt a wave of resentment that Lucy was bringing them all to this. His fingers closed around the memory stick and he pulled it out and shut the drawer. 'Got it. Right, sweetheart, I need to head off. You be good for Mummy, OK?'

'I'm always good,' she said reproachfully, and he hugged her, because it was true, she was a good girl and he loved her more than he could ever find the words.

'It's not for long,' he said, mentally crossing his fingers as he bent to kiss her goodnight. 'I'll see you again in a day or two.'

'Ring first,' Lucy said from the doorway. She was standing there with Lottie, and the baby was lean-ing out towards him and grizzling, so he took her and hugged her tight, crushing the lump in his throat and gritting his teeth.

'I'd better go,' he said, handing Lottie back and ruf-fling Megan's hair. 'I'll see you soon, guys.'

He let himself out, shutting the door behind him

without collecting any of the clothes he'd meant to get, and all the way back to the motel he wrestled with the lump in his throat.

'Right, where are we going for coffee?'

Coffee?

Lucy stared at Daisy, then shut her eyes. 'Sorry, I'd forgotten. It's been a bit...'

She bit her lip and looked away, and Daisy tutted and started to walk. 'Come on, we'll go back to mine. Ben bought some really nice coffee, and I made chocolate brownies yesterday. Sometimes a girl just needs chocolate.'

Lucy hesitated for a split second, then went with her. Ben and Daisy had moved recently to a lovely Victorian house a couple of streets away. She'd been itching to see it, but now, suddenly, it didn't seem important any more. Nothing did, apart from Andy, but Daisy's kindness called out to her, and she knew instinctively that anything she said would stay right there and she so needed a friend to talk to.

'What about the buggy?' she asked as Daisy opened the battered but beautiful old front door. 'The wheels are a bit muddy but Lottie's asleep.'

'Oh, you're fine. The floor's tiled. Bring her in.'

Daisy let Thomas out of his buggy and headed for the kitchen, and Lucy left Lottie sleeping and followed her, staring around at the shabby, tatty grandeur of the lovely old house.

'Excuse the mess, we've got quite a lot to do here,' Daisy said with a grin, reaching for the kettle, then her smile softened. 'Sit down and relax. You look shattered, Lucy.'

She sat, unwilling to talk about the mess her marriage was in and yet so desperate to pour it all out, to share the craziness that was her life right now.

Daisy put a cake tin on the table, plonked the cafetière down beside it with a couple of mugs and a jug of foamed hot milk, then sat Thomas in his high chair with a drink and a chunk of squidgy, gooey chocolate cake that Lucy just knew would go everywhere, but Daisy didn't seem to care in the least.

'Right,' she said, settling down and smiling at Lucy. 'Coffee?'

She let her breath out on a little huff and smiled. 'Please. That would be lovely. And some of that. It looks really good.'

Daisy put the coffee down in front of her, handed her chocolate sprinkles and a massive chunk of brownie and then stirred her coffee thoughtfully.

'Lucy, I don't want to invade your privacy,' she said gently after a pregnant silence, 'but—if you want to unload, it won't go any further, and I can see something's wrong. Is there anything I can do to help?'

'Do?' she asked, staring at Daisy and seeing concern in her eyes. They swam out of focus, and she looked quickly away. 'I wish. We're just—Andy's really busy, and he's been working stupid hours, and...'

'And?' Daisy prompted gently, and the floodgates opened.

'They asked him to work on Sunday and he said yes, but he'd promised the kids he'd do something with them and I just flipped.'

'Everyone needs a good row now and then,' Daisy said pragmatically.

'But it wasn't a good row,' she said, remembering

the bitterness, the acrimony, the stubborn thrust of his jaw. 'That would have been fine. This—this was an awful row, and I told him to go. I thought—I was just calling his bluff, but he went. He just—went. And I let him go, Daisy,' she said, swiping at her nose because it was suddenly running and her eyes were welling and there was a sob just itching to get out if she'd only let it.

'Oh, Lucy...'

Daisy wrapped her hand in hers and squeezed, and the simple gesture pushed Lucy over the brink. She felt the tears well over and splash down her cheeks, but she couldn't stop them, and with a muffled murmur Daisy hugged her gently and let her cry, then shoved a tissue in her hand and let her talk.

'He just doesn't seem the same. I know it sounds crazy, but I feel as if I don't know him any more. He's not who he was—and it's since Lottie. I thought he wanted another baby, but ever since she was born he's been really strange—distant, distracted, as if we aren't really there half the time. And he's got the most amazing sense of humour normally. He's so funny, so sharp, and that's just gone. It's like living with a stranger.'

'Ben said the ED's been bedlam since James went on holiday, and I gather the maternity leave locum's been a bit flaky.'

'Flaky? Try downright skiving. She's never there. That's why I wasn't at book club on Friday night. And instead of saying they should shut the department and send everyone to another ED, Andy just takes another shift, and then another one, and they walk all over him, because he can't just let people down, but the kids—'

She broke off, biting her lip, and Daisy sighed and topped up her coffee. 'Tough choices.'

'Impossible,' she went on. 'The nearest ED is miles away, and time is so important, but so is family. You're a doctor, you know what it's like, the hypocritical oath that tells you to put everyone before your own, so we always seem to come last.'

'Oh, tell me about it. I've threatened to kill Ben before now, but I'm just as bad. We were in Theatre delivering some twins the night before our wedding, and I really wonder what would have happened if they'd needed us on our wedding night.'

Lucy smiled wryly. 'I do understand what it's like for him. I know how it is, but—I just feel, if I don't fight for our marriage, then who will? Not him, he didn't even realise it's going down the pan. And this stupid, stupid course he's taken on—really, I could kill him for that, because of all the unnecessary things…'

'What's it on?'

'Oh, I don't know. Something to do with stabilising patients with massive trauma—juggling acts, really. He gave me an assignment to proof-read the other week and I couldn't understand a word of it. And I'm a doctor.'

Daisy tipped her head on one side thoughtfully. 'Is he depressed?'

'Daisy, I have no idea. I don't think he's got time to be depressed, but he's exhausted, I know that, and Lottie's not going through the night properly yet, and I'm starting work again in two weeks, and I…'

'You're at your wits' end,' Daisy filled in gently. 'I can understand that. When's the course finish?'

'The exam's on Friday week, and then it's done. And James is back, and they had a new locum yesterday, Andy said, so maybe it'll sort itself out, once the pressure's off and we can all think straight. Well, that's what I'm hoping,' she added, and closed her eyes and sighed. 'Oh, I feel so disloyal talking to you about this—'

'Don't be stupid. You're just letting off steam. We all need to do it, and it won't go any further. And if there's anything I can do to help, just ask. Anything. The kids can stay over—whatever.'

'Oh, Daisy—that's so kind of you.'

'Rubbish. That's what friends are for. And since you're here, you can give me a hand. What do you think of this curtain fabric for the sitting room?'

It was a fortnight he could have done without, but at least the staffing crisis seemed to have been resolved now it was too late, he thought bitterly.

He went to the hospital, worked his shifts and no more, and every other evening he popped in and saw the children. Then Lucy, the girls and the dog went away to her parents for half term, he checked out of the hotel and went home, and he put his head down and worked until he was ready to drop.

And on the Friday of half term he went down to London to sit the exam, and he was so tired he could hardly answer the paper. He knew exactly what he wanted to say, but he just couldn't find the words, and he caught the train home kicking himself because it was all such a phenomenal waste of time. He'd have to re-sit it, he knew that, because he'd screwed up so badly on a couple of the questions, but in the meantime his marriage was on the rocks and he'd resorted to lying to his children.

And it looked as if it had all been for nothing.

CHAPTER THREE

THEY were due back from her parents' at lunchtime on
Sunday. He was working until three, having swapped
Friday with James, and then he was going home to see
the children and hopefully talk to Lucy.

He had Monday off, and he'd thought they could
spend the day together while the children were at school,
but she was starting work at the practice that morning,
apparently, so it was tonight or who knew when.

But first he had to get through the day, and it was
another of those days. Cold, windy and as unpromis-
ing outside as it was in the department, and he was too
tired to deal with it all.

Amongst the sports injuries and nose bleeds and dog
bites was the inevitable night owl who'd sobered up and
realised she'd hurt herself after falling off that table
last night, and another who'd fallen down the stairs of
a nightclub and fractured her skull and had only realised something was wrong this morning when she
couldn't see straight.

They tried his patience, but it wasn't really their fault.
He knew that, and it wasn't only them. There were the
people who'd lain suffering all night and finally come
in when the pain had become impossible to ignore. One

was a query heart attack, another had an agonising kidney stone. He shunted them off to the appropriate departments, and then a gust of wind brought a tree down on a car, and an elderly woman with head injuries was brought in.

'Jean Darby, front seat passenger,' he was told. 'GCS thirteen at the scene, now ten, she's had oxygen and tramadol.'

'Is the driver on his way in?' he asked, trying not to worry about Lucy and the children out on the road in this weather, but the paramedic shook his head, his face filling in the details and ratcheting up the apprehension Andy was feeling.

He frowned and picked up her left hand. There were three rings on it—a wedding ring, an engagement ring and an eternity ring.

He stared at it. He still hadn't got Lucy the eternity ring he'd promised her when she was pregnant with Emily. Three babies later, she still didn't have it. Another item on that blasted list of ways in which he'd failed her. Failed all of them.

He put his family out of his mind and focused on the patient who'd very likely just lost her husband of many years. For now, she needed him. His family would be fine. They'd be home by now, and he'd see them later. Unlike this poor woman, who would never see her husband again, and might never see her family.

He knew how that would feel for them. He'd lost both his parents together in an accident, only a few years ago, and he'd felt reamed out inside.

He stroked her hand, squeezing it comfortingly.

'Hello, Jean. Can you hear me? You're in Yoxburgh Park Hospital. You've had an accident in the car.'

'Dennis,' she mumbled. 'Where's my husband? I need Dennis. Please find him…'

Her words were slurring worryingly. It might have been the drugs, but he didn't think so. She wasn't really responding, and he whipped out his pen light and shone it in her eyes. Sluggish pupils. Not good. His hand shook and he put the pen light back in his pocket.

'OK, Jean, just try and rest, he's in good hands. Will somebody contact CT and X-ray, please? We need a scan and a full head and neck series. And bloods. We'll need group and save, and—'

He stumbled, the familiar list eluding him, and he just waved a hand. 'Do a full set of bloods—all the usuals. And five minute obs, and get Neuro down here, Kazia. And someone contact the family, please. They need to be here now.'

Leaving the SHO in charge, he walked out, needing a break, a change of air—something. He had pins and needles in his hand now, and flashing lights.

A migraine? He'd had a few recently, although he hadn't mentioned it to anyone. Nothing major, just a bit of tingling for a few minutes. Painkillers, he thought, and went to find the sister in charge.

'Got a migraine. Any pills you can give me?'

'Sure. We'll have to write them up. What do you want?'

He tried to think of the drug names, and couldn't. 'Something strong,' he mumbled, and took them from her hand, his fingers shaking.

'Andy, are you OK?'

'I'm fine. Just tired and I've got a headache. I had that exam on Friday—I've been overdoing it.'

She looked at him sceptically, and he tried to smile,

but it was all too much effort, so the moment he'd swallowed the pills he turned on his heel and walked back to Resus to see the woman.

Joan? Jane? He picked up the notes.

'Jean. How are you feeling?' he asked, but she didn't answer.

'I think she's got a bleed,' Kazia said softly, and he nodded.

'Um—Neuro on the way?'

'I'm here,' a familiar voice said from behind him, and he sighed with relief. He didn't need to deal with a junior, and nor did Jean.

'Raj, hi. Um—this is Jean—er—Darby—Kazia, would you fill us in?'

'Sure,' the SHO said, shooting him a strange look and taking over. He didn't mind. The words were escaping him, slithering away into the corners, hiding in the dark.

He propped himself against the Resus trolley and watched and listened as Raj ran through a quick neurological screen and then nodded.

'She needs to go to Theatre, but it's not looking good.'

It wasn't. In fact, it was considerably less than good, and that moment her pupils blew and she arrested. They worked on her, Andy doing chest compressions, Raj checking her pulse and haunting the monitor, but the odds were stacked hugely against her anyway, and after a few unsuccessful minutes Raj put his hands over Andy's and stopped him.

'This is pointless. She's gone, Andy.'

Damn. He straightened up and looked around, knowing he was right but gutted nonetheless. 'All agreed?' he asked, and everyone nodded.

He stared at the clock for an age, but he couldn't seem to get the words out. 'Time of death twelve thirty two,' he said after a long pause, and he stripped off his gloves, threw them in the bin and turned to the neurologist.

'Thanks, Raj. Sorry—waste of your time,' he said, his voice hitching slightly as if they were reluctant to come out, and Raj frowned and tipped his head on one side, searching his eyes.

'No problem. Got a minute?'

'Yeah, sure. Are the family here yet?'

'They're on their way.'

'OK. Find me when they're here. I want to see them.'

'Andy, now,' Raj said softly, and taking his elbow he steered him out of Resus, and then stopped in a quiet bit of the corridor. 'OK, what's going on? You're not yourself.'

'Don't know. I've got a migraine. Flashing lights, pins and needles—that sort of thing.'

'History?'

He shook his head. 'Not really. Bit. I've had a few in the last couple of months.'

'Have you been drinking?'

He shook his head. 'No. God, no. I'm just—tired.'

Raj took his hands. 'Squeeze.'

He squeezed, but even he could feel that his right hand wasn't working properly, and he felt his blood pressure kick up a notch as his heart started to pound. What the hell was wrong with him? The endless possibilities started spooling through his head, but he couldn't make sense of them.

'I think we need to take a proper look at you. Let's find somewhere quiet.'

He took him to a room reserved for patients kept in under observation, and laid him down, prodding and poking and shining lights in his pupils, making him count fingers and follow things with his eyes.

'What day is it?'

'Sunday, and I shouldn't be here, I should be with my kids.'

Raj smiled. 'I know the feeling. What's the time?'

He stared at the clock. 'Nearly ten past one.'

'Come on, I want more than that.'

'Thirteen oh eight,' he said after a second.

'Better. What do you give a child with anaphylaxis?'

'Um—' He swore, and looked away. 'Sorry. I can't...'

'Don't worry. Give me the words that go with these. Bread and...?'

'Butter.'

'Chalk and...?'

'Cheese.'

'What's the opposite of up?'

'Down.'

'And the opposite of accept?'

'Um—reject. Raj, what are you doing?' he asked, a bit shortly because, dammit, for a fraction of a second the word had eluded him.

'Trying to work out what's wrong with you, because something is and I don't think it's just migraine. I could be wrong, but I want you to have a scan. Shall we call Lucy?'

He felt a finger of fear creep up his spine as things started to fall into place. The struggle he'd had answering the question paper—the words he'd known but not been able to find. The tiredness. The loss of motor control in his right hand. The paper he'd been going to use for his assignment, that he'd not been able to understand. And adrenaline. How could he not have remembered adrenaline for anaphylaxis? He *knew* that!

'No. Don't call her. She's busy with the kids.' Hell, he couldn't even manage a simple opposites test without pausing to think, and the finger of fear turned into an icy hand clutching at his throat. 'Um—I need to see the family of that woman.'

'No, you don't. Someone else can do it. Stay here. I'll get someone to take you down to CT.'

'No! I can—' What? What could he do? Nothing, it seemed. He was so, so tired, but he got up anyway, and walked down to the scanner under his own steam. He wasn't being pushed through his own hospital on a stretcher. Lucy would know about it before he was even in the scanner, but it seemed a hell of a long way there and he could have sworn it had moved.

He sagged back against the pillows and gave in as a fleet of people appeared and took over in the scanner room.

They gave him an injection of contrast medium, and he felt it flash through his body in a hot wave as they slid him inside the body of the scanner.

'Keep nice and still and just breathe normally. That's great.'

It seemed like for ever, but it was only a few minutes before he was called into Raj's office. 'We've got the results.'

'And?' he said, his voice edgy.

Raj frowned, and he knew instantly he wasn't going

to like what was coming. 'Not good news, I'm afraid. There's a mass over the left side of your frontal lobe.'

He turned the screen so Andy could see it, and as he stared at it he felt the blood drain from his head, and his heart rate kicked up as the adrenaline began to surge through his body. It looked huge, menacing.

Life threatening?

He hauled in a breath. 'What kind of mass is it? Come on, Raj, I'm a doctor, give it to me straight. Could it be a bleed?'

'No. It isn't a bleed. It could be a tumour of some sort. It's overlapping the superior temporal gyrus and Broca's area, part of your speech centre, which I think is why you're struggling to express yourself. There's some weakness on your right hand side, as well, because the motor area's right there, too. Does that make sense? Stop me if you don't understand anything. I don't want to assume you just know what I'm talking about.'

He nodded. Oh, he knew, all right. He only wished he didn't. 'No, it all makes sense.' Far too much sense. He swore, softly but succinctly, and closed his eyes. 'That's why I can't find words,' he mumbled. 'Thought I was just tired.'

'You are tired. You will be tired. You'll need an MRI scan in the morning, which will give us more information so we can decide on a course of treatment. And you'll need referring to a specialist centre.'

'What if it isn't treatable?'

Raj frowned again. 'We'll cross that bridge if we get to it. Until we know what kind of mass it is exactly, I don't want to speculate, but it'll need a biopsy for accurate diagnosis.'

He felt his muscles tighten in a flight response. For

two pins he'd get up and run away, but that was ridiculous. He was a doctor. He knew about this stuff. He
could deal with it. He breathed in and out slowly, and
then nodded again.

'OK,' he said, and forced himself to stay there and
listen to what Raj was saying.

'This has obviously been growing for some time.
You say you've had symptoms for a while?'

'Mmm. We've got a new baby. Seven months—
nearly eight. She's still not going through the night
properly. And I've been doing a course. Lot of work.
I've just done the terminal exam.' God, he was tired,
and talking was so hard. The words were just sliding
away. 'Thought I was just tired because of everything,
but obviously not.'

'OK. Why don't you have a rest now? We'll take you
up to Neurology and settle you in a side room while
we run a few more tests, and I'll come and talk to you
again soon.'

'No. Can't we do this quietly?' he asked, feeling a
sudden rush of desperation. 'I don't want Lucy knowing. Not until we know more. I don't really need to go
to the ward, do I?'

Raj frowned. 'Not really, not if you don't want to.
I can do the tests here. I don't need to keep you in tonight if you'd rather I didn't, but I'll take the bloods
today so we can get started, and we'll do the scan first
thing tomorrow and take more of a history, and go from
there. You can go home as soon as I've got the bloods,
if you want.'

'I do want.'

It would be easier, he thought as Raj quickly filled
several tubes with blood, if he had a home to go to

where he was welcome, but he didn't, not if Lucy had anything to say about it, he thought with bitterness and a shiver of apprehension. Then the practicalities hit him. His car was here, in the hospital car park, and even though he knew what the answer would be, still he asked the question.

'Can I drive?'

Raj shook his head, and Andy felt his life ebbing away from him.

'I'm sorry. Not for a while. Press that with your finger. And you can't work, either. I'm signing you off sick until further notice.'

He stared at the plaster Raj stuck over the needle site. Further notice? How long was that, for heaven's sake?

A month? A year?

For ever?

It was six thirty, over five hours since Raj had yanked him off the emergency department and into an alien universe.

He walked into the ED, went to his office and phoned James, the clinic lead, and told him the news.

'Don't spread it around. I don't want the details of this out. Just tell everyone I'm off sick. Tell them it's stress. Tell them whatever lie you like, I don't care. Just—don't tell them that.'

'OK. Andy—if there's anything I can do...'

'Yeah. Thanks.'

He hung up and left the building, wondering when— if—he'd ever come back in here again in an official capacity.

'Are you all right, Mr Gallagher?'

He gave the receptionist a fleeting smile. 'Yes, Jane, I'm fine, thank you, or I will be after a few days' rest.'

Lies again, but he wasn't telling her what he wasn't telling his own wife yet. He contemplated getting her to call him a cab, but he was still reeling from the news and it was just as easy to walk home, and the fresh air might clear his head.

He gave a grunt of laughter. Fat chance. It would take more than a bit of fresh air to clear this monster out of his head.

He collected a few things from the car, eyed it with regret and walked home in the tail end of the wind which had killed Jean Darby and her husband earlier today. He thought of her distress as she was asking about him, her rings, the years of love they represented, all gone in an instant.

At least he was still alive, and, if it came to that, he'd have time to say goodbye…

It was almost seven by the time he got home, and he walked into a scene of domestic chaos, welcomed by the dog and the children, but not by Lucy who was swiping at Lottie's face and hands with a baby wipe.

'I thought you were coming at three. We've been expecting you,' she said reproachfully.

Because he'd promised, he thought, and felt sick. 'Sorry. I got held up,' he said, truthfully if a little economically, and she gave a soft snort and turned away. He sucked in a breath and turned to his children, dredging up a smile.

'So, kids, did you have a good time with Grannie and Grandpa this week?'

'Yes, it was brilliant,' Emily said, her eyes sparkling. 'We went to the zoo, and I touched an elephant's trunk and it was all rough and hairy and scratchy, and the end was sticky and disgusting. It was awesome.'

He laughed, a hollow, rather desperate sound, and then listened to Megan talking about the monkeys, and then Em had a story about the meerkats, and they would have been there all evening if Lucy hadn't cut it short.

'Bedtime, girls. You need to go upstairs and put your dirty clothes in the bin while I bath Lottie, then you can have a bath and get to bed. You've had quite enough excitement this week and it's a school day tomorrow.'

'Daddy, will you read to us?' Megan asked, her eyes so like Lucy's pleading with him.

'Yes, darling. Of course I will.'

'Can I choose our story?' she asked, but then Em chipped in and they started arguing about which story they wanted.

'I'll read them both. And I'll read one to Lottie. In fact,' he said, ignoring Lucy's glare, 'why don't I go and bath her while you two put all the toys away?'

And lifting his sticky little daughter out of the high chair, he carried her upstairs and into the bathroom, still slightly numb inside. 'You're a mess, little one,' he said, turning on the taps and stripping her of the food-magnet clothes and trying not to speculate on whether he'd see her grow up. See her walk. Hear her call him Daddy...

He checked the mat in the bottom of the bath to make sure the temperature indicator hadn't changed colour, then checked it with his hand, and finally lowered her into it.

'What a little grub you are!' he said lovingly, the numbness thawing to leave an agonising ache in its place. 'Where's that sponge?'

He cleaned her face tenderly, washed the food out

of her hair and blew a raspberry on her tummy, making her giggle.

She grabbed his face, scrunching his cheeks up with her fingers, her sharp little nails gouging into his skin. 'Ouch, little monkey. That hurts,' he said, and he gently prised her fingers off and straightened up, chuckling as she giggled again and made another swipe for his nose.

'Why *are* you so late, Andy?'

The soft voice behind him almost made him jump. It shouldn't have done. He'd known she'd come up the moment she could, to challenge him.

'I told you, I was held up.'

'But it's too late. They've been waiting for you since three. Why couldn't you be here then? Why can you never, ever do what you say you're going to?'

He gritted his teeth, unwilling to tell her the truth, at least until he had some answers. 'I got held up,' he repeated. 'I told you that. And I know it's late, but they're still up, and like I said, I wanted to spend some time with them.'

'You should have been here earlier. They've got school tomorrow, and you'll only get them overexcited and they won't sleep properly, and it's my first day at work tomorrow, you know that. I wanted a quiet evening to prepare.'

'So go and prepare. I'm not stopping you. Far from it. And I've moved back in, by the way.'

'No.'

'Yes,' he said, equally firmly. 'I'm not a cat, Lucy. I've told you that before. You can't just put me out of the door when it suits you. This is my home, too.'

'Not in front of the children,' she murmured warningly, and turned to hug Megan who'd run up to her.

'We've put all the toys away. Can Daddy bath us, too?'

'I expect so. He seems to be Superman tonight.'

And with that she walked off, leaving him with Megan hanging over the edge of the bath and splashing a giggling Lottie, while he fought back the stinging in his eyes and wondered when and how it had all gone so horribly wrong.

"'And they all lived happily ever after.'"

Why did they all end like that? It cut through him like a knife, slashing him with the uncertainty of his future, the exact diagnosis lurking just out of reach, the fear of the unknown gnawing at his insides and racking him with grief.

'More!' Emily said, but Megan's eyes were drooping, and he knew Emily would soon fall asleep.

'No,' he said, although in truth he could have carried on all night, under the circumstances, cuddled up with his precious little daughters. 'Come on. Snuggle down, Megan. Emily, back in your own bed, darling. Time for sleep now. You've got school tomorrow.'

He shut the book and put it down on the pile, tucked them in and kissed them both goodnight, then turned off the light and pulled the bedroom door to, leaving just a chink of light to chase away the monsters.

Lottie was fast asleep long ago, lying flat on her back, little arms thrown up above her head, her rosebud lips slightly parted. She reminded him so much of Emily at the same age.

He closed her door again, leaving the same little chink of light, and went into the bedroom that until now he'd shared with Lucy. She was sitting on the bed, stony faced, waiting for him.

'Have you been here all week?'

'There didn't seem to be any point in staying in the hotel when you weren't even here to object,' he pointed out.

'But we're back now, so are you going to explain why you think you're staying here tonight? Why you've just moved back in without asking me? I thought we were going to discuss this?'

'We are—and I don't *think* I'm staying here, I *am* staying here, and I don't have to explain to you,' he said stubbornly, because tonight, of all nights, explaining was the last thing he wanted to do. 'I have every right to be here. Anyway, don't worry, you won't have to share a bed with me. I can sleep in the attic.'

'Good,' she said, dashing a hope he hadn't even realised he was harbouring, and he swallowed hard and opened his side of the wardrobe, pulling out clean clothes for the morning.

'If you're hungry, you'll have to go and forage in the kitchen. You were so late I just assumed you weren't coming, so I haven't got anything cooked for you.'

'I'm not hungry,' he said truthfully. 'I've eaten.' Sandwiches from the staff canteen at lunchtime and a couple of biscuits with a cup of tea in Raj's office, but he wasn't telling her that.

He could feel her eyes boring into him, hear her mind working.

'I thought the idea was you'd get your exam out of the way and then we'd talk. Strikes me there's not been a lot of talking, so how come you think it's all right to move back?'

'I need to be here. There are things I need in the study, stuff I want to sort out,' he said, again truthfully, even if it was only part of the truth this time. 'And I want to spend time with the girls. Read to them.' Like tonight, maybe for the last time. 'I thought that was what you wanted?'

'Is that why you just read them five stories?'

Had he? Probably. Five hundred wouldn't have been enough.

'Guilt's an ugly thing,' she went on. 'You can't make it all up to them on one night, you know. It needs a concerted effort, change of lifestyle. And so far you aren't doing so great, are you?'

He closed his eyes and counted to ten. 'I'm well aware of that,' he said, his teeth gritted. 'I'm going to put this stuff upstairs, and then I'm going in the study. You don't need to bother about me. I'll be out first thing in the morning, you won't even see me.'

'Where's your car? How did you get home?'

'I walked. It's at the hospital. The service light came on. The garage are going to pick it up tomorrow.'

Lies again. This was the first time he'd lied to her. The first out-and-out lies, at least, in all their marriage, and now he was doing it all the time. He'd tell her the truth tomorrow, but for tonight he'd just wanted to spend time with the girls without having to deal with Lucy's emotions. It was hard enough dealing with his own, and now he just wanted to be alone so he didn't have to pretend any more. And he certainly didn't want to start talking about their future, not when he didn't even know if he had one.

Scooping up his things, he walked out of their bedroom, flicked on the upper landing light and walked firmly up the stairs. He wasn't going to weaken. He wasn't going to go downstairs and sit with her, and pour his heart out.

Anything could happen. Until he'd had a biopsy there was no knowing what they'd find. It might be easily treatable, or it might be highly aggressive. And then where would Lucy be?

No. If she was angry with him, if she was ready to make a break from him, then he'd let her, for her sake and the children's. It would be so much easier for them that way. And anyway, a large part of him was still angry with her for issuing that ultimatum two weeks ago. If she could do that, if she was prepared to throw it all away without giving him a chance, then maybe it really *was* over.

So he put his things in the larger attic bedroom, went downstairs to make himself a drink and a sandwich and shut himself away in the study. He had things to check—wills, details of his pension and bank accounts, life assurance, mortgage—all sorts of things needed to be looked at, put together, so if the worse came to the worst, Lucy wouldn't have a nightmare to deal with. And it had to be done while he was still able to do it.

Ignoring the flicker of dread, he pulled open the drawer at the bottom of the bookshelves and pulled out the file.

It was all in order. He'd known it was, but he'd had to check. When, like Jean and Dennis Darby, his parents had died together in an accident, their affairs had been in chaos. It had taken him ages to sort it all out, and he'd vowed that his family would never have to deal with the mess he'd been left with.

It was typical of them, though. He'd loved them

dearly, but they'd never made a plan and stuck to it in their lives. His schooling had been constantly disrupted by their moves from one opportunity to another, and he'd grown used to making new friends and working hard to catch up in every new school. He'd done it because he'd had no choice, but he hadn't enjoyed it, unlike his parents who thrived on every challenge life threw at them.

It hadn't all been bad, he remembered fondly. His childhood had been filled with love and laughter, but it had also been riddled with upheaval and financial uncertainty, and he'd vowed his own children wouldn't have to put up with the same chaotic lifestyle, and they certainly wouldn't find his affairs in total disarray if anything happened to him.

But there was no mess. He'd already taken care of that, and if the worse came to the worst…

The flicker of fear made his chest tighten, but he ignored it. He wasn't going to dwell on the dark side of this. Not until and unless he had to. He made another drink and carried his laptop back up with him. He'd spend the rest of the evening researching all the things that could be going on in his head, to take his mind off his disintegrating marriage to the woman he loved with all his heart.

And then tomorrow, hopefully, he'd have some answers.

She sat there on the bed, listening as he walked up and down the stairs. He spent a few minutes in the study, then eventually he went back up to the attic bedroom, closing the door with a quiet but somehow final click.

The sound made her breath hitch, and she closed her eyes and squeezed them tight shut.

Why had he come back? She was just getting her head around being here without him, and now he was back and she felt unsettled and restless and sad.

Was it just guilt about the children that had brought him back tonight? Or had he intended to try and win her round, but she'd put him off by being defensive?

She'd seen the look in his eyes when he was talking to the girls, when he'd first walked in, and he'd looked—gosh—grief stricken, for a moment? So did that mean her plan was working, that finally it had sunk in just how much he was needed by all of them? How much he hurt them every time he broke a promise?

He'd shut himself away now—keeping out of her way so as not to intrude? She didn't think so. And he wasn't really working, despite what he'd said. If he'd been working, he would have been in his study as usual.

Maybe he felt it wasn't his any more, but that was ridiculous because he was the only one who used it, by and large. Their books were stored in there, shelf after shelf of reference books and novels and autobiographies, DIY books and How-To books, all the family photograph albums from their first holiday together through to Lottie's first few months, and all their household bills and things were filed in the cupboards at the bottom, along with all the important stuff, like birth certificates and their marriage certificate and the wills.

But it was his study, always had been, and recently it had been the place he'd retreated to more and more. So why not tonight?

She went down to the kitchen and saw an open bottle of wine on the side. He must have taken a glass upstairs.

She poured herself a glass and hesitated. Should she go up to him? Talk to him again, find out what was really motivating him? Maybe he was waiting for her, hoping she'd go up to him.

Maybe that was why he'd chosen a bedroom, she thought, rather than the study, and she ran her tongue over suddenly dry lips.

She felt a fizzle inside her, a tingle of something that could have been fear or then might have been excitement. She sipped the wine, put it down and squared her shoulders. Only one way to find out, she told herself, and headed for the stairs.

Then stopped, and walked back into the kitchen.

No. She wasn't going to make it that easy for him. If he wanted to make it up to her, to them, then he could come and talk to her. He knew where she was, and she was damned if she was going to fold first. And anyway, she reminded herself, nothing had changed. He'd been four hours later tonight than he'd said he'd be.

No. Let him sweat.

Ignoring the wine, she made herself a cup of tea, went through some information from the practice, watched a little television and went to bed, to find the lingering scent of his aftershave clinging to the sheets and tormenting her dreams.

He was up and showered and dressed by the time Lottie woke, and he went down and scooped her out of her cot and cuddled her as he carried her into their bedroom.

'Someone needs you,' he said, and Lucy emerged from the bedclothes looking rumpled and warm and so beautiful he nearly weakened.

'You're dressed.'

'I've got an early appointment,' he said glibly, kissing Lottie and handing her over.

'When are you going to see the children again?'

He sucked in his breath silently. 'I don't know,' he said honestly. 'I'll give you a call.'

'OK.'

'Good luck with work today. Hope it goes well.'

'Thanks. It's only the morning. I'll be fine.'

'I'm sure you will.'

Then, because he just couldn't help himself, because she was propped up against the pillows with Lottie suckling noisily at her breast and the scene was tearing holes in his heart, he leant over and pressed his mouth to hers in a hard, brief kiss of farewell.

'Goodbye, Lucy,' he said.

And then before he could make a fool of himself and pour it all out, he walked away, glancing in on the girls just to torture himself a little more before he carried his bag downstairs. He left his laptop in the study. He wouldn't need it today. Maybe never.

He let himself out of the front door as the taxi drew up outside, and as it pulled away he glanced back and saw Lucy standing at the bedroom window. He lifted a hand, and then looked away before he crumbled and asked the driver to stop.

He had to do this—had to go to the hospital and face the future, and he had to do it alone.

CHAPTER FOUR

RAJ was waiting for him in the MRI suite, and he shook his hand and then ushered him through to the changing cubicle.

'You know the form. I'm afraid you need to take everything off and put on the gown. There's a locker you can put your things in. Any metalwork we need to know about?' he asked, and Andy shook his head.

'No. All me.'

'Good. Don't forget to take off your watch and any jewellery, and come out when you're done. We're ready to go.'

No time to run away, then.

Not that he was going to, but it was ludicrously tempting.

He was taken through to the MRI scanner and lay down on the bed, his head towards the hollow tube where the scan would take place. Someone connected him up to the headphones, and left him there.

This was it, then. He'd get his answers now, thanks to this miracle machine which could see inside him with astonishing clarity. For a second, he wished it had never been invented.

'Right, lie as still as you can, but breathe normally,'

a voice said through the headphones, and the scanner bed started to move.

He'd told people about them, but he'd never understood what noisy, confined things they were until he was posted into it. He hated tight spaces, always had, and his pulse rocketed.

He fought the fear, crushed it down as the thing whirred and clonked for what seemed like an age, and then at last it was over and they slid him out and Raj came and stood beside him.

'OK?'

'I'll live,' he said, and wondered if that was actually true. 'Can I see it?'

'Sure. Get your clothes on and we'll go up to my office.'

Five minutes later Raj sat him down as they scrolled through the images.

Shocking images, of the mass inside his head.

They weren't meaningless to him, of course, and certainly not meaningless in terms of their possible implications, but he knew Raj could understand far more from these slices of his brain than he ever would.

'I can't give you any definite answers,' he said quietly. 'I'm sorry, the only way is a biopsy, and I need to refer you for that. This is going to take specialist equipment we simply don't have, and I want to fast-track you. I won't beat about the bush, this is big, and I think you're deteriorating fast now. Do you have any preference for neurosurgeons?'

He felt a wave of nausea and crushed it. 'Yes. David Cardew. I trained with him, and I still see him quite often at conferences and things. I think he's got a good reputation.'

Raj nodded. 'He is good. Do you want to give him a call, or shall I?'

'I'd better break the news first. Will you talk to him then?'

'Sure.'

He called his old college friend, and got his voice-mail, so he rang the hospital and was put through to his secretary.

'I'll get him to call you straight away,' she promised, and two minutes later his mobile rang.

'Andy, hi, how're you doing?'

'Not great,' he said without preamble. 'David, I've got a problem. A mass on the left side of my temporal lobe. It's over Broca's, and it's not small.'

David swore softly. 'Got the scans? Who's your consultant?'

'Rajiv Patel. He wants to fast-track me. He's right here with me—want to talk to him?'

'If I could.'

He handed the phone over, and sat there listening to a one-sided conversation that he'd rather not have heard. There was the truth, after all, and then the whole truth.

Frankly, he could have done with a bunch of lies.

'He wants to talk to you again.'

He took the phone back. 'Get everything you need?'

'Yeah. Give me a few minutes to look at these—Raj is sending them over now. I'll call you, but from what he says, you need a biopsy. I've got a slot tomorrow, if that helps.'

'Tomorrow?'

'I can't do it today, much as I'd like to.'

He laughed. 'I didn't expect you to. I was thinking, maybe, a week or so.'

'No. Let me look at the images, and I'll come right back to you.'

He slid the phone back into his pocket and met Raj's eyes. 'So—he says he could do the biopsy tomorrow.'

'Yes. I'm sorry, Andy. I wish I could have told you something better, but I can't. You'll be in good hands, though.'

'Yeah. Thanks, Raj. I'll let you know what he says.'

He got himself a coffee from the café and went and sat in his car outside, for want of anywhere more private to wait, and while he was there he called the garage and asked them to collect the car and service it. He couldn't just leave it at the hospital indefinitely and at least they could return it to his home.

'Well, I think it's a meningioma, arising from the arachnoid membrane surrounding the brain, rather than a tumour in the cerebral cortex itself,' David said when he called back a short while later.

'That's good news, isn't it?' he asked, checking before he allowed himself to feel relieved.

'Very good news. If you're going to have a brain tumour, it's the one to have. That said, it's pretty extensive. It's right over Broca's area, which seems to control the way we express words rather than understand them. I understand from Raj you've got a slight speech loss— expressive aphasia, so you can understand everything but not speak as fluently, and it's also affecting the motor control of your right side, especially your hand, but that you can understand everything that's said. Does that make sense to you, fit your symptoms?'

'Yes. Mostly I'm fine. It's only complicated stuff, really, or odd things that I'm having trouble with. And my right hand's been shaking for a while, off and on. I thought it was just stress and tiredness. It's all much worse when I'm tired.'

'Yes. It would be, because you're compensating with all the day-to-day things, and it's only the really high-level stuff that you've lost at this stage. So—surgery. I'm pretty sure I'm right about it being a meningioma, so I think we'll bypass the biopsy and just cut to the chase. I'd like to operate tomorrow, if that's all right with you?'

'Tomorrow?' he echoed, shocked. 'I thought you'd only have time to do a biopsy?'

'No. I had a long elective procedure booked, but the patient's had to cancel, he's got flu. So I have a long enough slot. Otherwise we might be talking a couple of weeks and from what Raj has said, I don't want to leave you any longer than I have to. Can you get down here today so we can run a few more tests and take a thorough history?'

'Um—sure. Where's the clinic?'

'I'll email you the link. It's easy to find. And don't worry about it, Andy. We'll get you sorted. This is the kind of stuff I deal with every day.'

Was it? He was glad he was sitting down, because he felt the blood leave his head and a wave of nausea swept over him. It suddenly all seemed incredibly real. 'Um—how are you intending to do it?'

'Awake craniotomy. It's too large for an endoscopic technique, and I need access to the margins to make sure I've got it all. And I need you awake because of the speech implications. We'll need to map the language areas.'

Under normal circumstances he would have found

the idea fascinating. Not today. 'Can you tell from the scans if it's benign or malignant?'

'Not without a biopsy which we'll do at the same time, but it hasn't invaded the cerebral cortex or the dura as far as I can tell from the scans, so that's a positive sign. However, it does look as if it's following some of the tight fissures in Broca's area. And that has implications for the prognosis.'

He didn't like the sound of that. 'Permanent implications?' he asked warily.

'I hope not. It could, however, be significant post-op. You might find you lose your speech totally or almost totally for a while until the swelling and bruising caused by the surgery has healed and your brain's recovered from the sustained pressure of the tumour. That's why I want to do it as soon as possible.'

'How long's a while?' he asked, wondering if he'd ever practise medicine again. Not if he couldn't speak fluently, couldn't pull important information out and share it, that was for sure.

'Days. Weeks. Months, possibly, for the really high-level stuff to come back.'

'So I'll be off work for a long time?'

'Maybe. I'm hoping it won't be too long. Maybe a couple of months.'

'But that's assuming it's not malignant and it hasn't migrated into the brain tissue?'

'Andy, this is all speculation. I can't tell you any more until I've operated on you tomorrow. And I really need to do it while you're awake. Are you OK with that?'

Was he? He sucked in a long, slow breath, and nodded. It was the best way. He'd seen documentaries about it but now it had a new relevance, so last night he'd been reading up on it, watching video clips on the internet, and knew that they used electrodes to identify parts of the brain used for specific functions, so they knew which parts were important for which tasks. And for that mapping process, he'd have to be awake and responsive.

He swallowed. 'Yes. I'm fine with it.'

And then he thought about Lucy, and shut his eyes. 'I should tell my wife.'

'You still haven't told her?'

'No. I wanted to know more.' And now he did, there was no excuse for delaying.

'Do you want me to talk to her?'

'No. I'll tell her. It'll be better coming from me.'

But she rejected his call. She was probably still at work, he told himself, but even so, he needed her, needed that contact desperately, and as he walked home to pack his bags, he felt more isolated than he'd ever felt in his life.

She didn't answer the phone.

She was in a café with Daisy Walker, with Lottie and Daisy's Thomas in high chairs making a mess with biscuits, and they were talking about nothing in particular while her heart was quietly breaking. She'd watched him go this morning, seen him wave, and it had seemed so—so *final*, really. She'd really hoped, now the exam was out of the way, that finally they'd talk and find a way to bridge this gulf between them, but he hadn't shown any sign of wanting to talk to her last night, and she'd hardly been able to concentrate all morning at work.

She was glad she'd arranged to meet Daisy for coffee after she'd finished her surgery. Anything rather than sitting at home and wallowing in self-pity for the rest of the day.

And when the phone rang, she hesitated, just in case it was him, but she couldn't ignore it. It might be the school.

It wasn't. It was Andy.

She hesitated, then rejected the call. She didn't want to talk to him now. She'd call him back later, when she was alone. But not yet.

'How about another coffee?' she asked Daisy brightly. 'I can't be bothered to go home and tackle the washing.'

'Nor can I. I'll get them. What was yours? Skinny decaf cappuccino?'

'Please.'

But then it ran again, while Daisy was still rummaging in her bag for her purse, and she answered it this time.

'Andy, I'm a bit busy at the moment, I'm having coffee with Daisy. Will it keep?'

'Not really. I need to talk to you pretty urgently.'

'I only saw you this morning. How can it be that urgent?' she asked, impatient with him because everything—*everything*—always had to be done to suit him, and she'd spent the whole morning in knots.

'D'you know what? Forget it,' he said crisply, and hung up.

And then Daisy's phone rang. 'Sorry, I need to take this, it's Ben,' she said, and she answered it, then looked across at Lucy and frowned thoughtfully. 'I don't know.

No, she hasn't mentioned it and she's just spoken to him. Yes, I'll ask her. OK, darling. Thank you.'

She sat down again. 'Lucy, that was Ben,' she said softly. 'He said to ask you how Andy is.'

'Andy? I don't know. He was fine this morning when he went to work. Why?'

'Because he didn't go to work today. He's off sick, apparently, and Ben saw him coming out of Raj Patel's office. And yesterday he had a CT scan.'

'*What?*'

Her blood ran cold. Raj was a neurologist. And he'd had a CT scan? Why hadn't he told her last night? Was that what he'd been phoning to tell her just now? And she'd all but told him to go to hell...

'Lucy?' Daisy took Lucy's hands in hers, her face concerned. 'Talk to me.'

'He just rang me,' she said, her voice sounding hollow and far away. 'He said it was urgent, and I told him I was busy. Daisy, I've got to go to him. I had no idea there was anything wrong...'

She broke off, sucking in a breath, trying to keep calm.

'What can I do?' Daisy asked, quietly and calmly taking command of the situation.

Oh, help, the children. 'Could you have Lottie? Just for now. I don't even know where he is.'

'Ring him.'

She rang, and eventually he picked up. She didn't even let him speak, just pitched in, distraught.

'Andy, where are you? Are you at the hospital still? Why didn't you tell me you were sick?'

She heard a quiet sigh. 'I tried, Lucy,' he pointed

out, and she felt the guilt spiral. 'I'm at home, but not for long. I've got to go to London.'

'Not without me. Whatever it is, you're not going without me. I'm coming home now. Don't you dare leave without me.'

She scrambled to her feet, gathering up her things, her heart racing. 'Daisy, we have to go to London—'

'Go home. I'll take Thomas home and come round in the car to pick Lottie up. I'll look after her, and the dog, and I'll get the girls after school. You don't have to worry about a thing. Go—shoo.'

She went, hurrying along the pavements with the buggy, dodging pedestrians and feeling choked with fear, and then he was opening the door and she fell into his arms.

'I'm so sorry—'

'Shh. Don't upset Lottie. Just help me pack.'

'Can I come? I know I've been a complete bitch to you, but please let me come, whatever it is.'

'Of course you can come. And you haven't been any worse than me, but I can't do this now, Lucy. I know things are a mess. I just—not now, OK?'

The doorbell rang, and she snatched it open and let Daisy in. 'Daisy's going to have the children.'

'Bless you,' Andy said, and hugged her. 'Thanks.'

'I'll get some stuff.' She ran upstairs on legs of rubber, threw things for all the girls into a bag and handed it to Daisy, then kissed Lottie goodbye and put her into the car seat that Andy must have moved. 'I'll call my parents—they'll come and get them from you. Here, give them my keys. Thank you so, so much.'

'No problem. Come on, Stanley. In the car.'

She loaded the dog into the boot with the bag of

clothes, and as she pulled off the drive Andy headed for the stairs.

'I need to pack,' he said, and went up, leaving her to follow. There was so much he wanted to tell her, so much he needed to say, but there was a gulf between them that not even this could bridge adequately.

'Talk to me,' she pleaded. Her eyes were wide with fear and shock, and he could feel her shaking all over. 'Andy? What's going on?'

'I've got a brain tumour,' he said, curiously detached.

'A brain tumour?'

He nodded. 'David Cardew thinks it's a meningioma,' he said, and she went chalk white and sat down suddenly on the bed, her fingers threaded through his and locked on tight. He gripped back, curiously relieved that she'd come home to him. Not that it changed anything, but—

'How did you find out? What made you think there was anything wrong?'

'Raj spotted it yesterday. He came to the ED, and he noticed I was stumbling over my words, and he did a CT—'

'Why didn't you say anything? Last night—you came home, and you didn't say anything! Why ever not?'

'I just—I wanted it to be normal,' he said, and she could see his jaw working. 'I wanted—'

He couldn't go on, so she finished the sentence for him, her heart breaking.

'You wanted to read to the girls,' she whispered, and he nodded.

'Raj fast-tracked me to David Cardew, and he says after the op I might lose my speech for a while.'

She closed her eyes, the implications only just sinking in. 'Where is it?' she asked, dreading the answer. 'This tumour?'

'On the side of my left frontal lobe. Over Broca's.'

She flinched, the significance not lost on her. 'Does he think he can get it out?'

'I think so. He's going to operate tomorrow morning. That's part of the hurry. It's causing the aphasia.'

The aphasia she hadn't even noticed, but come to think of it, he'd been less communicative, less talkative and certainly not himself. 'Expressive aphasia.'

'Yeah. I can understand everything—well, not everything. I read a research paper the other day and couldn't understand it, but that could have been because it was pretentious crap. It's finding words. It's driving me nuts. I can't—I know exactly what I'm trying to say, it's all there, I just can't find the exact words. Most of the time it's fine, I can wing it, but difficult stuff—it's just not there, and some of the easy stuff is getting harder. And it's getting rapidly worse.' He hesitated, then went on, 'I thought I was just tired, but my hand's been funny, as well. Shaking. Weaker. I've been ignoring it—in denial, I suppose, but it's because the tumour's over the motor control area for my right side, as well as Broca's, so it's having a motor effect, as well.'

Which was why his handwriting was untidy. So many clues, and she'd missed them all. Lucy felt sick. Sick with fear, sick with guilt, sick with worry.

'I'm so sorry—'

'No. Not now, Luce. I can't do this now. I know our marriage is a mess, and this doesn't change it, and it'll probably be worse afterwards, but I can't deal with that now. I just need to get through this.'

She nodded numbly. 'OK. Can I stay with you? I

know I kicked you out, but it wasn't because I don't care. I do care. I care a lot—so much. Please let me stay with you.'

His fingers tightened, and he nodded. 'Course you can,' he said gruffly.

He wrapped his arms around her and held her tight, and she clung to him, her body shaking all over with reaction. He could feel her crying, feel the sobs breaking free, and he lifted her face and kissed away the tears.

'Don't cry.'

'I can't help it,' she said brokenly. 'I can't lose you.'

'Don't—you won't lose me. I'm here.'

She touched his cheek, her fingers trembling. 'I love you.'

He gave a ragged groan and gave up. He needed her, as he'd never needed her, and he bent his head and took her mouth in a long, frenzied kiss, his fingers tunnelling through her hair, his hands all over her, searching for her skin, dragging the soft sweater out of the way and sliding his hands around her ribcage.

So soft. So sweet. God, he'd missed her. And if the operation went wrong...

She was tugging at his shirt, but there wasn't time for that and he hauled up her skirt, unzipped his trousers and pushed her back onto the bed, driving into her with a desperate groan.

It wasn't subtle. It was frantic and messy and fraught with emotion, and the end when it came left him reeling.

He dropped his head on her shoulder and sucked in a breath, and her hands gentled, stroking his shoulders, sliding down his back and soothing him tenderly.

'I love you,' she murmured, and he lifted his head

and stared down into her tear-filled eyes, and felt his own flood.

'Lucy, this doesn't change things. I don't want you feeling you're stuck with me because of this. If the surgery doesn't work out—'

'Shh.' She pressed her finger to his lips and eased away from him. 'Come on, we have to pack. We've got a train to catch.'

'Mr Gallagher? Mr Cardew will see you now.'

He stood up. 'Coming?'

She nodded and got to her feet, and went in with him, her legs like jelly.

David greeted them warmly, but then dispensed with the pleasantries and got straight to the point.

'I'm sorry about the unseemly rush, but you probably don't mind. Right, this is what we're dealing with.'

She looked at the images on the screen in front of them, and she felt Andy's fingers thread through hers again and tighten. She squeezed back, and kept his hand firmly in hers while David talked to them.

He told them exactly what he planned to do, and she was shocked by the extent of the pale shape sprawled across the left side of his frontal lobe.

All the way there she'd convinced herself it could only be tiny, just a trivial little blip pressing on his brain, but there was nothing slight or trivial about it, she realised in dread, and the fallout from the surgery could be huge. And that was assuming that it was benign.

The significance of it wasn't lost on Andy, either, she realised, because as David started explaining in detail what he intended to do, his fingers tightened on hers again and she could feel the tension vibrating through him.

She felt overwhelmed, staring at the extensive mass that David was planning on slowly and painstakingly dissecting out. It followed every line and contour of his speech area, snuggling down into every nook and cranny. Getting it out will be a nightmare, she thought. What if he loses his speech completely? What if he can't ever talk to me again? Or the children?

She thought of his dry wit, the hilarious stories he told at dinner parties, his effortless eloquence. He had an opinion on just about everything, and expressed himself so fluently, so clearly, so lucidly. If he couldn't do that, couldn't even manage the normal everyday communication of essentials, the frustration would kill him, even if the tumour didn't.

'I want to operate first thing tomorrow morning,' David was saying. 'We've discussed this briefly, but I'll go over it again. We'll give you all kinds of lovely happy drugs, take you into Theatre and give you a brief anaesthetic while we remove the area of skull over the tumour, and then we wake you up. If you can tolerate it, and it should be pain free, we'll take a biopsy of the tumour and get it sent off, and then we'll ask you to talk to us and read out loud until we've established what part of the affected area is controlling what, and then we'll know what we can and can't achieve. If you get speech arrest at any point in the procedure, we'll have to assess where to go from there.'

He'd be in Theatre for ages, she thought numbly. Awake, and lying there trying to concentrate while they carefully nibbled away at this insidious thing inside the head of the man she loved.

'How long will it take?' she asked, knowing it could only be a guess but struggling for any kind of common sense from this.

'A few hours. Four, maybe, at the most? We'll keep you in overnight tonight, Andy, and run some more tests before the morning. I've got a speech and language therapist coming to do a pre-op assessment, and she'll repeat that tomorrow after the procedure and then she'll be working with your local SLT as necessary in the next few weeks or months. You're welcome to stay here, Lucy; there's a reclining chair and some blankets in the room, and we'll keep updating you with progress tomorrow as we go.'

'How long will I be in?' Andy asked, his voice sounding rusty and unused.

'It depends how you are. Probably one night post-op. Maybe not even that. Once you're stable and I'm satisfied there are no post-op complications, you can go home. I'll get them to show you to your room now and they can start to clerk you.'

It was a lovely room, a single room off the quiet ward overlooking a tree-lined courtyard, and Lucy perched on the edge of the reclining chair while Andy paced restlessly.

'What about the children?' he asked, worrying about them, about the fact that he hadn't been able to see them and explain—might never be able to explain. 'Will your parents be all right to have them that long?'

'They'll be fine. They're going to stay at ours. Daisy's got my keys. I'll call them later, and we'll update them again tomorrow. After the op. When I know—' She broke off. When she knew he was alive?

When she knew he wouldn't die? *When she knew that he'd never talk again?*

Damn, she was crying, and while she mopped herself up Andy just stood there staring numbly out of the window.

'Sorry,' she said, sniffing. 'It's just such a shock.'

He nodded. 'I know.'

He looked as if he was going to say more, but then there was a knock on the door and a smiling woman came in armed with a folder.

'Hi, are you Andrew Gallagher?'

'Yes. Andy. And this is my wife, Lucy.'

'Hi, there. I'm Kate North, I'm the speech and language therapist. Is it OK if I call you Andy and Lucy?'

'Sure.'

'Right, I don't know how much you know about this. A fair amount, I imagine? I gather you're both doctors?'

'Yes, that's right,' Lucy said, warming to her. 'So—what happens now?'

'I'd like to do a test to establish where you are at the moment with your speech, Andy. Is that OK?'

'That's fine. Go ahead.'

'Do you want me to leave?' Lucy asked him, wondering he'd want her there or if he'd feel less uncomfortable without her.

He shrugged, but Kate gave her an encouraging smile. 'I'm fine with you staying. You're the person he talks to most, so it's actually quite useful for you to know what we do and how we establish speech loss, and you can give me an idea of what you would have expected him to be capable of.'

She nodded. 'I would be interested,' she admitted.

'I'm a GP, so I have lots of stroke patients I refer for SLT. It would be very useful to see it in action.'

'Sure. Right, let's start.'

It was simple. Dead easy, he thought, having no trouble at all with any of the exercises. Then they shifted up a gear, and he had the odd hesitation, but Kate didn't seem fazed by it and moved on.

And he began to struggle. Really struggle, with things he *knew*. And it shook him.

As if she realised that, she shut her folder and smiled. 'OK, I think we've done enough now. I'll be able to tell after the op just how much of an effect, if any, it's had on you, and I'll pass that onto the SLT you'll be working with at home in Suffolk so she knows where to start.'

He nodded, and with a reassuring smile and a handshake, she left them again.

'Wow. That was quite intensive,' Lucy said, but he didn't reply. He was still busy taking in the shocking extent of the holes in his expressive language ability that her tests had revealed, an extent he'd been blissfully unaware of except for the odd moment of frustration.

No. More than that, if he was honest, but nothing that couldn't have been put down to distraction or tiredness. But the tests she'd just done proved to him beyond any doubt that this was serious and significant.

And in that moment, it went from theory to reality.

There were other tests.

Swabs for MRSA, even though they'd been done in Yoxburgh on Sunday. Bloods, ditto. A full physical examination from the anaesthetist, and another talk-through of the procedure, as if he wasn't well enough aware of what they were going to do to him.

In a gap in the middle he spoke to the children, assured them that he was all right, told them he loved them and then handed the phone to Lucy because his throat closed up so he couldn't speak.

'Are they OK?' he asked when she hung up, and she nodded.

'I think so. They've had supper and they're about to get ready for bed. My parents send their love, and Daisy and Ben said break a leg, apparently. Oh, and Stanley's dug a hole in the lawn.'

He gave a tiny, twisted smile, and then another nurse came in for another set of obs and the merry-go-round started all over again.

And then finally, at seven o'clock, they were left alone.

'So what happens now?' he asked a nurse who popped in to check his notes.

'Supper. You have a choice—there's a menu here, or if you'd rather you can go out for dinner. There's a nice Italian place round the corner.'

'Can we do that?' he asked, sounding stunned.

'Yes, sure. Just don't have anything too heavy, and don't drink too much.'

'One glass of wine?'

She smiled. 'One glass of wine is fine. Go out of the door, turn right and right again, and it's in the mews, about half way down on the left. Be back by nine, if you can.'

She walked out, and Andy let out a tiny, amazed huff of laughter and looked at Lucy. 'Well, are you coming?'

'Absolutely.'

She stood up and pulled on her jacket, and Andy

shrugged into his coat and opened the door for her, looking as if he'd been reprieved.

He held out his arm, and she tucked her hand into the crook of it and they walked out together into the chilly November night, arm in arm, for all the world like any other married couple.

If only…

CHAPTER FIVE

THEY found the restaurant easily, and because it was Monday night and quite early, there was a table free.

'So, what do you fancy?' he asked, scanning the menu.

'Nothing, really. It's just nice to get out of the hospital.'

He put the menu down and smiled at her, his slate blue eyes curiously intense. 'Forget it, Lucy. Let's forget everything for the next couple of hours. Just you and me, a nice meal, a glass of wine.'

Because it might be the last conversation they ever had.

She held his eyes for an age, spellbound by that strange intensity, and then nodded and looked down at her menu. 'OK. I'll have the crayfish arrabiatta, and then probably tiramisu. And a glass of prosecco, I think.'

'Sounds good to me.'

He hailed the waiter, placed the order and then took her hand, his eyes gentle now, warm and tender. 'Thanks for coming with me.'

She swallowed. 'I wouldn't have let you come on your own. I've missed you. It's felt—wrong.'

He ignored that. 'Tell me about work. How did it feel going back?'

'OK, I suppose. I was a bit worried about Lottie at nursery, but she was fine.' And you, only you weren't fine, were you, she thought, but didn't say it. 'Actually, I'd better let them know I won't be in for a while.'

'Why not?'

'Because I'll be looking after you.'

'No, you won't. I'll be fine. And anyway, we weren't talking about that,' he said with a smile that didn't seem to reach quite to his eyes. 'Tell me about Ben and Daisy's house. Have you seen it yet?'

She let it go for now. Curiously liberating, she realised, and smiled back, playing along with him because really, what else could they do? And it *was* nice to sit and talk to him as if nothing so momentous was going to happen tomorrow.

'Yes. Yes, I have seen it, a couple of times, and it's lovely, but I think they're mad. I'm so, so glad we bought a modern house because we just wouldn't cope. We still haven't got round to painting it, and all we have to do is open a tin of emulsion. They've got to strip wallpaper and replaster half of it, and the kitchen's huge, but at the moment it's almost bare and they're pretty much camping in it. She was telling me what they're going to do, and it'll be really lovely when it's finished, but—wow.'

'You always said you fancied a Victorian house.'

'No. I said I love them,' she corrected, picking up an olive and chewing it thoughtfully. 'I didn't say I'd want to live in one. The flat was enough to put me off for life.'

He laughed softly. 'It was a nightmare, wasn't it? Do you remember that night of the storm, when the plaster cornice fell down in the bedroom and nearly smashed the chest of drawers?'

'I don't think I'll ever forget it! And the landlord never did fix it. We had a hole in the ceiling for a year, and every time it rained, it dripped into a bucket.'

'That was a long time ago.'

'It was, and it should have been awful, but we had fun. We used to go out for walks and house-hunt every Sunday.'

'We did. And then we found our little house.' His thumb stroked rhythmically over the back of her hand, his smile nostalgic, and she ached to hold him. Instead she fed him an olive.

'I loved that house. And it was much better than the flat.'

'Only slightly. It was in a pretty tired state, and it had a wasp's nest in the roof instead of leaks,' he reminded her.

She laughed. 'I'd forgotten that—but it was ours, so it didn't seem to matter. It had a lovely rose bed down the side of the garden, though, and that gorgeous old brick wall behind it. Beautiful. They smelt amazing, those old roses. I really missed them when we sold that house.'

'You always loved roses,' he murmured. 'You had them in your bouquet. Real ones, scented, out of your mother's garden. They were beautiful. You were beautiful. You still are.'

Her eyes filled, and she looked down, a soft wash of colour flooding her cheeks. It was years since she'd blushed, he realised. Years, maybe, since he'd complimented her. What a waste.

'Lucy?'

She looked up, and saw sorrow and regret in his eyes.

'Don't, Andy. Not now. It really doesn't matter.'

She took his hand in hers, tracing the lifeline with her fingertip, wondering what secrets it held for their future.

'Scusi, Signora.'

She let his hand go and sat back so the waiter could set her plate down, and the moment was gone...

'Lucy?'

She turned her head towards him, lying in the bed close by her side. 'Mmm?'

'Come here. I want to hold you.'

She sat up, the light blanket sliding off her shoulders, and searched his face in the dim light. 'We can't!' she whispered.

'Of course we can, we're married. And anyway, who's going to know?'

'They'll come in and do your obs.'

'No, they won't. Not till the morning.'

He was right, they wouldn't, and she couldn't sleep, not when all she wanted to do was hold him. And she guessed he couldn't sleep, either, which was more significant, because tomorrow was going to be a very challenging day for him.

She slipped into bed beside him and rested her head on his shoulder, and his arm curled warm and firm around her back, his hand splayed over her hip as their legs tangled together.

'That's better,' he said softly, and within minutes he was snoring quietly, his chest rising and falling evenly as he slid into sleep. She could hear his heart beating steadily under her ear, feel the shift of his ribs under her hand with every breath.

'I love you,' she whispered silently, hot tears leaking unbidden from the corners of her eyes.

She did love him.

He might not be perfect, but he was her rock, her anchor in the choppy sea of life, and she lay there holding him, the man she'd loved for so many years, surrounded by the muffled sound of the London traffic and the quiet footfalls of the nurses in the corridor outside, keeping vigil over him until the noises outside the door signalled the start of the day.

Then she slipped quietly out of his arms and stood at the window, watching the first faint streaks of dawn lighten the sky while she waited for the curtain to rise on the next act.

He was given a pre-med, and the 'happy drugs' David had talked about, the sedative that would keep him calm throughout the procedure, and David came to see him.

'How are you?'

'Looking forward to it being over.'

'I'm sure. Lucy, have we got your mobile number so we can keep in touch?'

'Yes. But I'll probably be here for most of it. Is that all right?'

'Of course. Do whatever you want. Any more questions, either of you?'

They shook their heads, and he squeezed Andy's hand. 'See you in there. You'll be fine. I'll look after you.'

He nodded, and David went out, closing the door softly behind him and leaving them alone.

'Do you want to speak to the girls?' she asked, and he nodded again, so she rang home and he talked briefly to both of them. Lucy was sitting beside him, perched on the edge of the chair, her hands clenched together as she watched him. His eyes were bright when he handed back the phone.

'OK?'

He nodded, unable to speak, teetering on the brink of his control. He was OK, he supposed, in a way—as OK as it could be when you'd just spoken to your children for what might be the very last time. Except…

He turned to face her, his heart thumping.

'Luce, I've written something for the kids, and for you. It's upstairs in the attic bedroom, in the top drawer of the bedside table. If anything happens—'

She caught her breath, and hastily blinked away the tears. 'Nothing's going to happen,' she said firmly, crushing his hand. 'You're going to be fine. You heard him. He's going to get it all out, and you'll be fine.'

His smile nearly broke her heart.

'Give it to them. If you need to.'

She sucked in a breath and blinked back a fresh wave of tears.

'Of course I will. But I won't need to. David won't let anything happen to you.'

But they both knew it wasn't all down to David and his skill, and as the minutes ticked by, the tension mounted and it was almost a relief when they arrived to take him to Theatre.

He rested his head back and closed his eyes, and Lucy held his hand until they kicked the brakes off the bed.

'Time to go,' they said, pausing.

'Good luck. I love you,' she said softly as she kissed him goodbye, and as they wheeled him away she didn't hear his answer. It could have been, 'I'm sorry,' but she wasn't sure.

Her heart lurched, and she pressed her hand to her mouth to hold back the cry.

Don't be sorry. Just live. Anything else we can deal with. Just—live...

It was the longest morning of her life.

He'd been taken down to Theatre at seven fifty, and despite what she'd said about waiting there, she suddenly needed to be outside, so she went to the little café on the corner near the restaurant, and bought herself a cappuccino and a biscotti to dunk in it, and phoned her mother.

'How is he?' she asked.

'Um—he's gone to Theatre a few minutes ago. Because it's a meningioma David's confident he can get all of it without causing any damage, but it's over his speech centre, Mum, and—' She broke off, struggling with tears, and her mother waited.

'Sorry. It's just all a bit much. How's Lottie? I had to express some milk this morning, and I didn't bring the breast pump so it was a bit tricky. Was she all right with the bottle?'

'She's fine. We're all fine. She woke once in the night but she settled again. She's spreading her breakfast in her hair at the moment, but apart from that everything's going well.'

Lucy laughed and then sniffed. 'Sorry. She does that. Are the girls OK? Andy just wanted...'

'I know. Actually I think it was a good idea, because they were really worried about him and they seemed reassured. I wish I could come and be with you, darling, but I guess I'm more use here. Is there anything I can do?'

'Cuddle Lottie for me,' she said, and then had to fight back the tears again.

'Hey, come on, you're made of sterner stuff than that,' her mother said, ever practical. 'I thought I'd change your sheets—he'll need clean sheets when he comes home. And someone's been in the attic, so I've changed those sheets, too, and done all the rest of the washing, and your father's taken the girls to school and then he's going to walk the dog.'

'Thank you, Mum. I don't know what we would have done without you.'

'Well, you aren't without us, and that's what families are for. You just sit tight, and let us know how it goes, and don't worry about the girls, they're OK.'

'Thank you.'

She finished her coffee, then couldn't suddenly bear to be so far from him, so she went back to the hospital and paced around his room.

And then the phone rang, and it was David. 'Lucy, I've got Andy here for you,' he said. 'We've done the craniotomy and the biopsy, and we've woken him up and he's quite comfortable, so we're about to go ahead with the surgery, but I thought you might like to talk to him.'

And then Andy was on the line, to her astonishment, sounding slightly drowsy otherwise but utterly normal.

'Hi, Luce. How're you doing?'

'Oh—I'm fine,' she said with a little gasp. 'I can't believe I'm talking to you. How are you? How is it?'

'OK. It's a bit surreal. There's a frame holding my head still, and I can't see anything, but I can hear them all talking and I gather they're inside now and they're about to start debulking it, I think. They're going to do some mapping, find out which areas do what, but I can't feel a thing. I thought it would hurt, but it's fine. Just—weird.'

'Gosh. It's amazing to talk to you. I'm glad it doesn't hurt. Are you really OK?'

'Yeah, I'm fine. It's good. Interesting. How are the girls?'

'OK. Lottie was spreading breakfast in her hair when I spoke to Mum.'

She heard him chuckle, and then someone said something and he said, 'Oh. I've got to go. They're going to start the serious stuff, so I have to count and read out loud and wiggle my fingers and things. I'll see you later.' There was a tiny hesitation, then he murmured, 'Love you.'

He hadn't said that in so long it almost took her breath away. 'Love you, too,' she said, and then the phone went dead and she sat down on the chair with a plonk and waited, his softly murmured words echoing poignantly in her head.

They updated her once they'd done the initial mapping to identify the functioning areas under the tumour, and again when the biopsy result came back.

She was in a little park when that call came, strolling aimlessly around and watching children kicking up the autumn leaves, and she rang her mother.

'It's benign,' she told her, and burst into tears.

'Oh, Lucy, that's fantastic! I'm so glad. Darling, talk to your father, I'm a bit tied up with Lottie.'

There was a slight scuffle, then her father came on the line.

'Hi, darling, I gather it's good news. How is he?'

'Fine,' she gulped, sucking in a breath and swiping away the tears. 'He's going to be fine. It's very deep, and it's going to take them a long time to get it all, apparently, but then it shouldn't regrow and he'll be fine.'

'And his speech?'

'I don't know. I spoke to him in Theatre before they started removing the tumour and he sounded fine, but I don't know how he'll be when it's over. It's just a case of waiting now.'

'Well, let us know when he's out. We're thinking of you.'

'Thanks. Give Lottie a hug.'

'Will do.'

She looked at her watch. It was nearly twelve. Four hours since he'd gone to Theatre, over three since she'd eaten anything. No wonder she was feeling shaky and pathetic.

She went back to the café and ordered another coffee, but decaf this time so she didn't end up with palpitations. She was close enough as it was. She bought a sandwich to go with it but she only picked at it, her appetite in tatters.

And then she went back to his room to wait, and almost immediately she had a call to say he was in Recovery and doing well.

'Is he talking?'

'Yes, but that will probably change in the next few hours,' David told her. 'We had a bit of a struggle to get the last part out, so it might take a while for him to recover completely, but I'm hopeful he won't have any lasting deficit. He'll probably get worse in the next few days, and then he'll slowly start to get better. We'll see how he is tomorrow. I'd like to keep an eye on him for twenty four hours, but then I think you should be able to take him home some time tomorrow afternoon.'

'That sounds good,' she said shakily. 'Thank you, David. Thank you so much.'

'My pleasure. I'll see you both in a while, but he should be with you shortly.'

He was awake when they brought him back, but drowsy.

'Hi there,' she said, and he smiled slightly and lifted his hand.

'Hi,' he said, after a second. 'OK?'

'Yes, I'm fine. Pleased to see you. How are you?'

'OK. Tired. Very…long.'

'I'm sure it was. Why don't you have a sleep now? I'll be here.'

He grunted softly, his eyes drifting shut, and she sat there beside him and watched him sleep while the nurses quietly came and went.

She'd expected his head to be bandaged, but there was just a strip of dressing stuck on the suture line, a narrow channel shaved in his hair around three sides of a square, above his left ear and over his temple. At a glance you might not even notice there was anything amiss, she thought, especially since his hair was long overdue for a cut. Given a couple of weeks, it would be invisible.

'Will he be in pain?' she asked one of the nurses, and she shook her head.

'No, he shouldn't be. He will have been given something in Theatre so it won't be hurting him now. He should be quite comfortable, and he'll be discharged on painkillers. They usually manage very well post-op.'

That was reassuring to know. It seemed bizarre, impossible, that David had been inside his head, meticulously dissecting out that huge and threatening mass she'd seen on the scan images. Even more bizarre to know that it had been growing there for who knew how long. Had it changed him? Sucked away his personality? He'd certainly been different, but was that all down to the tumour, or something else?

Well, it was gone now, and only time would tell if that had been the cause. Whatever the reason, she was determined to get their marriage back on track. She knew it wouldn't be easy, but they would get there, she promised herself.

Come hell or high water, they would get there.

He slept off and on for the rest of the day.

David came to see him, and he sat up and shook his hand and seemed OK. Until he tried to speak, and then the words just weren't there.

'Don't worry,' David said. 'You were fine during the op, you didn't suffer any significant speech arrest while we were working, and you were talking well all through it, so this is temporary, OK? It's all still there, it's just a case of giving it time, and I think within a few days you'll be starting to see a real improvement. I know it's frustrating, but it's not for ever. Hold that thought, OK?'

'OK,' he said, David's words swirling around in his head, some of them meaningless. 'Wh—wha—whe…'

'When can you go home?'

'Yeah. Go—home.'

'Tomorrow, I think. We'll do another scan, and then

you can leave once I'm happy everything's as it should be. You probably don't want to go on the train, so you could either book a cab or arrange for someone to pick you up.'

He nodded, turning to Lucy. 'You—um—'

'I'll get my father to come. OK?'

'OK,' he said, sagging back against the pillows. 'Good.'

'Has Kate North been yet?'

'No,' Lucy told him. 'Will she come today?'

'Yes. She's got a chart with pictures of things that you can point to, so you can ask for what you want to help you get through these early days, and all sorts of other ideas. I'll page her, get her to come and see you, and I'll be back in the morning. You're doing really well, Andy. Hang in there. I'll see you later.'

He patted him on the shoulder and left them, and Andy turned away, but not before she'd seen the bleak expression in his eyes.

He should have expected it.

He'd been warned. He'd known it was possible that he'd lose his speech for a bit, but it was scary the way the words had just gone, vanished into thin air.

He was surprised he could think so clearly. Not in words, not really, more concepts. Feelings.

Frustration, relief, impatience.

Thirst.

There was a glass and a bottle of water on the locker beside him, but his right hand was being a bit uncooperative, and he didn't fancy his chances of getting the lid off.

'Do you want a drink?'

He nodded carefully, and Lucy came round to the other side of the bed, back into his line of sight, and poured him a glass of water. He lifted his right hand, changed his mind and took it with his left.

Bliss. It tasted amazing. Cool and sweet and clean. He drained it and handed it back, and she put it down and perched on the bed beside him.

'The girls send their love. I've spoken to them, told them you're all right and you're going to be OK. They told me to give you a cuddle.'

She leant forwards with a smile and put her arms round him, and after a second he lifted his arms and slid them round her, easing her closer so her head was beside his, her cheek against his right temple so that his nose was buried in her hair. It smelt of her shampoo, soft and fragrant, achingly familiar and oddly reassuring.

He only let her go when Kate North came into the room, and as Lucy straightened up he could see moisture under her eyes.

'Hi there,' Kate said, pulling up a chair as Lucy moved away to stand by the window, surreptitiously swiping the last trace of tears from her cheeks and staring out into the gathering gloom of the early evening.

The nights were drawing in, the days shorter and shorter.

Would he be talking by Christmas?

And would they still be together?

Yes. He loved her. He'd said so. She hugged the thought to her heart. Whatever was coming, they could deal with it together...

Kate gave him a chart.

* * *

He hated it. Hated having to point, but it beat lying there trapped in a silent prison where everybody else could talk except him. He could manage some words. Simple stuff, greetings and so on, meaningless things, but to ask for a specific thing seemed infinitely harder and absolutely beyond reach.

But he was alive. He told himself that, again and again, over the course of the next few hours, but when the morning came the little bit of speech he'd had seemed to have slipped away and even thinking was harder. And his right arm was even less useful, so that Lucy had to help dress him when David said he could go home.

Her father came, and he sat in the front with the seat reclined, dozing most of the way, and then he heard the crunch of gravel and opened his eyes.

'Home,' he said, after groping for a moment, and Lucy smiled at him, her eyes misting.

'Yes. Home. Come on, let's get you inside and have a cup of tea.'

And then the girls were running out, slinging their arms around him and hugging him, the dog pushing in and licking his hand, and he felt his eyes filling and welling over.

Odd, because he actually didn't really feel any emotion, just a curious numbness. 'Tea,' he said, and the girls led him inside, one on each hand, towing him through the door and into the sitting room with Stanley at their heels, then Megan was climbing up on the sofa beside him and peering at his head.

'Careful, darling,' Lucy said, but he didn't seem worried, just put his arm round her and hugged her, Emily on the other side and the dog stuck on his leg, gazing at him adoringly. So far, so good, she thought, but not for the first time she wondered exactly what it would be like living with a man who couldn't communicate.

He wasn't the most long-suffering, and she didn't imagine for a moment that he'd be a good patient, but he was alive, he was going to stay alive, and he should get better.

One step at a time, she told herself. One day at a time, one hour—one minute.

'Tea?'

He nodded. 'Tea,' he repeated, but there was no answering smile, and she turned away before he could see the tears in her eyes.

Her mother was in the kitchen boiling the kettle, and without a word she put her arms round Lucy and held her. When she moved away, her mother searched her face and tutted.

'He'll get better. Isn't that what David said? That this is temporary?'

She nodded. 'Yes. It's just—I know it's crazy, but I wasn't really expecting him to be like this. Not speaking, maybe, but—he's not reacting to things, not responding, really, and his right hand's uncooperative—Mum, it's almost as if he's had a stroke.'

'Don't forget that the surgery itself is the equivalent of a brain injury,' her mother pointed out gently. 'It's tough. His brain is irritated, swollen, it needs time to recover from the insult. It's like concussion. He will be all right. He just needs time. Give him a few days.'

She sucked in a breath and nodded. Her mother was a nurse, and she'd worked in a head injuries unit for years. She knew what she was talking about, and these weren't just platitudes. She knew that, just as she knew everything her mother was telling her. But...

'Where's Lottie? I could do with feeding her to take the pressure off.'

'In her buggy in the utility room, sleeping. She dozed off on the way back from school and I thought I'd leave her, but she's had over an hour. Why don't you have your tea first and get Andy settled in, then you can feed her when she wakes up?'

She nodded again, picked up the tea tray and carried it through to the sitting room.

'Come on, girls, give your father a bit of room,' she said, setting the tray down, and they went and lay on the floor in front of the television. Stanley would normally have been there with them, with Megan draped over him, but he stayed by Andy's side, his head rested on his master's knee, eyes fixed on him.

Andy's right hand was lying on the dog's head, and she put his mug down in reach of his left hand, out of Stanley's way.

He just looked at her, meeting her eyes expressionlessly before picking it up. They didn't look like his eyes, she thought in surprise. They were just flat slate, dulled, without any of their usual expressiveness.

And then she thought of his eyes on Monday, when they'd gone out for dinner to the little Italian restaurant and his eyes had burned with that curious intensity. Now, it was as if the curtains had been closed on his soul, shutting her out, and she couldn't even tell if he was in there any more.

And she wanted to weep for him. For herself. For the children. For all of them.

Please, David, be right. Let him get it all back.
The alternative was unthinkable...

CHAPTER SIX

IT WAS odd, how little he felt.

No pain, no anything, really.

Except tired. He was ridiculously tired, and after he'd finished his tea he got up and walked towards the stairs.

'Andy?'

Lucy was there, catching up with him in the hall and looking at him in concern. He wanted to tell her he was tired, but the chart wasn't around and he couldn't find the word for sleep, so he just closed his eyes. He could feel himself swaying, and her hand wrapped around his arm and steadied him.

'Do you want to go to bed?' she asked softly, and he sighed with relief and nodded, and she tucked her arm around his waist. 'Come on,' she murmured, and went up with him to their bedroom, helping him out of his clothes. His overnight bag was there, and he found his wash things and took them into the bathroom, and by the time he came out she'd closed the curtains and turned back the bed.

He crawled into it, closed his eyes in relief and crashed into oblivion.

'Is Daddy all right?' Emily asked, snuggling up beside her when she came back down, and she nodded and hugged them both. Lottie was stirring, and her mother brought her through and put her on Lucy's lap, and while she fed her, she sat there with her three girls and talked quietly to them about their father.

'He's going to be fine, but he might not be able to speak very much for a few days.'

'Did they cut his tongue off?' Megan asked, looking ghoulishly fascinated, and she laughed and shook her head.

'No, darling, but the bit of him in his head that tells his mouth what to say is very sore, and it just needs to rest for a bit and get better. You know when you fall over and get a bruise, it hurts for a bit and then in a few days it's all gone? Well, it's like that, as if his brain's got a bruise on it, and it just needs to get better.'

'Then will he be able to talk to us again?'

'Yes, he should be.'

She crossed her fingers behind Lottie's back as she said it, hoping she was right. 'So, tell me what you've been doing at school today. Did you have a fun time?'

'No,' Emily said, snuggling closer. 'I cried. I was worried about Daddy.'

'I cried, too,' Megan said, but Lucy wasn't sure if she was just copycatting. 'But we did painting, and it was fun. I did a picture for Daddy but it was wet so I had to leave it there.'

'I'm sure he'll be really pleased when you can bring it home,' she said, leaning over to kiss her. Lottie was standing on her legs and jumping now, and she held her baby firmly and smiled at her.

'You look happy. Did you miss me?' she said, but her mother just laughed at her.

'Of course she missed you, they all did, but they've

been as good as gold, haven't you, girls? And they helped me cook last night. They were good girls.'

'They are good girls,' she said, hugging them all, and Lottie snuggled into her neck and blew a nice wet raspberry.

Her father looked at his watch. 'Lucy, darling, I hate to do this to you but we really ought to head off, if you're OK now? We just dropped everything and walked out, and I can't remember if I locked the back door, so we really should go home.'

'Of course you can go,' she said guiltily, putting Lottie safely on the floor and getting up to hug them both. 'Thank you so, so much for all your help.'

'Don't mention it—and keep in touch.'

'Of course I will.'

They hugged and kissed the children, and then her father patted her cheek gently, as if she was still his little girl. 'You take care of that man of yours. I know he's not always the easiest, but he's a good man, and I know how much you love him. You'll get there.'

She swallowed. How did he know there was anything wrong? She hadn't said a word—but this was her father, and maybe words just weren't necessary.

'Ring me when you're home,' she made them promise, and shutting the door behind them, she shepherded the children back into the kitchen, scooping Lottie up on the way, and set about cooking supper.

She was exhausted herself, more than ready to call it a day, and by the time she crept into bed beside Andy two hours later, she could hardly keep herself awake.

'Andy?' she whispered, and he turned his head and just looked at her. 'Are you OK? Do you need any supper?'

He shook his head. 'Y-you,' he said haltingly, and he reached for her, pulling her into his arms and resting his face against hers. 'Better,' he mumbled, and then she felt him relax again, his body slumping into sleep, and she snuggled down under the quilt, her head on his shoulder, and fell instantly asleep.

She was woken at eleven by Lottie crying, and she stumbled out of bed and went into her room, to find Andy standing by the cot stroking her and crooning softly.

'Come here, little one, it's all right,' she said, lifting her out and hugging her.

Andy handed her the feeder cup of water she'd brought up earlier, and she flashed him a smile and offered the baby a drink, then settled her again. She went down without fuss, miraculously, and they went back to bed, but Andy paused, sitting on the edge looking thoughtful.

'Are you OK? Do you need painkillers?'

He shook his head and pointed to his mouth.

'Hungry?'

'Mmm.'

'I'll go and raid the fridge. I'm hungry, too, I haven't really eaten.'

So she went downstairs and made ham sandwiches and tea and took them back to bed, and they lay propped up against the headboard, eating their midnight feast and sitting in companionable silence.

There, she thought. We don't really need to talk. Not all the time. And they snuggled down again under the duvet, curled together like spoons so she could feel his chest against her back, his arm warm and firm and heavy over her waist, his fingers splayed across her abdomen.

The last time they'd been in this bed together they'd made love, she remembered sadly, clutching at each other in desperation, one last frenzied reaching out before it might have been too late. How good it felt to be back here with him, warm and safe and on the mend. Right then, nothing else mattered.

She closed her eyes, slipped back into sleep and didn't stir till morning.

'Luce.'

She prised her eyes open and saw Andy standing over her with Lottie grinning and reaching out to her from the safety of his arms.

'Hello, little one,' she said, pushing herself up the bed and taking the baby from him. 'Are you all right to carry her? Don't overdo it.'

He just raised an eyebrow and disappeared into the bathroom, and she turned her attention back to the hungry baby.

'OK, OK, I'm here. There you are.'

She'd been surprised that her milk hadn't dried up while she'd been away, because her expressing hadn't been astonishingly successful. Maybe nature was cleverer than that, and in times of such stress it knew when to shut down and when to start up again. She'd been relieved to feed her last night, though, and again this morning, and she sensed that Lottie was relieved, too, to get her mother back.

Andy came out of the bathroom, disappeared down the stairs and came back a minute later, and in the distance she could hear the kettle.

'Is that a hint for early morning tea?' she said with

a smile, and for the very first time since the operation, his mouth quirked.

'I'll take that as a yes,' she said, and changed the baby's nappy and put her back next to him. 'Don't let her fall off the bed,' she warned, and he rolled his eyes, so she grinned and walked away, her heart lighter than it had been for days.

When she went back, Lottie was sitting on his chest, holding his hands and beaming at him. He blew a raspberry at her, and Lottie grinned and said, 'Da-da.'

She stared at the baby, astonished. 'When did you learn to say that?'

'Da-da,' she said again, and Andy's eyes filled.

'Oh, Lottie. You clever, clever little girl,' she said, putting the tray down and getting back into bed beside them, delighted. 'Now, practise this. Mum-mum-mum—come on. Mum-mum-mum.'

'Da-da-da,' Andy said, and Lottie laughed out loud and grabbed his face, getting dangerously close to his scalp wound, so Lucy prised her off and cuddled her, then found her a toy other than her father to play with and handed him his tea.

Of all the times for her to come up with her father's name, there couldn't have been a better one, she thought contentedly.

Lucy didn't go to work that day, but she did on Monday because he told her before the weekend that he'd be fine. Somehow. A mixture of pantomime and pointing at the calendar and miming using a stethoscope.

She'd nodded and phoned the surgery and said she'd be in on Monday, and she'd gone, taking the children to school and Lottie to nursery en route.

'It's only for three hours. I'll see you soon,' she

promised, and kissed his cheek and went, ushering the children out.

The sound of the door closing behind them reverberated around the silent house, and he leant back against the sofa cushions and sighed with relief.

So good not to have to think, or try and speak, or smile. He didn't feel like smiling. Didn't *feel* at all, really. It had been a hectic weekend, the children so pleased that he was there and seemed all right that they'd bounced excitedly around like puppies, and although it was wonderful to be home, wonderful to see them again and be surrounded by the chatter, he was exhausted, and he was glad they'd all gone out, Lucy included. Especially Lucy, maybe, because he felt she was watching him, searching for any slight sign of improvement, and he felt he was failing her.

At least his hand was improving. He'd been able to do up his shirt buttons today without help, although it had taken ages, but that didn't matter. What else did he have to do?

Nothing. So that was what he did.

The whole time she was out, he just sat there, staring into the garden and doing exactly nothing while outside the house the world all carried on as normal.

Would he ever be part of it, as he'd been before? Would he ever be normal again? He kept trying to reassure himself, but as the days had gone by and his speech hadn't returned, he'd grown more and more despondent.

Had David been wrong? Was the damage to his brain permanent?

Would he never be able to speak again?

* * *

Julie Harding, the local SLT Kate North had recommended, came that afternoon, after Lucy was home.

She'd been given a report by Kate, and she came armed with exercises and games and a whole bunch of stuff that just scared him because there was so much he couldn't do.

He could understand everything she said, could repeat it, mostly, but couldn't find it inside his own head without a prompt. But she came every day, and every day he got a tiny bit better, and in the meantime he had homework.

Ridiculously simple tasks, like matching pairs of words, copying words by writing them underneath—that sort of thing. And sometimes he even got it right.

He was boiling over inside, seething with impatience, scared because the longer it took, the more worried he was that it would never come back and he'd be trapped in a world of silence.

No. Not silence. Everyone else was talking, but he just couldn't join in, and he felt more and more remote.

Lucy didn't seem to know what to do with him, either. She'd tried to talk to him, but he couldn't respond so he'd just withdrawn, and she'd given up. He couldn't blame her. He couldn't talk to her, couldn't ask for anything, only demand it if he could find the word or failing that point to the loathsome chart.

He thought he'd go mad.

Some days he thought he already had.

It didn't really hurt. His scalp was a little sore, the whole area tender, but there was no headache, just a curious feeling of nothingness for the first few days.

At first he was ridiculously tired, but after that he was just plain bored. He couldn't read, or only with

huge effort and he was saving that for his SLT homework. He could understand the television, but there was
a limit to how much daytime TV he could cope with,
so as a change from that he'd started walking aimlessly
around the streets killing time. He had the dog with
him, so at least it looked as if he had a purpose, but in
reality he didn't.

And then feelings began to creep back in.

Frustration. Anger. Grief, for the loss of so much
of himself.

And need. Need for Lucy. The need to hold her, to
be held by her. The need to touch her, to kiss her, to
take her to bed and make love to her until they were so
close he didn't know where he ended and she began.

But he didn't. He didn't know how to ask, and she
didn't offer, and anyway, she'd kicked him out before all
of this had happened, and they still hadn't sorted it out.

Maybe never would, if he couldn't talk to her. That
ate at him like acid, but without words there was nothing he could do apart from bottle his frustration and
his feelings.

So he kept his distance, and she kept hers, and he
felt dead inside.

She was worried about him.

She knew a lot about expressive aphasia from her
work as a general practitioner, and it was hard to tell just
how much aphasics understood because it was hard to
get feedback. At the moment, certainly, she was pretty
sure Andy understood just about everything, which was
good news. And before the op, only the high-level stuff
had been badly compromised—like the research paper
he'd talked about, which like so many of them could

well have been impenetrable—so there was an excellent chance that he'd get it all back with time, along with his speech.

Knowing that, she was surprised that he'd shown so little interest in the television or radio. He just sat in silence, staring into space, or went out for walks with Stanley. He often did that—just went out for a walk, the faithful Labrador at his side. She had no idea where they went, or what they did, and she didn't like not knowing, just in case anything happened to him, but he seemed physically well so what could she do?

The incision had healed well and she'd taken the sutures out, but apart from that she hadn't really touched him. He just didn't seem to want her to, and that hurt.

She only had herself to blame, of course, because she'd thrown him out, but he was so withdrawn it worried her, so when Julie came on Friday morning she intercepted her while Andy was in the garden prowling round and looking frustrated as he waited for her arrival.

'I don't know what to do with him,' she said. 'He's just not himself, and I can't get him to try to talk at all— well, not just to chat. It's only basic, essential communication, as if he's afraid to try anything else.'

'He probably is. He's not a man who's used to failure, is he? And he probably sees this inability to speak fluently as failure, so he'd rather not set himself up to fail. Try doing it while you're doing something else together, like washing up or cooking or gardening. What's he like with the children? They're usually pretty good ice breakers.'

'Good, but he's not really speaking to them, he just watches them and looks sad.'

She nodded thoughtfully. 'I've got a game—it's great because it's not patronising. Lots of cards with photos on, and you have to put the things into different categories. It's got all sorts of levels it can be played at, and you could do it as a family. It's really good for the kids. It's in the car, I'll get it, but I would ask you to look after it because I've only got the one set and I'm supposed to be trialling it.'

'OK. Sounds good. I'm sure the kids will love it. Maybe they can do it while I'm cooking?'

'Good idea. You've got a brilliant family kitchen. What age is your eldest?'

'Emily? Seven. Coming up for eight.'

'So she's reading well?'

'Yes. She's quite good.'

'Great. I'll suggest it to him. Leave it to me.'

'Can't,' he said, when Lucy showed an interest in it later.

'It's funny that that's one of your best words,' she said drily. 'How about "yes" or "why not" or "try"?'

He just looked at her and walked away, picking up his coat and letting himself out of the house, Stanley at his heels, and she sighed and dressed Lottie up warmly and pushed her to school in the buggy to pick the girls up.

And found Daisy there, picking up Florence because they had her most weekends. It was the first time she'd seen her since his op, and she suddenly realised how lonely she was feeling.

'Hi there,' she said, and Daisy smiled at her and hugged her.

'Hi. How's it going?' she asked, and Lucy shrugged, squashing the urge to cry. It would have been so easy to give in to it, but she wouldn't let herself.

'OK,' she said. 'Sort of. Physically he seems fine, he's recovered well and I've taken his sutures out, but he's a bit down in the dumps, I think, and he won't speak unless he absolutely has to. I think he's bored and fed up, and I can see that.'

'You ought to get him out a bit, start having a social life again,' Daisy suggested. 'Why don't you come for dinner?'

'I've got a better idea. Come to us. We owe you big-time for all the help you gave us over his op, and anyway, you haven't got a kitchen so it's a bit of an empty threat.'

Daisy laughed. 'True. OK. When? We're free this weekend—we're only having Florence tonight as a favour to Jane and Peter, and then they're having both children tomorrow night because we were supposed to be going out, but it's been cancelled, so we're at a loose end if that's any good?'

'Brilliant. Come at seven thirty. We should have the girls in bed by then.'

'Done. Can I bring anything?'

'Yes. Your sense of humour. It's a bit lacking at the moment at home.'

'Oh, Lucy.' Daisy hugged her again, and for the briefest moment she let herself lean on her friend.

And then Daisy was easing away, and smiling at someone over her shoulder. 'Well, if it isn't the man himself. Hi, soldier. How are you?'

'OK,' he said, and he smiled, but it didn't really reach his eyes.

Daisy wasn't fazed. 'Neat scar,' she said, peering at his hair with a grin. 'Amazing. Did they put anything useful in there while they had the chance?'

He gave a short huff of what might have been laughter, but he seemed to relax a fraction, and Lucy let out a sigh of relief.

'I've invited Ben and Daisy to dinner tomorrow night,' she told him as they walked home, and he stopped dead and stared at her.

'Can't,' he said, looking pressured and frustrated. 'Can't—speak.'

'I've told you about "can't",' she said gently, taking his arm and hugging it as he pushed the buggy. 'You don't have to speak, you can pour wine. That'll be useful.'

He did that humourless, empty little laugh again, and she wondered if it had been such a good idea inviting them, after all. Well, she'd find out tomorrow.

'What shall we give them to eat?' she asked, clearing up the breakfast things as he finished his coffee the next morning, the newspaper untouched beside him.

He shrugged and shook his head.

'I don't know, either. Any suggestions? Meat? Fish? Curry? Roast?'

'Curry,' he said instantly.

She glanced across at him, wondering if this was too big a challenge, because he still wasn't really reading and he might need to look at the recipe. And his hand was still a little shaky, although much better than it had been last week. Could he do it? One way to find out.

'Only if you cook,' she said innocently. 'I'm rubbish at it. You always do the curries.'

He shrugged again. 'OK.'

She cracked then, not wanting to push him too far. 'I'll help. What kind of curry?'

He frowned thoughtfully, squawked and flapped his elbows, and she laughed without thinking.

'Chicken curry?' she tried, and he nodded.

'Chicken. Chicken pas—um. And—' He broke off, drawing a P on the table. 'Pil...'

'Pasanda, and pilau rice?' He nodded, his shoulders dropping as the frustration eased. 'OK,' she said. 'And we can get poppadoms and chapattis—what about a pudding?' She pushed away from the worktop and fetched a notepad and pen. 'I'm going to have to go to the supermarket. I know we haven't got enough mango chutney and I think we're short of rice.'

And then she had a brainwave. There was no need for them all to go shopping, and while she was out they could try out that game. She scribbled a list, then straightened up and looked at him.

'How would you feel about me leaving you with the girls and going shopping with Lottie? Is that OK? Are you happy looking after them?'

'We'll look after Daddy,' Emily said, cuddling up to him, and he tucked her under his arm, kissed the top of her head and nodded.

'OK.'

'Why don't you try that game Julie left yesterday?' she suggested casually, and put it on the table. 'Here— Emily, you read the instructions out.'

Heart in mouth, she went off to the supermarket, hoping she hadn't caused havoc at home, and came back to find Megan and Emily kneeling up and leaning over the table, and Andy looking smug.

'Daddy's really good at it,' Megan said, sounding disgusted. 'It's too hard.'

'No, it's not, you just have to think,' Em pointed out,

but Andy cut them off by tidying away the game and coming over to help her unpack the shopping.

She gave him a hug, and he hugged her back, holding on a second or two longer than she'd expected, and she tipped her head back and saw something new and different in his eyes. Something warm and interesting and much more like the old Andy.

Thank goodness for that. She'd been so afraid she'd pushed him too hard by leaving him with the girls to play the game.

She smiled, went up on tiptoe and kissed him, lingering for a moment, and then busied herself putting everything away, her body singing. That look in his eyes needed following up. Not now, though. Now, she had a supper party to prepare for, and the house was far from ready. But later…

'Right, you cook, I'll clean. Em, Megan, will you keep an eye on Lottie, please?'

It was good to see Ben again.

Surprisingly good, and he found himself smiling as Ben came in armed with two bottles of wine and a box of chocolates, dumped them on the table and shook his hand.

'Hey, Andy, it's great to see you,' Ben said, and hugged him briefly, slapping him on the back. 'You're looking good. How are you?'

He grunted and shook his head. 'OK—talking—not…great.'

'Well, that makes a change,' Ben said drily. 'I might get a word in edgeways. May I?' He lifted his hair out of the way and checked the suture line. 'Very tidy. Nice job.' He dropped the lock of hair. 'They've got a good locum covering you, by the way,' he added, 'but I think they miss you. It's all a bit quiet in there without your sharp tongue and razor wit.'

Andy rolled his eyes, for want of a better expression, and Ben chuckled. 'Come on, get the wine open. Working on the principle that there was some serious celebrating to do, we walked, so let's not hold back.'

Andy laughed, a real laugh that caught him by surprise, and got the corkscrew out. 'Here—you. Busy.'

And he turned back to the curry, stirring and tasting it. Ben followed him, dipping the tip of his finger in and sucking it.

'That's nice. Very nice. Did you cook it?'

He nodded.

'Can I have the recipe?'

'Not another curry recipe!' Daisy said, laughing. 'He's got loads. It's the only thing he can cook, so I hope it's not too hot. I don't want to have the baby tonight, it's not due for weeks yet.'

Andy shook his head. 'No. Um…' He found himself tracing the letter on the worktop. 'Pas…' he groped, and then Ben bailed him out.

'Pasanda? It is mild, Daisy, and you'll love it. In fact, it's probably nicer than mine, dammit.'

'Oh, perish the thought,' Daisy said, laughing, and then pushed a wine bottle towards him. 'I thought you'd been given a job? I think Andy's tongue's hanging out there, and I could do with a drink if you've got anything soft.'

'That was a great evening. The curry was gorgeous. Thank you, darling.'

'W-wel—' Damn, where was the word?

'Welcome?' she offered, and he nodded.

'Yeah. Welcome. Good idea.'

She smiled. 'I thought so. Time for bed?'

He looked at the kitchen table. She'd cleared it at some point, probably while she'd been making the coffee and he'd been talking to Ben. Or the other way round, more likely. Whatever, the dog couldn't get to any leftovers, the dishwasher was on and there was nothing to stop them going to bed.

He felt curiously hesitant, though. Not that he wasn't tired, but she looked lovely tonight, and he wanted her. Wanted to touch her, to hold her, to kiss away the little streak of chocolate on her lip and then plunder her mouth. He just didn't know how to say so without sounding clumsy and awkward.

'Come on,' she said gently, taking him by the hand and leading him towards the stairs.

'Dog?' he said, but she just shook her head.

'I put him out a few minutes ago. He's fine.'

He followed her, letting her lead him into the bedroom and close the door quietly but firmly behind them.

Then she turned and went up on tiptoes and pressed her mouth softly to his.

'Thank you,' she murmured.

'Why?' he asked, for want of a better word.

'For cooking for us. For having a go, and doing it so well, and not just saying "can't".'

She pulled his shirt out of his trousers and unbuttoned it, slowly and systematically, and when she looked up, her eyes were warm and welcoming, and it turned out he didn't have to say anything, didn't have to ask.

His heart pounding slightly, he cupped her face in

his hands, bent his head and took her mouth in a long, slow, lingering kiss that left both of them wanting more.

'Luce,' he murmured, nuzzling her neck, trailing his tongue over the hollow of her throat where he could feel her pulse picking up, too. He slid his hands up under her top, cupping her breasts, soft and warm, achingly right in his hands. He slipped the catch on her bra and moved it out of the way, letting the weight of them fill his palms, and she moaned softly and slid the shirt off his shoulders.

He let it drop to the floor behind him, then peeled off her top over her head and unfastened her jeans, sliding them down over her hips, snagging the little lace knickers on the way and pushing her gently back onto the edge of the bed.

She sat down and obediently picked up her feet, one at a time, so he could strip her jeans away, and then she reached for his belt. It was ages since they'd done this, slowly and deliberately seduced each other, and she found herself smiling.

'What?' he asked, and she looked up and met his eyes.

'Nothing. It's just nice.'

'Mmm.'

She hooked her thumbs in his waistband and pulled his trousers down, then he bent and kicked them off, heeling off his shoes at the same time and kicking them out of the way. Slowly, deliberately, she peeled down the soft, clingy jersey shorts, and he pushed her gently backwards onto the bed, lifted her legs and tucked them under the quilt and slid in beside her, drawing her back into his arms.

His mouth found hers, and she threaded her fingers through his hair and then froze.

'Oh—did I hurt you?'

'No.'

'Sure?' She levered herself up on one elbow and leant over him, pressing her lips to his hair, resting her cheek against the side of his head over the healed wound.

His hands slid up her back, warm and firm, and he eased her away and found her mouth again, and she forgot about his surgery, forgot about everything except lying there in the arms of the man she loved.

He knew just how to touch her, when to go slow, how to keep her hanging on until she was sobbing with frustration, and then how to set her free, timing it perfectly so they fell apart together, clinging to each other, then coming slowly back to earth with soft stroking touches, tender caresses, light, lingering kisses.

'Nice,' he said drowsily, and then he rolled to his back, pulled her into the crook of his arm and drifted off to sleep.

CHAPTER SEVEN

HE SLEPT better that night than he'd slept since his operation.

Amazingly, so did Lottie. Lucy crept out of bed and took her downstairs when she woke at six, put the kettle on, let the dog out of the kitchen and curled up on the sofa to feed the baby.

A few minutes later she realised that Stanley had disappeared, and she took Lottie upstairs and found the dog installed on the bed, licking Andy's hand vigorously and trying to look cute.

'Stanley,' she said warningly, and his tail wriggled guiltily as he slid off the bed.

'Sorry,' Andy said, looking every bit as guilty, and she shook her head and laughed.

'You're both naughty. No dogs upstairs. Here, cuddle Lottie,' she said, and handing his daughter over, she took Stanley back down, fed him and let him out into the garden while she made the tea, then she shut him and his wet paws in the utility room again and went upstairs to find Emily and Megan on the bed, too.

She went back down, brought them up drinks and climbed back into bed.

'When did we last do this?' she asked him, and he shrugged.

'Ages,' he said eventually, and she nodded.

'So, girls, what do you want to do today?'

It was predictable. Megan wanted to feed the ducks, Emily wanted to play the game Julie had lent them so she could see if she could win, and Lottie had what she wanted. She was busy pulling hairs out of Andy's chest and making him wince, but he didn't really seem to care and she thought he probably had what he wanted, too.

His family, all around him, and for once the time to enjoy them without guilt.

He looked up at her and smiled, and she knew she was right. If only he could keep it up when he went back to work, she thought, but that was a long way away and in the meantime there were ducks to feed and games to play.

'Can we have bacon and eggs for breakfast?' Em asked, and Andy looked hopeful.

'Andy, what do you want?' she asked, not letting him get away with that, and he just smiled knowingly.

'Bacon. Egg. Um—' He turned his hand sideways and chopped it down, then pressed an imaginary button.

'Toast!' Emily said victoriously. 'Daddy wants toast.'

'Tea or coffee?'

'Coffee. And marm...marma...'

'Marmalade!'

'Em, you have to let Daddy say the words,' she said gently. 'It just takes him a bit longer. I tell you what, why don't you say the beginning of what you want, and let him guess?'

'OK. Saus.'

'Sausages,' he said after a moment, and Emily clapped her hands and bounced on the bed.

'Well done! And tom.'

'Tomato.'

'Mummy, what do you want?'

'Pain au...'

'Chocolat,' he finished, the hesitation barely perceptible.

'You're getting too good. You do realise we don't have all of these ingredients?' she pointed out, but by the time they'd finished their tea and they'd all washed and dressed, the mini supermarket round the corner was open, so she sent Andy and Emily off with Stanley and a shopping list, and Megan entertained Lottie in front of the television while she laid the table.

They came back with extras.

Mushrooms, and another bottle of milk, and, because they had no pain au chocolat, some chocolate spread and croissants so she could make her own.

He put the bag down on the worktop, came up behind her and nuzzled her neck. 'Hi, gorgeous,' he murmured, and she turned her head and beamed at him.

'What do you want?' she asked teasingly, and he raised an eyebrow and grinned.

'Insatiable,' she murmured, trying not to laugh, and gave him a job.

'I won!'

Andy sat back and folded his arms and frowned at the game. Beaten by his seven year old daughter, he thought in disgust, but then he caught Lucy's eye and she winked, and he just smiled and let it go.

He'd get his revenge in time. His speech was getting better by the hour, or so it seemed today, so maybe David had been right and once the inflammation had gone down he'd be back to normal.

He'd said weeks to months. Maybe it really would be only weeks, and it wasn't yet two.

Plenty of time yet, and in the meantime, he was rediscovering his family, and the joy of spending time with them.

He looked out of the window, and saw that the rain which had threatened earlier had gone, and the sun was shining weakly through the trees.

'Ducks?' he suggested, and Megan leapt to her feet, fed up with a game she couldn't win and wanting to be out and about.

'I'm carrying the bread,' she said, grabbing the new loaf and running to the door. He followed her, took it away from her and said, 'No. Old bread. And—coat.'

She ran back to the kitchen, grabbed the other loaf of bread and was back at the door, one arm in her coat, the other one struggling because the sleeve was inside out. He sorted her out, then put Lottie's coat on and tucked her in the buggy, by which time Stanley was at his side, tail lashing, whining softly in anticipation.

'She always carries the bread,' Emily grumbled, but Lucy had appeared with an empty sandwich bag and she split the bread, ending the squabble before it started, and they set off to the park.

'There's Florence and Thomas!' Megan yelled, and they ran over to the others, leaving them to follow with Lottie.

'Hi! I was about to ring to thank you for last night,' Daisy said as they drew closer, 'so you've saved me the trouble. It was really lovely.'

'Yes,' Andy said, frowning in concentration but still smiling. 'Great. Thanks.'

'Thanks?'

'For—coming.'

'Oh, Andy.' She hugged him, her spontaneous warmth bringing a lump to his throat. 'It was a pleasure. It was great to see you.'

'I want that recipe,' Ben reminded him. 'Don't forget.'

'I'll remind him,' Lucy said. 'Are you heading for the ducks?'

'Yes. Are you?'

'Of course. It was Megan's turn to choose what to do, and she always wants to feed the ducks.'

'Well, why don't we feed them together, and then go back to our house for tea? I'm sure we've got some biscuits of some sort, and then Andy can realise how lucky he is having a sensible house to look after!'

Ben just groaned, and Andy slapped him encouragingly on the shoulder. 'Idiot,' he said cheerfully, and Ben laughed wearily.

'Tell me about it.'

'Nice house, isn't it?'

'Night—night—um,' Andy said as they walked away.

'Nightmare?' she suggested with a wry grin, and he nodded.

'Yup. Nightmare. Nice. But—sheesh.'

'Yeah. See what I mean about ours? Manageable.'

He grunted, but he had a thoughtful look and Lucy wondered why. Surely he wasn't contemplating a renovation project?

'You don't want one like that, do you?' she asked, and he laughed.

'No.' Firmly, definitely, no hesitation at all.

'Thank goodness for that,' she said, smiling, and

tucking her arm through his, she walked along beside him, keeping a close eye on Megan and Emily who were sharing the lead and holding onto Stanley.

Bless him, he just walked beautifully along beside them both, as good as gold. It was all down to Andy. He'd trained the dog from day one—but that was before everything had gone wrong.

She put that thought out of her mind. He was home now, and although he wasn't back at work, he seemed genuinely different, and he obviously wanted to be with them.

And hopefully the change would be permanent.

'Going to—hos…' he announced the next day.

'Hospital?'

'Yes.'

She was getting ready for work, and he'd said he'd drop the girls at school and take Lottie to the nursery, so they were all up and dressed, but there'd been no mention of the hospital.

'What for? Why are you going? Are you all right?' she asked, going into panic mode a bit.

'Fine. See—Raj and—James.'

'Oh. OK. Have a good time.' She kissed them all goodbye, then kissed him again. 'I'll see you later. You might get something nice for lunch.'

'OK.'

He dropped the girls off, took Stanley to the park and then home, and walked to the hospital. He hadn't been there since he'd walked home two weeks ago exactly, almost to the hour, and he felt a shiver of unease.

What would it be like going back?

Difficult, was the answer. He went to the Neurology

clinic and asked to speak to Raj. Well, he managed his name, but not much else, which wasn't really helpful, and because the receptionist didn't know him and he couldn't explain, she was reluctant to disturb him.

'He's consulting,' she said. 'When he's free I'll see if he can fit you in. What's your name?'

'Andy. Andy—Gall—Galla…'

Raj came out of his consulting room at that moment, and he saw Andy standing there and came straight over. 'Andy, how are you? How's it going?'

He sighed with relief and frustration. 'OK. Not—not great.'

'I wouldn't say that. Come on in.' He took him into his room and sat him down. 'I've had a report from David Cardew, and I would say you're doing well. It sounds as if it was pretty extensive.'

He nodded. 'Yes. But—slow.' Hell, he was worse, because he was trying to pass on precise information, not just chat, and it was much more challenging. 'Speech—slow.'

'He said you had speech loss after the op, but he's very confident it's transient.'

'Good. Doing—head in,' he said, stumbling over every word, and then laughed wryly. 'Raj—thank you.'

'You don't need to thank me. I'm glad I was able to help. Have you been down to the ED yet? They miss you.'

'Ben—said.'

'Ben?'

Oh, damn. He couldn't remember his name. 'Um—babies,' he groped, and Raj nodded.

'Walker.'

'Yeah. Ben Walker. Going—now to ED.'

'Good, they'll be pleased to see you. How's the SLT going?'

He nodded. 'OK. Slow. All slow.'

Raj smiled. 'You're too impatient, Andy. Enjoy the holiday. Have fun with the kids. They grow up all too fast.'

He nodded again. They did. It seemed like minutes since Lucy had told him she was pregnant, and Lottie was eight months old now. Eight months old, and could say 'Da-da'. That was worth all of this. He just needed to remind himself from time to time.

He said goodbye to Raj, and walked over to the ED.

And was mobbed.

He didn't need to speak. They probably all knew he couldn't, really, but it was amazing to see them, and he was hugged and kissed by nurses who under normal circumstances would have given him a wide berth, and slapped on the back by the lads.

And then James, the clinical lead, dragged him off to his office and gave him a coffee and told him how much they missed him.

'We want you back, but we know it's going to be a while,' he said.

'Want to come, but—' It was pointless trying to say any more. Those few words were enough to underline quite clearly his inadequacy. 'How—locum?'

'OK. Good. Not as good as you, of course.'

'Of course,' he repeated drily, if a little slowly.

They swapped grins, and then James' pager went off, so he followed him and stood outside Resus looking in and feeling swamped by frustration. He could see from here what was wrong, what was needed, knew exactly what to do, he just couldn't *tell* anyone.

And until he could, he'd be a danger to his patients.

James glanced up, and he smiled at him and lifted his hand and walked away, leaving them to it.

There was no sign of him when she got home with Lottie, and the dog was missing.

It might have meant nothing, but she had a bad feeling about it. Apart from anything else, he'd said he'd pick something up for lunch for them, and so she'd been expecting him to be there. She scoured the house for a note, then realised he probably couldn't write her one.

He'd gone to the hospital.

Had one of his friends dragged him off to the café for lunch? Unlikely. They all seemed to be too busy for lunch, but Lottie was getting grizzly, so she opened the baby a jar of food and was spooning it into her when she heard the utility room door open.

'No!'

He followed the sodden, muddy dog into the kitchen with an apologetic wince. 'Sorry. Door open.'

'That's OK. Are you all right?'

He ignored that, stared at her and swore softly. 'No lunch. Sorry.'

There *was* something wrong, she knew it now. 'Don't worry. We'll go to the pub. I'm just giving Lottie something, and she can come with us and have a nap in her buggy. They won't be busy.'

He nodded, but he didn't look overjoyed, just took the dirty dog back out to the utility room and came back a few moments later without him. 'Muddy.'

'He is. Where did you go?'

He frowned. 'Trees,' he said, when the word he was

looking for evaded him. So frustrating. He was ready to punch the walls, but it wouldn't help.

'The spinney?'

'Yeah. Spinney,' he repeated, trying to rebuild the memory for that word, but it didn't work like that, he knew.

'Right, little monkey, let's clean you up and you can have pudding in the pub.' She made a bottle quickly, threw it in the changing bag with a pot of apple and mango puree, and pulled on her coat. 'Coming?'

He'd taken off his coat, but it was his dog-walking coat and she saw he was swapping it for a thick fleece. He put the buggy in the boot, then automatically went to the driver's side of the car. She saw him grit his teeth as he went back to the passenger side and got in, and she wondered what had happened, because he'd been fine that morning.

'How did you get on at the hospital?' she asked him when they were settled by the fire in the pub.

He stared out of the window at the sea surging against the breakwaters off the prom, and sighed. 'OK. Saw Raj.'

'Did you thank him?'

He nodded. 'Saw James. Everyone was—nice.' More than nice, but how to say it?

'And?' she prompted, sensing more.

'So stupid,' he said softly, his voice taut. 'Watched them—Resus—know everything, but just—can't.'

'Oh, Andy. You will be able to. Darling, it's only two weeks tomorrow since the operation. You're much better than you were. The words are starting to come, much better. And your hand's fine now. It's such early days. Just enjoy it—treat it like a holiday.'

'What Raj said. Holiday. But not, is it? Not holiday. And—what if…?'

'Andy, no. Don't start thinking like that. Just take each day as it comes. Starting right now. Lottie needs pudding. I think the ideal person to give it to her is the only person whose name she can say.'

And she handed the pot and the spoon to him, and went off to order their meal.

'Da-da-da,' Lottie said, smacking her hands on the tray of the high chair, and he stared at her, this miracle that was their child, and gave up. Maybe everyone was right. Maybe he should just enjoy the holiday, take it day by day and have fun, and let his speech take care of itself.

'Good girl,' he said, ripping the foil top off the dessert and dipping the spoon in it. 'Open.'

She opened her mouth, like a baby bird with a gaping beak, and he spooned yellow gloop into it and felt glad to be alive.

Well, something had changed, she thought, threading her way back through the tables.

Lottie was beaming and covered in pudding, and Andy was smiling at her and laughing and scooping the drips off her chin with every appearance of enjoyment.

'Da-da,' Lottie said, and he grinned, and she smiled.

That was it. Bless her, Lottie had charmed him out of his grumps and made him smile, and she could have scooped her up and hugged her, but she was covered in yellow slime and Lucy was wearing one of her few decent jumpers.

'Have you two spread that quite far enough?' she asked mildly, plucking a baby wipe from the packet and swiping it over her face. Two minutes later she was clean as a whistle, out of the high chair and snug in Andy's arms, having her bottle, so Lucy settled back and picked up her fizzy water and watched them.

It was good to see him with Lottie. He'd spent far too little time with her, and she adored him. Maybe there was truth in the saying that absence made the heart grow fonder.

'I ordered you fish and chips.'

He shot her a smile. 'Good. Brain—food.'

She laughed. 'Not when it's in batter,' she said drily, but there were times to worry about Omega 3 and times to have fun, and today was definitely the latter.

'I've got something to tell you,' she remembered. 'I saw a man today—a Mr Darby. He said you treated his mother two weeks ago in the ED, and she died. It was on the Sunday of the storm, just after we got home from my parents, I suppose, the day Raj saw you. He lost both his parents when a tree fell on their car, his father in the car and his mother in the hospital later. He recognised the name and asked if we were related, and I said yes, and he told me he'd wanted to thank you, but you weren't there. He said he'd been told you'd gone off sick, but that you'd apparently worked really hard on her.'

'Jean,' he said, remembering her face, remembering the worry she'd felt about her husband. Remembering the cluster of rings on her finger. 'Who—told him?'

'One of the nurses spoke to him. She said you were holding her hand, stroking it and trying to soothe her, and that you wouldn't give up and they had to stop you.'

He hadn't wanted to stop. He'd held her hand, seen the rings, and he'd felt a huge wave of sadness when she'd died.

'Last patient,' he said. 'Head—injury. Raj came.'

'And took you away for a CT scan, which is why you didn't see the relatives.'

He nodded. 'Sad. Both parents. Like me. Maybe— better together.'

'Better that they'd gone together, like yours did?'

He nodded.

'Her son thought so. He said she would have been lost without him. They'd been married for fifty seven years.'

'Wow. Long time.'

'It is. I told him I'd pass it on to you. He asked how you were.'

'What'd you say?'

'I told him you were getting better.'

He nodded slowly, and then smiled, glancing down at Lottie in his arms. She'd fallen asleep, her arm flopped out to the side, head lolling, and he eased her into the buggy without waking her.

He was getting better.

And he would be a doctor again.

One day.

Julie came at three, just a few minutes after they were home, and Lucy left them to it and went to get the girls. She took the car, because Lottie was asleep in her cot and might not stay there, and she didn't want to be out long, and when they got back she heard voices upstairs.

'She's lovely. How old is she?'

'Eight months.'

'And is her name Lottie, or is that short for something?'

'Charlotte,' he told her, his voice carrying clearly. 'Liked—Lottie, though. No, Lottie. Keep still.'

He was changing her nappy, Lucy realised, and she was on the point of running upstairs to take over when she realised he was talking with less hesitation. Still slowly, a little haltingly, but almost properly. And he'd been better at lunch, once he'd relaxed.

Progress. Tiny steps but each one was massive progress, and they were happening hour by hour as his brain recovered. Overwhelmed, she went into the cloakroom, shut the door and put her hand over her mouth to stifle a little sob.

He was getting better. He was.

Finally, after two weeks of painfully slow progress, he was getting better, and the relief was immense. She hadn't realised how wound up she'd been, how desperately worried for him. For all of them, really, because if he'd stuck at that, he would have been really difficult to live with.

Thank goodness she'd never have to find out just how difficult.

She came out of the cloakroom just as they came downstairs, Lottie in his arms smacking his face with her hands and laughing, and she caught Julie's eye and smiled.

Julie gave her the thumbs-up, and she nodded. So it wasn't her imagination.

Unable to stop the smile, she veered off into the kitchen, put the kettle on and made a celebratory cup of tea.

Better, he realised, didn't mean cured.

Emily needed help with her reading, and Lucy was upstairs with Lottie, changing her nappy.

'Can't—do it,' he said, hating the admission, seething with frustration, because it was so simple, so ridiculously damned easy, and Emily looked crestfallen.

'Never mind,' she said gently, climbing onto his lap and hugging him. 'Mummy will help me.'

He hugged her back, his eyes stinging with tears. He wanted to help her, wanted to be the one to do it, otherwise what was the point of him being there at all?

Being anywhere?

'Hey. What's up?'

He looked at Lucy, her face creased in concern, and he lifted Emily off his lap and walked away. He could hear her explaining, the words coming so easily to her, and Lucy's murmured response sounded reassuring and comforting.

He wanted to reassure and comfort—wanted not to have caused the need for that reassurance in the first place.

'Andy?'

He was in his study, the room which had always been his retreat, only now it felt like a torture chamber, filled with things he couldn't understand or deal with. Including Lucy.

She closed the door softly behind her and slid her arms around his waist. 'What's up, darling?'

'Em needed—reading. Couldn't—'

He let out a growl of frustration and slammed his hand into the wall, and Lucy let him go and came round in front of him.

'Hey, come on. David said it would take time.'

'Want to help,' he said, his eyes stinging again, and she made a soft sound of comfort and went up on tiptoe, drawing his head gently down and kissing him. Her lips were soft and warm and yielding, and he sank into the kiss, hating that he was so needy and yet absorbing the comfort she offered because he was so lonely and isolated.

'So much—want to say,' he mumbled.

'I know. It'll keep. Be patient.'

'Mmm. Have to.'

'I'm sure we can find other ways to communicate.'

He lifted his head and looked down into her eyes, seeing not only the promise but also the sorrow. Not pity, he realised, but genuine sorrow that this was happening to him. To them.

He kissed her again, just a soft, lingering brush of his lips on hers, and then he let her go.

'Want me—bath girls?'

'Please. I've done Em's reading with her but I need to feed Lottie.'

'OK.' He kissed her again, just because it felt so good, and then he went and rounded up the girls.

His frustration was still there, but for now, at least, it had moderated to the point where he could deal with it, thanks to Lucy. And hopefully, if he could only hang on, it would get easier to deal with.

Over the next few days his speech improved hugely, and every little improvement merited celebration.

Sometimes they went out for coffee and cake, sometimes they went to the pub for lunch, and sometimes, if Lottie was napping, they went into their bedroom, closed the door and made love, then lay there tangled in each other's arms dozing or talking softly until Lottie stirred.

Bliss.

Then on Friday, while they were lying in bed in the aftermath of another stolen moment, she had an idea. 'You have to see David in London on Wednesday, don't you?'

'Yes.'

'Why don't we ask Ben and Daisy if they can have the girls for the night, and drop Lottie off at my parents and spend the night in London? Maybe go to a show, even, and then we can come straight home after you see him. I don't have to work on Tuesday or Wednesday, and it would be so nice, wouldn't it? I think we both deserve a treat.'

He stared at her for a moment, then nodded slowly. 'Yes. Lovely. If they don't—mind.'

She asked them that evening, and they didn't. None of them minded—not Ben and Daisy, or her parents, and least of all Emily and Megan who thought it was a brilliant idea going for a sleep-over in the middle of the week. And amazingly Ben and Daisy even wanted the dog.

'Ben's father's a vet and his childhood was overrun with pets, and he really misses having dogs around,' Daisy said. 'And we've always said it would be fun to have a dog, but we can't get one until we've finished doing up the house, so to borrow Stanley would be lovely, so long as he won't chase Tabitha.'

'No, he's fine with cats, he's terrified of them, and feel free, you can have him any time you want,' Lucy said, laughing, and hung up and told Andy.

'Great,' he said, and he smiled, his eyes lighting up in a way they hadn't done for ages. 'So—what show?'

'I don't know. Let's look on the internet, see what there is. What do you fancy?'

'Something fun,' he said, after a moment's hesitation. 'Musical? But not too big. Not noisy. Don't want noise.'

'OK.'

They found a show, in a tiny venue, a function room in a restaurant off the Kings Road. The ticket price included dinner, and it looked perfect. The only problem was that it was sold out.

'Ring,' he suggested.

She didn't hold out any hope. The act was hugely popular, cripplingly funny according to the reviews, and she didn't think they stood a chance, but someone was looking after them.

'I've just had a family group of twenty cancel, and I had eighteen people on my waiting list, so, yes, I can offer you a table for two, but you are so lucky.'

'I know,' she said, grinning and giving Andy the thumbs-up, and he just shrugged and made his 'I told you so' face, so she stuck her tongue out, paid for the tickets over the phone and then did a little happy dance.

She had such a good feeling about this now.

'OK. Hotel,' she said, coming back to the sofa and snuggling up to him at the computer. 'How about the one we stayed at the night you proposed to me? That's close.'

And full of happy memories.

'OK,' he said, nodding.

It was eye-wateringly expensive, but they gave them an upgrade to a room at the back overlooking the gardens, and threw in breakfast.

'Done,' she said, and paid, trying not to think about how long their savings might last if Andy could never return to work. He had critical illness cover, but was it good enough?

She stopped the negative thoughts. There was a lot of water to go under their bridges before they needed to worry about that, and for now she felt they both needed a treat.

So it was costing them a small fortune. So what? She didn't care about anything except Andy and his recovery, and if it helped to bring them closer together, then she was all for it, because he seemed to be holding something back.

Despite his willingness to make love to her whenever they had the chance, he still wasn't talking about *them*, wasn't talking about the future.

He was spending time with the children, much more time, and seemed to be doing his best to make up for all the hurt he'd caused in the run-up to his exam, but time with her seemed—what?

Less romantic than she'd like it to be? Less loving? He hadn't said 'I love you' since she'd spoken to him in the operating theatre, and now she was wondering if he'd really meant it then or if it was just David's 'happy drugs' talking. Or because he'd secretly been afraid he might die, and thought he'd leave her with that last thought to cherish?

Or because he really did love her, but it had taken something that drastic to get him to admit it.

Why? Was he still hurt because she'd thrown him out? It was a possibility, but until he could speak fluently again, she didn't want to force the issue and frustrate him.

Maybe, though, she could use this time together alone to create some new, romantic memories, to set the tone for their future. Not family time, not family memories, but something special between just the two of them.

And maybe then, given enough provocation, he'd tell her again that he loved her.

CHAPTER EIGHT

THEY left the car at her parents' house in Essex, got a taxi to the station and caught the train into London.

It took them less than an hour door to door, and when they checked in, the memories came flooding back.

Lucy was busy at the desk, and he let her deal with it while he looked around the foyer. The restaurant was through there, he thought, the place where he'd proposed to her over dinner. He hadn't done anything crazy like go down on one knee, but it had still been pretty public once she'd let out that little shriek and flung herself into his arms.

Where had all the years gone?

'Hey, what's up?'

He stared around, then looked down into her gentle green eyes. 'Just remembering. So long ago.'

'It's not that long. Come on, let's go and find our room.'

It was lovely, on the inside corner of the L-shaped building, so that the window was angled and they looked down into a mass of greenery where the gardens of all the houses that backed onto the area were mingled together out of sight of the busy streets.

It would be stunning in summer, she thought, but

even in winter it was green and fresh and calming, a sort of secret oasis in a desert of stone and concrete.

She turned to him, about to comment, and found him sprawled out on the bed watching her, his eyes almost indigo.

'Come here and lie down.'

'Are you tired?'

'No.'

'Oh. I see,' she said, smiling and walking slowly towards him, swaying her hips provocatively. He raked her with his eyes.

'Good.'

'Mmm. I hope so.'

'Complaining?'

That was a big word. It made her smile. That, and the idea that she'd ever complain about Andy's lovemaking.

'Absolutely not. Never.' She took off her coat and hung it up, unzipped her boots and put them neatly in the corner under the coat, then slipped off her trousers, her jumper, the thin silky vest top underneath, her heart pounding with anticipation. He might not be able to speak to her fluently yet, but there was nothing wrong with his powers of expression, and when she glanced at him she saw his eyes on her body, flames dancing in them as she peeled off her clothes one by one.

If she'd ever doubted that he still wanted her, the doubt went in that moment, burned away by the fire in his eyes.

He didn't take them off her for a second, just lay there, scarcely breathing, watching her as she undressed for him.

Lovely. Beautiful.

His?

Maybe. He hoped so. He really, really hoped so, but if things didn't improve a lot, could he ask her to stay with him? There was so much he wanted to say, so much they needed to talk about, but he just couldn't. A conversation as important as that couldn't be bungled by his stupid lack of words, and he knew it was sensible to wait until he could really say what he needed to say.

Probably starting with 'sorry'. Hell, he could say that now, but on its own it was hardly enough, and she had some apologising to do, as well.

But in the meantime...

'Come here,' he said again, gruffly this time, and she went to him, dressed only in the skimpiest lacy underwear.

He tried to sit up, but she put a hand flat on his chest and pressed him back, then slowly, deliberately, she unbuttoned his shirt, then slid his belt buckle free, her fingers taunting him as she unfastened his trousers and slid the zip down.

He'd kicked his shoes off, and she patted his hips so he lifted them and peeled his trousers slowly down his legs. His clingy jersey shorts left little to the imagination, and she made a soft purr in her throat and ran her hands back up his legs, skimming past his hips, then settled herself over him.

She didn't say a word, and nor did he, just lay there and let her torture him exquisitely until he couldn't stand it.

It didn't take long.

She rocked against him, once, twice, and he cracked, sitting up and taking her face in his hands and kissing her as if he'd die without her. Maybe he would. He didn't know, and he didn't want to find out.

She slid his shirt down over his shoulders and off his arms, and then pushed him back, trailing her hands down over his chest and easing away the soft jersey that was separating him from her.

He swallowed hard, his breath jammed in his throat until she shifted her hips and took him deep inside her. Then he let it out in a rush, his hands reaching up and drawing her down so he could kiss her.

The lace of her bra chafed against his chest and he groaned and cupped the soft fullness of her breasts.

'Lucy,' he groaned, and she moved, killing him inch by inch, the sweet torture finally too much.

He snapped, rolling her under him, plundering her mouth as his body drove into her, his hands seeking, finding, worshipping.

She splintered in his arms, taking him with her over the edge, and he dropped his head into the hollow of her shoulder and waited for his heart to slow and his breathing to return to normal.

Then he rolled carefully to his side, taking her with him, their bodies still locked together, and he held her close against his heart.

'Very good idea, that,' he said lazily, and she laughed softly, her breath drifting over his skin.

'I thought so.'

'What time do we—go?'

'Not yet.'

'Good. Little nap,' he said, suddenly drained, and slid gently into sleep in her arms.

The show was amazing.

They'd walked there from Kensington, hurrying a

little because they were in danger of being late, but they were there in good time in the end.

They went for a simple meal of hot chicken salad with ciabatta twists, with a good Pinot Grigio and a wicked dessert with a million calories and enough chocolate even for her.

And as the desserts were served, so the act started.

She was worried at first. Andy had seemed tired after their impromptu lovemaking, and she wasn't sure if he would be able to keep up with the pace of the jokes, but he was having no trouble, and she hadn't seen him laugh so much in ages.

Or herself, come to that. She thought she was going to split her sides at times, and she saw Andy wipe tears from his cheeks at one point.

Fun, he'd said, his only specification apart from music. This was both. Witty, exquisitely observed, the songs were hilarious, the volume wasn't excessive and they couldn't finish their desserts because it was too dangerous to eat at the same time.

They drank the wine, though, and ordered coffee, and she thought he'd choke on it at one point he was laughing so hard.

'That was—fantastic,' he said, when it was over and they were walking back to the hotel, the applause still ringing in their ears. 'Really, really fantastic. Thank you.'

'Don't thank me. It was you who chose it, you who made me call them. I wouldn't have bothered, and I'm so glad I did.' She lifted her head and looked up at him, tucking her hand in his arm. 'Do you know that's the first time I've heard you really laugh since your operation? And it's months and months since you've laughed as much as that. It was so nice to hear.'

'It felt—really good.' He pulled his arm away from her and looped it round her shoulders, tucking her closer to his side, and they ambled back along the streets, passing Harrods on the way.

Their Christmas window display was up, blazing with light, and they strolled past, fascinated and enthralled.

'It's amazing. They really do Christmas,' she said, and found herself wondering what their own Christmas would be like.

'Not long now,' he said. David had said two months, maybe. That would take them up to the start of the New Year. He wondered now if that was too optimistic. He was certainly feeling much better, but he was a very, very long way off being able to go back to work.

Financially, it didn't worry him. He was off sick on full pay for months yet, and when that came to an end he had good critical illness cover—his parents' fiasco had taught him that lesson. But from a personal point of view, he wondered what on earth he would do to fill the time. There was a limit to how often he could make love to Lucy, although he'd yet to reach it.

They arrived back at the hotel and went up to their room, the rumpled bed a teasing reminder of their afternoon's activities. He took her coat and hung it up, then drew her back against his chest, nuzzling the side of her neck.

'Tired?' he asked, and she shook her head.

'No. Do you want tea?'

'No. Just you.'

She turned in his arms, slid her hands up into his

hair and pulled his head gently down until his face was in reach.

Her lips feathered softly over his, and with a quiet sigh of contentment he eased her closer and took the gift she was offering.

Their appointment was for ten and he had to have a scan first, so they went down for breakfast at seven, checked out at eight and made their way across London in the rush-hour scrum.

'OK?' she asked, glancing up at him as they walked in, and he nodded. He'd been relaxed last night, but today the tension was back and she wondered if he was worried.

He didn't need to be, but then he couldn't see his progress as she could.

First stop was an MRI scan to see how things were, and then David greeted them warmly, armed with the results and a broad smile.

'Well, the scan looks great. How's it going? Speech coming back?'

'Sort of,' he said. 'Still hard. Worse if I—*need* to say something. Exact words—really difficult.'

'That figures. You've got a massive vocabulary, so if you're just winging it, there are lots of words to choose from so you can take the first one off the pile that fits. If you have to be exact, as you say, you have to dig deeper and that's what you're going to find. And that will get better, but it's what I meant by the higher level stuff. This will improve quickly, the everyday stuff, as your brain recovers from the insult of the operation. The harder things, the more specific, the most critical—

these will probably take longer and they will have implications for your career in the short term. Have you been back to the hospital?'

'Yes. Watched them. In Resus. Knew it—all, David. But—no words. I couldn't—*tell* anyone. Couldn't dir... um...'

'Direct?'

'Yes. Couldn't direct. Couldn't give—instructions. Couldn't lead. It's my job—'

'OK. Let's just take you back three weeks. You could hardly say a word. You've just told me perfectly lucidly what's going on at the moment. This is huge progress, Andy. Huge progress. I think that tumour had been pressing on your brain for months, and you'd just learned to compensate. The pressure's off now, but it's a bit like a memory foam mattress. It takes time to recover, time for the imprint to fade. And you have to give yourself that time.'

He nodded. 'OK.'

'How are you feeling otherwise? Physically recovered?'

He saw Lucy shift slightly out of the corner of his eye, and shut the images of her in their hotel room firmly out of his mind. 'Yeah,' he said in as normal a voice as possible. 'Physically, fine. Still a bit tired, but OK.'

'Are you having fun? Getting out and enjoying life?'

He nodded, smiling at the memory. 'Yes. We stayed—last night in—hotel, and went to—show. Very, very funny. Really good. Laughed a lot.'

'Excellent. I'm glad you're laughing again. That's a very good sign. You need to do more of the same. Get out there and enjoy life and do things with your family. Lots of fresh air, lots of physical activity and then puzzles, crosswords, all the things the SLT is suggesting, and don't worry about it. You're doing really well. I'm very pleased, considering how tricky the surgery was, but I really wanted to make sure I'd got everything, and I have, so this is it. No more treatment, just recovery. And that's just a question of time.'

'Always time,' Andy said as they walked away from the hospital. 'Story of my life.'

'Well, you're impatient, and you always expect to be able to do too much too quickly, so it doesn't surprise me at all that you're being impatient now, but I'm glad he's so pleased. The scan certainly looked different.'

'Didn't it? Much better. Feels better. Didn't know it felt wrong, but it did. Odd.'

'I'm just glad Raj spotted it.'

'Wouldn't have been—long. Getting worse, quickly.'

'You were. I'm still cross with myself for not realising.' Cross and gutted that she'd thrown him out when he'd been so ill, when she should have realised, if she'd looked at it dispassionately instead of in anger, that there *was* something wrong. Something serious. 'I should have seen it—should have recognised it. I'm so sorry.'

'Don't. My head, but I didn't, not really.'

'No, I think you did, I think you were just in denial. And you were never there, so I wasn't talking to you very much, there wasn't much opportunity for me to notice the changes. I still should have realised it was more than just tiredness and distraction instead of sending you away.'

'Well, here now,' he said, pausing in front of a café and smiling wryly. 'Fancy coffee?'

She smiled up at him and tucked her hand in his arm, happy to stretch out this time alone with him a little longer. 'Why not?'

Lottie was pleased to see them, and Lucy was very pleased to see her, too. Nature, it turned out, wasn't as clever as she'd thought when Andy had his operation, and her bra was feeling really tight.

'Has she been OK?' she asked, settling down on the comfy chair in the kitchen to feed her while her mother made them sandwiches for lunch.

'Fine. She's such an easy baby, she loves everybody.'

'Yeah. She loves them in the night, too, usually. She often wants to play.'

Her mother gave a wry smile. 'Yes, she seemed quite happy to see me at two something when she woke and wanted a drink. She was pretty disgusted when I settled her back down again and left her, but she went to sleep in moments.'

'She does, the little tinker.'

'So, how was your evening?' her mother asked, and Lucy tried not to blush.

'Lovely. We had great fun. Thank you so much for having her so we could do that. Andy was going to come on his own and I think it was really worrying him. He's still not confident having to talk to strangers. He thinks they won't understand. He's got a card that explains that he can't speak fluently but do you think he'll use it?'

'He's proud, Lucy. He's proud, and he's not used to being inarticulate. He's probably the most articulate and eloquent person I've ever met, and it must come hard to him when he can't even answer the phone or send a text or ask someone the way.'

She nodded. He'd had that problem when he'd gone to the hospital and the Neurology out-patients receptionist hadn't known who he was or what he wanted. And it had taken him ages to tell her about it.

'Never mind, he's much better, so I'm sure it won't be long. And I'm glad you had a lovely time. You deserve it.'

It had been lovely. Wonderful. Romantic and funny and full of secret, intimate moments, but he still hadn't said those three little words.

Oversight?

Or something more significant. Maybe he didn't love her. Maybe he was happy taking all the sex she could offer him, but didn't really care about her one way or the other.

No. That was wrong, she was sure of it. She was just being silly, wanting it all on a plate, and she needed to worry about the important things and forget it.

They'd had a great time, he'd been told he was recovering well, and maybe that was it, maybe the consultation had been hanging over him?

Time, she told herself, but the mantra was wearing thin for both of them, and she just wanted everything back to normal.

She thought of the sparkling festive Harrods window they'd strolled past on the way back to the hotel. Less than five weeks to go to Lottie's first Christmas, but at least she knew she'd have Andy at home this time. Last year he'd been at work on Christmas Eve and again on

Boxing Day, and the children had missed him. They'd all missed him.

This time—this time, she promised herself, it would be special.

So, it was down to him.

OK. He could do that. He knew the tumour had been removed completely and wouldn't regrow, so he could concentrate on his recovery, but in the meantime, until he could go back to work, he had to find some meaningful way to fill his days.

His SLT exercises had been a chore until now. Suddenly, they became a challenge. He tackled them as he tackled everything, head on and with gritted teeth.

Crosswords, puzzles, reading and writing exercises, and listening to people speaking.

The radio was the easiest way to do that, because he could be busy doing other things at the same time.

Like painting.

Lucy had talked about how glad she was they hadn't bought a Victorian house that needed work, because they hadn't even got round to painting the rooms in their own, but she'd had two young children when they'd moved, and a part-time job, and he'd just started in his first consultant's post, so they'd had bigger fish to fry.

Not now.

Now, he had nothing *but* time, and so on Monday morning, he started to decorate. They even had the paint for the kitchen in a cupboard in the utility room, so the first thing he did was strip everything he could off the walls, scrub them down with sugar soap to get rid of the film of grease from cooking, and then Lucy came home from work with Lottie to find him cutting in the paint round the edges of the doors and windows.

'What are you doing?' she asked, looking a little stunned.

'Painting?'

She let out a tiny, slightly puzzled breath and said, 'OK,' and then tried to put Lottie down. 'Um—Andy, where's the high chair?'

'Dining room.'

'OK. Um—did we discuss this?'

'Yes.'

'When?'

He shrugged. 'You got the paint.'

'Two years ago. Why now?'

'Why not? Nothing to do.'

Oh, no. Not again. 'Have you had lunch?'

'No.'

'I'll make sandwiches,' she said, looking round at her devastated kitchen in confusion. If she'd known, she would have made supper last night and had it ready to go in the oven, but as it was she hadn't, and it didn't look like her kitchen was going to be hers again anytime soon.

She retrieved the high chair, fed the baby a jar of chicken something, gave her some banana to mash up and spread in her hair and made a stack of ham, cheese and pickle sandwiches.

'Lunch,' she said, and he got off the ladder, to her relief, and came and ate.

'Good. Thanks,' he said, still chewing, and got up and carried on.

'Don't you want a cup of tea?'

'When it's made.'

She sighed, wiped the banana out of Lottie's hair and put her on her play mat with a pile of bricks. 'Want me to help?' she asked.

'No, you're OK. Play with Lottie.'

So she did that. She played with Lottie, kept the dog out of the way and she watched her kitchen turn from the fairly gaudy yellow it had been up to now into a muted pale putty colour that went much better with the tiled floor. With everything, really.

'That's great. Well done,' she said, admiring it when she got back from the school run. 'What do you think, girls?'

'It's nice. Daddy, can you paint our bedroom next?'

'OK. What colour?'

'Pink,' Emily said instantly.

'I want purple,' Megan said, and they started to fight.

'How about one wall pink, and one wall purple, and the others white? That will go with your curtains,' she suggested.

Andy just raised an eyebrow in disbelief and cleared away the tools. He still had the woodwork to do, but at least the kitchen walls were done.

'Utility next,' he said. 'Then your room. But no fighting.'

It was down to Lucy to sort out the squabble, of course. They ended up compromising on pale lilac for the window wall, paler pink for the other walls and the ceiling white. Megan's bed was against the window wall and Emily's was opposite, so that way they each had their own colour.

'I want my own room,' Emily said to her later when she was clearing up after supper. 'I don't want to share. I don't like purple.'

'Well, that's tough. It's only a bit of purple, and the spare room's for when Grannie and Grandpa come to stay, or your cousins.'

'But they can go in the attic.'

'No, they can't. You can both go up there and have your own room when you're older. For now, I want you and Megan together on the same floor as us, OK?'

'OK. But I want it pink.'

'No. You have to compromise. We've talked about this. It's only one wall, Em. You'll cope. Where's your father? Do you think he'd like to read to you tonight?'

'He can't, Mummy. You know he can't read.'

'He can a bit, or you could read the story and he can help you if you get stuck. You can help each other.'

'OK,' she said, brightening up.

But he was decorating the utility room.

She leant on the doorframe and folded her arms and stared up at him as he worked. 'Andy, the girls want you to read to them.'

'I'm busy.'

'And they're growing up.'

He opened his mouth, shut it and looked at the wall. 'OK. Do it later.'

He cleaned up his hands, peeled off his painting shirt and went up to the girls' bedroom. She followed, ready to step in if it all got too much for him, but it seemed fine. She heard the little shrieks of glee, and him shushing them so they didn't wake Lottie, and then she heard the soft, hesitant rumble of his voice.

Em had to help him with some of the words, and at one point she took over and then he had to help her, and then Megan read a bit, and Lucy sat on the stairs and listened to them and felt her eyes filling.

'Hey,' he said, coming to sit beside her on the stairs a few moments later. 'What's up?'

'I was just remembering you reading to them, the night before your MRI, when you knew there was something wrong but not what it was exactly. And you read them a million stories, and I was just sitting in the bedroom and fuming at you for coming home and sleeping in our bed while I was away, and you didn't say a word about what was going on. I should have known there was something dreadfully wrong—'

'Ah, Luce,' he said softly, and slid his arm round her shoulders. 'Can't do this yet. No words for it—too much to say, and want it right. But—it's good to be here.'

'It's good to have you here—so good. There was a time when I really thought I might lose you—'

'Shh. Not going anywhere. Just need time.'

'You can have time. You can have as long as it takes.'

His arm squeezed her, and then he got up and carried on down the stairs.

'Where are you going?'

He looked back up at her. 'Painting,' he said, as if it was obvious, and he disappeared into the utility room.

She followed him. 'Want some help?' she offered, and waited for the rebuff, but it didn't come.

He stared at her for a second, then smiled. 'OK. Great.'

'Back in a tick.'

She ran upstairs and changed into scruffy clothes, then went back and helped him.

Well, sort of. It wasn't a big room, and inevitably they got in each other's way, of course.

And then he cornered her, reaching over her head to

touch up a bit she'd missed, and when he looked down he smiled.

'Got paint on you,' he said, rubbing a smear off her cheek. She wriggled against him, and he felt his body roar into life.

'Are you—distracting me?' he asked, stumbling over the words a little but his laughing eyes more than expressive.

'Mmm. Apparently.'

He felt her hand slide down inside his jeans and circle him, her eyes alight with mischief and desire, and he sucked in his breath.

'Hussy.'

'Mmm.'

The children were upstairs in bed, asleep, and there was nothing to stop them, nobody to see. He put the brush down and turned back to her, smiling, and finished what she'd started.

There.

It was finished. Two coats of emulsion on all the walls in the kitchen and utility, and tomorrow he could start on the girls' bedroom.

They washed the brushes and roller, changed into their night clothes and went and sat down in the sitting room with a glass of wine.

'Well done,' she said with a smile. 'That was a good idea.'

'Talking about painting?'

Her smiled widened. 'All of it. Especially *that* bit. But it does look nice. And it was fun doing it together.'

'Still talking about painting?' he said, and she laughed and punched his arm gently.

'Girls' room tomorrow,' he said, and her smile faded.

'No! There's too much to do before you can paint their room, Andy. It's full of stuff, and they need to sort it out. You can't just pile it all in a heap in the middle and sling a dustsheet over it.'

'Why?'

'Because they need to clear it up,' she repeated. 'They have to learn—if they want it painted, they clear it up and put their toys away. And anyway, isn't Julie coming?'

'Yes. Damn.' He sighed shortly, and rammed a hand through his hair without thinking and winced. 'I'll do it after.'

'No! Andy, please, listen to me! Where's the fire?'

He sighed again, a longer sigh this time, and slumped back against the sofa. Lord, he was tired. 'OK. Do it another day.'

'You do that. You need to pace yourself.'

'I'm fine, Luce. Don't fuss me. I'm bored. I can't do—nothing. Going crazy.'

'I know.' She reached out her hand and laid it on his leg. 'Why don't we do something else together tomorrow?'

'Like?'

'Taking Lottie swimming. She loves it, and it's much easier with help. She's a bit of a wriggler and she could roll off the changing mat and fall on the floor now. I can't take my eyes off her.'

'Can't change with you.'

'You can. They have family changing rooms.'

They did? He didn't know that—because he'd never been swimming with her? He hadn't, he realised. He had in the summer, when they'd spent a few days at Center Parcs, but not here at home in Yoxburgh.

'OK,' he agreed. It might be nice to go swimming and burn up a few lengths in the pool. He was getting flabby and unfit with all the sitting around, and he hated it.

He opened a puzzle book and tackled a simple crossword, but he couldn't think of any of the answers. Well, not many. Still, at least he could read the clues now and they made sense. He tried another one, then tackled the Sudoku puzzle over the page, but he just couldn't get it.

He was tired, he realised. He could have done it in the morning, but now it just defeated him, so he threw the book back on the coffee table, put his feet up and went to sleep.

Idiot. He'd exhausted himself.

Lucy sighed softly and went and made herself a cup of tea in her smart new kitchen. It smelt strange, but in a good way, and he'd done a good job, but at what cost?

He really needed to learn to pace himself better, but he never had, he always worked at things until he'd burned out.

Well, no, that wasn't true. Before his parents died he'd been more relaxed, but since then he'd been—obsessive?

Strong word, but maybe the right one. It had definitely changed him, changed his attitude to a lot of things. Nothing was ever left to chance now, and she sensed it was a backlash from the chaotic and random childhood his parents had inflicted on him.

He'd always been a grafter, though, ever since she'd known him. It was just the way he was, but he needed to take it easy now. She'd have to keep an eye on him, stop him overdoing it in future. She took her tea back into the sitting room, curled up in the other corner of the sofa and channel-hopped until bedtime. Then she turned off the television and leant over.

'Hey, sleepyhead,' she said, shaking him gently, and he opened his eyes and stared at her blankly for a moment.

'Oh. I was asleep. Sorry.'

'Come on, it's time for bed.'

He got stiffly to his feet, his right arm and neck aching from the painting. He flexed his shoulder, cupping it in his hand, and she slid her fingers under his and rubbed it.

'You've overdone it.'

'Maybe,' he admitted. 'Swimming will help.'

'Or I can give you a massage.'

'In bed?'

'If you're good.'

He smiled lazily. 'I'm always good.'

'Cocky, too.'

The smile turned into a grin. Suddenly he wasn't feeling so tired, after all...

Baby-swimming, he remembered belatedly, wasn't really swimming at all.

Mostly it involved kneeling in the shallow water of the baby pool, swooshing Lottie back and forth in the water while she shrieked with glee and splashed her hands. And drank it.

Every time her face got close to the water, her tongue came out and she tasted it. And then a child jumped in and a tidal wave sloshed over her head and she came up smiling.

'She doesn't care, does she?' he said, slightly surprised, but Lucy just shrugged.

'She's used to it. We come nearly every week, if we can, and I bring the girls in the holidays.'

It was a whole other way of life, he realised, and he'd missed it all because he'd been at work. Crazily, he felt excluded, and he turned the baby in his arms and hugged her. She beamed and blew a noisy wet raspberry on his shoulder, making him laugh, and then he looked up and met Lucy's eyes.

The expression in them warmed his heart, and he gave her a slow, smiley wink. She smiled back and held out her arms, and he turned the baby round. 'Where's Mummy?' he asked, and started forwards, holding her out in front of him. 'Catch Mummy.'

Mummy dutifully made a scaredy face and swam backwards, but they caught her easily and Lottie squealed with delight and snuggled her little arms around Lucy's neck and hugged her.

It brought a lump to his throat, and he suddenly felt overwhelmed.

'I'm going to swim,' he said, and left them to it, retreating to the emotionless monotony of the big pool where he carved his way up and down until his muscles screamed and his lungs were gasping.

Then he hauled himself out and nearly fell over, his legs buckling slightly under his weight. He was astonished at how exhausted he felt, how incredibly heavy. He'd been deceived by the buoyancy of the water. So, so unfit.

He looked for Lucy, and saw her in the little café

overlooking the pool. She'd changed and was giving Lottie her bottle, and he glanced at the clock and realised he'd been swimming for nearly an hour. No wonder they'd given up on him.

Guilty and frustrated, he changed quickly and joined them.

'Sorry. Forgot the time,' he said. 'Want a coffee?'

'Please. I didn't bring my purse, and I couldn't get your attention.'

She watched him as he walked to the counter and ordered their coffees, something he wouldn't have been happy doing even a week ago. So much progress, and yet he seemed curiously restless and unsettled since they'd got back from London.

Take the decorating, for instance. And the puzzles and crosswords—he'd become obsessed with them. Still, it was paying off in the improvement to his language skills, but the swimming? He'd been driving hard, pushing himself with every length, and she'd watched the frustration burning through him with every stroke.

Because David had suggested he should do puzzles and SLT and keep himself fit? Probably. And Andy being Andy, he was doing it his way—flat out. His parents had a lot to answer for.

She sighed and sat Lottie up, wiping a dribble of milk off her chin, and she craned her neck as she caught sight of him. 'Da-da,' she said, and Lucy smiled wryly and handed her to him once he'd put the coffee down.

'Your turn, I think,' she said, and sat back with her coffee and watching him bonding with his little girl while his coffee grew cold, forgotten.

CHAPTER NINE

'So what was that about?' she asked as they walked home. 'All that power-swimming? Were you trying to kill yourself?'

'Sorry. I just felt a bit—crowded.'

Crowded? By his eight month old daughter? When he was used to a frantically busy ED department? She nearly laughed, but she was still cross.

No, not cross. She'd *been* cross, when he'd taken himself off to the big pool to swim for ages, but when she'd gone to look for him and seen the driven way he was tearing up and down in the water, she'd been worried. And now he said he'd felt crowded.

Was this why he'd been taking himself away from the family so much, because he'd found it all a little uncomfortable?

'How, crowded?' she asked, unable to work it out and not wanting to let it rest.

'I don't know. Just—emotional.'

And he didn't show his emotions easily, she knew that. Especially in public.

'Hey,' she said softly, hugging his arm as he pushed the buggy up the hill. 'It's OK.'

'No, it's not. I said I'd help, but I didn't. I just feel—I don't know. Useless.'

'Oh, Andy, you aren't useless! Of course you aren't useless! You did a brilliant job of painting the kitchen and utility yesterday—'

'You were mad with me.'

'No, I was just a bit surprised, and worried for you, really. I didn't want you overdoing it.'

He had overdone it. He knew that. He'd overdone it in the pool, too, but he had to push himself. It was what he did, and he didn't know any other way.

'What if I don't get better, Luce?' he asked bleakly. 'What if I can't go back to work?'

'You will be able to! You heard David—you're making great progress.'

'Not great enough. Better, but not right yet. Nothing like.'

'You always were impatient, weren't you? You want everything done yesterday. It'll come. You just have to wait.'

So he waited.

He worked at his exercises, he listened to the radio while he painted the girls' bedroom once they'd cleared it up, and he started jogging again, taking Stanley out for a run in the morning instead of just a walk. He and the dog got fitter, the house got painted, but still he wasn't right.

'When can I go back to work?' he asked Julie one day after his SLT session.

'I can't say. It's not a straight line graph, Andy. You're working hard at it, but your brain won't recover faster than it's able to.'

'Christmas?'

'I can't say. Possibly.'

'But—unlikely.'

'Realistically, I think so. It's only three weeks away.'

It was?

That surprised him. He hadn't registered the passage of the days, but he'd seen Lucy dressing Megan up in something for the nativity play at school, so of course it was coming.

'You're getting there, Andy. You've made huge strides, and I'm impressed with how conscientious you've been. Don't get despondent. It'll happen when it's ready.'

If one more person told him that, he'd scream.

He showed her out, then went and found Lucy.

'About Christmas.'

'What about it?'

'Are your parents coming?'

'I haven't even thought about it,' she told him. 'I had thought they might, but that was before…'

She tailed off, and he raised a wry eyebrow.

'Before you kicked me out?' he said, the memory still raw.

She closed her eyes briefly and nodded. 'But now— well, I don't know. What do you want to do?'

'Stay here. Just us.'

'That would be nice. We hardly saw you last year, or the year before.'

'I'll be here this year,' he said, not as a promise, but because it seemed less and less likely that he'd be any-where else at this slow and frustrating rate.

'Good,' she said, kissing his cheek as she reached up to a cupboard to put the mugs away. 'Talking of

Christmas, do you want to go shopping? I haven't even started yet, and I'm normally done by now.'

Christmas shopping? He hadn't done it for years—two, at least. She'd got everything, including her own present. He'd asked her what she wanted, told her to get it and last year he hadn't even wrapped it.

Deluged with guilt, he smiled at her. 'Yeah. Let's go shopping. Now.'

'Dr Gallagher?'

They were walking along the main street looking in the shops when the voice stopped them, and Lucy turned.

'Excuse me. I'm sorry to intrude, but—is this your husband, by any chance?'

Lucy stared at the man for a second, then registered. 'Oh, hello. Sorry, I didn't—yes, he is my husband. Andy, this is Mr Darby. I told you I'd met him. You were with his mother when she died.'

The man held out his hand. 'I wanted to thank you, sir, for everything you tried to do for my mother. Their car was hit by a tree and my father was killed instantly, but my mother was taken to the hospital and they told me you worked tirelessly to try and save her. You probably don't even remember her.'

He shook his hand, remembering another hand he'd held, frail and gnarled, with three well-worn rings on her finger, symbols of a loving relationship with the husband she'd just lost. His last patient—ever?

'Of course I remember her. She was a real lady. Very worried about your father. Kept asking for him. We tried, but there was nothing we could do, no more that could have been done. So sorry we couldn't save her,' he said gruffly.

'Don't be. Without my father she would have been utterly lost, and they'd had a good life—very happy. They'd always said they wanted to go together.'

He nodded. His parents had said the same thing. They'd had a good life, spent all of it having fun, and none at all dedicated to the trivial details like wills or bank records, but they'd died happy. Maybe they'd had it right, after all?

'Still tough, losing them both together. I'm glad you stopped us. I hate loose ends, but I was ill and couldn't talk to you.'

'Yes, they said. I hope you've recovered? I expect your wife's been looking after you? She's an excellent doctor.'

He smiled ruefully, touched by his concern. 'Yes, she is, and I'm getting there, thank you.'

'Well, I won't hold you up. Have a good Christmas with your family.'

'We will. And you.'

They watched him walk away, and Andy let out a long, slow breath. There was so much more he could have said, so much more he should have said, but because it mattered, the words had flown, yet again, like startled birds from a tree at dusk, and left him almost monosyllabic and stumbling.

Damn.

'Nice man,' Lucy said. 'His mother obviously made a real impression on you.'

He nodded. 'Mmm. Real lady, even though she was dying. You could tell that. Hard for the family, though.

It's tough losing both parents, even if it makes them happy.'

'You found it really tough, didn't you?'

He nodded. 'Just such a mess, as well.'

'I remember. It took you nearly a year to sort out the paperwork.'

Which was why his affairs were so meticulously sorted, he thought. One less thing for him to have worried about in the last few weeks. Just in case anything unforeseen had happened...

They walked on, strolling past a jewellers, and he glanced in the window. They had a display of antique rings, just the sort of thing that Lucy loved. She didn't even look at the window, though, just kept on walking, talking about the children and what they should get them.

Well, he knew what he was getting her. Seeing Jean Darby's son had jogged his conscience, and tomorrow, while she was at work, he'd buy it.

Whatever 'it' turned out to be. He'd know when he saw it.

The shops were heaving, the good old Christmas songs being belted out in every one, and he found himself singing along. Odd, how he could sing all the words fluently, when he struggled to say them on demand.

A different part of his brain, Julie had told him, and it seemed she was right, because after they came out of one of the shops he carried on singing softly, and Lucy gave him a quizzical smile.

'You sound happy.'

He grinned, the plan forming in his mind. 'I am. It's fun. What's next?'

They managed to get most of the presents on her

list, but not all, and the following day Lucy announced that she was going to a big toy shop on the outskirts of a nearby town.

'Are you coming?'

'No, don't think so. I've got to do my SLT and other stuff. You go. I'll have Lottie, if you like.'

'Sure?'

He smiled. 'Yes, I'm sure. We'll muddle through together.'

'You haven't seen my engagement ring, have you, by the way? I took it off in the bathroom last night when I was bathing Lottie and I can't find it.'

'No. I'll look for it. It'll be somewhere.'

In his pocket, but he didn't tell her that. 'You go, have fun, I'll see you later.'

'OK. Well, I won't be long. Two hours, max.'

'OK.'

That didn't give him long, so as soon as she was off the drive he put Lottie in the buggy and walked briskly back to the jewellers.

'I'm looking for an eternity ring for my wife,' he said to the assistant. 'She likes antique rings. We walked past yesterday and I saw some in the window, but I couldn't really look. I want it to be a surprise. It has to go with this.'

He showed her Lucy's engagement ring, and she took him outside so he could point out the rings he liked, but there were none that were quite right.

'I want—oh, can't remember what it's called. Smooth setting, no claws, like this one, so it doesn't catch on things.'

'Cushion set.'

'Yes, that's it.'

'In gold, or platinum?'

'Gold. Her other rings are gold.'

'We've just had one in that might answer. If you could hold on, I'll see if it's been cleaned yet.'

She went out the back, and reappeared with the ring in her hand. 'This is it. The diamonds are very good, apparently, so it's going to be expensive. I'm not sure if we've got a final valuation. Would you like to speak to the jeweller?'

He stared at it, a strange feeling coming over him. He could picture it on Lucy's finger, see her hand worn and old, the ring still there even though the knuckle had grown thickened with age. Would they still be together then, as much in love as the Darbys had evidently been? He hoped so.

'Yes, please.'

A man emerged from the back, an eyeglass hanging round his neck. 'I gather you're interested in this ring.'

'Yes. I want an eternity ring for my wife. I promised her one eight years ago but I just haven't got round to it.'

'Ah.' He smiled. 'Well, this is a beautiful ring. It belonged to the grandmother of a friend of mine and he asked me to sell it for him. He didn't like to part with it, but there's nobody in the family for him to leave it to; he said it was too beautiful to go in a drawer and he wanted it to be loved.'

He held it in his hand, stroked his finger over the smooth setting, turned it so it caught the light. 'I can see why. It's lovely.'

'It's a very good ring. A little worn, but nothing that can't be repaired. And the diamonds are flawless. Beautiful diamonds.'

They were. Even though they were cushion set, when the light caught them they sparkled like fireworks.

'What size ring does your wife take?'

'I don't know. I've brought her engagement ring with me if that helps? She wears it all the time so I guess it still fits.'

'Perfect. Let me check.'

It was the right size, and he just knew Lucy would love it. The price was irrelevant, and he would have paid twice as much. 'Does it need repair?'

'A little. It's been worn next to another ring and the shoulder needs rebuilding. The setting's a little thin and it would be hard to match a diamond as good as these if you lost one.'

'Go for it,' he said.

He paid for it, slipped her engagement ring back into his pocket and walked home. He bought some nice ham from the deli on the way past, and arrived back just as Lucy turned onto the drive.

'Perfect timing,' he said, the ring burning a hole in his pocket. 'I bought some ham. You make lunch, I'll sort Lottie out.'

He changed the baby's nappy, and then went into the kitchen just as Lucy put a pile of sandwiches on the table.

'I found your ring,' he told her, handing it to her. 'It was in the bathroom.'

'Really? I looked there. I must be going blind. Never mind. Thanks.'

'So, how did your shopping trip go?' he asked her, trying not to look guilty.

Well, was the answer. She brought two bulging carrier bags in from the car as soon as they'd had lunch, and they spent the next two hours wrapping presents and hiding them in the loft ready for Christmas.

'Right, that's all the presents done,' she said. 'Well, except yours. What do you want? Any ideas?'

He shook his head. 'Nothing you can give me,' he said, trying to smile, and her face fell and she hugged him.

'Oh, darling. It's really early days. Don't give up. It'll all be fine.'

'I know,' he said, even though he didn't. 'How about you? What do you want?'

She smiled a little shakily. 'The same thing as you. I guess we might have to wait a little longer for our Christmas presents.'

Except he had hers, or he hoped he did.

He'd been promised the ring would be ready in time, and he felt a tingle of anticipation. He couldn't wait to see her face when he gave it to her. He knew she'd love it.

He went into work the next day, and cornered James in a rare quiet moment.

'Can we have a word?'

'Sure. You're sounding better.'

'That's what I want to talk to you about. I want to come back to work.'

'Ah. Coffee?'

'Yeah. Shall we go to the café?'

'Good idea.'

They got their coffees and settled in a corner of the café out of the way of the other customers. 'So—you think you're ready to come back?'

He remembered his conversation with Jean Darby's son, the way the words had vanished, and shrugged.

'I'm getting there. I'm just not sure what I have to do to prove it. I suppose there are procedures—boxes to tick?'

'Oh, bound to be. I was talking to Occupational Health, and they said they'd need a report from your neurosurgeon, and another from your speech and language therapist.'

He nodded. 'What about if I come back under supervision?'

'The same, I think,' James said. 'In fact, I'm sure they'd insist on it, at least for a month or so.' He sighed and stirred his coffee, then met his eyes again. 'Look, Andy, it's none of my business, but why are you rushing this? Why not just take the time and enjoy your family? God knows you're lucky enough to have one.'

He felt a stab of guilt. James was only two years older than him, but he'd been widowed for ten years, as long as he and Lucy had been married.

'I know I'm lucky, but what good am I to them if I can't work?'

James gave an ironic little laugh. 'I know you, Andy. You're nothing if not organised, and I'd be astonished if you don't have really good critical illness cover, not to mention substantial savings and a cast-iron pension scheme with guaranteed equity. If you can't work, your family will still be taken care of.'

He felt himself colour slightly. 'OK. Rumbled.'

'So go home, get well, enjoy them all and come back when you're ready and not before. You don't want to get back and find you're out of your depth because you've rushed it.'

He was right. Frustrated, but knowing it made sense,

he went home and resigned himself to another few weeks of pottering aimlessly.

Or, he thought, he could do something about the garden. They'd talked for ages about having a bigger patio to take advantage of the sun, and even if he didn't do that, there were a million other jobs he could do out there.

So he changed into scruffy clothes, pulled on his boots and his dog walking coat and went out into the garden, secateurs in hand, and cut down all the perennials. There was a shrub that had grown wildly out of control, and he cut it back, too, and shredded it, and then another one because it looked out of balance after he'd hacked the first one back.

By the time he'd finished it was almost dark, the compost bin was full and the girls were home, so he went inside and sat down at the dining table to help them with their homework.

If he could do nothing else yet, he could do that, he thought, but it seemed they didn't need him. Homework was making sure their costumes were all ready for the nativity play, and that was Lucy's department, so he took himself off to the study and tried to read the paper that had flummoxed him before.

It was no better. In fact, it was worse, and in sheer frustration he shredded it, changed into his running clothes and took the dog out for a run along the dimly lit pavements.

It was a good job he did, because as he ran past the Walkers' house, he glanced at it and saw Daisy leaning on the front door, panting.

He stopped in his tracks and went up the path. 'Daisy?'

'Oh—Andy! Oh, I'm so glad it's you. I've gone into labour and I can't get hold of Ben. Can you call him for me? He's gone late-night shopping and he probably can't hear over all the Christmas jingles.'

'Of course I'll call him. What are you doing outside? You'll freeze. Where's Thomas?'

'Inside. I'd just put him to bed and I heard a car pulling up, so I came out to see if Ben was coming and it just hit me.'

'Let's get you back in, you'll be freezing.'

He led her back inside, told Stanley to sit and called Ben while she leant over the sink and moaned softly.

'OK, he's on his way. What can I do?'

'Nothing. Stay with me. It feels a bit—ah!'

'Daisy, don't do this to me,' he muttered under his breath, but it seemed she was, so he shut the dog out in the utility room and made Daisy comfortable on the kitchen floor on some towels he found in the airing cupboard.

She was kneeling up, draped over a chair, rocking and moaning softly, and he knelt beside her and rubbed her back.

'Oh, Ben, where are you?' she was asking, and he nearly laughed because it so exactly echoed his thoughts.

The last thing—absolutely the last thing—he needed was to end up delivering the baby of a colleague who was an obstetrician! But he'd done it before, and no doubt he could do it again, if the need arose. He just hoped it didn't.

'It's OK, Daisy, you're doing fine, just hang on,' he said, but she couldn't, it seemed. Unless he was mistaken, the baby was coming any moment.

'OK, Daisy, pant,' he urged. 'Don't push.'

'Got to push!'

'No. Just pant, little light breaths. Come on, you can do it,' he pleaded.

And then, just when he thought he was going to have to deliver it, he heard a key in the front door and Ben was there.

He took one look, rinsed his hands hastily and caught his baby as she emerged purple and furious into the world.

Redundant now, Andy left them in peace and went upstairs to Thomas, who was screaming in his cot.

'Hey, little guy, you've got a sister,' he said, picking him up and cuddling the fractious child as he walked along the landing. 'Isn't that clever of Mummy?'

'It would have been cleverer of Mummy to have re-alised she was in labour a little earlier,' Ben growled affectionately from the bottom of the stairs. 'Bring him down. She's respectable for a minute.'

Andy carried Thomas downstairs and into the kitchen, a lump forming in his throat. Daisy was smiling down at the baby in her arms, Ben was looking swamped with emotion and it was getting pretty mutual.

'Anything I can do?'

'Yes. Put Thomas in his high chair and hold the baby while I sort Daisy out.'

He handed him the streaky little bundle, and he sat down at the kitchen table next to Thomas and chatted to them both while Ben took care of his wife.

He could hear Stanley whining softly, and then his phone rang, so he slid it out of his pocket and spoke to Lucy.

'I'm at the Walkers'. Daisy just had the baby. I

ran past and she was in the front garden looking out for Ben.'

'What! What is it? Are they all right?'

'A girl, and they're fine. Ben's home now, just in time. I'll stay here for a bit, as long as they need me, and then I'll come home, OK?'

'OK. Are you all right?'

He laughed softly. 'I'm fine. Just fine. I'll see you soon.'

He was fine, he realised. This was what life was about, not going back to work before he was ready. What was that saying? Nobody ever died wishing they'd spent another day at the office?

And anyway, there was still plenty more to do at home.

The feeling of euphoria lasted a whole three days.

Then an envelope arrived from the exam board, dropping innocently to the mat in a clutch of Christmas cards.

'This is for you,' Lucy said, handing it to him at the kitchen table, and he put his mug down and stared at it as if it was poisoned.

'Well, aren't you going to open it?'

'No point,' he said flatly. 'I know what it says.'

'How do you know?'

'Because I screwed up!' he yelled, losing it. He slammed his chair back and it hit the wall, and Lottie started to cry, but he wasn't there to see it. He'd gone, grabbing his coat and disappearing out of the door.

The sound of the slam reverberated around the house, and Lucy picked the baby up and shushed her comfortingly. 'It's all right, darling, Daddy's just struggling a bit,' she said, struggling herself against the tears.

'Da-da,' Lottie said, peering over her shoulder, her bottom lip wobbling.

'He'll be back,' she said reassuringly, but she needed reassurance as much as Lottie, because she wasn't sure when he'd be back, or what mood he'd be in.

She stared at the envelope lying harmlessly on the table where he'd dropped it like a hand grenade.

Should she pull the pin out?

'You passed.'

He stopped in the doorway and stared at her. She was sitting on the stairs, the letter in her hands, and the house was quiet. Lottie must be asleep, he realised, and closed the door quietly.

'So what?' he said. It made no difference. He couldn't use the qualification, and all the course had done was ruin his marriage.

'So what? What do you mean, so what? You really wanted to do this course. You said it was important. If it wasn't important, why the hell did you do it?'

'I have no idea,' he said, and snatching the letter from her, he took it into the study and shut the door firmly.

It was a minute before he could look at it, and then the print blurred. Of all the useless pieces of paper...

He filed it, just because he was like that, and when he came out she was upstairs with Lottie, changing her nappy.

'I'm going in the garden,' he said, and got the shredder and loppers out of the shed and started savaging the hedge that bordered the drive. It was hanging over the gravel, restricting the turning space, and it needed cutting back.

So he cut it.

Hard.

Lucy watched him from the bedroom window, wincing as he decimated the bushes. Hopefully they'd recover, she thought, and she finished putting away the washing and carried Lottie downstairs, putting her on her play mat with a pile of toys while she wrote the last of the Christmas cards.

She made herself a cup of coffee to help the task along, but she just felt sick. She hated it when he was so upset, hated it when she couldn't reach him, but in this mood he was best left alone to work it out for himself.

She pushed the coffee away, finished the cards and put Lottie in the buggy. 'We're going to the post office,' she told him, pausing beside him on the drive.

He didn't stop, just grunted and carried on hacking, and she winced again and left him to it. There was nothing she could do to help him, and there was something she'd been meaning to do for days.

She went to the post office, bought a card and some flowers and a present for Thomas, and took them round to Daisy.

'Wow, you're looking well,' she said when Daisy opened the door.

'I am. I'm so grateful to Andy, he was amazing, so calm. I was just totally freaked out. He's a good doctor.'

She swallowed. He *was* a good doctor, but would he ever get the chance to practise again?

For the first time ever, a seed of doubt crept into her mind, and she wondered how he'd cope with that. Not well, if the hedge was anything to go by.

'Do you want a cuddle?' Daisy asked, and handed her the baby.

So small. So fine and dainty and tiny, the little fingers clinging instinctively to hers. She felt a huge lump in her throat and swallowed hard.

'She's beautiful. She's very like you.'

'Well, good, because Thomas is the spitting image of Ben and it strikes me I've done all the work so far,' she said with a laugh. 'Fancy a coffee? You can have it with or without caffeine.'

She stared at the baby. 'Can I have tea?' she said, a little thoughtfully. She couldn't be. Surely not? Even though her cycle hadn't returned yet, they'd been careful.

Except once, the day he'd been told he had a tumour, the day they'd gone to London to see David Cardew. And again in the utility room, she remembered. OK, twice, then. But even so…

'Are you all right?' Daisy asked, and she looked up and met her eyes and found a smile.

'I'm fine. Just amazed at how tiny she is. I'd sort of forgotten how small they are.'

'I know. She makes Thomas seem enormous. Biscuit?'

'Thanks.'

It was plain, thankfully, just a simple shortcake biscuit, and she dunked it in her tea and nibbled it and chatted to Daisy while her thoughts whirled round and round.

CHAPTER TEN

THE hedge was trashed.

She'd known it would be, but then he started on the back garden and she couldn't watch it any longer so she tackled him about it.

'Andy, what are you doing?' she asked. 'I know you're angry and frustrated, but you can't just take it out on the garden. There won't be anything left at this rate.'

He straightened up, threw the loppers down on the ground and pushed past her in the doorway.

'Hey, Andy, talk to me.'

'There's nothing to say.'

'There is. Please. Come on. Don't be mad with me.'

'I'm not mad with you. I'm just—'

He stopped, standing there in the kitchen with a closed look on his face, and she put her arms round him and held him. He didn't move, didn't react, didn't return the embrace, and she felt despair swamp her.

She let him go and put the kettle on.

'I've been to see Daisy,' she told him. 'The baby's beautiful.'

'I know. I was there, remember? Their perfect baby in their perfect house in their perfect life—'

'Andy! What the hell's got into you? We've got a pretty good life—'

'Have we? You didn't think so a few weeks ago. You threw me out, remember?'

She felt sick. 'We just needed space.'

'Space? How much space do you need? You told me not to come back.'

'Is that what this is all about? Because you got your work/life balance in a knot?'

'It wasn't in a knot. They were short staffed, they needed cover, and it's my job. I wasn't prepared to let them down by failing in my duty. I've worked damned hard to get where I am, and I've done it all for us. Everything I've done, I've done for us. You know that, but it's not enough. It's never enough. It doesn't matter what I do, it's wrong. I spend too much time at work, too much time away from the family neglecting the house and the garden, and it's wrong. And then I'm here and I do it and it's wrong again.'

'But you're just overdoing it. You're so driven all the time. You say it's for us, but it's not, it's for you, because you're obsessional and you can't seem to see that. Sometimes I think I don't know who you are any more!'

'I just want things to be right,' he said stubbornly. 'That doesn't make me obsessional.'

'It does if your priorities are wrong,' she said gently.

'How is making sure my family is cared for wrong?' he asked, his voice curt.

She sighed and stepped back, searching his eyes. 'It isn't. But it's not everything. We don't just need you working for us like some kind of robot. We need the human side of you, the loving father. And I want the man I married.'

Except he seemed to have disappeared without trace. He still hadn't told her again that he loved her, not since he'd been under the influence of David's 'happy drugs'. Maybe she should ask him for some more of them and slip them into Andy's tea.

Or maybe she should just accept that he didn't love her, after all, was just doing his duty because that was the kind of man he was, and he'd never shirk his duty, not to anyone.

In which case, she just hoped to goodness she wasn't pregnant, because the last thing they needed was yet another child for him to feel dutiful about.

She turned away.

'It's the nativity play tomorrow morning, and Megan's torn her costume so I've got to go over to the school and see if I can fix it,' she said, and putting Lottie in the buggy, she left him to get on with whatever he wanted to do, because right then, she was all out of words on the subject of their marriage.

She didn't even know if she still had one.

He'd massacred the garden.

He stood in it, staring at the mess he'd made and wondering what had possessed him.

Guilt? Grief? Uncertainty?

All of them, probably.

Lucy was right. Ever since his parents had died, he'd been driven, and it was wrecking their lives. And the garden, apparently. He cleared up the prunings, shredding them and scattering the shreddings under the shrubs because there was no room for them in the compost bin, and then he put the tools away and show-ered and went into town.

He'd had a call from the jewellers to say that the ring was ready, and he needed to collect it.

It looked beautiful. The repair was seamless, the worn side built up so that the diamonds were secure, and it was dazzling.

Would she even want it? She'd told him just a few hours ago that she didn't know who he was. Well, he didn't, either. She wanted the man she'd married, but he wasn't that man any more. That man had been articulate, calm under pressure, good in a crisis, able to handle anything that came into the ED with confidence. Now, he couldn't even recall the names of the drugs.

How could he ask her to bind herself to him for eternity?

He went with Lucy to the nativity play in the morning. The children were desperately excited, and Emily didn't seem to believe that he was coming.

'Will you really be there?' she asked, and he felt the crush of guilt again.

'Yes, Em, I'll really be there. I promise.'

And he was, sitting somewhere in the middle with Lucy, Lottie climbing around on his lap and jumping up and down and grabbing his hair until Lucy took her away because she was tugging on his still-tender scalp.

When the girls came on stage, he could see Emily scanning the crowd looking for them, and she spotted him and beamed. He swallowed. He'd missed all of the plays to date, but so did most of the fathers. It was pretty much unavoidable and there were children whose fathers commuted to London on a daily basis. They were surely never there.

But Ben was there, on paternity leave now, with

Thomas and Daisy at his side and the new baby in his arms, watching Florence, and they looked across and smiled. The perfect family? Maybe. Lucky them, he thought bleakly.

James was right. He should enjoy this time with his family, relish every moment of it because he was lucky to have it. So he did. He laughed, he got a lump in his throat when Emily got her words right, and he tried not to laugh when Megan tripped over her costume.

It was an interesting nativity play. The wise men brought peace, harmony and co-operation, the stable was a garden shed and Mary and Joseph were on their way to visit their family, the Christmas story with a twist.

Peace, harmony and co-operation, he thought. If only. Lucy had hardly spoken to him since yesterday, and she looked peaky and troubled. He thought of the ring, stashed safely in a locked drawer in his desk. Would she accept it?

He had no idea.

'Did you like me? I got my words right!' Emily said, bouncing with excitement as they walked home laden with shoebags and PE kit and paintings.

'You did. Well done.'

'And did you see me? I nearly felled off the stage!' Megan told him.

'But you didn't, and you were very good. You were both good.'

'Florence wanted to have Henrietta as baby Jesus, but Daisy wouldn't let her. She said she was too small and she might cry, so we had Jasmine's doll. It wees.'

'Does it?' he said, trying not to laugh.

'Only if you give it water,' Emily said. 'Miss Richards said we couldn't give it water so it wouldn't wee on the stage.'

'Good idea,' he said, glancing at Lucy, but her smile was strained and she didn't look at him, and his heart sank.

So much for peace and harmony...

'Can we put the tree up, Mummy? Please, please!'

Megan was fizzing with excitement, but Lucy felt hollow inside. Only not so hollow.

'I expect so, if your father can get it out of the loft.'

'Can we have a real one?' Emily asked, tugging at him. 'They smell so lovely.'

'Can we?' he asked Lucy, knowing she'd have an opinion.

'We can't all fit in the car with a tree.'

'I'll go, then,' he said, and then remembered. 'Or I'll look after the children, rather, and you can go.'

'They've got them at the garden centre round the corner. It's only a few hundred yards. Can you carry it that far?'

'I expect so, if it's not eight foot tall.'

'Right. Well, you take the girls and I'll stay here with Lottie and find the decorations,' she said, so they put their coats on and headed off.

The girls all but dragged him to the little garden centre, and as soon as they arrived he knew he was in trouble.

'Daddy, look! They've got Santa's Grotto! Please can we go and see him? Please please please please *pleeeeeease*!'

He looked down at Emily, her little face beseeching, and then Megan, eyes like saucers, bouncing next to him and joining in the begging, and he crumpled.

'I'll call Mummy,' he said, and pulled his phone out. 'Luce, hi. We may be a while. They've got Santa.'

'Oh, the girls'll love it!'

She sounded wistful, as if she'd like to be there. And why not?

'Why don't you come?' he urged, suddenly needing to have all of them together for this. 'Bring Lottie down. It's her first Christmas and she's never seen him. We'll wait for you.'

'OK,' she said, and he grinned at the girls.

'Mummy's coming and bringing Lottie to see him, too,' he told them, and their little faces lit up.

'Yay! We can see him! We can see Santa!' Emily squealed, bouncing on the spot.

'I tell you what, shall we go and choose a tree while we wait, and they can keep it for us till we go?' he suggested, hoping the distraction would help to keep a lid on their excitement until Lucy got there.

It worked, to his relief. They found the trees, all lined up against the fence, and started to look through them, discussing their flaws and failings. They were a motley collection, because it was only two days to Christmas and they'd left it a bit late to choose a real one, but it was what Emily wanted, and he wanted to give her what she wanted this year, because last year he hadn't even been here for most of it.

He chose the bushiest one which seemed well balanced, and they paid for it and had it put on one side. By the time they'd done that, Lucy had arrived with Lottie, to his relief, so with the girls fizzing with excitement again they went and queued outside Santa's Grotto.

It was pretty makeshift, but the girls didn't seem to mind, and after a mercifully short time they reached the front of the queue and went in together as a family.

'Three beautiful little girls? Ho-ho-ho,' the jolly Santa said, beaming. 'Come and sit here and tell me your name,' he said to Emily, and she perched on the stool beside him and told him her name.

'And what do you want for Christmas, Emily?' he asked cheerfully.

'I want my Daddy to be better,' she said, her eyes welling, and Andy felt as if he'd been hit in the chest.

He sucked in a breath and met the startled man's eyes.

'Has your Daddy been ill?'

She nodded. 'He had something nasty growing in his head and it was pressing on his brain, but they cut it out and now he's getting better, but it's too slow and it makes him cross and he makes Mummy cry.'

Oh, God. Why, *why* had he thought this was a good idea?

'I'm OK,' he said, his voice ragged with emotion. 'Em, I'm OK, darling. I'm getting better.'

'Really? Promise?'

'Really. Really and truly, I promise. I'm just bad tempered because it's taking a long time, and I'm sorry. I don't mean to be...'

He felt Lucy squeeze his arm, and he sucked in another breath and tried to crush down the emotion that was overwhelming him.

'I'm sure you don't,' their Santa said softly. 'Well, young lady, I'll have a word with the elves and we'll see what we can do, but I think if you were to give your Daddy a cuddle, it would be all the Christmas present he would need, and I'm sure it would make him feel much better.'

She nodded, sniffing, and he leant forwards and patted her hand. 'Is there anything else you'd like?'

She shook her head. 'Not really. Just my Daddy back.'

'Well, why don't you go and give him that cuddle and see if it works?' he suggested gently.

She ran to him, burying her face in his coat, and he hugged her close, lifting her into his arms and cuddling her tight. He left Lucy dealing with Megan and Lottie. He had no idea what Megan asked for, or what Lottie made of the strange man with the crazy beard and the funny costume. He just held Emily tight until she stopped clinging to him, and then he kissed her gently and put her down, and they walked out together, Em's hand firmly in his.

'Are you OK?' Lucy asked quietly, and he could see that her lashes were clogged with tears.

'Just about,' he said gruffly. 'Luce, I'm sorry. I didn't know I made you cry.'

'Shh,' she murmured, her voice gentle. 'It's OK, Andy. It's just been a bit tough for all of us, but we're getting there.' They walked through the shop part, and she suddenly stopped and clapped her hands together. 'Hey, girls, why don't we go and choose some more decorations for the tree?'

Bless her for distracting them. They found a 'Baby's First Christmas' bauble for Lottie, and a little red stocking to hang on the fireplace with the others, and a new angel for the top of the tree. And then they collected the tree and he carried it home.

By the time they got there he was regretting not

going for a scrawny one, but once it was in the pot and his arm had stopped aching, he was sure it would be fine.

'It's a bit crooked, Daddy,' Em said, snuggling up to him and studying it thoughtfully.

It was. The trunk kinked half way up and then carried on straight up, so if they looked at it side on they could see it, but it went in a corner so it didn't really matter. And Emily was right, it did smell lovely.

'Daddy, Daddy, you have to do the lights,' Megan said, dragging them out of the box.

'Carefully. Give them to me.'

He untangled them, which would have been easier without his helper, and threaded them round the tree, and then the girls and Lucy hung the baubles on it, Em and Megan doing the lowest ones, Lucy standing on a chair while he held it steady so she could do the higher ones.

She leant over to put the new angel on the top and he put his hands on her hips and anchored her, then lifted her down and kissed her. Just a fleeting touch of his lips, but she seemed a little distracted and he didn't know why.

'That looks lovely,' she said, smiling brightly, but he could see it didn't quite reach her eyes. 'Good work, everyone. Shall we have some tea and cake?'

'Yay, cake!' Em said, dancing into the kitchen on tiptoes, and he cleared up the boxes and put them back in the loft, wondering what was wrong with Lucy.

Was she getting round to telling him that this would be their last Christmas together as a family? He didn't know, and he'd given up trying to second-guess her, but then he hadn't realised that he'd made her cry, either.

Feeling slightly sick with apprehension, he went back down to the kitchen.

'Don't give me any cake,' he told her. 'I've got things to do.'

And he shut himself in his study, sat down at his desk and unlocked the drawer. The ring, nestled in its original velvet box, sparkled at him mockingly.

'Oh, Lucy,' he sighed, and shut the drawer, locked it again and took Stanley for a walk.

The supermarket would be a nightmare, and going there was the last thing she wanted to do after she finished her surgery on Christmas Eve morning. She hadn't wanted to work the shift, and she remembered the grief she'd given Andy just a year ago because he'd been working Christmas Eve.

She felt such a hypocrite, and racked with guilt, because she realised now that sometimes you just had to do what you had to do, no matter how unwelcome it might be.

Like the last-minute shopping. She'd done most of the shopping a few days earlier, but there were a few things she still had to get, so she dived into the supermarket on the way home and got the rest.

Not that she felt like cooking. The queasiness she'd been feeling for the last week or so was still there, lurking in the background, and just to set her mind at rest she picked up a pregnancy test on her way to the checkout.

It burned a hole in her handbag all the way home, and she unloaded the shopping, opened the fridge and saw the turkey and the stuffing, and drew the line.

She'd do it tomorrow morning. No doubt the children would be up at six at the latest, so there'd be plenty of time to stuff it and get it in the oven in time. They were watching a film on the television, Andy in the middle, Lottie asleep on his lap and the girls on either side snuggled up against him.

Taking the slim box out of her handbag, she went upstairs to their bathroom, locked the door and opened the packet.

'Is that everything?'

'I think so,' he said. 'I hope so. There seems to be a lot.'

The girls were finally in bed asleep, and they were on the floor by the tree, stacking presents for the children.

'They're all for the children,' she told him, feeling flat and despondent and tearful. 'I haven't got you a present. I didn't know what to get you. It's not that I didn't want to give you anything, I just feel I don't know you any more, and I had no idea what you'd like.'

His eyes softened. 'Oh, Lucy, you don't need to give me anything.'

'There is one thing,' she said, her heart hitching a little. 'It's not really a present, and I don't know if you'll even want it, but it's a bit late to worry about that now. It's not the sort of thing you can take back.' She took a deep breath, then said, 'I'm pregnant.'

'Preg—? Oh, Lucy.' He gathered her into his arms, cradling her against his chest and feeling the joy burst in his heart. 'Oh, that's amazing,' he said, not knowing whether to laugh or cry. 'How could you think I wouldn't want another baby?'

'Because you didn't want Lottie?'

He was stunned. 'Of course I wanted her! I love her to bits.'

'But you were never here for her, you hardly paid any attention to her when you were here, and I thought you didn't want her, didn't love her. Didn't love any of us any more.'

'Of course I love you. I love all of you—Lucy, how could you think that?'

'Because you never *tell* us. The only time in ages you've told me that you love me, you were under the influence of David's "happy drugs".'

He swallowed hard, remembering the burning, desperate need to say those words to her. 'I thought it might be my last chance, that if I lost my speech permanently, I'd never be able to say it again. I didn't know if you'd want to hear it, but I wanted you to know. Just for the record. And I know I've been difficult. I know I'm not easy to live with, I know I drive myself too hard, I know I try and overcompensate because of my parents, go too far the other way, but it doesn't mean I don't love you. I do love you. I love you so much it's hard to find the words, even under normal circumstances.'

'Well, you seem to be doing all right at the moment,' she said tearfully.

He gave a hollow laugh and shook his head, then stood up and lifted a tiny little parcel from the tree.

'This is for you. I don't know if you'll want it, or if it's the last thing in the world you want from me, but it's how I feel about you, and I should have shown you years ago. But I don't want you feeling pressured by it. I love you. I want to make our marriage work, I always have, and I'm not very good at it, but I'm willing to try, and the last thing I'm going to do is walk away from you, ever. But if you want to walk away from me, if that's what's right for you, then I'll understand, because I'm not the man you married. I don't know what's going to happen about my speech, I still have problems, and I may never be able to go back to my job again, and that changes things, I know that, so I can't ask you to stay if you feel it's wrong for you.'

She stared at him, then down at the tiny parcel he'd put in her hands. There was a fine gold ribbon round it, and she pulled the bow and it fell away. The paper was meticulously folded round it, perfectly creased, and she unwrapped it and a small velvet box fell into her hand.

It had a tiny gold clasp on one side, and hinges on the other, and it looked very old. A ring box?

She lifted the catch and opened the lid, and gasped.

'Andy!' she breathed, and then her eyes flooded with tears. 'Oh, Andy, it's beautiful.'

'It's an eternity ring,' he said gruffly, 'because that's how long I'll love you.'

Tears cascaded down her cheeks, and she lifted the ring out of the box and gave it to him, her fingers shaking.

'Put it on my finger, please?' she asked him softly, and with hands that shook slightly, he slid it on. It settled there next to her other two rings as if it had been made for it, and she stared down at them and sniffed.

'Oh, Andy, it's perfect. Where did you find it?'

'In the jewellers' in town. It had only just come in the day before, and it had to be cleaned and repaired, because it was a little worn on one side, but it just seemed to have your name written all over it, and it was the right size.'

'How did you know?'

'I took your engagement ring with me.'

'The day I couldn't find it,' she said, realising what he'd done.

He nodded.

'I can't believe you thought I didn't love you any more,' she said.

'You haven't told me recently, either,' he pointed out. 'I've been too busy making sure all the boxes were ticked, and you've just been left to muddle along in the chaos that I've left behind.'

She nodded.

'We've been pretty rubbish, haven't we?' she agreed.

'We have. Shall we start again?'

'Good idea. I love you. And it doesn't matter to me if you go back to work or not, you're still the man I love and you always will be. I just might have to hide the garden tools.'

He laughed softly, then his smile grew tender. 'I love you, too. And I'm sorry you had to throw me out to get me to come to my senses. Thank you for standing by me through all of this. It would have been so easy to walk away, especially the way I've been.'

'It would never be easy to walk away from you,' she said, remembering the day he'd gone. 'I thought my heart would break when I heard that door close behind you. And when I realised you were so ill, when I thought I might lose you for ever—'

He scooped her up in his arms and settled down with her on the sofa, cradled on his lap. 'You haven't lost me. You'll never really lose me, whatever happens. I'll always love you.'

'I hope so. I'm banking on it.' She went quiet for a

moment, then tilted her head so she could see his eyes. 'What was in the letter?'

He went very still, then gave a wry smile. 'Ah. A lot of soul-baring. I'm surprised you didn't read it.'

'I didn't want to. I thought—I'd rather you told me yourself.'

He nodded. 'I've still got it. It's in my desk.'

'Can I read it?'

He hesitated briefly, then nodded again. 'Sure. I'll get it.'

He shifted her off his lap, brought it to her and then sat down quietly at the other end of the sofa.

Fingers trembling slightly, she peeled up the flap of the envelope and pulled out the single sheet. The writing was untidy, the ink smudged in places.

Tears?

She flattened it out with her hand and started to read.

My dearest, darling Lucy
If you're reading this, it's because it's all gone horribly wrong. I hope you never have to. As I write, I'm filled with dread for what the future holds for us all. Not for me. I'm not afraid for me, but for you and the children, because I know the impact of losing your parents is devastating, and I can't bear to think of the children growing up with that sadness hanging over them. I know you'll be amazing with them, loving and support-ive, and I hope in time you'll find someone to sup-port you, too, hopefully someone who won't let you down as I have.

This is the hardest thing I've ever had to write, and I don't know where to start, except to say

I'm sorry that I've somehow hurt you or let you down. I never meant to. Everything I've done, I've done for you, for the family, but that doesn't seem to have been what you wanted. It's too late now to change, too late to do anything about it except to apologise with all my heart for failing you, for letting our marriage get brushed aside by other things.

You have been my reason for living, the only thing that's got me through the tough times, the best thing that's ever happened to me. The ten years I've been privileged to be with you have been the happiest and most fulfilling of my life, and I'm gutted at the thought that all of that might be gone, wiped away by this crazy thing in my head.

Even if I live, I might be unable to function normally, might be unable to communicate or understand, paralysed—who knows? And I cannot bear the thought of you tied to me under those conditions. If that is what's happened, then please, PLEASE, don't stay with me. I want you to be free, to find a new life with the children, a life of peace. I don't want you staying with me out of guilt or pity, trapped in an impossible situation because of a vow you made to a different man, the man I used to be. I love you far too much to bear that.

Be happy, my darling. Be free of guilt and pain and fear. Love our children for me, and when they ask about me, try and remember the good times. All my love,
Andy

She felt the tears sliding down her face. One dripped onto the letter, making another smudge to join the others his tears had caused.

She couldn't speak. There was nothing she could say. Maybe nothing *to* say, nothing that mattered any more.

She stood up and walked over to him, curled up on his lap and let him hold her as she cried away the grief and pain and fear that she'd held trapped inside her for months. And then she lifted her head, and kissed away his tears.

One year later...

'Mummy, Mummy, Daddy's home!' Emily shrieked.

Lucy came out of the kitchen wiping her hands on a tea towel, and kissed him. 'Hi,' she said, her eyes smiling. 'How was work?'

How was it? Great, was how it was. Great that he was back, great that, after a month of supervision, he'd been passed as fit to work alone since May. He'd done what James had suggested, taken his time, waited until he was sure he was all right rather than rush it and go back too soon, and he'd spent that extra time with his family.

And as a result of that experience, he'd only gone back part time, job sharing with a woman who had a young family, and it was panning out really well. He had time for the children, time for Lucy and time for himself. It was a win-win situation, and he loved it.

'Work was fine. Good. Surprisingly quiet, thankfully. How are you? Are you coping with all the Christmas chaos?'

She chuckled. 'I'm fine. I'm glad you're home promptly, though.'

'I promised I would be,' he said pointedly, and she smiled, because these days, if he promised something, he did it. No messing. No ifs or buts, nothing getting in the way, because he'd learned that he wasn't indispensable to anyone but his family, and they always came first, without exception.

'It's so nice to be home with you,' he said softly. 'I didn't know what I was missing before.'

She smiled and kissed him again, lingering this time a moment longer. 'Mum and Dad have arrived. Go and say hello and then come and open a bottle. You're off now for three days, and I intend to make sure you relax.'

'You do that,' he said, grinning, and he went into the sitting room and scooped Daniel off the floor. 'Hello, monster, how are you?' he asked, tucking the giggling baby into the crook of his arm and greeting his in-laws warmly. 'I think Lucy's got some champagne in the fridge. Can I tempt you?'

'I think that would be lovely,' Lucy's mother said, getting to her feet and kissing his cheek.

They followed him into the kitchen, and he stole a slice of bread with smoked salmon on it. 'Yum. Hi, Lottie. Hi, Megan.'

'Hi, Daddy,' they chorused, and he handed Daniel over to his grandfather and popped the cork on the champagne, then raised his glass.

'Happy families,' he said, and the adults echoed him.

'It's not happy families, silly, it's Happy Christmas!' Megan told him, laughing, but he just grinned at her and hugged her.

'Same thing, isn't it?' he said, and over the top of

her glass Lucy smiled at him, her eyes filled with love
and laughter.

'Definitely. I couldn't have put it better myself…'

* * * * *

HER LITTLE
SPANISH SECRET

BY
LAURA IDING

This book is dedicated to the Milwaukee WisRWA group.
Thanks to all of you for your ongoing support.

First published in Great Britain 2012
by Mills & Boon, an imprint of Harlequin (UK) Limited.
Harlequin (UK) Limited, Eton House, 18-24 Paradise Road,
Richmond, Surrey TW9 1SR

© Laura Iding 2012

ISBN: 978 0 263 89212 3

Harlequin (UK) policy is to use papers that are natural, renewable and recyclable products and made from wood grown in sustainable forests. The logging and manufacturing process conform to the legal environmental regulations of the country of origin.

Printed and bound in Spain
by Blackprint CPI, Barcelona

Dear Reader

Like many of you I've spent years as an armchair traveller, learning about other countries and other cultures by reading rather than visiting.

Last year I had the tremendous opportunity to visit Seville (pronounced Sevilla), in Spain. My family and I had a great time, and when I returned home I had this story whirling around in my head about how an American woman falls in love with a Spanish surgeon.

Miguel and Kat originally meet in the US, when Miguel is an exchange student, but when they meet again Kat is visiting Miguel's home city of Seville. Sparks flash and the passion that they shared once before returns in force. But can they create a life together coming from such different cultures? Will true love conquer all?

I hope you enjoy reading Miguel and Kat's story as much as I enjoyed writing it. Don't hesitate to visit my website or find me on Facebook—I love to hear from my readers.

Sincerely

Laura Iding

www.lauraiding.com

Recent titles by Laura Iding:

DATING DR DELICIOUS
A KNIGHT FOR NURSE HART
THE NURSE'S BROODING BOSS
THE SURGEON'S NEW YEAR WEDDING WISH
EXPECTING A CHRISTMAS MIRACLE

**These books are also available in eBook format
from www.millsandboon.co.uk**

PROLOGUE

Four and a half years earlier...

Kat had never seen so much blood—it pooled on the floor and stained the walls of the O.R. suite. Dr. Miguel Vasquez, along with two other trauma surgeons, had worked as hard as they could to stop the bleeding but to no avail. Their young, pregnant patient and her unborn baby had died.

After the poor woman's body had been sent to the morgue, Kat was left alone to finish putting the supplies and equipment away while the housekeepers cleaned up the blood. Only once they were finished did she head over to the staff locker room. Thankfully, her shift was over, she was exhausted. Yet as tired as she was physically, she was emotionally keyed up, and couldn't get the horrific scene from the O.R. out of her mind. They hadn't had a case like that in a long time.

After she changed out of her scrubs into a pair of well-worn jeans and a short-sleeved sweater, she found Dr. Vasquez sitting in the staff lounge, holding his head in his hands. He looked so upset and dejected that she stopped—unable to simply walk away.

"Please don't torture yourself over this," she urged

softly, as she sank down beside him on the sofa close enough that their shoulders brushed. "Her death wasn't your fault."

Miguel slowly lifted and turned his head to look at her, his eyes full of agony. "I should have called the rest of the team in earlier."

"You called them as soon as you discovered her abdomen was full of blood and they came as soon as they could," she corrected. "No one knew she was pregnant, it was too early to tell."

"I should have examined her more closely down in the trauma bay," he muttered, more to himself than to her. "Then we would have known."

"Do you really think that would have made a difference?" she asked softly. "Even if the other two surgeons had been notified earlier, they wouldn't have been able to come right away. Dr. Baccus said they were resuscitating a patient in the I.C.U. All of us in the O.R. suite did the best we could."

He stared at her for a long moment, and then sighed. "I can't help thinking about what I should have done differently. I know we can't save every patient, but she was just so young. And pregnant. I can't help feeling I failed her."

She put her hand on his arm, trying to offer some reassurance. "If three of the best trauma surgeons in the whole hospital couldn't save her or her baby, then it wasn't meant to be."

A ghost of a smile played along the edges of his mouth, and she was glad she'd been able to make him feel a little better. Because what she'd said was true. Everyone talked about Miguel's skill in the O.R. He could have stayed here in the U.S. once his fellowship was finished, even though he'd made it clear that wasn't part of his plan.

She reluctantly slid her hand from his arm and rose to her feet. But she'd only taken two steps when he stopped her.

"Katerina?"

She hesitated and turned to look back at him, surprised and secretly pleased he'd remembered her first name. They'd operated on dozens of patients together, but while she'd always been keenly aware of Miguel, she had never been absolutely sure he'd noticed her the same way. "Yes?"

"Do you have plans for tonight? If not, would you join me? We could get a bite to eat or something."

She wasn't hungry, but could tell Miguel didn't want to be alone, and suddenly she didn't either. Word amongst the O.R. staff was that Miguel wasn't in the market for a relationship since his time in the U.S. was limited, but she ignored the tiny warning flickering in the back of her mind. "I don't have any plans for tonight, and I'd love to have dinner." *Or something.*

"Muy bien." He rose to his feet and held out his hand. She took it and suppressed a shiver when a tingle of awareness shot up her arm.

But she didn't pull away. Instead, she stayed close at his side while they left the hospital together.

CHAPTER ONE

"Down, Mama. *Down!*"

"Soon, Tommy. I promise." Katerina Richardson fought a wave of exhaustion and tightened her grip on her wriggly son. She couldn't imagine anything more torturous than being stuck in a plane for sixteen hours with an active soon-to-be four-year-old. She didn't even want to think of the longer flight time on the return trip.

Plenty of time to worry about that, later. For now they'd finally arrived in Seville, Spain. And she desperately needed to get to the hospital to see how her half sister was doing after being hit by a car. The information from Susan Horton, the coordinator for the study abroad program, had been sketchy at best.

"I can't believe the stupid airline lost my luggage," her best friend, Diana Baylor, moaned as they made their way out of the airport to the line of people waiting for taxis. "It's so hot here in April compared to Cambridge, Massachusetts. I'm already sweating—I can't imagine staying in these same clothes for very long."

Kat felt bad for her friend, who'd only come on this trip in the first place as a favor to her, but what could she do? Diana's lost luggage was the least of her concerns. "Don't worry, I'll share my stuff or we'll buy what you need."

"Down, Mama. Down!" Tommy's tone, accompanied by his wiggling, became more insistent.

"Okay, but you have to hold my hand," Kat warned her son, as she put him on his feet. She'd let him run around in the baggage claim area while they'd waited for their luggage, but even that hadn't put a dent in his energy level. She was grateful he'd slept on the plane, even though she hadn't. Kat grabbed hold of his hand before he could make a beeline for the road. "Stay next to me, Tommy."

He tugged on her hand, trying to go in the opposite direction from where they needed to wait for a taxi. Thank heavens the line was moving fast. Her son was as dark as she was blonde and if she had a nickel for every person who'd asked her if he was adopted, she'd be rich. Even here, she could feel curious eyes on them.

"No, Tommy. This way. Look, a car! We're going to go for a ride!"

His attention diverted, Tommy readily climbed into the cab after Diana. They all squished into the back seat for the short ride to their hotel. "Hesperia Hotel, please," she told the taxi driver.

"Hesperia? *No comprendo* Hesperia." Their cab driver shook his head as he pulled out into traffic, waving his hand rather impatiently. *"No comprendo."*

Kat refused to panic and quickly rummaged through her carry-on bag to pull out the hotel confirmation document. She handed it to him so he could read the name of the hotel for himself. He looked at the paper and made a sound of disgust. "Es-peer-ria," he said, emphasizing the Spanish pronunciation. "Esperia Hotel."

Properly chastised, she belatedly remembered from her two years of high-school Spanish that the H was silent. Being in Spain brought back bittersweet memories of Tommy's father, especially during their three-hour layover in Madrid. She'd briefly toyed with the thought of trying to find Miguel, but had then realized her idea was ludicrous. Madrid was a huge city and she had no idea where to even start, if he'd even be there, which she seriously doubted. He may have studied there but it was possible he'd moved on. "*Sí*. Hesperia Hotel, *gracias*."

The taxi driver mumbled something unintelligible and probably uncomplimentary in Spanish, under his breath. Kat ignored him.

"Are you going to the hospital today?" Diana asked with a wide yawn. "I'm voting for a nap first."

"I doubt Tommy will sleep any time soon," she reminded her friend. "And, yes, I'm going to head to the hospital as soon as we get the hotel room secured. I'm sorry, but you'll have to watch Tommy for a while."

"I know," Diana said quickly. "I don't mind." Kat knew Diana wouldn't renege on her duties, seeing as Kat had been the one to pay for her friend's airfare, along with footing the hotel bill. Kat hadn't minded as she'd needed someone to help watch over her son. "Wow, Kat, take a look at the architecture of that building over there. Isn't it amazing?"

"Yeah, amazing." Kat forced a smile, because Diana was right—the view was spectacular. Yet the thrill of being in Europe for the first time in her life couldn't make her forget the reason they were there. The knot in her stomach tightened as she wondered what she'd discover when she went to the hospital. Susan Horton, the director of the study abroad program at Seville

University, had called just thirty-six hours ago, to let her know that her younger half sister, Juliet, had a serious head injury and was too sick to be flown back to the U.S. for care.

Kat had immediately made arrangements to fly over to Seville in order to be there for her sister.

She and Juliet hadn't been particularly close. And not just because of the seven-year age gap. They had different fathers and for some reason Juliet had always seemed to resent Kat. Their respective fathers had both abandoned their mother, which should have given them something in common. After their mother had been diagnosed with pancreatic cancer, Kat had promised her mother she'd look after Juliet.

Juliet had gone a little wild after their mother's death, but had settled down somewhat after she'd finished her second year of college. At the ripe old age of twenty-one, Juliet had insisted on studying abroad for the spring semester of her junior year. Kat had been forced to pick up a lot of call weekends in order to pay for the program, but she'd managed. To be fair, Juliet had come up with a good portion of the money herself.

Kat felt guilty now about how she'd been secretly relieved to put her younger sister on a plane to Spain. But even if she'd tried to talk Juliet out of going, it wouldn't have worked. Juliet would only have resented her even more.

How had the accident happened? All she'd been told was that Juliet had run out into the street and had been hit by a car, but she didn't know anything further.

Getting to the hotel didn't take long, although there was another hassle as she figured out the dollar to Euro exchange in order to pay the cranky cab driver. As soon as Diana and Tommy were settled in the hotel room, Kat asked the front-desk clerk for directions to the hospital. She managed to figure out how to get there on the metro, which wasn't very different than using the subway back home.

Seville's teaching hospital was larger than she'd expected and that gave her hope that Juliet was getting good medical and nursing care. Kat found her sister in their I.C.U and walked in, only to stop abruptly when she saw Juliet was connected to a ventilator. Her stomach clenched even harder when she noted several dark bruises and small lacerations marring her sister's pale skin.

"Dear heaven," she breathed, trailing her gaze from her sister up to the heart monitor. She'd done a year-long stint in the I.C.U before going to the O.R. so she'd known what to expect, but had hoped that Juliet might have improved during the time it had taken her to make the travel arrangements and actually arrive in Seville.

A nurse, dressed head to toe in white, complete with nurse's cap on her dark hair, came into the room behind her. Kat blinked back tears and turned to the nurse. "How is she? Has her condition improved? What is the extent of her injury? Can I speak to the doctor?"

The nurse stared at her blankly for a moment and then began talking in rapid Spanish, none of which Kat could understand.

Kat wanted to cry. She desperately paged through the English/Spanish dictionary she held, trying to look up words in Spanish to explain what she wanted to know. *"¿Donde esta el doctor? ¿Habla Ingles?"* she finally asked. Where is the doctor? Speak English?

The nurse spun around and left the room.

Kat sank into a chair next to Juliet's bed, gently clasping her half sister's hand in hers. Maybe the age difference, and completely opposite personalities, had kept them from being close, but Juliet was still her sister. With their mother gone, they only had each other.

She had to believe Juliet would pull through this. Her sister was young and strong, surely she'd be fine.

Kat put her head down on the edge of Juliet's bed, closing her eyes just for a moment, trying to combat the deep fatigue of jet lag and her fear regarding the seriousness of her sister's injuries.

She didn't think she'd fallen asleep, but couldn't be sure how much time had passed when she heard a deep male voice, thankfully speaking in English. She lifted her head and prised her heavy eyelids open.

"I understand you have questions regarding the condition of Juliet Campbell?"

"Yes, thank you." She quickly rose to her feet and blinked the grit from her eyes as she turned to face the doctor.

His familiar facial features made the room gyrate wildly, and she had to grasp the edge of her sister's side rail for support. "Miguel?" she whispered in shock, wondering if she was dreaming. Had thoughts of Tommy's father conjured up a mirage? Or was it just the doctor's Hispanic features, dark hair falling rakishly over his forehead, deep brown eyes gazing into hers, that were so achingly familiar?

"Katerina." His eyes widened in surprise, and she couldn't help feeling relieved to know she wasn't the only one knocked off balance at this chance meeting. For several long seconds they simply stared at each other across the room. Slowly, he smiled, relieving part of the awkwardness. "What a pleasant surprise to see you again. How are you?"

She tightened her grip on the bed rail behind her because her knees threatened to give away. "I'm fine, thanks." She struggled to keep her tone friendly, even though for one beautiful night they'd been far more than just friends. Yet despite her fanciful thoughts during the Madrid layover, she hadn't really expected to see Miguel again.

He looked good. Better than good. Miguel was taller than most Latino men, with broad shoulders and a golden skin tone that showcased his bright smile. His dark eyes were mesmerizing. If not for his full name, Dr. Miguel Vasquez, embroidered on his white lab coat—she'd for sure think this was a dream.

She knew Juliet's condition needed to be her primary concern, but she had so many other questions she wanted to ask him. "I'm surprised to find you here in Seville. I thought you lived in Madrid?"

He didn't answer right away, and she thought she saw a flash of guilt shadow his dark eyes. She glanced away, embarrassed. She didn't want him feeling guilty for the night they'd shared together. Or for leaving so abruptly when notified of his father's illness. It wasn't as if they'd been dating or anything.

Neither was it his fault she'd let her feelings spin out of control that night.

When she'd discovered she was pregnant, she'd called his cell phone, the only number she'd had, but the number had already been out of service. She'd assumed he hadn't kept his old American phone once he'd returned to Spain. She'd looked for him on several social media sites, but hadn't found him. After about six months she'd stopped trying.

"I live here," he said simply. "My family's olive farm is just twenty minutes outside Seville."

"I see," she said, although she really didn't. Obviously, she hadn't known much about Miguel's family. She could hardly picture him growing up on an olive farm. She'd simply assumed because he was a Madrid exchange student that he'd lived there. She forced a smile, wishing they could recapture the easy camaraderie they'd once shared. "How's your father?"

"He passed away three and a half years ago." The shadows in Miguel's eyes betrayed his grief.

"I'm sorry," she murmured helplessly. She'd known that Miguel had needed to return to Spain when his father had been sick, but she was a little surprised that he'd stayed here, even after his father had passed away.

During the night they'd shared together he'd confided about how he dreamed of joining Doctors Without Borders. When she hadn't been able to get in touch with Miguel once she'd discovered she was pregnant, she'd imagined him working in some distant country.

Why hadn't he followed his dream? He'd told her about how he was only waiting to be finished with his family obligations. And his father had passed away three and a half years ago. He should have been long gone by now.

Not that Miguel's choices were any of her business.

Except, now that he was here, how was she going to tell him about their son?

Panic soared, squeezing the air from her lungs. She struggled to take a deep breath, trying to calm her jagged nerves. Right now she needed to focus on her sister. She pulled herself together with an effort. "Will you please tell me about Juliet's head injury? How bad is it? What exactly is her neuro status?"

"Your sister's condition is serious, but stable. She responds to pain now, which she wasn't doing at first. She does have a subarachnoid hemorrhage that we are monitoring very closely."

A subarachnoid hemorrhage wasn't good news, but she'd been prepared for that. "Is she following commands?" Kat asked.

"Not yet, but she's young, Katerina. She has a good chance of getting through this."

She gave a tight nod, wanting to believe him. "I know. I'm hopeful that she'll wake up soon."

"Katerina, I have to get to surgery as I have a patient waiting, but I would like to see you again. Would you please join me for dinner tonight? Say around eight-thirty or nine?"

She blinked in surprise and tried to think of a graceful way out of the invitation. She knew he was asking her out from some sense of obligation, because they'd spent one intense night together.

But she needed time to get the fog of fatigue out of her mind. Time to think about if and when to share the news about Tommy. Obviously Miguel deserved to know the truth, but what about Tommy? Did he deserve a father who didn't want him? A father who'd made it clear he wasn't looking for a family?

She didn't know what to do.

"I'm sorry, but I'm sure I'll be asleep by then," she murmured, averting her gaze to look at her sister. "I just flew in today and I'm a bit jet-lagged."

She steeled herself against the flash of disappointment in his eyes. Juliet's well-being came first. And Tommy's was a close second.

As far as she was concerned, Miguel Vasquez would just have to wait.

Miguel couldn't believe Katerina Richardson was actually here, in Seville.

He allowed his gaze to roam over her, branding her image on his mind. She wasn't beautiful in the classical sense, but he'd always found her attractive with her peaches and cream complexion and long golden blonde hair that she normally wore in a ponytail. Except for that one night, when he'd run his fingers through the silk tresses.

To this day he couldn't explain why he'd broken his cardinal rule by asking her out. Granted, he'd been devastated over losing their patient, but he'd been determined to avoid emotional entanglements, knowing he was leaving when the year was up. He knew better than to let down his guard, but he'd been very attracted to Katerina and had suspected the feeling was mutual. That night he'd given up his fight to stay away.

But then the news about his father's stroke had pulled him from Katerina's bed the next morning. He'd rushed home to Seville. His father's condition had been worse than he'd imagined, and his father had ultimately died twelve painful months later. His mother was already gone, and during his father's illness his younger brother, Luis, had started drinking. Miguel had been forced to put his own dreams on hold to take over the olive farm, which had been in the Vasquez family for generations, until he could get Luis sobered up.

His visceral reaction to seeing Katerina again

stunned him. He hadn't allowed himself to miss her. Besides, he only had three months left on his contract here at the hospital and he'd be finally free to join Doctors Without Borders.

And this time, nothing was going to stop him. Not his brother Luis. And certainly not Katerina.

He shook off his thoughts with an effort. Logically he knew he should accept her excuse, but he found himself pressing the issue. "Maybe a light meal after siesta, then? Certainly you have to eat some time."

There was a wariness reflected in her green eyes that hadn't been there in the past. He wondered what had changed in the four and a half years they'd been apart. He was relieved to note she wasn't wearing a wedding ring even though her personal life wasn't any of his business. He couldn't allow himself to succumb to Katerina's spell—he refused to make the same mistakes his father had.

"You've described my sister's head injury, but is there anything else? Other injuries I need to be aware of?" she asked, changing the subject.

He dragged his attention to his patient. "Juliet was hit on the right side. Her right leg is broken in two places and we had to operate to get the bones aligned properly. She has several rib fractures and some internal bleeding that appears to be resolving. Her head injury is the greatest of our concerns. Up until late yesterday she wasn't responding at all, even to pain. The fact that there is some response now gives us hope she may recover."

Katerina's pale skin blanched even more, and his gut clenched when he noted the tears shimmering in her bright green eyes. They reminded him, too much, about the night they'd shared. An intense, intimate, magical night that had ended abruptly with his brother's phone call about their father. She'd cried for him when he'd been unable to cry for himself.

"When can she be transported back to the United States?" she asked.

The instinctive protest at the thought of her leaving surprised him. What was wrong with him? He wrestled his emotions under control. "Not until I'm convinced her neurological status has truly stabilized," he reluctantly admitted.

Katerina nodded, as if she'd expected that response. "Are you my sister's doctor? Or just one of the doctors here who happen to speak English?" she asked. Her gaze avoided his, staying at the level of his chest.

"Yes, I'm your sister's doctor. As you know, I'm a surgeon who does both general and trauma surgery cases."

"Do any of the nurses speak English?"

Seville didn't have the same tourist draw as Madrid or Barcelona, which meant not as many of the locals spoke English. Miguel had originally learned English from his American mother, who'd taught him before she'd died. He'd learned even more English during his time at the University of Madrid. In fact, he'd earned the opportunity to live and study medicine in the U.S. at Harvard University.

There he'd ultimately become a doctor. And met Katerina. He dragged his thoughts out of the past. "No, the nurses don't speak much English, I'm afraid."

She closed her eyes and rubbed her temples, as if she had a pounding headache. Once again he found himself on the verge of offering comfort. But he didn't dare, no matter how much he wanted to.

"I would appreciate periodic updates on my sister's condition whenever you have time to spare from the rest of your patients," she said finally.

The way she turned her back on him, as if to dismiss him, made him scowl. He wanted to demand she look at him, talk to him, but of course there wasn't time. Glancing at his watch only confirmed he was already late for his scheduled surgery. "I'd be happy to give you an update later today, if you have time at, say, four o'clock?" He purposefully gave her the same time he normally ate a late lunch, right after siesta.

She spun around to face him. "But—" She stopped herself and then abruptly nodded. "Of course. Four o'clock would be fine."

He understood she'd only agreed to see him so that she could get updates on her sister, but that didn't stop him from being glad he'd gotten his way on this. "I look forward to seeing you later, then, Katerina," he said softly.

He could barely hide the thrill of anticipation racing through him, knowing he'd see her again soon, as he hurried down to the operating room.

CHAPTER TWO

"So what do you think? Do I really need to tell Miguel about Tommy?" Kat asked, after she'd caught up with Diana and Tommy at the park located right across the street from their hotel. The park was next to a school and seeing all the kids in their navy blue and white uniforms playing on the playground wasn't so different from the preschool Tommy attended back in the U.S.

"I don't think you should do anything yet," Diana advised. "I mean, what do we know about the custody laws in Spain? What if Miguel has the right to take Tommy away from you?"

The very thought made her feel sick to her stomach. "Tommy is a U.S. citizen," she pointed out, striving for logic. "That has to count for something."

"Maybe, maybe not. I don't think you should say anything until we know what we're dealing with. Miguel is a big important doctor at the largest hospital here. Maybe he has connections, friends in high places? I think you need to understand exactly what you're dealing with if you tell him."

Kat sighed, and rubbed her temples, trying to ease the ache. Lack of sleep, worry over Juliet and now seeing Miguel again had all combined into one giant, pounding headache. "And how are we going to find out the child custody laws here? Neither one of us can speak Spanish, so it's not like we can just look up the information on the internet."

"We could check with the American Embassy," Diana said stubbornly.

"I suppose. Except that seems like a lot of work when I'm not even sure Miguel will bother to fight me for Tommy. During our night together he told me his dream was to join Doctors Without Borders. He made it clear he wanted the freedom to travel, not settling down in one place."

"Except here he is in Seville four and a half years later," Diana pointed out reasonably. "Maybe he's changed his mind about his dream?"

"Maybe." She couldn't argue Diana's point. She still found it hard to wrap her mind around the fact that Miguel was here, in Seville. She'd stayed with her sister for another hour or so after he'd left, slightly reassured that Juliet's condition was indeed stable, before she'd come back to the hotel to unpack her things. Seeing Miguel had made her suddenly anxious to find her son.

Tommy was having a great time running around in the park, chasing butterflies. As she watched him, the physical similarities seemed even more acute. She realized the minute Miguel saw Tommy, he'd know the truth without even needing to be told.

Although Miguel wouldn't have to see him, a tiny voice in the back of her mind reminded her. Tommy could stay here with Diana and in a couple of days hopefully Juliet would be stable enough to be sent back to the U.S. Miguel didn't need to know anything about their son.

As soon as the thought formed, she felt a sense of shame. Keeping Tommy's presence a secret would be taking the coward's way out. Diana was worried about the Spanish custody laws, but Kat had other reasons for not wanting to tell Miguel about Tommy. Being intimate with Miguel had touched her in a way she hadn't expected. When she'd discovered she was pregnant, she'd been torn between feeling worried at how she'd manage all alone to secretly thrilled to have a part of Miguel growing inside her.

She knew he hadn't felt the same way about her. Men had sex with women all the time, and lust certainly wasn't love. She knew better than to get emotionally involved. In her experience men didn't remain faithful or stick around for the long haul. Especially when there was the responsibility of raising children. Her father and Juliet's father had proven that fact.

She gave Miguel credit for being upfront and honest about his inability to stay. He hadn't lied to her, hadn't told her what he'd thought she'd wanted to hear. It was her fault for not doing a better job of protecting her heart.

Telling Miguel about Tommy opened up the possibility that she'd have to see Miguel on a regular basis. If they were raising a child together, there would be no way to avoid him. She would have to hide her true feelings every time they were together.

Unless Miguel still didn't want the responsibility of a son? There was a part of her that really hoped so, because then he wouldn't insist on joint custody.

Now she was getting way ahead of herself. Maybe she could tell Miguel about Tommy and reassure him that she didn't need help, financially or otherwise, to raise her son. She and Tommy would be fine on their own. The way they had been for nearly four years.

"Don't agonize over this, Kat. You don't have to tell him this minute, we just got here. Give me a little time to do some research first, okay?"

"I guess," she agreed doubtfully. Diana was clearly concerned, but she was confident that Tommy had rights as an American citizen. "I won't do anything right away, although I really think I'm going to have to tell him eventually. I tried to call him when I discovered I was pregnant, even tried to find him on all the popular social media websites. Now that I know he's here, I need to be honest with him."

"Then why do you look like you're about to cry?" Diana asked.

"Because I'm scared," she murmured, trying to sniffle back her tears. "I couldn't bear it if Miguel tried to fight for custody."

"Okay, let's just say that the Spanish law is the same as the U.S. regarding joint custody. You mentioned he wasn't wearing a wedding ring, but we both know that doesn't always mean much. Miguel might be married or seriously involved in a relationship. Could be the last thing on earth that he wants is to fight for joint custody."

"You're right," she agreed, even though the thought of Miguel being married or involved with someone didn't make her feel any better. "Okay, I need to get a grip. Maybe I'll try talking to Miguel first, try to find out about his personal life before springing the news on him."

Diana nodded eagerly. "Good idea. Meanwhile, I'll see if I can call the U.S. embassy to get more information."

Kat nodded, even though deep down she knew she'd have to tell him. Because Miguel deserved to know. Besides at some point Tommy was going to ask about his father. She refused to lie to her son.

The spear in her heart twisted painfully and tears pricked her eyes. As difficult as it was to be a single mother, she couldn't bear the thought of sending Tommy off to be with his father in a far-away country. Although she knew she could come with Tommy, no matter how difficult it would be to see Miguel again.

If Miguel was truly planning to join Doctors Without Borders, maybe all of this worry would be for nothing. She and Tommy would go back home and continue living their lives.

Tommy tripped and fell, and she leaped off the park bench and rushed over, picking him up and lavishing him with kisses before he could wail too loudly. "There, now, you're okay, big guy."

"Hurts," he sniffed, rubbing his hands over his eyes and smearing dirt all over his face.

"I know, but Mommy will kiss it all better." Holding her son close, nuzzling his neck, she desperately hoped Miguel would be honorable enough to do what was best for Tommy.

Kat returned to the hotel room to change her clothes and freshen up a bit before going back to the hospital to see Juliet and Miguel. She'd left Diana and Tommy at the local drugstore, picking out a few necessities for Diana to hold her over until her luggage arrived. They'd also picked up two prepaid disposable phones, so they could keep in touch with each other. After fifteen minutes, and with the help of one shopkeeper who did speak a bit of English, they had the phones activated and working.

The metro was far more crowded towards the end of the workday, forcing her to stand, clinging to the overhead pole.

At her stop, she got off the cramped carriage and walked the short distance to the hospital. The temperature had to be pushing eighty and by the time she arrived, she was hot and sweaty again.

So much for her attempt to look nice for Miguel.

Ridiculous to care one way or the other how she looked. Men weren't exactly knocking down her door, especially once they realized she had a son. Not that she was interested in dating.

She hadn't been with anyone since spending the night with Miguel. At first because she'd been pregnant and then because being a single mother was all-consuming. But she didn't regret a single minute of having Tommy.

In the hospital, she went up to the I.C.U. and paused outside Juliet's doorway, relieved to discover Miguel wasn't there, waiting for her. Her sister had been turned so that she was lying on her right side facing the doorway, but otherwise her condition appeared unchanged.

She crossed over and took Juliet's hand in hers. "Hi, Jules, I'm back. Can you hear me? Squeeze my hand if you can hear me."

Juliet's hand didn't move within hers.

"Wiggle your toes. Can you wiggle your toes for me?"

Juliet's non-broken leg moved, but Kat couldn't figure out if the movement had been made on purpose or not. When she asked a second time, the leg didn't move, so she assumed the latter.

She pulled up a chair and sat down beside her sister, glancing curiously at the chart hanging off the end of the bed. She didn't bother trying to read it, as it would all be in Spanish, but she wished she could read the medical information for herself, to see how Juliet was progressing.

She kept up her one-sided conversation with her sister for the next fifteen minutes or so. Until she ran out of things to say.

"Katerina?"

The way Miguel said her name brought back a fresh wave of erotic memories of their night together and she tried hard to paste a *friendly* smile on her face, before rising to her feet and facing him. "Hello, Miguel. How did your surgery go this morning?"

"Very well, thanks. Would you mind going across the street to the restaurant to talk?" he asked. "I've missed lunch."

She instinctively wanted to say no, but that seemed foolish and petty so she nodded. She glanced back at her sister, leaning over the side rail to talk to her. "I love you, sis. See you soon," she said, before moving away to meet Miguel in the doorway.

As they walked down the stairs to the main level of the hospital, he handed her a stack of papers. "I spent some time translating bits of Juliet's chart for you, so that you can get a sense as to how she's doing."

Her jaw dropped in surprise and for a moment she couldn't speak, deeply touched by his kind consideration. "Thank you," she finally murmured, taking the paperwork he offered. Miguel had often been thoughtful of others and she was glad he hadn't changed during the time they's spent apart. She couldn't imagine where he'd found the time to translate her sister's chart for her between seeing patients and doing surgery, but she was extremely grateful for his efforts.

He put his hand on the small of her back, guiding her towards the restaurant across the street from the hospital. The warmth of his hand seemed to burn through her thin cotton blouse, branding her skin. She was keenly aware of him, his scent wreaking havoc with her concentration, as they made their way across the street. There was outdoor seating beneath cheerful red and white umbrellas and she gratefully sat in the shade, putting the table between them.

The waiter came over and the two men conversed in rapid-fire Spanish. She caught maybe one familiar word out of a dozen.

"What would you like to drink, Katerina?" Miguel asked. "Beer? Wine? Soft drink?"

"You ordered a soft drink, didn't you?" she asked.

He flashed a bright smile and nodded. "You remember some Spanish, no?" he asked with clear approval.

"Yes, *muy poco*, very little," she agreed. "I'll have the same, please."

Miguel ordered several *tapas*, the Spanish form of appetizers, along with their soft drinks. When the food arrived, she had no idea what she was eating, but whatever it was it tasted delicious.

"Do you want to review Juliet's chart now?" he asked. "I can wait and answer your questions."

"I'll read it later, just tell me what you know." She wanted to hear from him first. Besides, there was no way she'd be able to concentrate on her sister's chart with him sitting directly across from her.

He took his time, sipping his drink, before answering. "Juliet has begun moving around more, which is a good sign. She will likely start to intermittently follow commands soon. We have done a CT scan of her brain earlier this morning and the area of bleeding appears to be resolving slowly."

She nodded, eating another of the delicious *tapas* on the plate between them. There were olives too, and she wondered if they were from Miguel's family farm. "I'm glad. I guess all we can do right now is wait and see."

"True," he agreed. He helped himself to more food as well. "Katerina, how is your mother doing? Wasn't she scheduled to have surgery right before I left the States?"

She nodded, her appetite fading. "Yes. The result of her surgery showed stage-four pancreatic cancer. She died a couple months later." Despite the fear of being a single mother, at the time of her mother's passing, her pregnancy had been one of the few bright spots in her life. Things had been difficult until Juliet had gone off to college. Thankfully, her friend Diana had been there for her, even offering to be her labor coach.

"I'm sorry," he murmured, reaching across the table to capture her hand in his. "We both lost our parents about the same time, didn't we?"

"Yes. We did." His fingers were warm and strong around hers, but she gently tugged her hand away and reached for her glass. She tried to think of a way to ask him if he was married or seeing someone, without sounding too interested.

"I have thought of you often these past few years," Miguel murmured, not seeming to notice how she was struggling with her secret. He took her left hand and brushed his thumb across her bare ring finger. "You haven't married?"

She slowly shook her head. There was only one man who'd asked her out after Tommy had been born. He was another nurse in the operating room, one of the few male nurses who worked there. She'd been tempted to date him because he was a single parent, too, and would have been a great father figure for Tommy, but in the end she hadn't been able to bring herself to accept his offer.

She hadn't felt anything for Wayne other than friendship. And as much as she wanted a father for Tommy, she couldn't pretend to feel something she didn't.

Too bad she couldn't say the same about her feelings toward Miguel. Seeing him again made her realize that she still felt that same spark of attraction, the same awareness that had been there when they'd worked together in the U.S. Feelings that apparently hadn't faded over time.

"What about you, Miguel?" she asked, taking the opening he'd offered, as she gently pulled her hand away. "Have you found a woman to marry?"

"No, you know my dream is to join Doctors Without Borders. But I can't leave until I'm certain my brother has the Vasquez olive farm back on its feet. Luis has a few—ah—problems. Things were not going well here at home during the time I was in the U.S." A shadow of guilt flashed in his eyes, and she found herself wishing she could offer him comfort.

"Not your fault, Miguel," she reminded him, secretly glad to discover he hadn't fallen in love and married a beautiful Spanish woman. "How old is Luis?"

"Twenty-six now," he said. "But too young back then to take on the responsibility of running the farm. I think the stress of trying to hold everything together was too much for my father." He stared at his glass for a long moment. "Maybe if I had been here, things would have been different."

She shrugged, not nearly as reassured as she should be at knowing his dream of joining Doctors Without Borders hadn't changed. She should be thrilled with the news. Maybe this would be best for all of them. He'd go do his mission work, leaving her alone to raise Tommy. Miguel could come back in a few years, when Tommy was older, to get to know his son.

All she had to do was to tell him the truth.

Diana wanted her to wait, but she knew she had to tell him or the secret would continue to eat at her. She'd never been any good at lying and didn't want to start now. She swallowed hard and braced herself. "Miguel, there's something important I need to tell you," she began.

"Miguel!" A shout from across the street interrupted them. She frowned and turned in time to see a handsome young man, unsteady on his feet, waving wildly at Miguel.

"Luis." He muttered his brother's name like a curse half under his breath. "Excuse me for a moment," he said as he rose to his feet.

She didn't protest, but watched as Miguel crossed over towards his brother, his expression stern. The two of them were quickly engrossed in a heated conversation that didn't seem it would end any time soon.

Kat sat back, sipping her soft drink and thinking how wrong it was for her to be grateful for the reprieve.

"Luis, you shouldn't be drinking!" Miguel shouted in Spanish, barely holding his temper in check.

"Relax, it's Friday night. I've been slaving out at the farm all week—don't I get time to have fun too? Hey, who's the pretty Americana?" he asked with slurred speech, as he looked around Miguel towards where Katerina waited.

"She's a friend from the U.S.," he answered sharply. "But that's not the point. I thought we had an agreement? You promised to stay away from the taverns until Saturday night. It's barely five o'clock on Friday, and you're already drunk." Which meant his brother must have started drinking at least a couple of hours ago.

"I sent the last olive shipment out at noon. I think you should introduce me to your lady friend," Luis said with a sloppy smile, his gaze locked on Katerina. "She's pretty. I'd love to show her a good time."

The last thing he wanted to do was to introduce Katerina to his brother, especially when he was intoxicated. Luis had been doing fairly well recently, so finding him like this was more than a little annoying.

What was Luis thinking? If he lost the olive farm, what would he do for work? Or was this just another way to ruin Miguel's chance to follow his dream? He was tired of trying to save the olive farm for his brother while taking care of his patients. He was working non-stop from early morning to sundown every week. It was past time for Luis to grow up and take some responsibility.

"Go home, Luis," he advised. "Before you make a complete fool of yourself."

"Not until I meet your lady friend," Luis said stubbornly. "She reminds me a little of our mother, except that she has blonde hair instead of red. Are you going to change your mind about going to Africa? She may not wait for you."

Miguel ground his teeth together in frustration. "No, I'm not going to change my mind," he snapped. He didn't want to think about Katerina waiting for him. No matter how much he was still attracted to her, having a relationship with an American woman would be nothing but a disaster. His mother had hated every minute of living out on the farm, away from the city. And far away from her homeland. He was certain Katerina wouldn't be willing to leave her home either. "Katerina's sister is in the hospital, recovering from a serious head injury. She's not interested in having a good time. Leave her alone, understand?"

"Okay, fine, then." Luis shook off his hand and began walking toward the bar, his gait unsteady. "I'll just sit by myself."

"Oh, no, you won't." Miguel captured his brother's arm and caught sight of his old friend, Rafael, who happened to be a police officer. "Rafael," he called, flagging down his friend.

"Trouble, amigo?" Rafael asked, getting out of his police car.

"Would you mind taking my brother home?" He grabbed Luis's arm, steering him toward the police car, but his brother tried to resist. Luis almost fell, but Miguel managed to haul him upright. "I would take him myself, but I'm on call at the hospital."

"All right," Rafael said with a heavy sigh. "You'll owe me, my friend. Luckily for you, I'm finished with my shift."

"Thanks, Rafael. I will return the favor," he promised.

"I'll hold you to that," Rafael muttered with a wry grimace.

Miguel watched them drive away, before he raked a hand through his hair and turned back towards Katerina. As if the fates were against him, his pager went off, bringing a premature end to their time together.

"My apologies for the interruption," he murmured as he returned to the table. "I'm afraid I must cut our meal short. There is a young boy with symptoms of appendicitis. I need to return to the hospital to assess whether or not he needs surgery."

"I understand," Katerina said, as he paid the tab. She gathered up the papers he'd given to her. "Thanks again for translating Juliet's chart for me. I'm sure I'll see you tomorrow."

"Of course." When she stood, she was so close he could have easily leaned down to kiss her. He curled his fingers into fists and forced himself to take a step backwards in order to resist the sweet temptation. "I will make rounds between nine and ten in the morning, if you want an update on your sister's condition."

"Sounds good. Goodbye, Miguel." She waved and then headed for the metro station, located just a few blocks down the street.

Back at the hospital it was clear the thirteen-year-old had a classic case of appendicitis and Miguel quickly took the child to the operating room. Unfortunately, his appendix had burst, forcing Miguel to spend extra time washing out the abdominal cavity in order to minimize the chance that infection would set in. Afterwards, he made sure the boy had the correct antibiotics ordered and the first dose administered before he headed home to his three-bedroom apartment located within walking distance of the hospital.

It wasn't until he was eating cold leftover pizza for dinner that Miguel had a chance to think about Katerina, and wonder just what she'd thought was so important to tell him.

CHAPTER THREE

"LOOK, it's a shopping mall!" Diana exclaimed. Then
she frowned. "I almost wish my luggage hadn't shown
up this morning, or I'd have a good excuse to go buy
new clothes."

Kat nodded ruefully. She was surprised to find
Seville was a city of contrasts, from the modern shopping mall to the mosques and bronze statues straight
out of the sixteenth century. "A little disappointing in
a way, isn't it?" she murmured.

"Hey, not for me," Diana pointed out. "I mean, the
history here is nice and everything, but I'm all in favor
of modernization. Especially when it comes to shopping."

They'd walked to a small café for breakfast, and
found the shopping mall on the way back to the hotel.
"Maybe you can explore the mall with Tommy this
morning while I'm at the hospital, visiting Juliet."

"Sounds good. Although don't forget we plan on
taking the boat tour later this afternoon," Diana reminded her.

"I won't forget," Kat murmured. Sightseeing wasn't
top of her list, but it was the least she could do for Diana
as her friend spent a good portion of every day watching

her son. Besides, sitting for hours at the hospital wasn't going to help Juliet recover any quicker.

"Here's the metro station," Kat said. "Call me if you need anything, okay? I'll see you later, Tommy." Kat swept him into her arms for a hug, which he tolerated for barely a minute before he wiggled out of her grasp.

"We'll be fine," Diana assured her, taking Tommy's hand in a firm grip.

"I know." She watched them walk away towards the mall, before taking the steps down to the metro station to wait for the next train. Despite the fact that she still needed to break the news about Tommy to Miguel, she found she was looking forward to seeing him again. Last night, before she'd fallen asleep, Miguel's words had echoed in her mind, giving her a secret thrill.

I've thought of you often over these past few years.

She doubted that he'd thought of her as often as she'd thought of him, though. Mostly because of Tommy since he was the mirror image of his father. Yet also because Miguel had taken a small piece of her heart when he'd left.

Not that she ever planned on telling him that.

She needed to let go of the past and move on with her life. Whatever her conflicting feelings for Miguel, she couldn't afford to fall for him. They wanted different things out of life. She wanted a home, family, stability. Miguel wanted adventure. He wanted Doctors Without Borders. He wanted to travel. The only time they were in sync was when they had worked as colleagues in the O.R..

And, of course, during the night they spent together.

Walking into the hospital was familiar now, and she

greeted the clerk behind the desk in Spanish. *"Buenos dias."*

"Buenos dias," the clerk replied with a wide grin. One thing about Spain, most people seemed to be in a good mood. Maybe because they had a more laid-back lifestyle here. She found it amazing that the shops actually closed down for three hours between noon and three for siesta. She couldn't imagine anyone in the U.S. doing something like that.

Yet if the people were happier, maybe it was worth it?

Kat took the stairs to the third-floor I.C.U., entered her sister's room and crossed over to the bedside, taking her sister's small hand in hers. "Hi, Jules, I'm back. How are you feeling, hmm?"

She knew her sister wasn't going to open her eyes and start talking, which would be impossible with a breathing tube in anyway, but Kat was convinced patients even in her sister's condition could hear what was going on around them, so she decided she'd keep up her one-sided conversation with her sister.

"Seville is a beautiful city, Jules, I can understand why you wanted to study here. I wish I knew exactly what happened to you. No one here seems to know anything more than the fact that you ran into the road and were struck by a car. Can you hear me, Jules? If you can hear me, squeeze my hand."

When Juliet's fingers squeezed hers, Kat's knees nearly buckled in relief. "That's great, Juliet. Now wiggle your toes for me. Can you wiggle your toes?"

This time Juliet's non-casted left leg moved again. It wasn't wiggling her toes, exactly, but Kat was still thrilled at the small movement. Her sister was truly doing better. Juliet would probably only follow commands intermittently, but each day she'd improve and do better.

Exactly the way Miguel had assured her she would.

"Good job, Jules. I'm so glad you can hear me. You're still in the hospital in Seville, but as soon as you're better, you're going to be sent to an American hospital back home. Can you understand what I'm saying? If you can understand me, squeeze my hand."

Juliet squeezed her hand again, and relieved tears blurred her vision. Her sister was going to make it. Juliet might have a long road to recovery ahead of her, but she was going to make it.

"Katerina?"

At the sound of Miguel's voice she whirled around and quickly crossed over to him. "She's following commands, Miguel!" she exclaimed. "She's starting to wake up!"

He caught her close in a warm hug. "I'm glad," he murmured, his mouth dangerously close to her ear.

She wanted to wrap her arms around his waist and lean on his strength, but she forced herself to step away, putting badly needed distance between them. What was wrong with her? It wasn't as if she'd come to Seville in order to rejuvenate her feelings for Miguel. Better for her if she kept him firmly in the friendship category. As if their one night together had been an aberration.

One that had produced a son.

There was no reason to feel as if being around Miguel was like coming home. Truthfully, she'd never been farther from home.

"I'm sorry," she said, wiping her tears on the back of her hand while searching for a tissue. "I didn't mean to get all emotional on you."

"Here." He grabbed the box of tissues from the bedside table and handed them to her. "Don't apologize, I know how worried you've been."

She blew her nose and pulled herself together, forcing a smile. "I hope this doesn't mean you're going to send Juliet home right away, are you?"

"Not yet. I would like your sister to be completely off the ventilator and more awake before she's transported back to the U.S."

"Sounds good." She was relieved to know they wouldn't have to leave Seville just yet. Especially as she hadn't told Miguel about Tommy. A wave of guilt hit hard. Should she tell him now? No, this wasn't exactly the time or the place for a heavy conversation. Besides, Miguel was working, making rounds. No doubt he had many patients to see.

She was about to ask him what time he got off work when he reached over to take her hand in his. "Katerina, will you have dinner with me tonight?"

She hesitated just a moment before nodding her assent. Wasn't this what she'd wanted all along? A good time and place to tell him about his son? A quiet dinner with just the two of them would be the perfect time to give him the news. "Yes, Miguel. Dinner would be wonderful."

"Excellent," he murmured. His gaze was warm and she had to remind herself this wasn't a date. Her son's future was what mattered here, not her roller-coaster feelings for his father.

"What time?" she asked.

"We'll go early as I know you're not used to our customs yet. Shall we say eight o'clock?"

A wry grin tugged at the corner of her mouth because eight o'clock wasn't at all early back home. "All right. Where should I meet you?"

"I will pick you up at your hotel. Which one are you staying at?"

"We— I'm at the Hesperia hotel," she said, using the correct Spanish pronunciation while hoping he didn't catch her slip.

"Excellent. There is a wonderful restaurant just a few blocks away." He glanced at his watch. "I'm sorry, but I need to finish making rounds. Did you have any questions about the chart copies I gave you?"

She'd read through his entire stack of notes early that morning, before Tommy had woken up. "I noticed her electrolytes keep going out of whack—do you think that's because of her head injury?"

"Yes, brain injuries cause sodium levels to drop, but try not to worry as we are replacing what she's lost."

She'd noticed the IV solution running through Juliet's IV was similar to what they'd use in the U.S. Except for the equipment being a little different, the basics of medical and nursing care were very much the same.

"Thanks again, Miguel, for everything," she said in a low voice, trying to put the depth of her feelings into words. "I'm so relieved to know my sister is in such good hands."

"You're very welcome, Katerina. I'll see you tonight, yes?"

"Yes," she confirmed. After he left, she walked back and sat down at her sister's bedside.

She was lucky that Miguel was here. Not just because he spoke English, which was a huge help, but because she knew he was an excellent surgeon.

Ironic how fate had brought her face to face with

Tommy's father after all these years. Her previously suppressed feelings for Miguel threatened to surface and she took a long, deep breath, ruthlessly shoving them back down.

She needed to protect her heart from Miguel's charm. And even more importantly, she needed to preserve the life she'd built with her son.

Miguel finished his rounds and then took a break to call his brother. Unfortunately, Luis didn't answer the phone so he left his brother a message, requesting a return phone call.

He rubbed the back of his neck, debating whether he should go out to see his brother after work or not. He should have time before dinner as he wasn't on call this evening. But at the same time, going all the way out to the farm and back would take at least two and a half hours, and he didn't want to be late for his dinner date with Katerina.

Miguel was pleased Katerina had agreed to see him again tonight. He felt the need to make it up to her for leaving so abruptly after finding out about his father's stroke. The night they'd spent together had been incredible. There had always been the hint of awareness between them while working together in the operating room. At times it had seemed as if Katerina could practically read his mind, instinctively knowing what he'd needed before he'd had to ask.

He'd been tempted to pursue a relationship, but had told himself it wouldn't be fair since he wasn't planning on staying. Maybe if things had been different...

No, he'd made his decision. He'd already given notice at the hospital that he was leaving at the end of the academic year, which was just three months away. He'd first heard about Doctors Without Borders in Madrid from one of his colleagues. He'd quickly decided that he wanted to join as well once he'd finished his training. He'd known early on he didn't want to stay on his family's olive farm. He'd wanted to travel. To learn about other cultures. He'd jumped at the opportunity to study in the U.S. and now couldn't wait to join Doctors Without Borders.

So why was he torturing himself by seeing Katerina again? If he had a functioning brain cell in his head, he'd stay far away from her until her sister was stable enough for transport back home.

Katerina wasn't the woman for him. He knew he shouldn't measure all women against his American mother, but after living in both cultures he understood a little better why his mother had reacted the way she had. The two lifestyles were very different. Maybe if the olive farm hadn't suffered two bad years in a row, there would have been money for vacations back in the U.S. Would that have been enough for his mother? Or would that have only emphasized her loss?

Truthfully, he couldn't understand why his mother just hadn't purchased a one-way ticket to New York and returned home if she'd been so desperately unhappy here. Instead, she'd stayed to become a bitter woman who'd made all their lives miserable. Until she'd unexpectedly died of an overdose, which had been determined to be accidental rather than a suicide attempt.

Miguel shook off his dark thoughts and concentrated on his patients. He loved everything about being a surgeon. There wasn't nearly as much trauma here in Seville as in Cambridge, Massachusetts, but he didn't mind. One thing he never got used to was losing patients.

Especially young patients. Like the twenty-five-year-old pregnant mother they'd lost during his last shift in the U.S.

After finishing his rounds on the adults in his case load, he made his way over to the children's wing, which happened to be in the oldest part of the hospital. He wanted to visit Pedro, his young appendectomy patient. The young boy would need to stay a few days for IV antibiotics before he could be discharged.

This was the other part he loved about being a doctor in Spain. There weren't large children's hospitals here, the way there were in the U.S. He was glad to have the opportunity to take care of both children and adults, rather than being forced to decide between them.

"*Hola,* Dr. Vasquez," Pedro greeted him when he entered the room.

"*Hola, Pedro. ¿Como estas?*"

"*¿*English, *por favor*? I'm fine."

Miguel grinned and switched to English for Pedro's sake. The youngster was part of a group of teenagers in Seville who were committed to learning English. Many of them didn't bother, but even when Pedro had been in pain in the emergency department yesterday, the boy had informed him he was going to America one day.

"May I examine your incision?" Miguel asked politely.

Pedro frowned, probably having trouble with the word "incision", but lifted his hospital gown anyway. "It's healing well, no?"

"Very much so," Miguel said, pleased to see there were no signs of infection. Although the bigger problem

Pedro faced was an infection in the bloodstream from the burst appendix. "Where is your mother? I think you'll need to stay for a couple more days yet."

Pedro smiled broadly as he drew his hospital gown back down. "She's caring for my younger brothers and sisters. She'll be here soon. And I'm glad to stay, Dr. Vasquez, because you will have more time for me to practice my English with you, yes?"

Miguel couldn't help but grin at the awkwardly worded sentence. "Yes, Pedro. We will practice while you are here, but even after you go home, we can practice when you return to clinic to see me, okay?"

"Okay. Thanks, Dr. Vasquez."

Miguel went on to see his second patient, a young girl who'd sustained a compound fracture of her left arm. They had orthopedic specialists, but since the fracture wasn't complicated he'd simply set it himself and casted it.

Marissa's room was empty so Miguel went to find the nurse, only to discover that the young girl was getting another X-ray of her arm.

He decided to return to the I.C.U., vowing to come back to check on Marissa later, but as he reached the third floor, the entire building shook and the lights flickered and went out. It took him a moment to realize what had happened, even though he'd been through this scenario once before.

Earthquake!

Kat was about to leave the I.C.U., intending to head back to the hotel, when she felt the building shake with enough force to make her fall against the wall.

The lights flickered and then went out. She froze, waiting for them to come back on.

Juliet's ventilator!

Instinctively, she ran back down the hall to her sister's room, able to see somewhat from the daylight shining through the windows. She saw Miguel going into another room but didn't veer from her path. After rushing over to Juliet's bedside, she reached for the ambu-bag hanging from the oxygen regulator. She turned the dial up, providing high-flow oxygen as she quickly disconnected the ventilator and began assisting her sister's breathing.

She forced herself to calm down so she wouldn't hyperventilate Juliet, hardly able to believe that the power was still out. Didn't they have back-up generators here? What had caused the shaking? Did they have earthquakes here? And where was everyone? She'd hadn't seen anyone other than the glimpse of Miguel going into another patient's room.

After what seemed like forever, the lights flickered back on, but only part way, as if conserving energy. At least Juliet's ventilator and heart monitor came back on.

She connected the ventilator back up to Juliet's breathing tube, but before she could go out and find the rest of the hospital staff, Miguel showed up in the doorway.

"What happened?" she asked.

"Earthquake. Nothing too serious, probably about a five or six on the Richter scale. We've had one similar to this before. But I need your help."

Earthquake? She was a little shocked, but strove to remain calm. "Me? What for?"

"I've just been told that a very old tree fell against

the corner of the building and we need to evacuate the patients. They are all pediatric patients in the children's wing located on the fourth floor. As it is a weekend, we do not have full staffing. We could use an extra pair of hands if you're willing to stay?"

"Of course," she said, knowing she couldn't simply walk away, even though she needed to know her son was safe. She was tempted to call Diana right away, except that she didn't want Miguel to ask questions. So she promised herself she'd wait until she could steal a few minutes alone to call her friend.

"Let's go," Miguel said, and she followed him out of the I.C.U. and down the hall, trying to make sense of what was happening. Clearly, the earthquake must have caused the tree to fall on the hospital building. What other damage had occurred? And what about the hotel? Was everything all right there?

As they walked down the hall, she peered through the windows to look out over the city. She was relieved when she didn't see any evidence of mass destruction. As she followed Miguel, she hoped and prayed Tommy and Diana were someplace safe from harm.

CHAPTER FOUR

KAT was horrified to see the amount of damage the building had sustained when they arrived in the children's ward. Many of the younger kids were crying, but one older boy had already stepped up to take charge. He'd obviously gathered all the children on several beds located as far away as possible from the crumbled corner of the building.

"Good job, Pedro," Miguel said as they rushed in. "Where's your nurse, Elouisa?"

"I'm not sure, but I think she went to get medication," Pedro answered. Kat was impressed that the boy spoke English and seemed to accept the responsibility of staying here with the children alone.

Miguel's mouth tightened, but he didn't say anything else. "Okay, then, we'll need to transport the sickest patients down to the I.C.U. first."

"DiCarlo is the worst, I think," Pedro said, pointing to a boy who was lying listlessly in bed. Kat estimated there were at least a dozen kids gathered on three beds surrounding the obviously very sick boy. "Elouisa said something about how he needed more antibiotics."

"She should have stayed here with all of you. He can get his antibiotics in the I.C.U.," Miguel said firmly.

"I'll take him down, but do you think it's safe to use the elevators?" she asked warily. She didn't mind transporting the sick child downstairs but the thought of being stuck in an elevator alone with him was scary.

Just then Elouisa returned, hurrying in with an IV bag in her hand. She came straight over to DiCarlo's IV pump to prepare the medication.

Miguel said something to her in Spanish, which she assumed was something related to the care of the children. She responded in Spanish as well, even while she hung the IV antibiotic. When they finished their conversation, Miguel turned to her.

"Okay, you and I together will take DiCarlo in his bed down to the I.C.U. Elouisa has promised to stay with the children." He turned to Pedro. "I am counting on you to stay here and to help Elouisa until I can return, okay? Once we have DiCarlo safe in the I.C.U., we can find other beds for the rest of you."

Pedro nodded. "I understand Dr. Vasquez. You should have trust that I will wait here for you."

"Good, Pedro. Thank you."

"Give me a quick rundown on DiCarlo's condition," she said to Miguel as Elouisa used an old-fashioned crank to lift the bed higher off the floor so it would be easier for them to push him. "I need to understand what to watch for."

Miguel set a small bin of emergency supplies on DiCarlo's bed, and again she was struck by the similarities between medical care here in Seville and in the U.S. When she worked in the I.C.U., they would always take a small pack of emergency supplies on what they called road trips, when patients needed to leave the I.C.U. to go down for certain X-rays or CT scans.

Miguel started pushing the boy's bed towards the elevator as he gave a brief report.

"What started as pneumonia has turned into full-blown sepsis. He's been fighting the infection as best he can, but he's had heart trouble since he was born so he's not as strong as most children his age."

She digested that bit of information as they left the children's ward through a long, empty hallway. As they waited for the elevator, which seemed to take a very long time, she looked down at DiCarlo's wan features, hoping and praying he'd survive the infection.

Miguel's impatience was obvious when he stabbed the elevator button a second time.

"Where is everyone?" she asked. Miguel's features tightened. "We were short-staffed to begin with, but some left, wanting to check on their loved ones. I honestly didn't think we would lose this many staff members."

She could understand why some staff had felt compelled to leave, and worry over the safety of her son gnawed at her. She pushed her fears aside. For one thing, Diana would have called her if something bad had happened. Their hotel was new and sturdy. Surely they'd be safe. The elevator arrived and she helped Miguel push DiCarlo's bed inside. The doors closed and she pushed the button for the second floor when suddenly the boy began coughing so hard his face turned bright red.

"Miguel, he's having trouble breathing," she said urgently, reaching for the dial on the oxygen tank and turning the knob to give him more oxygen. "Do we have a pediatric ambu bag?"

"Yes, along with intubation supplies." Miguel opened

the small bag of emergency supplies and pulled out the ambu bag. "We can intubate if we have to."

She hadn't assisted with an intubation since the time she'd worked in the I.C.U., but she nodded anyway. She gently placed the small face mask over DiCarlo's mouth and nose, and used the ambu bag to give him a couple of breaths.

DiCarlo squirmed beneath the ambu bag, fighting her at first, but then abruptly went limp, and she quickly reached over to feel for a pulse. "Miguel? His pulse is fading fast."

"I'll have to intubate him now, rather than waiting until we reach the I.C.U." He took the laryngoscope in his left hand and then gently slid the endotracheal tube into DiCarlo's throat. She took Miguel's stethoscope from around his neck and listened to the boy's lungs to verify the tube was in the correct place. Thankfully, it was. She quickly connected the ambu bag tubing to the end of the endotracheal tube so she could give DiCarlo several breaths.

Miguel secured the tube with tape and then gestured behind her. "Check his pulse and then push the button again. The doors have already closed."

She'd never heard the elevator ding. She made sure DiCarlo's pulse was stable before she turned around to hit the button for the third floor. This time it only took a couple of minutes for the doors to open.

She was very happy to see the critical care area. "Which bed?" she asked, as she walked backwards, pulling the bed as Miguel pushed, keeping one hand on the child's endotracheal tube.

"Twelve," he directed.

She knew the basic layout of the unit from visiting

her sister and quickly pulled the bed towards the vacant room number twelve. Nurses came over and assisted her with getting DiCarlo connected to the heart monitor overheard.

"Gracias," she murmured, smiling weakly. She glanced up and was reassured to note that DiCarlo's pulse had stabilized. Miguel spoke to them in Spanish, and they quickly brought over a ventilator. She stepped back, allowing the staff room to work.

Crisis averted, at least for the moment.

She hesitated, not sure if she should go back down to the children's wing alone or wait for Miguel. He was still examining DiCarlo, and the grave concern in his gaze as he listened to the boy's lungs wrenched her heart.

Would he look at Tommy like that?

Just then he glanced up and caught her staring at him. She swallowed the lump in her throat, holding his gaze for a long moment. Watching him, the way he was so gentle with DiCarlo, gave her hope and reassurance that he would never do anything to hurt their son. Including taking him away from her.

"He's fine for now," Miguel said, putting his stethoscope away. "Give me a few minutes here while I make sure his orders are up to date."

"Of course," she murmured, turning away, her hand on her phone. Outside DiCarlo's room, she made sure she was out of Miguel's hearing distance before she quickly pressed the number for Diana, holding her breath while she waited for an answer. Diana's voice brought instant relief. "Kat? Are you okay?"

"Yes. Are you and Tommy safe? Was there damage to the hotel?"

"We lost power for a while, and there seems to be a lot of confusion, but we're fine. No damage to the hotel that we know of."

Kat closed her eyes with relief. "I'm so glad. Listen, I have to stay here for a bit yet—will you be okay for a while?"

"Sure. We'll be fine."

"Thanks, I'll check in with you later." She closed her phone just as Miguel came around the corner of the nurses' station. She quickly tucked the phone back into her pocket.

"Ready to go?" Miguel asked.

"Of course." She felt bad for deceiving him, but obviously this wasn't the time or place for a conversation about his son. As they walked together toward the stairwell, their hands brushed lightly. A tingle of awareness shot up her arm.

"So, maybe I should apply to be a nurse here, huh?" she said jokingly, in a feeble attempt to break the closeness that seemed to grow deeper between them every moment they spent together.

"Are you planning to stay?" he asked, in shocked surprise. The brief flash of horror in his eyes pierced the tiny balloon of hope that had begun to grow in her heart.

"No! Of course not. That was a joke, Miguel." Ridiculous to be hurt that he didn't want her to stay. She preceded him down the stairwell, wondering if he'd change his opinion once she told him about Tommy.

She had to tell him about his son. The sooner, the better.

Miguel mentally smacked himself on the side of the head, understanding from the stiffness in her shoulders and the sharpness of her tone that he'd inadvertently hurt her.

He hadn't meant to make it sound like he didn't want her to stay. He'd just been taken aback by her statement, especially after they'd worked together to save DiCarlo. He couldn't help making comparisons with his mother. Maybe if his mother had been able to work in a career, other than helping his father run the olive farm, she would have been happier.

Could Katerina really be happy in Seville? And why did it matter as he himself wasn't planning to stay?

He hadn't slept well last night because all he'd been able to think about had been Katerina. And even now, in the aftermath of a small earthquake, he still wanted her.

But their situation was no different than it had been back when he'd met her in Cambridge. He'd already committed to Doctors Without Borders. He was finally going to live his dream. He couldn't start something with Katerina that he wasn't willing to finish.

A tiny voice in the back of his mind wondered if she'd be willing to go with him. But then he remembered Juliet. No, the Katerina he knew wouldn't pack up and leave her sister. Especially not when Juliet had a potentially long road of recovery ahead of her. Several months of rehab at least.

He pushed thoughts of Katerina possibly going with him to Africa aside to concentrate on the situation down in the children's ward.

Thankfully, Elouisa had kept her word, staying with the rest of the children. He was glad to see an additional staff nurse had come up to help.

"Which wing can we use as the children's ward?"

he asked, joining the group. "I'd like to keep them to-gether if possible."

"We can use the east wing of the third floor," Elouisa informed him. "I too would like to keep them together if possible. How is DiCarlo?"

"Very ill. We had to intubate him in the elevator," Miguel said. "You were right to make sure he received his antibiotic," he said by way of apology. He'd been upset to find the children alone, but he understood she'd prioritized the best she could.

"I was hoping to get him to the I.C.U.," Elouisa admitted. "But you were right, I shouldn't have left the children alone."

"Difficult decision either way, so don't worry about it." He noticed Pedro was listening to their conversation. He was impressed with how the boy had taken charge in Elouisa's absence. "Pedro, are you able to walk or would you like us to get you a wheelchair?"

Pedro practically puffed out his chest. "I can walk. I'm fine, Dr. Vasquez."

He could tell Pedro had some pain, but the boy wasn't about to admit it. He vowed to make sure Pedro took some pain medication as soon as they were all relocated in their new rooms.

Elouisa gathered up several wheelchairs and between the three of them they assisted getting all the children ready for transport. Pedro helped, as if he were a hospital staff member rather than one of the patients needing to be relocated.

The elevator was too small for everyone to go at once, so Elouisa and Pedro took three children first, while the second nurse, Maria, took two patients with her. Miguel and Katerina waited for the next elevator with their three patients. They were lucky there hadn't been more patients in the children's wing.

"Pedro's English is amazing," Katerina said while they waited for the elevator. "I'm impressed at how he seems to understand everything we're saying."

"He takes learning English very seriously as he is determined to go to America one day," he admitted. "You'd never know he had a burst appendix last evening, would you?"

Katerina's eyes widened. "No, I certainly wouldn't. He's doing remarkably well."

"Yes, but as his appendix ruptured, I want him to get a good twenty-four to forty-eight hours of IV antibiotics before he's discharged."

The elevator arrived and as they quickly maneuvered the three remaining patients into the elevator, Miguel found himself watching Katerina with awe. He'd always known she was an excellent O.R. nurse but seeing her interact with the young patients, managing to overcome the language barrier with smiles, simple words and hand gestures, he thought her skills would be better utilized in a position where she could care for awake and alert patients on the ward or in the I.C.U.

Or in the Doctors Without Borders program. They needed nurses to work with them, too.

Not that her career choices were any of his business.

It didn't take long to get the children settled on the east wing of the third floor. The entire layout of the area was very similar to the one where the building had collapsed. Even Pedro reluctantly took to his bed, and Miguel made sure he took a dose of pain medication that was long overdue.

Afterwards, he glanced at his watch, thinking he

should go up and check on DiCarlo. But he was hesitant to leave Elouisa here alone as Maria had been called away to help elsewhere. He walked up to the nurses' desk where Elouisa was busy organizing the charts. "Have you requested additional nursing support?" he asked.

"*Sí*, but so far Maria has not returned," she told him. "Thankfully, most of the children are very stable, especially now that DiCarlo is in the I.C.U."

"True, but I still think you should have someone with you. What if you have to leave the unit for some reason?"

Katerina stepped forward. "I can stay for a while," she volunteered. "I would just like a few minutes to check on my sister first."

He nodded, filled with gratitude. Even though Katerina wasn't licensed to practice nursing here in Seville, she could stay on the unit as a volunteer, offering a second pair of hands as needed. And her knowledge of nursing would be invaluable. He would feel much better knowing Elouisa wasn't here on the children's wing alone.

"Why don't you run over to see your sister, and I will wait here until you return?" he offered.

"*Gracias,*" she murmured. "I promise to be quick."

He couldn't begrudge her the chance to make sure Juliet's condition hadn't changed since they'd been up there. "I will need to check on her too, but I will wait for you to return."

"*¿Que?*" Elouisa asked, indicating she hadn't understood his conversation, so he quickly translated for her. "Both of you go and check on her sister," Elouisa said firmly. "I will be fine alone here for five minutes until Katerina returns. Pedro has been a huge help. He will get help in an emergency."

Miguel reluctantly agreed and led the way down to the I.C.U., using the stairwell as the elevator was so slow.

"You're going to have to make Pedro an honorary nurse, soon," Katerina teased as they walked towards Juliet's room. "Maybe after all this he'll decide to pursue a career in medicine?"

He chuckled. "There are not nearly as many male nurses here in Seville as there are back in America."

They entered Juliet's room and Katerina immediately crossed over to take her sister's hand. "I'm here, Jules," she said in a gentle tone. "Don't worry, you're still doing fine."

Juliet was moving restlessly on the bed, as if she was uncomfortable. Katerina tried to comfort her, talking to her in a soothing voice as Miguel took the clipboard off the foot of the bed and scanned the latest laboratory results and vital signs that had been recorded.

"Miguel?" He glanced up at Katerina's urgent tone. "Look! I think she's having a seizure!"

CHAPTER FIVE

"DISCONNECT the ventilator and use the ambu bag to assist her breathing," he directed quickly. He leaned over to hit the emergency call light and in less than thirty seconds two nurses came running in. He gave them orders in Spanish for a loading dose of IV dilantin followed by a continuous infusion. Also five milligrams of Versed to calm the effects of the seizure and for new IV fluids to correct Juliet's electrolyte imbalance.

His heart twisted when he saw the sheen of tears in Katerina's eyes. Thankfully, the seizure didn't last long, and within ten minutes he was able to put Juliet back on the ventilator. The medications he'd ordered worked beautifully, and Kat looked relieved when Juliet was resting quietly in her bed.

"She's going to be okay," he murmured to Katerina as they moved back, allowing the nurses to complete the dilantin infusion along with the new IV fluids he'd ordered. "This isn't a sign that her head injury is worse, but more likely as a result of her electrolyte imbalance."

Katerina rubbed her hands over her arms, as if she was cold, and he couldn't stop himself from putting a strong arm around her shoulders and drawing her close. "Are you going to do a CT scan of her head, just to be sure this isn't related to her intracranial hemorrhage?" she asked.

He hesitated because normally he wouldn't order such a test for that purpose. But he found himself wanting to reassure her in any way possible. "Let's wait to see how she does after the electrolytes are in, okay? If there is any change in her neuro status, I will order the scan immediately."

Katerina pulled away from him, turning to look at her sister, and he sensed she wasn't happy with his decision.

He wasn't used to explaining himself—especially not to a family member of a patient. "Listen to me, the earthquake has caused some chaos here in the hospital. I see now that your sister didn't get the new IV fluids I'd ordered during rounds. I truly believe, Katerina, her seizure is the result of an electrolyte imbalance."

She swiped a hand over her eyes, sniffed loudly and nodded. "All right, Miguel, we can wait to see how she does once the electrolytes are corrected."

He reached out to put a hand on her shoulder, wanting nothing more than to offer comfort, easing her fears. "I promise you, I'll take good care of your sister, Katerina."

For a moment he didn't think she'd respond, but then she suddenly turned and threw herself into his arms. Surprised and pleased, he hugged her close.

"I can't lose her, Miguel. I just can't," she said in a muffled voice. "I promised my mother I'd take care of her. She has to be okay, she just has to!"

Her despair tore at his heart. "I know, Katerina," he whispered, brushing his cheek against her silky hair, ignoring the shocked stares from the two nurses. "I know."

As soon as the IV medications were flowing according to his prescribed rate, the two nurses left them alone in the room. He continued to hold Katerina close, smoothing a hand down her back, giving her the emotional support she needed while trying to ignore the sexual awareness zinging through his bloodstream. He was stunned to realize how much he wanted her, even after all this time. And the feeling was impossibly stronger than it had been during the night they'd shared together four and a half years ago.

He hadn't left her by choice, returning home because of his father's stroke, but he hadn't sought her out afterwards, either. Had he made a mistake? Was he wrong not to have gone back to be with her again?

He pressed a kiss along her temple and the slight caress must have been too much for her because she pulled away abruptly, straightening her spine and swiping at the wetness on her face. "I'm sorry, Miguel. I don't know what's wrong with me. I'm usually not this much of a mess."

"Give yourself a break, Katerina. It's understandable that you're worried about your sister. And this has been incredibly stressful for all of us. Despite what you may think, we don't have earthquakes here often." He lifted a hand to wipe a strand of hair from her cheek. "You don't have to stay to help if you don't want to. Maybe you should go back to the hotel for some rest."

She bit her lower lip and he could sense her inner struggle, knowing she was tempted to take him up on his offer. But then she sighed and shook her head. "I can't leave Elouisa all alone with those sick children. I will stay, but only for an hour or so. Hopefully by then, some of the staff will have returned."

He nodded, admiring her strength and determination. "I would like to think so, too."

For a moment she simply stared at him, and then she totally shocked him by putting her hand on his chest and going up on tiptoe to kiss his cheek. It was everything he could do not to pull her into his arms for a real kiss. The feather-light touch was too brief and before he could blink, she drew away. "I'll see you later, Miguel," she whispered, before leaving to return to the children's ward.

His throat was so tight, he couldn't speak. He spent several long minutes wrestling his warring emotions under control. Part of him knew he was playing with fire, yet he couldn't stay away from Katerina. Couldn't keep himself at arm's distance. He longed to kiss her. To make love to her.

Taking a deep breath, he tried to relax his tense muscles. He hadn't forgotten their dinner plans for later this evening, but with the earthquake there was a possibility the restaurants would be closed.

But he refused to consider breaking their date. No, he could always cook for her at his place, if necessary.

The idea grew on him as he continued to make rounds on his patients. He would be happy to prepare Katerina a meal she would never forget. And maybe they could explore the attraction that simmered between them.

Kat tried to concentrate on distracting the children, but she couldn't stop worrying about her sister and her son.

Even though she'd spoken to Diana just a little over an hour ago, she wanted to talk to her again.

Tommy was pretty young to talk on the phone, but she needed to hear his voice, just for a moment.

She ducked into a bathroom, seeking a moment of privacy. She called Diana again, and her friend answered right away. "Hi, Kat."

"Diana, I'm sorry, but I'm still here at the hospital. Some of the staff left and I'm volunteering on the children's ward. How's Tommy?"

"He misses you, but we've been playing video games since the power has come back on. Truly, he's fine."

"Can I talk to him? Just for a minute?"

"Sure, just a sec. Tommy, say hi to your mama, okay? Say hi," she urged.

"Hi, Mama." Tears pricked her eyelids when she heard her son's voice.

"Hi, Tommy. I love you very much. Be good for Aunt Diana, okay?"

There was a moment of silence and then Diana came back on the line. "I know you can't see him, but he's nodding in agreement to whatever you said, Kat."

Knowing that made her smile. "I'm glad. I told him to be good for you. Diana, I'm sorry we can't go on the boat ride," she murmured. "Maybe things will be back to normal tomorrow."

"Sure. Just come back as soon as you can, okay?"

"I will. Take good care of Tommy for me." Kat had to force herself to hang up, or she'd be bawling again.

Okay, she needed to get a grip here. She was becoming an emotional basket case. She quickly used the facilities and then splashed cold water on her face, pulling herself together.

As she returned to the children's ward, she found herself looking for Miguel. Ridiculous, as he was obviously spending time with the sicker patients. She hoped DiCarlo was doing better as she made rounds on the sick children, pleased to note they were doing fairly well.

She saved Pedro for last, knowing he'd want time to talk. "How are you, Pedro?"

"Very good, miss," he said, although his smile was strained, betraying his pain.

"Please, call me Kat," she instructed, coming over to stand beside his bed. "When was the last time you took a dose of pain medication?"

He shrugged one thin shoulder and angled his chin. "I'm fine. I'm not sick like these other children."

"Pedro, you had surgery less than twenty-four hours ago," she reminded him gently. "Taking pain medicine is not a sign of weakness. You need to conserve your strength so your body can heal."

She watched as he seemed to consider her words. "Maybe it is time for a pill," he agreed reluctantly.

"I will ask Elouisa to come," she said, turning toward the door.

"Miss Kat?" His voice stopped her.

"Yes, Pedro, what is it?"

"Are you and Dr. Vasquez…" He paused and frowned, as if searching for the right word. "Boyfriend and girlfriend?" he asked finally.

She couldn't hide her shock. "No! Why would you ask something like that, Pedro?"

His dark eyes crinkled with humor. "Because to me it seems that you like each other very much," he said reasonably.

"Of course we like each other, we're friends, Pedro.

We're friends, nothing more," she said firmly, trying not to blush. The boy was too observant by far. She really needed to keep her emotions under strict control. "I will go and get your pain medicine, which you will take, okay?"

She didn't wait for his response, but went out to find Elouisa. So far, she and the nurse had managed to communicate with facial expressions and hand gestures, intermixed with brief phrases.

"Pedro—medication *para dolor*," she said, using the Spanish word for pain. She found it amazing how the occasional word from her two years of high-school Spanish flashed in her memory.

"*Sí,* okay." Elouisa seemed to know right away what she meant. As the nurse went to get the pain medication, she couldn't help glancing at her watch. She'd been here almost an hour, and as much as she wanted to stay and help, she also longed to return to the hotel to see her son.

Surprisingly, it was only two o'clock in the afternoon, although it seemed as if she'd been here at the hospital for ever. She vowed to stay just another thirty minutes and no longer. For one thing, she was very hungry. And for another, she wanted to hold her son close, kiss his cheek and reassure herself that he was truly okay.

Elouisa returned, holding out a small paper medication cup, very similar to the ones they used in the hospital back home. Kat and Elouisa went back to Pedro's room to give him his medicine.

They found him standing in the doorway, a frightened expression on his face. "Pedro? What's wrong?"

He brought his hand away from his abdomen, revealing a bright crimson stain spreading across his hospital gown. "I'm bleeding," he said, as if he could hardly believe it.

"Elouisa, call Dr. Vasquez, Hurry! *¡Rapidamente!*" The nurse rushed for the phone while she quickly crossed over to put her arm around Pedro's shoulders. "You've broken open your stitches," she told him calmly. "Come, now, you need to get back to bed."

Pedro murmured something in Spanish, and the fact that he was too stunned to practice his English worried her more than the blood staining his gown. She should have inspected his incision. "Stay still, Pedro, Dr. Vasquez will be here soon."

True to her word, Miguel strode in just moments later. "What happened?"

"I'm not sure," she was forced to admit. "I knew he was having pain, but I didn't realize he'd broken open his stitches."

"Everything he did today was too much for him." Miguel's compassionate gaze did not hold any blame.

"I should have examined his incision," she admitted softly. "I'm sorry, Miguel."

He shook his head as he turned toward Pedro. "Do not take this on yourself, Katerina. Will you please get me some gauze dressings? I need to see how bad the wound looks."

She knew he was trying to offer Pedro some privacy and quickly left the room, searching for the supply cart. She found the gauze without too much trouble and then returned to Pedro's room, hovering outside the doorway until she knew the boy was adequately covered.

"Do you have the gauze?" Miguel called, indicating it was safe to enter.

"Yes." The sheets were arranged so that his body was

covered except for his belly. The small gaping hole in Pedro's abdomen worried her, although she tried not to let it show. "Will he need to go back to surgery?" she asked as she opened the gauze packet for him, keeping the contents sterile.

He took the gauze with his gloved fingers and turned back to Pedro. "I'm afraid so. Pedro, I will need to fix this open incision right away, understand?" He spoke in Spanish too, likely repeating what he'd said.

"I understand," Pedro murmured.

"You'll need to talk to his mother. I'll ask Elouisa to get hold of her."

"Thanks."

She left the room, and made sure Elouisa understood she needed to call Pedro's *madre* before she returned. Miguel had just finished dressing the wound, stepping back and stripping off his soiled gloves. "I will call down to surgery to make sure they have a room available and staff to assist."

She chewed her lower lip nervously. "And what if they don't have staff to assist?" she asked.

Miguel hesitated. "I'm afraid I will have to ask for your assistance, Katerina. You are a skilled O.R. nurse and we have worked together many times."

She opened her mouth to protest but stopped herself, realizing Pedro was listening to the interaction between them. She didn't want to say anything to upset the boy. "I can certainly help as needed," she agreed.

Miguel hurried away, apparently to make the necessary phone calls. She forced a reassuring smile on her face as she crossed over to Pedro's bedside, taking his hand in hers. "You're going to be fine, Pedro. Dr.

Vasquez is a very talented surgeon. He will fix you up in no time."

"Will you assist him, Miss Kat?" Pedro asked, his eyes betraying a flicker of fear. "If there is no one else?"

"Of course I will do whatever is needed, Pedro. Don't you worry about a thing, okay? You're going to be fine."

"Gracias," he murmured, tightening his grip on her hand.

When Miguel returned, the tense expression on his face told her without words that her help would be needed. "There is a theater available, but the staff nurses who have stayed and the surgeon on call are busy with a trauma patient. Either Pedro waits until they are finished or you come down to assist me. It's your choice, Katerina. I know I have asked a lot from you today."

She didn't hesitate, knowing she could never let Pedro down. "I will be happy to help," she said firmly.

Miguel flashed a grateful smile. "Thank you, Katerina. This is a small surgery and shouldn't take too long."

She glanced down at Pedro's small brown hand clasped tightly in hers. She couldn't have left him any more than she could have left her own son. "I know. Remember, Pedro, Dr. Vasquez and I have worked together often in America. We made a good team."

"Yes, we did." Miguel's soft tone reminded her of the night he'd made love to her. She needed to protect her heart from his lethal charm.

"Dr. Vasquez?" Elouisa poked her head into the room and said something about Pedro's mother. Miguel excused himself and went out to take the call.

Within minutes he'd returned. "Your mother will try

to be here soon, but I'd rather not wait if that's okay. I need to repair the incision to protect against infection."

"I know. It's okay, she has my younger brothers and sisters to care for. I will be fine."

Kat's heart went out to Pedro, bravely facing surgery without his mother being here to hold his hand, to kiss him and to wish him well. She could tell Miguel felt the same way, from the way his gaze softened as he looked down at Pedro.

"You are very brave, Pedro," Miguel murmured. "I am extremely proud of you."

The simple words brightened Pedro's face and he beamed up at Miguel as if he were some sort of miracle worker. She couldn't help wondering about Pedro's father, why he wasn't here if his mother was home with the other children.

Miguel oozed confidence and kindness at the same time. Obviously, he cared very much for children. First DiCarlo and now Pedro. Both were patients under his care, but she knew that was only part of it.

Miguel would be the same way with his own child. With Tommy. The truth was staring her in the face.

As they wheeled Pedro's bed down to the elevator to go to the surgical suite, she knew that she couldn't put off telling Miguel about his son for much longer. She didn't know if he still planned on keeping their dinner date, so much had happened since then.

But even if their dinner plans had to be cancelled, she would have to tell him. Tonight.

No more excuses.

CHAPTER SIX

MIGUEL worked as quickly as he dared, first exploring the open wound in Pedro's abdomen and then irrigating with antibiotic solution. He believed the wound might have opened from a combination of an infection starting to take hold internally along with Pedro's physical exertions during the earthquake disaster.

He was lucky to have found an anesthesiology resident willing to stay after his shift. And Katerina was doing a phenomenal job of being his assistant. They settled into the old familiar routine as if the four and a half years hadn't gone by.

"Three-O silk," he said, but before he finished his statement Katerina was already handing him the pick-ups prepared with the suture. He grinned, even though she couldn't see behind the face mask, and gave his head a wry shake. "You always did have a way of reading my mind, Katerina."

She went still for a moment and he wondered if he'd somehow offended her. When she remained silent, he couldn't help trying to make amends.

"My apologies. I truly meant that as a compliment."

She lifted her head and looked at him, her beautiful green eyes probing as if she could indeed read his internal thoughts. "No apology necessary, Miguel," she finally said lightly. "I was thinking that I was glad that our roles weren't reversed and you were the one trying to read my mind."

"Really?" Closing the small incision didn't take long and he turned to face her as he set the pick-ups back down on the surgical tray. "Now you have piqued my interest. What is it you don't want me to read in your mind, I wonder?"

"Surely you don't expect me to answer that, do you?" Her green eyes crinkled at the corners, making him believe she was smiling. He relaxed, realizing he didn't like the thought of her being angry with him. "Pedro will be all right, won't he?"

"Yes, certainly. He must rest, though, and take care of himself. No more playing hero."

She nodded and there was a hint of relief in her gaze. "Good. That's very good."

She backed away from the surgical field and he had to bite back a protest, even though he knew her volunteer shift was over. Truly, she'd gone well above and beyond the call of duty. When she stripped off her face mask, he followed suit. "Katerina, I hope you will still allow me to take you to dinner this evening?"

She hesitated, and he sensed she wanted to refuse, but she surprised him by turning back to face him. "Of course, Miguel. But I need to return to my hotel for a bit. I'm still feeling the effects of jet-lag."

He couldn't blame her. The hour was still early, just three-thirty in the afternoon, and as much as he wanted to take her straight to his home, he couldn't begrudge her some down time. Especially not after everything she'd done for them today. "I will see you in a few hours, then?"

"Yes. I'll be ready." She glanced once more back at Pedro, where the anesthesiology resident was reversing the effects of his anesthesia, before she turned and disappeared through the doorway in the direction of the women's locker room.

He instantly felt isolated and alone after Katerina left, which was completely ridiculous. He stepped back, allowing the anesthesiologist to wheel Pedro's cart over to the recovery area.

As he washed up and changed his clothes, he spent time considering what meal he would prepare for her tonight. He wasn't a stranger to the kitchen. Living on his own, he'd been forced to learn how to cook, but he wanted to be sure the meal was to Katerina's liking.

For some odd reason he couldn't help feeling that tonight was incredibly important, a turning point in their renewed relationship.

And he was determined to make their evening together special.

"Mama!" Kat braced herself as her son launched himself at her, his chubby arms wrapping tightly around her neck.

"Oh, Tommy, I missed you so much!" She held him close, nuzzling his neck, filling her head with his scent, eternally grateful to have him in her life. The more difficult times of being a single mother were easily forgotten during joyous moments like this.

"We were just going to try and find something to eat," Diana said with a tired smile. "I'm glad you came home before we left."

"I'm so hungry I could eat a bear," Kat murmured, still holding Tommy close. For once her active son seemed content to stay in her arms. "I'm surprised you didn't order room service."

"Can't read the room-service menu, it's in Spanish," Diana muttered with a heavy sigh. "Besides, we've been cooped up in here long enough. Believe it or not, there is a small café that's open just a few blocks away. We should be able to get something to eat. I have to tell you, the earthquake was a bit scary. There's one person behind the desk downstairs who speaks English and told us to stay in our rooms for a while. But I've been looking outside and haven't seen much damage."

Kat hadn't seen much evidence of damage either, and wondered if the tree outside the hospital had been partially dead already to have fallen on the building. "I'm so glad you're both safe."

"We're fine. We took a walk and found a couple of broken windows and a couple of uprooted trees. Nothing too awful."

"All right, let's go eat." She knew she had to tell Diana her plans for later that evening. But first she desperately needed something to eat. The gnawing in her stomach was almost painful.

While they ate, she explained how she'd helped out at the hospital in the children's ward, including doing surgery on a thirteen-year-old boy. As much as she didn't like being away from Tommy, she couldn't deny the satisfaction she'd felt by helping out.

"Hmm." Diana sat back in her seat, eyeing Kat over the rim of her soft drink. "So basically you spent the entire day with Miguel, huh?"

Kat finished the *tapas* they'd ordered, not exactly

sure what she was eating but enjoying the spicy food just the same, before answering. "Yes. And you may as well know I'm having dinner with him later tonight."

Her friend's eyes widened in horror. "No! You're going to tell him?"

"Don't," Kat said in warning, glancing at Tommy slurping his soft drink loudly through a straw. "Not now."

"But…" Diana sighed heavily, understanding that Kat didn't want to have this conversation with Tommy sitting right there. "I haven't had time to call the embassy," she complained in a low voice. "You agreed to wait."

"Doesn't matter." Kat was pleased to note how Tommy enjoyed the Spanish food. Must be part of his natural heritage, a trait passed down to him from Miguel. "Trust me when I tell you I know what I'm doing."

But Diana was shaking her head. "You don't know Miguel well enough yet," she protested.

"We worked together all day, moving the sick pediatric patients out of the children's wing. I helped him intubate a small child in the elevator and operate on a young boy. I know enough, Diana. You have to trust me on this."

Diana didn't say anything more, although the disapproval in her expression was clear. Even though Kat knew she was doing the right thing, she understood why her friend was worried. Seeing Miguel at the hospital today, there was no denying the powerful standing he had within the community, not to mention being on friendly terms with a police officer. A minor detail she hadn't dared tell Diana about. She hadn't understood exactly what they'd been saying, but when the police officer had taken Miguel's brother away, she'd had the impression he'd acted out of friendship.

But deep down those reasons weren't enough to hold her tongue. She knew Miguel was incapable of hurting a child, especially his own son. And he'd been so incredibly nice and supportive of her. Right from the very beginning, when he'd translated Juliet's chart for her. Spending time together today had only made her admire him more. No matter what Diana said, she would not back down from her decision.

Telling Miguel was the right thing to do.

"I hope you're not making a big mistake," Diana said.

"I'm not. Are you finished eating? We could take a little walk, maybe check out the church over there." Kat was determined to change the subject. She had a good hour yet before she needed to return to the hotel room to shower and change.

Better she keep her mind occupied with sightseeing rather than dwelling on the sweet anticipation of seeing Miguel again.

Kat pulled on the only dressy outfit she'd packed, a long gauzy skirt with a white tank top that molded to her figure. She left her long blonde hair straight and loose, rather than pulled back in the usual ponytail, knowing Miguel preferred it that way.

"You're dressing up for him as if this is some sort of hot date," Diana observed mildly.

She couldn't deny it. "Wanting to look nice isn't a crime." She needed some semblance of being in control. And maybe a part of her wanted to remind Miguel of the night they'd shared. A night of passion. A night that had produced a son.

Tommy was already falling asleep, and Kat couldn't help feeling guilty that she was leaving, forcing Diana to stay in the hotel room again. "I promise we'll do more sightseeing tomorrow," she said by way of apology.

"It's okay." Diana shrugged, even though Kat could sense her friend's keen disappointment. "This is why you paid my way to come here, right? There's no way we could have predicted the added complication of Miguel."

Truer words were never spoken. She went over to give her best friend a quick hug. "Thanks for being here, Diana."

Diana hugged her back, her good humor seeming to return. "You're welcome. Now, you'd better go downstairs, Miguel might just decide to come up here."

"He can't. They would make him call up here first," she protested. Still, she quickly crossed over to her half-asleep son, brushed a kiss on his brow and murmured how much she loved him before taking the room key Diana held out for her and letting herself out of the hotel room.

The elevators seemed to take for ever, but since she didn't know where the stairwells were, she forced herself to be patient. When the doors opened to reveal Miguel standing there, she nearly screamed, her pulse leaping into triple digits.

"You scared me!" she accused, putting hand over her wildly beating heart. "What are you doing here?"

His teeth flashed in a bright smile, but he stood back, allowing her room to enter the elevator. "I'm sorry to have frightened you, but it's already five minutes past eight. I was worried you'd forgotten about our dinner date and had fallen asleep."

She struggled to breathe normally, but being in the small elevator so close to him was extremely nerve-racking. He was impeccably dressed in a crisp white shirt and black slacks, and his scent made her knees week. "How did you know what room I'm in? They're not supposed to tell you that. What if I didn't want to see you?" She was outraged that her privacy had been so easily violated.

"Hush, now, don't be so upset. The clerk at the front desk is one of my patients from the hospital. She knows I wouldn't hurt you."

As he spoke, the doubts Diana had voiced seeped into the back of her mind. Miguel knew everyone, had connections everywhere. He'd gotten her room number without any effort at all. What if he really did plan to take Tommy away from her?

She had to believe he wouldn't. But she wasn't willing to let him or the clerk off so lightly. "It's not right, Miguel. Just because she happens to know you, it doesn't mean she has the right to give you my room number. I intend to file a complaint."

He seemed taken aback by her biting anger. "I'm sorry, Katerina. The fault is mine. Please don't get her in trouble for my mistake."

She knew she was overreacting, but the near miss had rattled her. What if he'd gotten a glimpse of Tommy? She didn't want him finding out about his son by accident. Back in the hotel room she'd been confident they could work something out, but now she wasn't so sure.

It was tempting to beg off their plans, but keeping Tommy a secret was already eating at her. She couldn't hold off another twenty-four hours, so she did her best to relax and smile. "Okay, fine, Miguel. I won't file a complaint, although you know I have a right to be upset. You forget I'm a single woman in a strange country where few speak my native language. I have a right to be concerned about strange men being allowed up to my room."

He lightly skimmed a hand down her back in a caress so light she thought she might have imagined it. "You are right, Katerina," he murmured contritely, although with a hint of steel. "I would not be at all happy if any other man was allowed access to your room."

The macho tone put her teeth on edge, but when the elevator doors opened she quickly escaped, putting badly needed distance between them.

She needed to stay in control. This wasn't a date, and she realized she'd made a grave mistake by dressing up for him as if it were. She was on an important mission, one that would have a great impact on her son's life, his future. Her future.

This was not a date!

Miguel cursed himself for being so stupid. If he'd been patient, they wouldn't be starting the night off on the wrong foot with an argument.

Katerina was breathtakingly beautiful. He'd never seen her in a dress and it was taking all his will-power to keep his hands to himself. He'd wanted to sweep her into his arms, to kiss her the way he had over four years ago.

His car was waiting, and he gently cupped her elbow, steering her towards the vehicle. Of course she dug in her heels. "I thought the restaurant was close by?"

"Please, get in the car. The restaurant nearby is closed due to the earthquake." After a brief pause she did as he asked, sliding into the back seat. "I'm afraid I have another sin to confess," he murmured, once they were settled and the driver had pulled away from the curb.

Her brows pulled together in a frown. "Really? And what sin is that?"

He subtly wiped his damp palms on his pants, more nervous than he'd ever been in his life. He was used to women coming on to him, many made it no secret they wanted to be the one to help end his bachelor ways. But he suddenly cared what Katerina thought of him. It was telling that she hugged the door as if she might escape at any moment. He flashed his most charming smile. "I have made dinner for us tonight."

"You?" her eyebrows shot upwards in surprise. And then the full meaning sank in. "We're going to your home?"

She acted as if he intended to take advantage of her. Had he read her wrong? Was it possible that she didn't feel the same sexual awareness that he did? Or had his stupid stunt in going up to her room broken her trust? "If you'd rather not, we can wait until tomorrow to dine. Hopefully the restaurants will reopen by then. I'm more than willing to ask my driver to return to your hotel." He tried not to let his hurt feelings show.

There was a long pause before she let out a small sigh. "No need to go back, Miguel," she said softly. She lifted her gaze and he saw the faint glint of amusement there. "I must say, I'm stunned to learn you know how to cook."

He relaxed and lifted her hand to his mouth, pressing his mouth to her soft skin. "There are many things you don't know about me, Katerina."

She gasped and tugged on her hand, which he reluctantly released. "And maybe, Miguel, there are a few things you don't know about me."

He couldn't deny the burning need to get to know all her secrets. The driver pulled up to his home and she glanced out the window. "You live right by the hospital," she said, recognizing the landmarks.

"Yes, very convenient for those nights I'm on call," he agreed.

His home was on the top floor, and they rode the elevator up in silence. He unlocked the door and then stepped back, allowing Katerina to enter first.

"Wow, very nice," she murmured, and he was ridiculously pleased she liked his home. "Bigger than I expected for a man living alone."

She didn't sit, but wandered around looking at his things with interest. When she approached the hallway farthest from the kitchen, he said, "Feel free to explore. There are three bedrooms, although our rooms tend to be smaller than you're used to back in the U.S."

He turned to check on the food, which was being kept warm in the oven, and when he turned around he was startled to find her standing right behind him.

She was so beautiful, he ached. "Katerina, please don't be angry with me." He stepped closer, reaching up to thread his fingers through the silky golden strands of her hair. "I wanted tonight to be special."

A strange expression, something akin to guilt, flashed in her eyes, but then she smiled and he knew he was forgiven. "I'm not angry," she murmured.

"I don't think I've thanked you properly for your help

today," he murmured, moving closer still. She stared up at him, standing her ground, and he couldn't resist the soft invitation of her mouth for another minute. Without giving her a chance to say anything more, he gently cupped her face in his hands and kissed her.

CHAPTER SEVEN

KAT didn't know how she allowed it to happen but the instant Miguel kissed her, memories of the night they'd shared came rushing back to her, flooding her mind, making her melt against him. Instinctively, she opened her mouth, wordlessly inviting him to deepen the kiss.

One moment his mouth was gentle, the next it was demanding, needy, stirring up flames of desire she'd tried to forget, vowed to live without.

She'd missed this. Missed him. Missed the way he made her feel, alive, vibrant, attractive. She wrapped her arms tightly around his neck, hanging on for dear life as a storm of desire washed over her, nearly drowning her with its intensity.

"Katerina," he whispered, as he pressed soft, moist kisses down the side of her neck. "You are so beautiful to me. I've never forgotten you. Never."

For one long moment she almost gave in to his sinful temptation. His hand came up to gently cup her breast, his thumb stroking her nipple through the thin layer of cotton, and her body reacted, arching into his, desperately needing to feel his hands on her bare skin.

She wanted nothing more than to close her eyes and give in to the whisper of pure pleasure, but she wasn't that younger, carefree person any more. She was a single mother with responsibilities.

Appalled with herself, she quickly broke off the embrace, forcing herself to let Miguel go, stumbling in her haste to put the width of the kitchen table between them. She grasped the back of a chair so tightly her knuckles were white. "I'm sorry, but I can't do this. I didn't come here to—to pick up where we left off, Miguel."

She couldn't allow the flash of hurt in his eyes to get to her. Too bad if his macho pride had taken a low blow. He would survive. She had to think about Tommy now. She watched him struggle to pull himself under control and she was a little ashamed of herself for being glad he'd been as aroused as she had been. At least she knew for sure the attraction wasn't one-sided.

"Of course you didn't," he said slowly, as if articulating each word helped him to maintain control. "I promised you dinner and I always follow through on my promises."

Dinner? Food? He had to be joking. She couldn't have eaten a bite to save her life. She shook her head and took a long deep breath, before letting it out slowly. "Miguel, listen to me. I came here because I have something to tell you. Something very important." She forced herself to meet his gaze.

He seemed truly baffled and took a step towards her, and she instinctively took a quick step back. "What is it, Katerina? Are you all right? It's not…your health, is it?"

She couldn't help being touched that he cared enough to worry about her health. And if she was sick, would he stand by her? Or would he look for an excuse to leave? She didn't want to consider the answer to that question, so she ruthlessly shoved the thought aside.

Obviously, he wasn't going to be able to figure this out on his own. She'd have to come right out to say it. "I'm fine, Miguel. But there is something you should know." She took a deep breath and bravely faced him. "I have a son. *We* have a son. He will be four years old in a little less than three months."

He gaped at her in shock, and for several long seconds the silence was heavy between them. She wished she could read his mind to know what he was thinking. "A son?" he echoed, almost in disbelief.

"His name is Tomas. I named him after you." During the night they'd shared, Miguel had confided that Tomas was his middle name. And his father's name.

Miguel dragged a hand down his face, as if still hardly able to comprehend what she was saying. "I don't understand. How did this happen? We used protection."

She batted down the flicker of anger—hadn't she asked herself the same question while staring down at the positive pregnancy test? But having him think, even for a moment, that she might have done this on purpose made her grind her teeth in frustration. "Protection can fail, Miguel. I'm sorry to spring this on you so suddenly. You need to know I tried to find you after you left. I called your cellphone and searched for you on all the popular social media websites. When I couldn't find you, I assumed you were working somewhere remote with Doctors Without Borders, following your dream." She spread her hands wide. "I didn't know Seville was your home. Had no way of knowing you were here all this time."

Miguel looked in shock and he lowered himself slowly onto a kitchen chair. "A son. Tomas. I can barely comprehend what you are telling me."

Relieved to have the secret out in the open, she sank into a chair across from him and reached for her purse. "I have a picture. Would you like to see?" Without waiting for his reply, she slid Tommy's picture across the table. "He looks very much like you, Miguel."

He stared at the glossy photograph for several long moments before he dragged his gaze up to meet hers. "This is such a shock. I don't know what to say, other than that he's amazing. Thank you for bearing him."

There had really been no choice, not for her. The way Miguel stared at the picture, as if awestruck, made her a bit nervous. Was he already thinking of taking their son away from her? Beneath the table she linked her fingers together, tightly. "Miguel, I only told you about Tommy because you had a right to know. Please be assured, I'm more than capable of raising him. I don't expect anything from you."

For the first time since arriving in Spain she saw his gaze darken with anger directed at her. "I will not avoid my responsibility, Katerina," he murmured in a low tone. For just a brief moment she thought he looked upset, but then the fleeting expression was gone. In its place was grim resolution. "Of course I will provide for my son. And I would like to make arrangements to meet him. As soon as possible. I know Juliet will be here for a few more days, but I can make arrangements for the two of us to return immediately to the U.S."

She stared at him, realizing in some portion of her brain that Miguel didn't know Tommy was here in Seville with her. Was, in fact, sleeping soundly back in her hotel room. If she told Miguel he was there, she had no doubt he'd swoop in and wake him up, scaring the poor child to death. She strove to keep her tone level. "Miguel, be reasonable. He's a young boy, not yet four. He won't understand or recognize you. You will be a stranger to him. We need some time to think this through, to figure out what we're going to do. Besides, I don't want to leave Juliet yet."

Miguel slowly rose to his feet, staring down at her arrogantly. "If you think I will let you raise my son without me, you are sorely mistaken. I will be a part of his life, and nothing you do or say will change my mind."

The sick feeling in her stomach intensified as she stared up at him helplessly, knowing he meant every single word. And while she knew she'd have to share custody of Tommy with Miguel, she wasn't at all sure what that exactly meant regarding their future.

Would Miguel play at being a father at first but then lose interest in them? Would he decide to up and leave, just like her father had? The way Juliet's father had?

Seeing him with Pedro earlier, she'd thought Miguel would be a good father to her son. But now she couldn't prevent the doubts from seeping in. And she desperately needed time. Needed to understand exactly what the future truly held for them.

How much would she have to sacrifice for her son?

Miguel inwardly winced when Katerina eyes filled with wounded shock. He knew he'd crossed the line, had put her on the defensive by practically threatening her, but he couldn't seem to stop.

She'd borne his son. Had been raising him alone for years. Deep down he was outraged that he had been cheated of precious memories, yet logically he knew the situation wasn't her fault. He'd left to return home after his father's stroke, leaving Katerina to fend for herself.

He'd simply assumed she'd be fine. Bitter guilt for not talking to her again after he'd left coated his tongue. She'd had every right to believe he was working in some distant country—after all, he'd told her about his dream. And truthfully, if not for his brother's drinking problem, he would have already been in Africa, working with those in need. He wouldn't be here now, hearing the truth about having a son. And she'd searched for him, too.

For a moment his resolve wavered. For so long he'd dreamed of joining Doctors Without Borders. Now his dream would have to be put on hold once again. Indefinitely. Maybe for ever.

He squelched the feeling of despair and refused to allow himself to think about that now. Instead, he glanced once more at the glossy photograph of a young boy with light brown skin, dark hair, and big dark eyes. His bright smile was the only facial feature that resembled Katerina. He trailed his fingertips over the photo and had the strongest urge to hop onto the first plane to the U.S. to see Tomas in person.

"Miguel? I smell something burning," Katerina said in a tight voice.

He whirled around in surprise, having totally forgotten about the meal he'd prepared. He went over to pull the chicken dish from the oven, waving the smoke away. "I don't think it's too badly burned," he said, even though the chicken looked a bit on the overdone side.

"I'm not hungry," Katerina murmured. She pushed away from the table and rose to her feet. "I think it's best that I go back to the hotel now. We can discuss this more tomorrow."

He swung around to face her, unwilling to call an

abrupt end to their evening. "Don't leave," he said, his voice sharply commanding rather than pleading with her, the way he should. He forced himself to soften his tone. "If you could spare a few minutes, I would like to hear more about Tomas."

She stood indecisively, wringing her hands together, and he silently cursed himself for being so stupid. He'd frightened her, instead of reassuring her that he intended to be there for her and for Tomas. Maybe a part of him mourned the loss of his dream, but he refused, absolutely refused, to ignore his responsibilities.

He'd been selfish once, following his dream to study abroad, and his brother Luis had suffered for it. His father had suffered too. He would always regret not being there when his father had sustained his stroke. The fact that he'd saved countless patients' lives wasn't enough to make up for his failures regarding his family.

He couldn't bear to fail his son.

"There isn't much to tell," she protested. "He's hardly more than a baby."

Katerina avoided his direct gaze and he wished he could cross over and take her once again into his arms. Kissing her had felt like heaven and he'd nearly lost all control when she'd wantonly kissed him back.

"He's not stubborn, like his mother?" he asked, trying to lighten the mood by gently teasing her. "I find that difficult to believe."

She narrowed her gaze and flipped her long golden hair over her shoulder. "Believe me, Tommy gets his stubborn streak from his father."

He tried not to wince at the shortened version of his son's name. He didn't understand this American tendency to give nicknames rather than using given names. "I bet he's smart, then, too. Just like me."

Katerina rolled her eyes. "Of course he's smart. I read to him before he goes to bed at night and he has memorized every story. He attends preschool and already knows his letters and numbers."

Hearing about his son's life, bedtime stories and preschool caused helpless anger to wash over him. He'd missed so much. Too much.

She was right, his son didn't know him. He couldn't bear the thought of being a stranger to his own son. "I can't wait to see him, Katerina. I want to see him, to hold him in my arms. I feel like I've missed too much already."

Her expression went from tolerant amusement to frank alarm. "Miguel, you can't just barge into his life like a steamroller. You'll be a stranger to him. You have to give him time to get to know you. And what exactly are you suggesting? That we'll just move here to Seville to be near you? Neither one of us speaks the language here and, besides, Tommy is an American citizen. We have a life back home." As she spoke, Katerina edged closer to the door, her eyes wide with panic.

"I'm sorry, but this is too much stress for me to handle right now, Miguel. I came to Seville because of Juliet's injuries, remember? And after working all day, I can barely think straight. We'll talk tomorrow."

"Katerina…" he protested, but too late. She already had her hand on the front door. He knew he was pushing her too hard, too fast. "All right. We can talk more tomorrow. I'll be happy to take you back to the hotel."

"I'll ride the metro," she said, lifting her chin in the stubborn gesture he secretly found amusing. Except that her eagerness to get away from him wasn't at all comical.

"Katerina, please allow me to take you." When she still looked like a rabbit ready to bolt, he added, "If you insist on taking the metro, I will have no choice but to follow you. We will ride together."

Her mouth tightened, but after a moment she gave a small, jerky nod. "Fine. We'll take your car. But I'd like to go now, Miguel."

He couldn't think of a way to talk her out of it, so he simply nodded and reached for his cellphone. He called his driver, Fernando, and requested him to return right away. Fernando sounded surprised, but readily agreed. "My driver will be here in five minutes," he assured her.

Katerina didn't move away from the door, but simply looked at him from across the room, a long awkward silence stretching between them. He glanced over at the photograph of Tomas, still sitting on the kitchen table. "May I keep the picture of my son?" he asked in a low voice.

For a moment he thought Katerina was going to burst into tears, but she bit her lip and nodded. "Of course," she murmured in a husky voice. "I have others at home."

The way she said the word home, as if he wasn't included, made his temper flare, but he managed to hold his tongue. Thankfully, Fernando arrived quicker than expected.

Katerina didn't say more than a couple brief sentences on the way back to her hotel. He couldn't think of anything to say to put her mind at ease. Because even though he didn't want to upset her, there was no way on earth he was going to give his son up easily.

"Thank you for the ride," she said politely, when

Fernando pulled up in front of her hotel. "I'm sure I'll see you some time tomorrow."

He caught her hand before she escaped from the car. "Katerina, wait. How about if we agree to meet at eleven o'clock tomorrow morning? I will have finished making rounds by then. We'll meet in your sister's room and then we can go somewhere for a cup of coffee, okay?"

"Fine. I'll see you at eleven." She looked pointedly down at where his hand was locked around her wrist and he forced himself to let her go. "Goodnight," she said, and didn't wait for him to respond before slamming the door shut and practically sprinting into the lobby.

He watched her hurry away, trying not to panic at the realization that she could easily catch a flight home tonight, making it extremely difficult for him to find her. And his son.

"Ready, sir?" Fernando asked from the front seat.

He hesitated, fighting the urge to follow her upstairs to her hotel room before she could slip away, maybe for ever. He wanted to talk to her about how they would deal with this situation, to insist they finish their conversation right this minute.

He took several deep breaths, fighting to stay calm. Logically, he knew Katerina wasn't going to run away. She wouldn't leave Juliet, not when her sister had suffered seizures earlier that afternoon. Besides, no one had forced her to tell him about his son. Truthfully, Katerina could have kept Tomas a secret, simply returning home without telling him a thing. The fact that she had told him indicated she wanted their son to have a father. The thought calmed him.

"Yes, I'm ready, Fernando," he said, giving his driver the signal to leave. As they pulled away from the curb and headed home, Miguel sat back in his seat, his mind whirling.

He had until tomorrow morning at eleven to come up with a new plan. He needed some way to convince Katerina that Tommy would benefit from having them all be together as a family, rather than living apart. Surely she wanted such a thing as well, or she wouldn't have told him her secret.

Granted, the obstacle of living in different countries was no small thing. They both had family members to take into consideration as well. He had his brother Luis, who still needed support, and she had Juliet, who might need ongoing medical care.

The entire situation seemed impossible, but he was determined there would be a way to make things work out to everyone's satisfaction.

Grimly, he stared out through the night, knowing he would fight anyone and anything that stood in the way of establishing a relationship with his son.

CHAPTER EIGHT

KAT barely made it up to her hotel room where she collapsed in the chair beside the bed and buried her face in her hands, trying not to give in to mounting hysteria.

Miguel wanted to meet his son, and it sounded pretty certain that he would want custody. All this time she'd figured he wouldn't want the responsibility of having a family, yet he'd made it clear that he intended to follow her back to the U.S. in order to claim Tommy as his own.

"Kat?" Diana whispered from the bed. "Are you all right?"

She lifted her head and struggled to swallow her tears. Thankfully, Tommy was sleeping in the small roll-away bed as he would only be upset to see her crying. The room was dark, but they always left the bathroom light on in case Tommy needed to get up. "Fine," she whispered back, subtly swiping her hands over her wet cheeks. "We'll talk in the morning."

She wished Diana was asleep already too, because her emotions were too raw, too fragile to talk now.

Maybe Diana had been right to encourage her to wait before telling Miguel about Tommy. She wished she'd listened to her friend's advice. But it was too late now.

There was nothing to do except to move forward from here. Telling Miguel about his son was the right thing to do, but while she thought she'd prepared herself for the conversation, Miguel's reaction had overwhelmed her.

He'd assumed she'd left her son back home, and she hadn't possessed the courage to tell him otherwise. She could rationalize the reason was because Miguel would have come right up here to the room, demanding to see Tommy regardless of the fact that he was already asleep. Regardless of the fact that seeing a stranger might upset him.

But deep down she knew her reasons for keeping silent were far more selfish. She'd needed a little time to come to grips with how her life would change from this point on. Miguel's demand to return immediately to the U.S. had frightened her. The fantasy she'd harbored, where Miguel would allow her to continue to raise his son while he joined Doctors Without Borders, had exploded in her face.

She crept over to the side of the roll-away bed where Tommy was sleeping to gaze down at his sweet, innocent face. He was clutching his favorite stuffed animal, Terry the tiger, to his chest. She lightly brushed her fingers over his silky dark hair, being careful not to wake him up. She wanted to gather him close into her arms, as if to reassure herself that she wasn't going to lose him.

She pressed a soft kiss to the top of his head, before heading into the bathroom to wash her face and change into her nightgown. She crawled into her bed and stared blindly up at the ceiling, knowing she'd never relax enough to fall asleep.

Going back over the events of the evening, she couldn't help remembering, in vivid detail, the way

Miguel had kissed her. Before he'd known about Tommy. He'd clearly wanted her, his body's reaction had been no secret. Had he assumed that since they'd made love four and a half years ago she wouldn't think twice about doing so again?

It had been tempting, far more tempting that she wanted to admit, to give in to the passion that shimmered between them. Truthfully, Tommy was the main reason she'd pulled back. If not for her son, she knew that she and Miguel would have continued where they'd left off all those years ago.

Because she cared about Miguel. More than she should. And while they might be able to get along enough to share custody of their son, she wasn't sure how to get past her personal feelings for him.

"Mama, wake up!" Tommy said, climbing up on her bed. "I'm hungry."

Kat forced her gritty eyelids open, inwardly groaning. She'd been awake half the night, worrying herself sick about the future, and could easily have slept for several more hours. But as a parent she was used to putting her needs aside for her son. "I'm awake," she murmured, trying to focus on the clock across the room and wincing when she realized it was seven a.m.

"Do you want me to take Tommy down to the café for breakfast?" Diana asked as she came out of the bathroom. "You can probably catch another hour or so of sleep."

"No, that's fine. I want to come with you." Kat sat up, running her fingers through her hair. "I was thinking maybe we should go on the boat tour this morning, instead of waiting until later."

Diana's eyes lit up. "That would be great."

Kat didn't have the heart to tell her friend that by early afternoon she'd likely be arranging a meeting between Miguel and Tommy. Better to put that conversation off for a little while yet. "Give me fifteen minutes to get ready, okay?"

"Sure."

Kat freshened up in the bathroom, forgoing a shower to pull her hair back into its usual ponytail. During the long night, when she'd tossed and turned for hours, she'd decided Tommy needed his father, so she planned to present Miguel with her joint custody proposal. As much as it pained her, she thought that having Tommy spend summers here with Miguel, along with a few holidays, would probably be the least disruptive to their lives. And she could travel with Tommy to make sure things went well, at least for the first few years. She could only hope that Miguel would find parenting too much work. Although remembering the way he cared for the pediatric patients in the hospital, like Pedro and DiCarlo, she knew he wouldn't.

Tommy ran into the bathroom and grabbed her hand. "Mama, let's go."

"All right, all right. Slow down. Diana, do you have your room key?"

"Right here." Diana held it up.

"All right, here's mine. After we go on the boat ride, I'm going to head over to the hospital to see Juliet." And Miguel, although she didn't voice that last part.

"Do you want to stop on the way?" Diana offered.

She did, very much, but at the same time she was too afraid they'd run into Miguel. And since she'd promised Diana and Tommy a boat ride, she was determined to follow through on her promise. If she was back in the U.S., she could simply call the hospital to see how her sister was doing, but with the language barrier she had no choice but to actually go in to see Juliet for herself. And it didn't help that Miguel's eleven o'clock time frame hung over her head like a time bomb. "No, that's okay. Let's do the boat tour first."

As they left the hotel and walked down the street to their favorite breakfast café, she was determined to have this short time to play tourist with Diana and Tommy. A few hours alone, before their lives changed, for ever.

"Look at these bikes, Kat—isn't this the coolest idea?" Diana said as she gestured toward the bike rack located a few feet from the café. "I found out that this is a type of public transportation offered in Seville. For a small annual fee you can take one of these bikes, ride it to your destination, park it in another bike rack and then use it again to go home. No need to buy a bike of your own. These bike racks and bikes are located all over the city."

Kat smiled when she saw an elderly gentleman ride away on one of the red and white bikes, his front basket full of groceries. "Very cool idea."

"Have you notice the people walk or bike everywhere? No wonder they're healthier than Americans." Diana was starting to sound like a TV commercial sprouting the benefits of living in Seville.

"Remember, this is southern Spain where the weather is mild and we live in the northeast of the U.S. Biking in snow and ice isn't an easy task."

"Maybe," Diana murmured. "But I have to say, this trip has really opened my eyes to how other cultures thrive."

Kat couldn't disagree. They finished their breakfast and took the metro to the heart of the city, where the sidewalk vendors sold tickets for the boat tours. Tommy was happy to be on the move, running from one location to the other. She gave him room to run, knowing that his boundless energy had to be let loose some time.

They had to wait almost thirty minutes for the next tour, and Kat kept an eye on the time, knowing she needed to head back to the hospital in order to meet Miguel by eleven o'clock. As much as she wanted to enjoy the tour, her stomach was knotted with nerves.

The boat tour wasn't crowded this early in the morning and they had almost the entire upper deck of the boat to themselves. Tommy was thrilled when she lifted him up so that he could see over the railing.

The tour lasted almost an hour, and by the time they disembarked from the boat Kat knew they needed to head back toward the hotel. "No, we need to go this way, Tommy," she called, when he took off down the sidewalk.

Her son ignored her instruction and Diana glanced at her. "I'll get him," she offered.

"No, I'll go." Kat took off after Tommy, who was running and laughing as if they were playing a game of chase. She wanted to be mad at him, but just listening to him laugh made her smile. She gained on him and tried to get his attention. "Tommy, come on, now. We have to go for a ride on the metro."

A woman walking a dog was heading towards them and Tommy suddenly swerved right in front of them. The dog was on a leash but reacted instinctively by jumping up and nipping at him at the same time both Kat and the dog's owner shouted, "No!"

Tommy let out a wail as the dog's owner yanked the dog back and Kat rushed over, picking Tommy up and carrying him out of harm's way. "Shh, it's okay. You're okay, Tommy," she crooned as she tried to examine him for injuries.

Her heart sank when she found puncture marks in the fleshy part of Tommy's arm a few inches above the wrist. The wounds were bleeding, and she glanced up as Diana joined them, feeling like the worst mother on the planet. "The dog bit him."

Diana was a nurse too, and she looked at the wounds with a grimace. "We need to get that cleaned up right away."

"Yeah, but I think he'll need antibiotics too. Do they have clinics here? Or should we go straight to the hospital?" She hated knowing this was all her fault. She shouldn't have let Tommy run around. She should have anticipated something like this.

The dog owner was talking in rapid Spanish, clearly upset about what happened. Kat tried to smile, shaking her head. *"No comprendo Espanol,"* she said.

"They must have clinics," Diana was saying with a frown. But Kat had already made up her mind.

"We'll go to the hospital where Juliet is being cared for. I saw an emergency department there."

"Are you sure that's a good idea?" Diana asked. "We could run into Miguel."

"It's a risk, but Tommy needs good medical care. Miguel is a surgeon—chances are good that we'll be in and out of there without him knowing." And even if they weren't, she wasn't going to worry about Miguel's reaction at seeing them. Tommy's health was far more important.

Diana reluctantly agreed. Kat made sure they stopped in a restroom to wash the dog bite with soap and water, before taking the metro back to the hospital. As they walked into the small emergency room, Kat couldn't help glancing around for any sign of Miguel.

Tommy was, of course, her first concern. Miguel already knew about their son, but she didn't really want him to find out like this that Tommy was here in Seville. She would much rather tell him herself.

The woman at the desk in the emergency room didn't speak any English, and she showed her the dog bite on Tommy's arm, pulling out her Spanish dictionary to find the word for dog. *"Perro,"* she said, demonstrating the action of biting.

"Sí, un momento." The woman spoke to someone else in Spanish, and then took them back to a small exam room. Kat was glad to see the nurse bring in a wash basin.

She relaxed, feeling better now that they were actually getting medical care for Tommy. She glanced at her watch, realizing she was going to be late for her meeting with Miguel.

"I can stay with Tommy if you need me to," Diana offered, sensing her distress.

She slowly shook her head. "No, I can't just leave. Not until I know the wound is clean and that he'll get the antibiotics he needs."

If she had a way to call Miguel, she would. But as she didn't, she could only hope Miguel would have patience and wait for her.

Miguel arrived at the hospital early, unable to contain his excitement. He'd found a flight to Cambridge that was scheduled to leave early the next morning and he'd been tempted to go ahead and book it, except that he wasn't sure when Katerina's return flight was scheduled for. It wouldn't help him to get there before she arrived. Yet he was thrilled that he was closer than ever to meeting his son.

He went up to see how Juliet was doing, hoping that she would soon be stable enough to transfer home. He was pleased to discover that she was following instructions again and hadn't had any more seizures. Her electrolytes were back to normal, which was also a very good sign. He left orders to begin weaning her from the ventilator.

She wasn't quite ready for transfer back home but would be soon.

Since he was early, he decided to check on his other patients. First he checked on DiCarlo, who remained in the I.C.U. The boy was still critical, but his vitals were stable. From there, he headed over to the temporary children's ward to visit with Pedro.

"Hi, Dr. Vasquez," Pedro greeted him. The boy looked a little better, although still a little too pale and drawn. He didn't like seeing the dark circles beneath Pedro's eyes.

"Pedro, how are you feeling?" He crossed the room and checked the nursing notes on the clipboard. "Why aren't you taking pain medication?"

Pedro grimaced. "I don't like the way they make me feel."

"Maybe not, but I don't think you're getting enough rest. Sleep is very important. You will heal much faster if you take some pain medication at nighttime."

The boy flashed a wan smile. "You sound like Miss Kat. That same thing she explained to me yesterday."

Miguel nodded, sensing a bit of puppy love for Katerina in Pedro's gaze. "Katerina is a very smart lady. You would do well to follow her advice."

Pedro was quiet for a moment. "I thought she might come to visit me today."

He saw the stab of disappointment in the boy's eyes. "She is planning to come later, and I'm sure she will visit. I'll need to talk to your mother about keeping you here another day, Pedro."

"She won't care. She is too busy at home with my brothers and sisters."

Miguel wished there was something he could say to make the boy feel better. "That may be true, but you also help her, don't you? I'm sure she misses you."

"Of course." Pedro winced as he shifted in the bed. He put a tentative hand over his incision. "But I don't think carrying my brothers and sisters is a good idea right now."

"No, that would not be good," Miguel agreed. He lifted Pedro's hospital gown and gently peeled back the gauze dressing to examine his wound. The skin around the incision was a little red and he gently palpated the area to make sure there was no pus beneath the skin. There wasn't, but he decided to add yet another antibiotic just to be on the safe side. The risk of infection was high. "Looks good, but you have to take your pain medications. I need you to get up and walk the hallways. Staying in bed all day isn't healthy."

Pedro nodded. "Okay, I will do that."

Miguel called for the nurse and waited until Pedro had taken the ordered pain medication before he moved on to the next patient. He took his time making rounds, wanting to be sure to have everything finished before he spent time with Katerina.

He returned to Juliet's room at exactly eleven o'clock, frowning when he discovered Katerina hadn't arrived yet. He went back out to the nurses' station. "Has Juliet's sister been here to visit?" he asked in Spanish.

"No, Dr. Vasquez, she has not been here yet."

He gave a brief nod, hiding his impatience. He went back to DiCarlo's room, reviewing the chart to make sure his orders had been carried out, secretly watching for Katerina to arrive.

At eleven-thirty his temper began to simmer. Was it possible his worst fears had been realized? That she'd actually taken an earlier flight home in an attempt to hide Tomas from him? He didn't want to believe she would do such a thing, but as the minutes passed with agonizing slowness, he couldn't help believing the worst.

At noon he muttered an oath and left the hospital, calling his driver to take him to Katerina's hotel. He had to know she was still here in Seville. And if she was simply trying to avoid him, he would make certain she never did such a thing ever again.

His driver pulled up in front of the hotel and Fernando had barely put the car in park before Miguel shot out of the back seat, striding purposefully up to the front desk. "I need to speak with Katerina Richardson in room 212," he said.

"I will ring the room," the clerk said. After a few minutes he shrugged and hung up. "I'm afraid there is no answer."

"But she's still a guest here, right?" Miguel persisted. The time was almost twelve-thirty and most of the flights back to the U.S. left early in the morning, but there had been one early-afternoon flight.

"*Sí, señor,* she is still a guest. If you would like to wait, I suggest you have a seat in the lobby."

Miguel was too keyed up to sit in the lobby so he went back outside to let Fernando know he'd be staying for a while. He paced back and forth for several minutes, before taking a seat in the outside café adjacent to the hotel. He ordered a soft drink, although he was in the mood for something far stronger.

Within minutes a familiar voice reached his ears. "Walk, Tommy, don't run. Here, take my hand."

He went still, hardly able to believe his ears. Tommy? Slowly he turned in his seat in time to see Katerina walking up the sidewalk toward the hotel, holding the hand of a young boy.

The same boy in the photograph she'd given him.

Their son!

CHAPTER NINE

MIGUEL slowly rose to his feet, his anger towards Katerina fading as he drank in the sight of his son. Seeing Tomas in person was so much better than a photograph. The boy was so animated, Miguel could barely breathe.

Katerina abruptly stopped in her tracks, going pale when her gaze locked on his. But then she took a deep breath and said something in a low voice to her companion, a woman with dark hair who looked vaguely familiar, as she resumed walking.

He wanted to rush over and sweep his son into his arms, but remembering what Katerina had said yesterday about how he was a stranger to Tomas, it gave him the strength to stay right where he was. It wasn't until Katerina and Tomas came closer that he noticed the white gauze dressing on his son's left forearm.

"Hi, Miguel," she greeted him. "I'm sorry I missed you at the hospital. This is my son, Tommy, who had a small accident. And you remember my friend, Diana Baylor?"

He cleared his throat, striving to play along as if seeing his son in person hadn't completely knocked him off balance. "Of course I remember. Diana, it's good to see

you again. And this is your son, Tommy?" He purposefully used Katerina's dreadful nickname and crouched
down so he was at eye level with the child and wouldn't
seem so intimidating. "Hi, Tommy, my name is Miguel
Vasquez. I'm very happy to meet you."

Tomas stared at him with his large brown eyes and
shrank back toward his mother, as if suddenly shy.
Miguel didn't want to frighten the boy, but at the same
time he couldn't help being frustrated that his son didn't
know him.

He had to remind himself that the situation was his
own fault. Not Katerina's. And certainly not the child's.

"It's okay, Tommy," Katerina said, brushing a hand
over his dark hair. "Miguel is a good friend of mine.
Show him where the dog bit you on the arm."

Tomas held out his arm, the one covered in gauze.
"Bad doggy bit me," he said solemnly.

"Tommy, remember how you ran straight at the
doggy? He only nipped at you because he was scared,"
Katerina said, filling in the gaps of what had happened
for Miguel. "And the emergency-room nurse gave you
a lollipop, didn't she?"

There was a hint of red staining the child's fingers
and teeth as he nodded vigorously. "I'm a good boy."

"I'm sure you were a very good boy," Miguel said
with a smile, relieved to know that his son had received
appropriate medical care for the dog bite. Obviously,
this was the reason Katerina hadn't met him in her
sister's room. A very good excuse, except that it didn't
at all explain why she'd let him believe Tomas was back
in the U.S.

Although he'd assumed that, hadn't he? Katerina
hadn't lied to him, but she had withheld the truth.

He would grant her a pass on this one, but now that she was here, with Tomas, he was determined to spend as much time with his son as possible.

And Katerina had better not try to stand in his way.

Kat had been shocked to find Miguel waiting for her outside their hotel, but by the time she noticed him it was too late as he'd already recognized Tommy. At least now there were no more secrets. She could see Miguel wasn't happy with her, but there wasn't much she could do. This had already been a rough day, and it was barely one o'clock in the afternoon.

"Katerina, do you think the three of us could take a walk?" Miguel asked, as he rose to his feet. "No offense, Diana, but I'd like some time alone with Katerina and Tomas."

Diana crossed her arms over her chest and shrugged, glancing over at her. "Kat? What would you like to do?"

Kat knew her friend would stand by her, if asked, but she'd known that Miguel would want to spend time with his son and there was no good reason to delay. "We'll be fine, Diana. You deserve some down time anyway. Should we meet back here at the hotel in an hour or so? Tommy will be more than ready for his nap by then."

"Sure thing." Diana's gaze was full of suspicion as she glanced over at Miguel. "Nice meeting you again, Dr. Vasquez," she said politely, before turning to walk away.

"I'm getting the sense she doesn't like me very much," Miguel murmured after Diana was out of earshot.

"Diana has always been there for me when I needed her. She was my labor coach and has helped me out more times than I could count, especially on days when I needed child care when Tommy was sick." Her temper flared. She was unwilling to allow him to put down her friend.

Miguel winced as her barb hit home. "In other words, she blames me for not being there with you."

Kat glanced down at Tommy and decided this wasn't the time or the place to argue about the past. "You wanted to take a walk, so let's walk. There's a park not far from here, down the block and across the street."

Miguel nodded and fell into step beside her, keeping Tommy between them. "Yes, I played at that park often as a young boy. See that school there?" He gestured toward the white building across the street. "That's where both my brother and I attended school."

She remembered seeing the young kids all wearing their navy blue and white plaid uniforms running outside at recess. Today was Sunday, so there weren't any children playing now, but she couldn't help wondering if Miguel was insinuating that he wanted Tommy to attend the same school he had. She struggled to remain calm. "Yes, I saw the students playing outside in their uniforms the other day. I was struck by how similar the school was to ours back home."

"Tommy, do you like school?" Miguel asked, turning his attention to their son.

"Yeah." Tommy seemed to be slowly warming up to Miguel. "School is fun."

"Do you play games at school?" Miguel persisted.

"Yep. I play with my friends."

Kat couldn't help smiling as Miguel tried to have a conversation with their son. Too bad that having a rational conversation with an almost four-year-old wasn't easy. Miguel was lucky to get anything more than one- or two-word answers to his questions.

When they reached the park Tommy tugged on her hand so she let him go, allowing him to run over to the water fountain. He looked over the cement edge, peering into the water.

"I can't believe you didn't tell me he was here," Miguel said in a low tone. "Do you realize I almost booked a flight to Cambridge this morning?"

"I'm sorry, Miguel. But Tommy was already asleep and I couldn't risk you marching into the room and waking him up. Besides, I honestly planned on bringing him with me to see you today. Unfortunately Tommy's dog bite prevented me from meeting you at the hospital, as we'd planned."

He sensed the truth in her words and forced himself to relax.

"But why would you book a flight without discussing your plans with me?" she continued. "You can't bulldoze your way into Tommy's life, Miguel. What we want doesn't matter here. The only thing that matters is what's best for Tommy." She turned to face him. "I told you about our son, first because you deserved to know, and second because Tommy deserves a father. I would like to think we could work something out together."

"Joint custody?" Miguel's nose wrinkled in distaste. "Impossible with both of us living in two different countries."

"Not impossible," she countered. "Tommy could visit you in the summer and maybe over the holiday."

"While he lives the rest of the time with you?" Miguel asked. "I hardly think that arrangement is fair."

"Fair? Do you think it was fair to leave me pregnant

and alone? I tried to find you, Miguel, but you certainly didn't try to find me. So don't stand there and try to tell me what is or isn't *fair*."

There was a charged silence between them as Kat tried to rein in her temper. She'd long ago accepted that the night she'd spent with Miguel meant nothing to him. Yet deep down she had to admit there was still a small kernel of resentment.

"You're right, Katerina. I must accept responsibility for my actions."

Miguel's acquiescence shocked her. So much that she didn't have any idea how to respond.

"I can only ask that you give me some time now to get to know my son. And, of course, we will need to agree to some financial arrangements."

"I don't want your money, Miguel," she protested. "We're not rich, but we're not poor either."

"I insist," he said. And she could tell by the edge to his tone that there was no point in arguing.

She let out her pent-up breath in a silent sigh. "Fine. We can discuss that more later." She should be thrilled that he hadn't put up much of a fight. But as Miguel left her side to cross over to where Tommy was digging in the dirt with a stick, she couldn't help feeling a sharp stab of disappointment that apparently they wouldn't be raising their son together.

As a family.

Miguel wanted to protest when Katerina insisted it was time to head back to the hotel, but even he could see that Tomas was getting cranky. He didn't doubt her wisdom regarding the fact that their son needed a nap.

He cared for pediatric patients in the hospital, but

obviously he didn't know the first thing about raising a child. How was he to know that almost four-year-olds still took naps?

"Up, Mama, up," Tomas whined.

"Is your arm hurting you?" she asked, swinging the boy into her arms and cuddling him close.

Miguel wanted, very badly, to be the one to carry his son, but suspected his offer of assistance wouldn't be welcomed by Tomas. He'd started to make friends with his son, but the boy still clung to his mother for comfort.

"Yeah," Tomas said, burying his face against her neck.

"I'll give you something to make your pain go away when we get back to the hotel room, all right?"

"They gave you pain medication?" he asked in surprise.

"No, but I have children's ibuprofen at the hotel, although I suspect he'll practically be asleep by then, anyway."

Katerina was correct. Tomas had closed his eyes and fully relaxed against his mother by the time they approached the hotel lobby.

"Wait for me here," Katerina told him, as she stabbed the button to summon the elevator. "I'll only be a few minutes."

He stepped back, resisting the urge to follow her up to their room. He was surprised she'd asked him to wait, figuring she'd want nothing more than to put distance between them. Although it was possible she simply wanted updated information on Juliet.

True to her word, Katerina returned a few minutes later. "Thanks for waiting, Miguel. I'm planning to head over to the hospital, and figured we could ride the metro together."

"I'm happy to ask Fernando to drive us there," he offered.

A grimace flashed over her features, but then she nodded. "I can't get used to the idea of having someone drive me around, but that's fine."

He called Fernando, and then gestured towards a small park bench sitting beneath the trees. "Have a seat. Fernando will be here in a few minutes."

"Why haven't you learned to drive?" she asked.

"I do know how to drive," he said testily, even though, truthfully, it had been a long time since he'd sat behind the wheel. "Fernando is a former patient of mine. He has a wife and three children. He lost his job after his accident and subsequent surgery, so I hired him."

She didn't say anything until Fernando drove up in Miguel's sleek black car. "That was very kind of you, Miguel."

He shrugged and strode forward, opening the back passenger door for her. Once she was seated inside, he closed the door, went around to the other side and slid in.

"Take us to the hospital, please, Fernando," he said in Spanish.

"Sí, señor," Fernando said, his gaze resting curiously on Katerina.

"Juliet is doing better today," he said, as Fernando pulled away from the curb. "Her electrolytes are all within normal range and she's following instructions again. I left orders this morning to begin weaning her off the ventilator."

Katerina smiled and relaxed against the seat. "I'm

so happy to hear that. I feel bad I haven't been in there to see her yet today. Sounds as if she'll be ready to return home soon."

Now that he knew Tomas was here in Seville, he wasn't so anxious to pronounce Juliet stable enough for transport back to the U.S., but obviously he couldn't keep Juliet, or Katerina for that matter, hostage here. Maybe he'd be booking that plane ticket to Cambridge after all. "Perhaps," he responded slowly. "But I would like to make sure she's off the ventilator first."

She raised a brow, as if she was able to read his mind. But instead of pushing the issue, she changed the subject. "Tell me, how are DiCarlo and Pedro doing?"

"DiCarlo is still in the I.C.U., but his condition is stable," he admitted. "Pedro is doing well, too. He asked about you this morning. I think he was hurt that you didn't come to visit him."

"I'll visit him this afternoon," she promised. "He's a good kid, Miguel. I know his mother has several other children at home, but it breaks my heart to see him lying in that hospital bed all alone."

"Mine, too, Katerina," he murmured. There was no denying the soft spot in his heart he had for the boy. "His father is off for weeks at a time as a truck driver, so she isn't ignoring him on purpose. Regardless, I know he'll be thrilled to see you."

The ride to the hospital didn't take long. He put on his lab coat and then gave Fernando some well-deserved time off, seeing as he was close enough to walk home from the hospital.

"I'd like to see Juliet first," Katerina said as they entered the elevator.

"Of course." Several of the staff greeted him as they

walked down the hallway of the I.C.U., and if they were surprised to see him once again with Katerina, they didn't say anything to his face. No doubt, there was plenty of gossip going on behind his back and he was glad no one else knew about Tomas.

"Hey, sis, I'm back," Katerina said, as she crossed over to Juliet's bedside. "I'm sorry I couldn't be here earlier, but Tommy was bitten by a dog and I had to bring him to the emergency room."

Miguel was pleasantly surprised when Juliet opened her eyes and turned her face to look at Katerina.

"Juliet! You're awake!" Katerina took her sister's hand and leaned over to press a kiss on her forehead. "I was so worried about you."

Juliet looked as if she wanted to talk, but the breathing tube prevented her from making a sound. Before Miguel could step forward, Katerina took control.

"Don't try to talk—you still have that breathing tube in. But don't worry, Dr. Vasquez is trying to get that removed very soon. Which means you have to cooperate with him. You have to show us that you can breathe okay on your own. Can you understand what I'm saying?"

Juliet nodded and pointed to the tube, demonstrating with hand gestures that she wanted it out.

He crossed over to pick up the clipboard hanging off the end of the bed. "Good afternoon, Juliet. I can see here that your weaning parameters look very good."

Katerina glanced at him, her eyes full of hope. "Does that mean we can get the tube out now?"

He hesitated. Juliet had suffered a seizure just twenty-four hours ago, but he'd been convinced all along that she'd be fine once he got her electrolytes under control. "Let me listen to her lungs first," he said, replacing the clipboard and pulling his stethoscope from the pocket of his lab coat. Katerina went down to crank the head of the bed up so that Juliet was sitting upright. He helped her lean forward so that he could listen to her lung sounds.

"Well?" Katerina demanded when he'd finished.

Even though he knew that this meant Juliet would be discharged back to the U.S. soon, he nodded. "Yes, her lungs sound clear. I will get the nurse to come in and assist."

Katerina looked relieved and stood back as he and Maria, Juliet's nurse, took out her endotracheal tube.

"Water," Juliet croaked.

Katerina quickly came over to hold the small plastic cup and straw up so that Juliet could take a sip.

"Hurts," Juliet whispered hoarsely, putting her hand up to her throat.

"I know. Try to rest," Katerina said, putting a hand on her arm. "Breathe slow and easy. You're going to be just fine, Jules."

"Where's Mom?" Juliet asked.

Katerina tossed him a worried look. "Mom's gone, Juliet. She passed away three years ago."

"Remember, she's still recovering from her head injury," he murmured.

"Don't talk, Jules. Just relax."

"I thought you were a dream," Juliet said, rubbing her obviously sore throat.

"I'm not a dream. I came as soon as I heard. I love you, Jules. Very much." Bright tears filled Katerina's eyes.

Miguel slipped out of the room, giving the two sisters

time to be alone. He was pleased with Juliet's progress, even though he knew she still needed time to recover fully. Yet his heart was heavy as he went back to the nurses' station to write new orders. Obviously, if Juliet continued doing this well, she'd be stable enough to move to a regular room in the morning.

That would give him no choice but to deem her stable enough for transportation back to the U.S. as soon as arrangements could be made.

As he wrote instructions for breathing treatments and another chest X-ray in the morning, he vowed to let his boss know he needed a leave of absence as soon as possible. He couldn't bear the thought of Katerina and Tomas leaving so soon. He'd barely spent an hour with his son. And even though he would consider Katerina's proposed custody arrangements, he wasn't going to give up that easily.

There was no way he was going to settle for some long-distance relationship with Tomas. He was going to need that plane ticket after all.

CHAPTER TEN

KAT spent several hours with her sister, enormously relieved that she seemed to be doing so much better. But Juliet was also still very confused, not understanding that she was in Spain or that their mother was gone.

When Kat finally left, she was surprised to find Miguel sitting out at the nurses' station, clearly waiting for her. He rose to his feet when he saw her approach.

"Do you have time to visit Pedro?" he asked, meeting her halfway.

She nodded, ashamed to realize she'd completely forgotten about the young teen. "Of course. But you didn't have to stay, Miguel."

"I wanted to," he said simply.

She was touched by his dedication, even though logically she knew that he was glued to her side because of Tommy more than anything. Still, when he put his hand in the small of her back, her traitorous body reacted by shivering with awareness.

When the elevator doors closed, locking the two of them inside, the tension skyrocketed, his familiar scent filling her head. For a moment she couldn't think of anything except the heated kiss they'd shared.

She sneaked a glance at him from beneath her lashes,

wondering if she was losing her mind. Why did she have this strange attraction to him? She'd avoided personal entanglements with men because she didn't want to be left alone, like her mother had been.

Yet here she was, wishing for another chance with Miguel.

The doors opened and she stepped forward quickly, anxious to put space between them.

Thankfully, Pedro was a good distraction, greeting her enthusiastically. "Miss Kat! I'm so glad you came to visit."

"Hi, Pedro," she said, going over to take his hand in hers. She gave him a mock frown. "I hear you're not taking your pain medication as Dr. Vasquez ordered."

"Yes, I am," he corrected. "I took some earlier today when you were here, Dr. Vasquez. Don't you remember?"

Miguel sighed. "Pedro, that was almost eight hours ago. Do you mean to tell me you haven't taken anything since?"

He ducked his head sheepishly. "I wanted to wait until it was nighttime. You said that sleep was important."

Kat put her hands on her hips. "Pedro, you promised me you would take the pain medication."

"I'm sorry. I will take more tonight. Why are you so late here at the hospital?"

"Well, it was quite a busy morning," she said, as Miguel went out into the hall, probably to flag down Pedro's nurse. "I have a four-year-old son named Tommy and he was bitten by a dog so I had to take him to the emergency department to get antibiotics."

"I didn't know you have a son," Pedro said in surprise, and she belatedly realized she hadn't mentioned Tommy earlier. For a moment Pedro seemed almost disappointed by the news, but then he recovered. "Having a dog bite is very scary. Is he okay?"

"He's fine." She refused to look at her watch, not wanting Pedro to think she was in a hurry. Even though she knew Tommy would be up from his nap and ready to eat dinner soon. "But tell me how you're doing, other than not taking your pain medication."

"I walked today, the way Dr. Vasquez told me to. I went up to visit DiCarlo." Pedro grimaced and shrugged. "But I'm bored here with nothing to do all day. One of the nurses did play a word game with me, but she would only use Spanish words. How am I to learn English without practice?"

She'd noticed the game next to his bed. "How about we play a game before I leave? But our rule will be that we only use English words. Okay?"

"Really? You would do that for me?" He looked so happy that she wished she'd thought of it earlier.

"Of course." She pulled out the game and then sat next to his bed. She couldn't just leave, no matter how much she wanted to see Tommy.

"May I join you?" Miguel asked.

"Yes, more players will be more fun," Pedro said excitedly.

As Miguel pulled up a second chair, she realized Miguel would make a wonderful father.

But even as she acknowledged that truth, she knew there was no way to know for sure if he would be just as good a husband.

At the end of the second game Kat threw up her hands in defeat. "I give up. It's embarrassing to lose to both of you when I'm the one who speaks English."

Miguel flashed a conspiratorial grin at Pedro. "What do you think, amigo? Maybe we should have let her win one."

Pedro nodded. "I think we should have. It's only polite to allow a woman to win."

She rolled her eyes and stood. "I don't need either of you to do me any favors. You each won fair and square. But I'm afraid I need to go. Pedro, I'll visit again tomorrow, okay?"

"Okay. Thank you for staying," Pedro said. "I had much fun."

Miguel also stood. "I'll take you back to the hotel. And, Pedro, take your pain medication, please."

"I will." Pedro looked sad to see them go, but she'd already stayed far longer than she'd planned. She gave him a quick embrace before heading down the hall, anxious to get back to the hotel.

She glanced at Miguel as they waited for the elevator. "I can ride the metro back, there's no reason for you to go out of your way."

He didn't answer until they were inside the elevator. "I would like to see Tommy again, if you wouldn't mind. I thought I would take you all out for dinner."

She wanted to refuse, because being around Miguel was wearying. She was constantly on edge, trying not to let her true feelings show. But glancing up at him and seeing the hope in his eyes, she found she couldn't say no. "Tommy can't wait that late to eat. We usually have dinner at six or six-thirty."

"That's fine with me." When the elevator doors opened on the lobby level, he once again put his hand in the small of her back, gently guiding her. "I will take every moment possible to see my son."

She nodded, realizing with a sense of dread that they would have to make more specific plans for the future, especially now that her sister was doing better. How much longer would Juliet be allowed to stay in Seville? Probably not long. She swallowed hard and tried not to panic.

She wasn't surprised to see that Fernando was waiting outside for them. Now that she knew the reason Miguel had hired him, she found she was happy to have him drive them around. *"Buenos noches,* Fernando," she greeted him.

He flashed a wide smile. *"Buenos noches, señorita."*

"And that's pretty much the extent of my Spanish," she muttered wryly, as she slid into the back seat.

"I'd be happy to teach you," Miguel murmured after he climbed in beside her. "Tomas should learn both languages too."

She bit back a harsh retort, turning to gaze out the window instead. Her anger wasn't entirely rational, yet the last thing she needed was Miguel telling her how to raise her son.

Their son.

Her lack of sleep the night before caught up with her and tears pricked her eyelids. Telling Miguel about Tommy had been the right thing to do so there was no reason to be upset.

"Katerina, what is it? What's wrong?" Miguel asked. He reached over to take her hand and she had to struggle not to yank it away. "Becoming bilingual is a good thing. If my mother hadn't taught me English, I would not have been given the opportunity to study abroad. We never would have met."

And if they hadn't met, Tommy wouldn't exist.

She momentarily closed her eyes, struggling for control. "Miguel, can't you understand how difficult this is for me? Tommy has been my responsibility for almost four years. I was pregnant and alone. I did the best I could. Now it seems like you're planning to barge in and do whatever you want. Without bothering to consult with me."

His hand tightened around her. "Katerina, I am more sorry than you'll ever know about how I left you alone. I will always regret not keeping in touch with you after leaving the U.S. And not just because of the time I missed getting to know my son. But because I realize now how much I missed you."

She sniffed and swiped her free hand over her eyes. "You don't need to flatter me, Miguel. If I hadn't shown up here to visit my sister, we wouldn't have met again. You never would have tried to find me."

There was another long pause. "Katerina, do you believe in fate? Believe that some things just happen for a reason?" His husky voice was low and compelling. "It's true that my dream was to join Doctors Without Borders, and if not for the difficulties with my brother, I probably would not have been here when your sister required emergency care. But I was here. And you arrived with our son. What else could this be if not fate?"

"Coincidence." Even as she said the word, she knew it wasn't entirely true. Was there really some cosmic force at play here? Drawing the two of them together after all this time? She generally believed that hard work and taking responsibility for your choices was the way to get ahead, but she couldn't totally renounce Miguel's beliefs.

"Fate, Katerina," Miguel whispered. "I believe we were meant to be together."

Together? As in as a family? She didn't know what to say to that, and luckily Fernando pulled up in front of her hotel. She gratefully tugged her hand from Miguel's grasp and reached for the doorhandle. "*Gracias,* Fernando," she said, before climbing hastily from the car.

But as quick as she was, Miguel was that much faster. He caught her before she could bolt and gently clasped her shoulders in his large hands. "Katerina, please talk to me. Tell me what has caused you to be so upset?"

She tipped her head back and forced herself to meet his gaze. "I'm more overwhelmed than upset, Miguel. And I'm not sure how you can stand there and claim we were meant to be together. We're not a couple. We're simply two adults who happen to share a child."

One of his hands slid up from her shoulder to cup her cheek. "You can't deny what is between us, querida."

She was about to tell him not to call her darling, but he quickly covered her mouth with his, silencing her with a toe-curling kiss.

She told herself to pull away, even lifted her hands to his chest to push him, but instead her fingers curled in his shirt, yanking him closer as she opened for him, allowing him to deepen the kiss.

All the pent-up emotions she'd tried so hard to ignore came tumbling out in a flash of pure desire. She forgot they were standing on the sidewalk in front of the hotel. Forgot that Fernando was still there, watching them with a huge, satisfied grin.

Forgot that she wasn't going to open herself up to being hurt again.

Everything fell away except this brief moment. A stolen fragment of time when they were able to communicate perfectly without words.

"*Querida,* Katerina, I need you so much," he murmured between steaming-hot kisses. "I can't understand how I lived all this time without you."

She pulled back, gasping for breath, bracing her forehead on his chest, wishing she could believe him. Wishing he'd felt a tenth of what she'd felt for him back then.

"Kat?" the sound of Diana's shocked voice had her jumping away from Miguel.

"Good evening, Diana. Hello, Tommy." Miguel smoothly covered the awkward pause. "Katerina and I were just about to ask you both to join us for dinner."

Kat avoided Diana's accusing gaze as she went over and gathered her son close. "Hi, Tommy, I'm sorry to be gone so long. Are you hungry?"

Tommy nodded. "I'm starving."

"Well, then, let's get going," Miguel said. "I understand there is an American restaurant nearby that serves great food, including hamburgers."

As much as she enjoyed the tangy bite of Spanish food, the thought of a simple American meal was tempting. "We can go somewhere else," she offered.

"Actually, other than smaller places that serve only *tapas*, the main restaurants don't open this early," Miguel said with a note of apology.

"I'm all in favor of having good old-fashioned hamburgers," Diana said. "But let's hurry, okay? Tommy's bound to get cranky if he doesn't eat soon."

Kat couldn't help feeling guilty all over again. She

shouldn't have stayed at the hospital so long. And she really, really shouldn't have kissed Miguel again.

The American restaurant was within walking distance, so Miguel sent Fernando away for a couple of hours. Diana's sour mood evaporated as they enjoyed their meal. When they were finished, Miguel took Tommy over to play a video game, leaving the two women alone.

"Kat, do you think it's smart to get emotionally involved with Miguel?" Diana asked in a low voice.

"I'm already emotionally involved with him, Diana," she responded wearily. "He's Tommy's father, remember? It's not like I can avoid him."

"Avoiding him is very different from having sex with him."

"It was a kiss, Diana." Although she suspected that if they'd been somewhere private, without the added responsibility of caring for Tommy, nothing would have stopped them from making love. "Besides, we'll be going home pretty soon. Juliet woke up and is off the breathing machine. She's still confused, but she's doing a lot better. I'm certain she'll be stable enough to be transferred home very soon."

"Already?" Diana looked disappointed with the news. "But we've hardly had time to sightsee."

"I know. I'm sorry." She did feel bad that Diana had been stuck babysitting Tommy. "Maybe tomorrow I can take Tommy to the hospital to visit Juliet, giving you time to go see the cathedral. I hear it's spectacular."

"All right. But what about Miguel? What's he going to do?"

Good question. "I'm not sure, but I suspect he'll

come visit me and Tommy in Cambridge. After that, I just don't know."

Diana was silent for a moment. "Are you going to move to Seville?"

"No!" Kat stared at her friend in shock. "Of course not. What on earth gave you that idea?"

Before Diana could respond, Miguel and Tommy returned to the table. "We blew things up," Tommy said excitedly. "Bang, bang, bang!"

Kat grimaced and glanced at Miguel, who didn't look the least bit repentant. "Tommy has very good hand-eye coordination," he said proudly. "We scored many points."

They left the restaurant a little while later so that Miguel could enjoy this time with his son. They went for a long walk, enjoying the warm night air.

When they returned to the hotel, Tommy was definitely looking tired. "I'll take him upstairs, he'll need a bath before bed," Diana said.

Kat enjoyed giving Tommy his bath, but before she could utter a protest, Miguel spoke up. "Thank you, Diana. I have a few things to discuss with Katerina."

"No problem," Diana said with false brightness. "Say goodnight to your mom, Tommy."

"G'night." Tommy held out his chubby arms for a hug and a kiss. And then he shocked her by reaching over to give Miguel a hug and a kiss too.

"Goodnight, Tomas," Miguel murmured, as he finally set Tommy down on the sidewalk.

They stood for several moments until Diana and Tommy had gone into the elevator of the hotel. Kat rubbed her hands over her arms, suddenly chilled in her short-sleeved blouse and Capri pants, uncertain what exactly Miguel wanted to talk about.

"Katerina, would you join me for a drink?" Miguel asked, as Fernando pulled up.

A drink? Or something more? The kiss they'd shared simmered between them and suddenly she knew he planned to pick up where they'd left off before Diana had interrupted them.

"Please?" He reached over to take her hand in his.

She hesitated, feeling much like she had four and a half years ago when Miguel had asked her out after losing their young patient. But she was older now, and wiser. She shouldn't be a victim to her hormones.

When he lifted her hand and pressed a kiss to the center of her palm, her good intentions flew away.

"Yes, Miguel," she murmured. "I'd love to."

CHAPTER ELEVEN

MIGUEL could barely hide the surge of satisfaction when Katerina agreed to have a drink with him. He took her hand and turned to head outside where Fernando was waiting inside the car parked out at the curb.

"Where are we going?" she asked, when they stepped outside into the warm night air.

"My place will provide us with the most privacy," he murmured, gently steering her towards the car. When she stiffened against him, disappointment stabbed deep. "Unless you'd rather go somewhere else?"

He practically held his breath as she hesitated. Finally she shook her head and prepared to climb into the back seat of the car. "No, that's okay. Your place is fine," she agreed.

His relief was nearly overwhelming, and as he rounded the car to climb in beside her, it took every ounce of willpower he possessed not to instruct Fernando to break the speed limit to get to his apartment as soon as possible. Once he was seated beside her, he reached over and took her hand. "I want you to know, Katerina, I think you have done an amazing job with raising our son."

She glanced at him in surprise. "For some reason, I keep expecting you to be angry with me."

No, he was only angry with himself. "After tonight it is easier for me to understand your desire to protect Tomas from being hurt." He'd been surprised at the strong surge of protectiveness he'd felt when he'd spent time with his son this evening. "But I hope you can also trust me enough to know I would never willingly do anything to upset him."

"I do trust you, Miguel." Her soft admission caused the tension to seep from his shoulders, allowing him to relax against the buttery-soft leather seats. "Somehow we'll find a way to work this out."

He wanted to do more than to just work things out, but he refrained from saying anything that might cause an argument, unwilling to risk ruining their fragile truce. He wanted this time they had together to be special. So he kept her hand in his, brushing his thumb across the silky smoothness of her skin.

Katerina was always beautiful to him, no matter what she wore. Even dressed casually, in a short-sleeved green blouse that matched her eyes and a pair of black knee-length leggings that displayed her shapely legs, she was breathtaking.

Fernando pulled up in front of his apartment and he reluctantly let her go in order to open the door to climb out. She didn't say anything as they made their way up to his apartment. Once inside, he crossed over to the small kitchen. "What would you like to drink?" he asked.

"Um, a glass of red wine would be nice," she said, clutching her hands together as if nervous.

"Excellent choice." He pulled out a bottle of his favorite Argentinean wine from the rack and quickly removed the cork before pouring them two glasses. She stood awkwardly in the center of the living room as he approached and handed her the glass.

"I feel like I should make a toast," he murmured as he handed her one glass and tipped his so that the rims touched. "To the most beautiful mother in the world."

She blushed and rolled her eyes, taking a step backwards. "Exaggerate much?" she asked, her tone carrying an edge.

He wasn't exaggerating at all, but he could see she was struggling to hold him at arm's length, as if uncomfortable with drawing attention to herself. Or believing in herself.

That thought brought him up short, and he paused, wondering if his leaving so abruptly after their magical night together had caused her to lose some of her self-confidence.

If so, he'd wronged her in more ways than one.

"Katerina, why do you doubt my feelings?" he asked softly. "Surely my attraction to you is no secret by now. Four and a half years ago I succumbed to the keen awareness between us. And obviously that same attraction hasn't faded over time."

"But you still left," she pointed out.

"Yes, but if my father hadn't suffered his stroke, I'm sure that we would have continued to see each other." He knew that he wouldn't have possessed the strength to stay away. Even for her sake.

She eyed him over the rim of her wineglass. "You don't know that, Miguel. Rumor amongst the O.R. staff was that you didn't want any emotional attachments because you weren't planning to stay in the U.S. I doubt that you would have changed your mind about that, even for me."

He shouldn't have been surprised to know his plans had been fodder for gossip, but he was. There had been many women who'd expressed interest in him, and he'd often used that line to avoid entanglements. "I can't deny that I wasn't planning to stay. I didn't keep my dream of joining Doctors Without Borders a secret. And even then I was hesitant to start a relationship with an American."

She looked shocked by his revelation. "Why?"

He wished he hadn't gone down this path. "My mother was American and she wasn't happy living here in Spain. But that part isn't important now. Suffice it to say that had I stayed three more months to finish my trauma surgery fellowship, I would have been there when you discovered you were pregnant. If not for my father's stroke, we could have handled things very differently." He wasn't sure exactly how, but at least he would have known about his son.

She stared at him for several long moments. "Maybe. But playing the what-if game isn't going to help. We can't go back and change the past."

"I don't want to change the past, Katerina," he countered. "I wouldn't give up Tomas for anything. Yet this evening isn't about our son. It is about you and me."

Her lips parted in shock, making a small O, and she carefully set down her wineglass as if afraid she might drop it. "I don't understand."

Obviously he wasn't being very articulate. "Perhaps you would allow me to show you what I mean instead."

When she didn't voice an objection, he stepped closer and drew her deliberately into his arms. He didn't pounce but stared deep into her eyes so that she could read his intent and see the desire he felt for her. When she still didn't utter a protest, he lowered his mouth to capture hers.

She held herself stiffly in his arms, and just when he thought she would push him away, she softened against him and opened her mouth, welcoming his kiss.

Desire thundered in his chest and he gathered her closer still, pulling her softness firmly against his hard muscles and tipping her head back so that he could explore her mouth more fully.

He forced himself to take his time, savoring the exotic taste, when all he really wanted to do was to rip their clothing out of the way so that he could explore every inch of her skin.

"Miguel," she gasped, when he finally freed her mouth in order to explore the sexy curve of her jaw, the hollow behind her ear.

"Say yes, Katerina," he murmured between kisses. He wanted to make love to her, right here, right now. "Say yes."

He continued his leisurely exploration, kissing his way down her neck, dipping further to the enticing valley between her breasts, as if waiting for her answer wasn't killing him.

"Yes, Miguel," she whispered in a ragged voice, arching her back to give him better access to her breasts. "Yes!"

He didn't trust his voice so he swept Katerina up into his arms and strode down the hall to his bedroom, hoping and praying that she wouldn't change her mind.

* * *

Kat didn't allow herself to second-guess her decision, every nerve-ending was on fire for Miguel. She hadn't felt this way since their one and only night together. No other man made her feel as beautiful and desirable as Miguel did.

When he swept her into his arms, she pressed her mouth against the hollow in his neck, nipping and licking, savoring his scent and enjoying the way his arms tightened around her in response.

In his bedroom he flipped on a single lamp and then paused near the bed. He gently slid her body down the front of his so that she could feel the full extent of his desire. She shivered, but not with cold, when he unbuttoned her blouse and shoved the cotton fabric aside, revealing her sheer green bra and then ultimately the matching sheer green panties.

She was grateful she'd worn decent underwear, even though it didn't stay on long. She should have felt self-conscious to be naked before him, but she wasn't. His gaze devoured her as he quickly stripped off his own clothes.

"Katerina, *mi amore*," he muttered as he gently placed her on his bed, before covering her body with his. "I don't deserve you."

She was pretty sure he had that backwards, but then she wasn't thinking at all because he'd lowered his mouth to the tip of her breast. She writhed impatiently beneath him but he took his time, giving equal attention to both breasts before trailing kisses down her abdomen to her belly button. And then lower still.

There was a brief moment when she worried about the faint stretch marks along her lower abdomen, but when he swept long kisses over every single one, the last vestiges of doubt vanished. She was practically sobbing with need when he finally spread her legs and probed deep, making sure she was ready.

"Now, Miguel," she rasped.

His dark eyes glittered with desire but he simply shook his head and dipped his head again, this time replacing his fingers with his tongue. Something he'd done that first time they'd made love.

Her orgasm hit fast and hard, deep shudders racking her body. He quickly rose up, rolled a condom on with one hand before he thrust deep, causing yet another orgasm to roll over her.

She was sure she couldn't take much more, but he whispered to her in Spanish, lifting her hips so they fit more snugly together, gently encouraging her to match his rhythm. Slow and deep at first, and then faster and faster, until they simultaneously soared up and over the peak of pleasure.

Kat couldn't move and not just because of Miguel's body sprawled across hers. Every muscle in her body had the consistency of jelly, making it impossible to move even if she wanted to.

Which she didn't.

After several long moments Miguel lifted himself up and rolled over, bringing her along with him, so that she was now lying fully against him. She rested her head against his chest, listening to the rapid beat of his heart.

The chirping sound of a cellphone broke the silence and she froze, trying to remember if that was how her small disposable cellphone sounded. Was Diana calling because Tommy needed her? Maybe the dog bite on his arm was getting infected?

When Miguel muttered something in Spanish beneath his breath, she realized the call wasn't for her. It
was for him. There was a strong sense of déjà vu as she
remembered the phone call he'd received the morning
after the night they'd spent together. She forced herself
to lift her head, to look at him. "Do you need to get that?
Is that the hospital?"

"I'm not on call tonight," he said with a dark scowl.
"Whoever it is can wait."

After several rings the phone went silent and she
relaxed against him. When she shivered, he pulled up
the sheet and blanket to cover her. She would have been
happy to stay like this with him for the rest of the night,
but she knew she should go back to the hotel in case
Tommy needed her.

She couldn't help thinking about what he'd revealed
earlier about his mother being American and not liking
it here in Spain. She'd known his mother had spoken
fluent English, which had been how he'd picked up the
language so quickly.

But what did this all mean about the future?

A loud buzzer sounded, echoing loudly across the
apartment, startling her. Miguel muttered something
rude before pulling away from her.

He fumbled for his clothing, pulling on his pants before heading out to answer the door. She was grateful
he closed the bedroom door, giving her privacy.

She didn't hesitate but quickly found her clothes and
got dressed, hardly able to contain her curiosity about
who'd come to Miguel's home at ten o'clock at night.
She crossed the room, trying to listen, unsure if she
should go out there or not. When she heard a female

voice speaking in rapid Spanish she froze, the blood draining from her face.

Was it possible that Miguel was actually involved with a woman after all?

Miguel wasn't the least bit happy to see the woman his brother used to date standing on the other side of the door. He tried to rein in his temper. "What do you want, Corrina?"

"Luis is missing, Miguel. I need you to help me find him."

Corrina was a pretty girl with dark wavy hair, who for some unknown, self-destructive reason was still hung up on his brother, despite the fact that Luis had broken her heart more than once.

"Come in," he said rather ungraciously, stepping back to give her room to enter. "How do you know he's missing?"

"He spent last night at my place but this morning he was gone. I've looked everywhere for him, Miguel. He's not at home or working on the olive farm or at any of his usual hang-outs." Corrina's eyes filled with tears. "I'm afraid something has happened to him."

He suppressed a sigh. His brother wasn't exactly known for his tact and could very easily have been looking for an excuse to avoid Corrina. "Did you notify the police?"

"Yes, but they said there's nothing they can do." Corrina stared up at him defiantly. "I know everyone thinks he's avoiding me, but I don't think so. Something is wrong, Miguel. I feel it here," she said, dramatically putting her hand over her heart.

The concern in her eyes was real enough, but he

didn't share her fears. Besides, he didn't want to end things so abruptly with Katerina. Not again. Not when their time here in Seville was so limited.

But then his bedroom door opened and Katerina emerged, fully dressed, and with a sinking heart he knew their evening had already come to an end. "Excuse me, I was just leaving," she said, avoiding his gaze as she swung her purse over her shoulder and headed for the door.

"Katerina, wait. This is Corrina Flores, my brother's girlfriend. It seems she believes Luis is missing."

There was a flash of surprise on Katerina's face and she paused, glancing back with concern. He realized she'd assumed the worst, believing Corrina was one of his former lovers. He was frustrated by her lack of trust yet at the same time grimly pleased that she cared enough to be jealous.

"Missing since when?" Katerina asked.

"Just since this morning. I'm sure he's fine, there's no need to rush off." Selfishly, he wanted her to stay, needed her support as he looked for his brother.

She grimaced and toyed with the strap of her purse. "Actually, I really should go, Miguel. I want to be there in case Tommy wakes up. The dog bite may cause him some pain."

He understood, even though he didn't want to let her go. There was so much yet that they needed to discuss before he released Juliet to return home. He'd used the short time they'd had together to make love, rather than planning their future.

Something he couldn't quite bring himself to regret.

"All right, let me call Fernando, he'll drive you back to the hotel. Why don't we plan to get together first thing in the morning? I'll take you and Tommy out for breakfast and then we'll visit your sister."

"Ah, sure. But don't bother Fernando this late," she protested. "I'll take the metro."

"It's no bother. He's probably just finishing dinner and I'll need his assistance myself, anyway." He certainly wouldn't allow her to go back to the hotel alone. And as much as he wanted to spend more time with Katerina, he couldn't bring himself to ignore Corrina's concerns about Luis.

"I hope you find your brother," Katerina murmured.

"I'm sure we will. And it's about time he learns to take responsibility for his actions. Luis can't expect me to keep bailing him out." He didn't bother to hide his annoyance.

Corrina wisely kept silent as he called Fernando and then walked Katerina outside.

"Thank you, Katerina, for an evening I'll never forget," he whispered, hugging her close and giving her another heated kiss.

"Goodnight, Miguel," she murmured, breaking away from his embrace and climbing into the back seat of the car. He couldn't help feeling as if he'd said something wrong when she ignored him to chat with Fernando.

Grinding his teeth together, he had little choice but to shut the car door and step back, allowing Fernando to drive Katerina away. He stared after the red taillights, fighting the urge to demand Fernando return at once so he could figure out what had caused Katerina to be upset.

Annoyed with himself, and his brother, he reluctantly turned and went back upstairs to where Corrina waited. All he could think was that he'd better not find out that his brother was simply trying to avoid his old girlfriend or he wouldn't hesitate to box Luis's ears.

This was the second time his family problems had pulled him away from Katerina. And he was determined that it would also be the last.

CHAPTER TWELVE

THE following morning, Kat was surprised when Miguel didn't show up as promised. As Tommy was hungry, she and Diana took him out for breakfast. As they enjoyed fresh pastries, she couldn't help wondering if Miguel had found his brother or if he'd stayed up the entire night, searching for him.

"I'll take Tommy with me to see Juliet now that she's doing better," she offered. "That way you can go and see the cathedral before we have to leave."

"If you're sure you don't mind," Diana said, before shoving the last bit of pastry in her mouth.

"I don't mind at all." In truth she would have loved to see the cathedral too, but coming to Seville hadn't been a vacation for her. She'd only come because her sister had been injured.

And there was a strong possibility she'd be back in the not-too-distant future if Tommy was going to be spending time with his father. She glanced around, silently admitting that, as beautiful as Seville was, she couldn't really imagine living here.

Once again she found herself thinking about Miguel's mother. Clearly he'd avoided dating anyone back in the

U.S. because he didn't plan to relocate to the U.S. on a permanent basis.

And considering the problems he'd had with his brother, she couldn't imagine him changing his mind. Which left them where? Back to a joint custody but separate countries type of arrangement?

She would have been satisfied with that before, but not any more. Not since making love with Miguel. She wanted it all.

She wanted a true family.

"Mama, go. Now," Tommy said insistently.

"Okay, I'm ready." She paid the bill and then used a wet napkin to clean up Tommy's sticky fingers. "We're going to go visit Aunt Juliet. Won't that be fun?"

He nodded vigorously and dropped from the chair, making her grin at the amount of energy radiating off his tiny frame. Had Miguel been the same way as a child? She suspected he had been.

She started walking toward the nearest metro stop, holding Tommy's hand as they took the stairs down to the lower level. There was a strong possibility that if Miguel had gotten home late, he'd decided to simply meet her at the hospital.

Suspecting that her sister might have already been moved out of the I.C.U., she stopped at the front desk. "*¿Donde esta mi hermana*, Juliet Campbell?" Where is my sister?

There was a flood of Spanish that she didn't understand. When she looked blankly at the woman, she wrote down the room number and handed it to Kat.

"*Gracias,*" she murmured, looking down at Juliet's new room number, 202. "This way, Tommy," she said, steering him toward the elevator.

Juliet was sitting up at the side of the bed, finishing her breakfast, when they entered. Kat was very relieved to find her sister looking much better. She crossed the room to give Juliet a hug. "Hey, sis, how are you feeling today?"

"Kat! You brought Tommy, too?"

"Yes. Tommy, you remember Aunt Juliet, right? Can you say hi to her?"

"Hi," Tommy said, and then ducked his head, refusing to relinquish Kat's hand.

"Hi, Tommy. It's good to see you. Wanna see my cast?" Juliet said, moving the blankets off her right leg.

Ever curious, the cast was enough to draw Tommy forward. He knelt beside Juliet's right leg, lifting his fist to knock on the fiberglass cast.

"Don't worry, that's the one part of my body that doesn't hurt," Juliet muttered dryly.

"Are you in pain, Jules?" she asked, moving closer. "Dr. Vasquez told me that you had some cracked ribs, too."

"Everything hurts," her sister admitted. "And don't bother asking me what happened, I honestly can't remember."

"Don't worry, I'm sure your memory will return in time." Although there was certainly no guarantee. The numerous bruises and lacerations were already starting to fade, but Kat could well imagine that her sister's muscles were also still sore.

She wanted to ask her sister more questions, to make sure Juliet wasn't as confused as she had been yesterday, but they were interrupted by a knock at the door.

"Good morning, Juliet," a plump woman greeted her

sister. "And you must be Katerina Richardson. Nice to meet you in person."

Kat stared at the woman, certain she hadn't met her before. She would have remembered someone speaking English, for one thing. The familiarity of the stranger's greeting was unnerving.

"My name is Susan Horton and I'm the study abroad program coordinator. I'm the one who contacted you about Juliet's accident, remember?"

Of course she remembered now. So much had happened since the first day she'd arrived, she'd completely forgotten about the woman. "Yes."

"I'm glad you're both here," Susan said, "because we need to make immediate arrangements for Juliet's transfer back to the United States."

Kat tried to hide her shock. "So soon? Don't we need Dr. Vasquez to sign off on Juliet's case first?"

"There's another doctor covering for Dr. Vasquez today, and he's already given his approval. So, if you'd come with me, we'll begin making the necessary arrangements."

"Right now?" Kat cast a helpless glance toward her sister, before following Susan out of the room. She could only hope Miguel would show up soon or they might have to leave without saying goodbye.

Miguel shouldn't have been surprised to find Luis in jail. His friend, Rafael Hernandez, had finally called him to let him know Luis had been driving under the influence. He'd called Corrina to make sure she knew, but then he debated with himself over whether or not to post Luis's bond. It wasn't the money but the principle of bailing his brother out of trouble again.

In the end they wouldn't let him post bail until the morning. Which ruined his plans to meet Katerina and Tomas for breakfast.

"Thanks for picking me up," Luis said, wincing at the bright light.

"Luis, you're either going to kill yourself or someone else if you don't stop this," Miguel said with a heavy sigh. "You'd better figure out what you want to do with the rest of your life, and quick."

"Don't worry about me, just go on your stupid mission trip," his brother muttered, scrubbing his hand over his jaw.

"I'm not going to Africa, I'm going back to the U.S., at least temporarily." He glanced over to where Luis was slouched in the corner of the car. "I have a son, Luis. A son I didn't know about until just a few days ago. But he and his mother live in Cambridge, Massachusetts."

Luis lifted his head and peered at him with bloodshot eyes. "You're going to live there? With them?"

He hadn't realized until just now how much he wanted to be with Katerina and Tomas on a full-time basis, but he wasn't keen on living in the U.S. for ever. Yet he couldn't ask Katerina to move here, not when she had her sister to worry about. And even once Juliet was better, he didn't want to risk the same thing happening to Katerina that had happened to his mother. He couldn't wait to see Katerina and talk to her about his idea of moving to the U.S. temporarily.

"I'm not sure where I want to live, but I do want to be a part of my son's life," he said slowly. "But I can't leave you like this, Luis. You need help. Professional help."

His brother was silent for a long moment. "Will you let me sell the olive farm?" he asked.

Shocked by the question, Miguel nearly swerved into the other lane. "You want to sell the farm? Why? What will you do to support yourself?"

"I've always wanted to work in construction," Luis admitted. "I hate farming. I want to build things. Houses, buildings."

Build things? He turned to stare at his brother, stunned by his revelation. Granted, Luis had built a new warehouse on the farm last year, but all this time he'd had no clue that his brother hated farming.

"Are you sure about this, Luis?" he asked. "Once you sell the farm, there's no going back."

"I'm sure. Corrina's father wants me to help in his construction company. I've been trying to get up the nerve to ask you about selling the farm."

"Do you think working for her father is wise? You haven't treated Corrina very well these past few years."

"I know I've made a mess of my life," Luis said in a low voice. "But I really want to do this, Miguel. I know the farm has been in our family for generations, but I feel trapped there. It's too far from town, for one thing. I realized when I built the new warehouse that I gained more satisfaction from doing that than all the years I've spent picking olives. And I care about Corrina. I kept breaking things off because I couldn't imagine raising a family on the farm. I keep remembering how Mom died there."

He couldn't hide his surprise yet at the same time he understood how Luis felt. "Why didn't you say something sooner?" he asked.

"I was afraid you would be upset. You and Papa always talked about how the Vasquez farm had sustained families for generations. That it was a family tradition."

Miguel winced, knowing Luis was right. He hadn't stayed on the farm, choosing to go into medicine at the university as soon as he'd been able to. It shamed him to realize he hadn't ever asked Luis what he wanted to do. "I'm sorry, Luis. I never realized how badly you wanted to leave the farm, too."

"So you're not mad?" Luis asked, looking pathetically eager despite his rough night in a jail cell. "Because Señor Guadalupe once asked me about selling. I would like to call him to see if he's still interested. If he will buy the farm, I can start working for Corrina's father right away."

"I'm not mad, Luis," he said. "By all means, call Señor Guadalupe. If he's not interested, let me know. I'll see what I can do to help."

Fernando pulled into the driveway of the Vasquez olive farm, and for a moment Miguel simply sat there, staring out at the rows upon rows of olive trees.

It was a little sad to think of selling the farm to strangers, yet at the same time he was a doctor. A surgeon. Saving lives was important and satisfying. He'd never planned on working the farm himself, yet had he subconsciously forced Luis into the role because he hadn't wanted to let go of the past?

The idea was humbling.

"Thanks for the ride," Luis said as he climbed from the car.

"Let me know when you have a buyer lined up."

"I will." Luis looked positively happy and waved as Fernando backed out of the driveway. He then headed into the house.

"Are you really moving to the U.S.?" Fernando asked from the front seat.

He met the older man's gaze in the rear-view mirror. "Yes, for a while, Fernando."

Fernando nodded. "Señor Vasquez, I wonder if you would be so kind as to give me a reference before you go so that I can apply for a job."

Miguel mentally smacked himself in the forehead. Why hadn't he thought of this earlier? "Fernando, how do you feel about being an olive farmer?"

"I would be willing to learn."

He grinned and reached for his cellphone. Everything was going to work out just fine. Luis didn't need to bother Señor Guadalupe after all.

Fate had helped him out once again.

Kat could only sit in stunned silence as Susan Horton finalized her sister's travel arrangements. Everything was set. They would be leaving Seville by one-thirty that afternoon. It was the latest flight out, and they wouldn't arrive back in the U.S. until nearly ten o'clock at night, but when Kat had tried to protest, Susan had remained firm that Juliet would be on that flight, regardless of whether or not Kat wanted to go with her. Given that choice, she'd quickly arranged for additional seating for herself, Diana and Tommy.

She'd also called Diana right away, arranging to meet back at the hotel immediately. The airport was only thirty minutes away, but they would need to get there by eleven-thirty, two hours before departure time, and it was already almost ten now. They had just over an hour to get back to the hotel, pack and check out of the hotel.

She left the hospital, carrying Tommy to make better time. Luckily the metro ran often and it didn't take her long to get to the hotel. She didn't waste any time tossing stuff into their suitcases.

"I can't believe they're making us leave today," Diana said as she helped Kat pack Tommy's things. "Like letting your sister stay one more day would make such a big difference?"

"I know. Although I suspect if they had come to visit Juliet on Sunday, they would have made us leave on an earlier flight."

"I suppose. Okay, that's everything," Diana said. They'd worked like speed demons, and had managed to get everything together in twenty-minutes flat.

Kat made one more sweep of the room, making sure Tommy hadn't left anything behind. "All right, let's haul all this down to the lobby so we can check out."

"What about Miguel?" Diana asked, as they crowded into the elevator.

"As stupid as it sounds, I don't have his phone number." Miguel was on Kat's mind, especially after the night they'd shared, and because they still hadn't made plans for the future. Kat had hoped that Miguel would show up at the hospital before they left, but she hadn't seen him. And now they'd be leaving the hotel shortly. "I'm sure he'll figure out what happened once he discovers Juliet has been discharged." She wished she didn't have to leave without saying goodbye, though.

"Did you guys decide on some sort of joint custody arrangement?" Diana asked.

"I'm not sure if we really agreed on that or not," she said truthfully. She hadn't told Diana about the evening she'd spent making love with Miguel either. Had she done the right thing by saying yes to Miguel? If only she'd waited. Obviously, it would have been smarter of her to avoid getting emotionally involved. Again.

"Stay here with Tommy while I check out." Kat crossed over to the counter, asking for the bill and for a taxi to take them to the airport where they would meet up with Juliet.

They arrived at the small Seville airport with time to spare, so they stopped for something to eat. Kat could barely concentrate—she kept scanning the area, looking for any sign of Miguel.

Where was he? Surely once he'd gone to the hospital and realized Juliet had been discharged, he would know to come and find her at the airport. Something bad must have happened to Luis for him to not be here.

Unless he'd changed his mind about being a part of Tommy's life?

No, she couldn't believe that. Not after the way he'd made love to her. Not after everything they'd shared.

Although she couldn't help coming back to the fact that he'd never wanted to be with an American. Like her.

"Kat, look, there's your sister."

She looked over in time to see Susan Horton pushing Juliet in a wheelchair through the small terminal, followed by an airport employee wheeling Juliet's large suitcase. "Watch Tommy for a minute, okay?" Kat said, before hurrying over to her sister.

"Hey, Jules, how are you?" Kat tried not to be upset at the way they were being rushed out of there. "Are you in pain?"

"I have her pain medication right here," Susan said before Juliet could answer. The woman's brisk, impersonal attitude made Kat grind her teeth in frustration.

"Now, is there anything else you need? If not, I'll be leaving Juliet in your hands."

Kat wrestled her temper under control. "We'll be fine," she said, taking over the task of pushing Juliet's wheelchair.

"Are you ready to go through security?" Diana asked, holding onto Tommy's hand. They needed the assistance of two airport employees to manage their luggage.

She sighed, glancing back over the crowd of people one more time, wishing more than anything that Miguel would come. But there was still no sign of him. As much as she wanted to wait, getting Juliet and Tommy through the airport security line would be difficult and time-consuming. She didn't dare wait much longer.

"Sure thing. Let's go."

Going through security took far longer than she could have imagined, especially with Juliet needing so much assistance. She tried not to think about the fact that they would have to change planes four times, before arriving at home. Once they were finished with security, they put their carry-on luggage back together and made their way down to their assigned gate.

Diana flopped into one of the hard plastic chairs with a groan. "Somehow, going home isn't nearly as much fun," she muttered.

Kat pasted a smile on her face, unwilling to let on how much she was hurting inside, as she made sure Juliet was comfortable.

She'd really, really, expected Miguel to show up here at the airport. And now that he hadn't—she wasn't sure what to think.

Had he changed his mind about wanting to be a father to Tommy? Did he regret making love to her? She wished she knew more about Miguel's mother. He'd mentioned she'd died several years ago, when he'd still been in high school. Whatever had happened had made him determined not to become emotionally involved with an American.

With her.

Her heart squeezed with pain and tears pricked her eyes as she realized she'd foolishly fallen in love with Miguel.

CHAPTER THIRTEEN

MIGUEL strode into the hospital, knowing he was beyond late. He wasn't due to work today but he knew Katerina would come to visit her sister.

He walked into room 202 and stopped abruptly when he saw an elderly man lying in the bed. He frowned and glanced at the room number, making sure he had the correct one.

After murmuring a quick apology, he spun around and went back to the nurses' station. They must have moved Juliet to a different room for some unknown reason.

But, no, her name wasn't on the board at all. With a frown he picked up the phone, intending to call down to the front desk, when he saw his colleague, Felipe. "Felipe, where's my patient, Juliet Campbell?" he asked.

Felipe turned around. "Miguel, what are you doing here? I thought I was to cover your patients today?"

"You are, but I was actually looking for Juliet's sister, Katerina. What room did Juliet get moved to?"

Felipe looked puzzled. "I discharged her, Miguel. Señora Horton from the study abroad program wanted her to be sent back to the U.S., so I went ahead and gave the discharge order."

"What?" A knot of dread formed in his gut and he grew angry with himself for not anticipating that something like this might happen. He'd known the minute he'd given the orders to have Juliet transferred to a regular room that her time here was limited. "When? How long ago?"

Felipe shrugged. "I'm not sure, maybe two or three hours?"

Three hours? No! He struggled to remain calm as he glanced at the clock. It was almost eleven-thirty already. "Was that when you wrote the order? Or when she actually left?"

"I didn't pay attention," Felipe admitted. "Miguel, what's the problem? Clearly, she was stable enough to travel."

He forced a smile, knowing none of this was Felipe's fault. "I trust your judgment. Excuse me but I need to catch up with them." Before Felipe could say anything more, he left, lengthening his stride to hurry as he called Fernando, instructing his driver to meet him outside.

"We need to stop at home, so I can get my passport. From there we're heading straight to the airport," he said, the moment he slid into the back seat. A few days ago, when he'd reviewed flights out of Seville heading to the U.S., he'd noticed the last flight was at one o'clock in the afternoon.

He grabbed his passport, and not much else. He'd have to buy what he needed once he arrived in the U.S. Back in the car, he called the airline in an attempt to book a seat as Fernando navigated the city streets.

"I'm sorry, but we can't book any more seats at this time," the woman said. "We stop selling tickets two hours before the flight."

He resisted the urge to smack his fist on the counter. "I need to get on that flight. I'm sure you can make an exception."

There was a pause, and he held his breath. "I'll check with my supervisor," she finally said.

He tightened his grip on the phone, willing Fernando to hurry. But the traffic was heavy today, and they were moving at a snail's pace. The airport was normally a thirty-minute drive, and he could only hope and pray that the traffic would break soon. He had to get there in time. He had to!

"I'm sorry, Señor Vasquez. We are not able to sell you a ticket."

He closed his eyes and swallowed a curse. He forced himself to be polite. "Thank you for checking."

"Problems?" Fernando asked, catching his gaze in the rear-view mirror.

He shook his head. "Just get to the airport as soon as possible. I want to see Katerina before she leaves."

He'd have to buy a ticket in order to get past security, but at this point he was willing to do anything to see Katerina, talk to her one more time before she and Tommy boarded that plane. The panic that gripped him by the throat surprised him. He hadn't realized until she was gone just how much he cared about Katerina.

It wasn't just that he missed his son. Katerina would agree to share custody, he knew. But at this moment he didn't care about custody arrangements.

He cared about Katerina.

When the airline attendant asked for all passengers needing help to board, Katerina stood up. "I think that means us. Are you ready to go, Juliet?"

"Sure." Her sister already looked exhausted and they hadn't even started their long flight. Kat couldn't suppress a flash of anger toward Susan Horton for rushing Juliet out so fast. As Diana had said earlier, what was one more day?

Maybe she should have put up more of a fight, even though Susan Horton hadn't been interested in listening to reason. Besides, it was too late now. She bent over to release the locks on the wheelchair and then pushed her sister forward, leaving Diana and Tommy to follow.

Getting Juliet safely transferred into an aisle seat was no easy task. The only good thing was that they were given a spot in the front row of a section, leaving plenty of room for her leg that was still in a cast. Juliet groaned under her breath as she used the crutches, favoring her right side where she had her cracked ribs.

They were both sweating by the time they were finally settled. Diana and Tommy were immediately behind them, which was a mixed blessing.

"Tommy, stop kicking the seat," she said for the third time, trying not to snap at him. "It feels like you're kicking me in the back."

"Sorry, Mama."

"Do you want me to switch places with him?" Diana asked, leaning forward anxiously as if sensing her frayed nerves.

"No, he'll only end up kicking Juliet." She was tense and crabby but did her best not to let it show as her bad mood certainly wasn't Tommy's fault. Or Diana's. Or Juliet's.

She was upset because she'd really expected Miguel to come to the airport to find her. But for all she knew, he was still looking for his brother. She tried to tell herself that this way was for the better. Things had moved pretty fast between she and Miguel so a little time and distance would likely be good for both of them.

Yet regret at leaving Seville so abruptly filled her chest, squeezing her lungs. There hadn't been time to say goodbye to Pedro. As the plane slowly filled up with passengers, she wondered how Miguel would manage to find her in Cambridge.

If he decided to come at all.

Miguel purchased a ticket to Madrid and managed to get through security in time to find Katerina's plane had just started to board. He rushed over to the gate and swept his gaze over the group of passengers. After several long moments he was forced to admit they must have already boarded. Which made sense, as Juliet had a broken leg and had probably needed help to get into her seat.

He went up to the desk. "Excuse me, but I need to speak to passenger, Katerina Richardson. I think she may already be on the plane."

"I'm sorry, but there's nothing I can do. You're not allowed on the plane without a boarding pass," the attendant said with a false smile.

So close. He was so close! "Just five minutes. You could ask her to come back out here and I promise she'll be back on the plane in five minutes."

"I'm sorry, Señor, I can't help you." The woman's false smile faded and he could see a security guard making his way over. She glanced past him as if he weren't there. "May I help you?" she asked the next person in line.

Miguel quickly left the counter, preferring to avoid

the security guard. He still had a ticket to Madrid, and from there he was sure there would be a better selection of flights to the U.S. But considering his flight didn't leave for two more hours, he knew there was no chance in the world of arriving in time to see Katerina or Tomas.

He called his police friend, Rafael, asking for help in finding Katerina's address back in Cambridge. Rafael called him back within twenty minutes with the address. At least that was one problem solved.

With a heavy sigh he crossed over to his own gate and settled into one of the uncomfortable plastic chairs. He wished more than ever that he'd spent more time talking to Katerina last night, rather than making love. Not that he regretted that part. He just wished they would have talked first.

He could only hope she would be willing to listen, to give him another chance, once he arrived in the U.S.

Nineteen and a half hours later Kat, Tommy and Juliet finally arrived home. Diana had gone to her own apartment and Kat couldn't blame her friend for wanting to sleep in her own bed.

Kat was exhausted, but she was far more worried about her sister. Juliet's pain had gotten worse the more they'd moved, and changing planes and then taking a train back to Cambridge had obviously been too much for her.

She was tempted to take Juliet straight to the hospital, but since the time was close to midnight, she decided against it. Rest would be the best thing for her sister, so she helped Juliet get into bed before giving her more pain medication. She'd have to arrange for follow-up doctor's appointments in the morning.

Unfortunately, Tommy wasn't nearly as tired. Just like on the way over to Spain, he'd slept on the plane and she wanted to burst into tears when he started bouncing on his bed.

After several minutes of fighting she gave up. "Okay, fine, let's go downstairs and watch a movie."

She put in a DVD and stretched out on the couch, holding her son in front of her, determined to get in at least a short nap. With any luck, Tommy would be tired enough to sleep after the movie was over.

Between Tommy's messed-up sleep cycle and her sister's pain, Kat only managed to get about four hours of sleep. Not nearly enough, but she would just have to make do. After making breakfast and encouraging Juliet to eat, she spent a good hour on the phone, making arrangements for Juliet to be seen by a doctor who specialized in head injuries.

Her sister was still slightly confused, but she was certainly better than she'd been when the breathing tube had been removed. At least she wasn't asking about their mother any more.

There was a loud knock at her front door at ten-thirty in the morning, and Kat fully expected to see her friend Diana had returned.

When she saw Miguel standing there, she stared in shock, wondering if her eyes were playing tricks on her. She blinked, but he didn't vanish. As she stared at him, she realized he looked as disheveled as she felt, indicating he must have been traveling all night. On one level she was glad to see him, but at the same time his timing couldn't have been worse.

"Miguel? How did you find me?" She didn't mean to sound ungracious, but lack of sleep made it difficult to think clearly. She was shocked to see him, but she couldn't deny she felt a warm glow at the knowledge that he'd come all this way to find her.

"I just missed you at Seville airport. I'm sorry we didn't get a chance to talk before you had to leave." He stared at her for a long moment as if trying to gauge her reaction. "May I come in?"

She smiled, although her eyes were gritty with lack of sleep. "Sure, but unfortunately, we're just getting ready to leave. Juliet has a doctor's appointment with a neurologist at Cambridge University Hospital." She stepped back, allowing him to come into her home. She frowned when she realized he didn't have so much as a suitcase with him.

For a moment her tired brain cells couldn't make sense of it all. Was Miguel planning to stay here with her? No, it made more sense that he must have left his luggage back in his hotel room.

"I think that is a good idea," Miguel was saying. "The doctors there will make sure she's really okay. Is she still confused?"

"A little. Not as bad as before, though."

"She probably just needs a little time." Miguel fell silent and she wondered what he was thinking as he glanced around her small home. After her mother had died, she had taken over the house payments and promised Juliet her half when she graduated from college.

"Maybe we can get together later on?" she suggested, glancing at the clock. If they didn't leave soon, they'd be late.

"I could stay here with Tomas, if you think that would help," Miguel offered.

She opened her mouth to refuse, even though going to the doctor's appointment would be much easier without dragging Tommy along. Tommy had only met Miguel twice and she couldn't bear to leave him with someone he probably still considered a stranger. "I don't know if that's such a good idea," she said slowly.

Glancing over her shoulder, she noticed Tommy hovering in the kitchen doorway, staring at Miguel with wide eyes. He wasn't crying, but he wasn't rushing over to greet Miguel either.

"Please?" Miguel asked. "I think he'll be fine. He doesn't seem afraid of me."

"Tommy, do you remember Mr. Vasquez?" she asked.

Tommy nodded, sticking his thumb in his mouth, something he only did when he was really tired. And suddenly, knowing that Tommy would probably fall asleep sooner than later, she made up her mind to take Miguel up on his offer.

"All right, you can stay here with Tommy. I would suggest you put a movie on for him as he's probably going to fall asleep soon. His days and nights are a little mixed up from the flight home."

Miguel's smile warmed her down to her toes. "I think I can manage that."

She forced herself to look away, trying not to think about the fact that Miguel was here for his son first and foremost. Obviously, Miguel wanted more time to get to know his son. But she couldn't help feeling a pang of resentment that Miguel was acting as if the night they'd spent together hadn't happened. "All right, we'll be back in a couple of hours."

Miguel helped her get Juliet out to the car, before going back inside. Leaving him in her house felt weird, but she kept her attention focused on her sister.

She could only manage one crisis at a time.

Kat was thrilled when Dr. Sandlow announced that Juliet's head injury seemed to be resolving without a problem. After a long exam, blood work and a follow-up CT scan of her head, he'd decided Juliet was stable enough not to be admitted. "I'd like to see her back in a week," he said. "And she also needs to start attending physical therapy three days a week."

She tried not to wince, wondering how in the world she'd be able to return to work while taking Juliet to therapy three days a week. She still had at least another week of vacation time saved up, but after that was gone, she'd need to apply for a leave of absence.

Time to worry more about that later.

The appointment had lasted longer than she'd anticipated, which was fine, except that they'd missed lunch. She stopped on the way home and picked up a bucket of fried chicken, mashed potatoes and coleslaw in case Miguel and Tommy were hungry too.

She parked her car in the driveway, rather than pulling into the garage, so that it was easier to maneuver Juliet out of the front passenger seat. She was somewhat surprised that Miguel didn't come out to help as she hooked her arms under Juliet's armpits to help her stand.

"Are you okay?" Kat asked, as she grabbed the crutches from where she'd propped them against the door.

"Fine," Juliet murmured, although her upper lip was beaded with sweat.

"Just a few more feet and you can rest, okay?" Moving around was obviously good for Juliet, but it was almost time for more pain medication. The way Juliet winced and groaned with every single swing of the crutches made Kat feel bad.

They managed to get into the house without incident and she immediately steered her sister towards the guest bedroom. Once Juliet was settled, she went back out to the main living area to look for Miguel and Tommy.

She found them on the sofa in the living room, both of them asleep. Miguel held Tommy close against his chest.

She stared at the two of them, father and son, feeling abruptly alone. The two had bonded while she'd been gone and Tommy clearly needed his father the same way Miguel needed him. She should be thrilled that they were together at last.

But she couldn't shake the sense of desolation. All this time she'd told herself she wanted a family. But she'd had a family, with Tommy and Juliet.

Now she was forced to realize what she really wanted was for Miguel to love her as much as she loved him. But did Miguel have the capability of loving her the way she wanted him to? Would he stick by her and Tommy not just in the good times but through the bad times as well?

Or would he leave the minute things got rough, just like her father?

CHAPTER FOURTEEN

MIGUEL felt a soft weight being lifted off his chest, and his arms tightened, instinctively holding on. He forced his eyes open and found Katerina leaning over him, her exquisite green eyes snapping with fury.

Confused, he tried to comprehend what he'd done to upset her. For a moment he didn't even remember he was in the U.S., until he glanced down to see Tomas was fast asleep on his chest. Abruptly all the memories tumbled to the surface.

"Let him go, Miguel. I need to put him down in his bed," Katerina said curtly. Still foggy with exhaustion, he released his hold so that she could lift their son into her arms. He instantly missed the warmth radiating from Tomas' soft body.

She disappeared from the living room and he used the few moments alone to pull himself together. How long had he been asleep? He couldn't remember.

With a guilty glance at the clock, he knew he'd slept longer than he should have. A part of him was disgusted that he'd wasted a good hour sleeping when he could have been making up for lost time with his son.

Although they would have plenty of time to get to know each other. Wouldn't they? On the long flight to the U.S. he'd finally realized that where he and Katerina lived wasn't important. Being together was all that mattered.

He kept waiting for the reality of his decision to sink in, but he didn't have the itchy feeling of wanting to leave. Was it possible that joining Doctors Without Borders really wasn't his dream?

Had it just been a way to escape?

He frowned and stretched in an effort to shake off his deep thoughts. Lifting his head, the distinct scent of fried chicken made him realize how hungry he was. He followed his nose into the kitchen.

There were bags of food lying haphazardly on the table, as if they'd been set down in a hurry. Before he could reach for one, Katerina returned.

"Tommy will be down soon, he wouldn't go back to sleep." Her slightly accusing gaze made him wonder if she believed that was his fault. Maybe it was. "We'll have lunch and then you'll need to leave, Miguel. I can't deal with you right now. I have Tommy and Juliet to care for."

He wanted to argue, but the lines of fatigue on her face tugged at his heart. She looked so exhausted he wanted to sweep her up and take her to bed. But, of course, he couldn't.

Somehow he'd thought she'd be happy to see him. But so far she'd seemed more annoyed. Had he misunderstood her feelings towards him? His heart squeezed in his chest.

He told himself to have patience, even though it wasn't easy. Tomas came running into the room and he helped Katerina pull out the fried chicken, mashed potatoes and coleslaw. He noticed that she made sure

Tomas had some food on his plate and that she made a plate for her sister, before worrying about eating anything herself.

"I'll be right back," she murmured, taking the food down the hall towards a small bedroom. He felt guilty all over again, knowing that Katerina had managed to get Juliet inside without his assistance.

He watched Tomas eat, determined to wait for Katerina. She returned quickly enough, dropping into a chair across from him.

"How is she?" he asked.

"Sleeping. Dr. Sandlow said she's fine, though. She needs to start physical therapy three times a week. I'll help her with her lunch later." She took a healthy bite of her chicken, and then seemed to notice he hadn't eaten. "Don't you like fried chicken?" she asked.

"Of course. Who doesn't?" He flashed a reassuring smile before turning his attention to his own plate. He wanted to help her, but sensed he was treading on thin ice. For some reason, she'd been angry with him for falling asleep. Either because she thought he'd put Tomas in danger, or because he'd slept when she couldn't. Or maybe because he'd made himself at home. Regardless, he knew he could help ease her burden by staying, if she'd let him.

"Lean over your plate, Tommy," she said gently when pieces of fried chicken dropped from his mouth and hit the floor. "Don't make a mess."

"No mess," Tomas said with his mouth full.

"Is the shopping mall still located a few miles from the hospital?" he asked. "I need to purchase clothes and toiletries."

She frowned. "Did the airline lose your luggage?"

"No. I didn't bring anything except my passport. I was racing to catch up with you and Tomas. As you'd already boarded the plane, they wouldn't let me talk to you. I ended up going through London to get here."

She looked shocked to hear he'd followed her. After several long moments she finished her meal and sat back in her chair. "Yes," she murmured. "The shopping mall is still there."

"Katerina, we need to talk." He glanced at Tomas, who was starting to wiggle around in his booster chair. He was tempted to smile at how their son had smeared mashed potatoes and gravy all over himself.

"Not now. As I said, I have other things to worry about at the moment. Tommy needs a bath and then I need to care for my sister. I'm sorry, but I'm afraid you'll have to wait until I get things caught up around here." She stood and picked up Tommy. "Goodbye, Miguel."

She turned and left, no doubt intending to give Tomas a bath. He wanted nothing more than to help, but she'd made her wishes very clear.

With a sigh he pushed away from the table and began clearing the dirty dishes, storing the leftovers in the fridge. Maybe she wanted him gone, but he wasn't about to leave this mess for her. Not when she looked like she was dead on her feet.

He wanted to believe that Katerina was just tired and jet-lagged, that she didn't mean what she'd said.

But since he'd arrived, she hadn't given any indication of wanting to pick up their relationship where they'd left off. If not for his brother going missing, they would have had time to talk. To plan. Surely there was a way to make this work? Surely Katerina felt something for him?

So why was he feeling as if she wished he hadn't come to the U.S.?

As he washed and dried the dishes, he racked his brain for a way to bridge the gap that had somehow widened between them.

Because if she thought he was giving up that easily, she was dead wrong.

Kat ran warm water and bubble bath into the tub for Tommy, knowing she'd been unfair to Miguel. He'd come all this way, had actually followed her to the airport in Seville, flying all night, only to have her demand that he leave. She hadn't even asked about Luis.

She set Tommy into the tub, kneeling alongside to keep a close eye on him. Tommy played in the water, splashing bubbles everywhere. She was so exhausted, so emotionally drained that she didn't even notice bubbles had landed on her hair.

She'd been badly shaken by the sight of Miguel holding Tommy, both of them looking adorable as they'd slept. She was a terrible mother to be jealous, even for an instant, of her son's love for his father. And the sad truth was that Tommy didn't even know that Miguel was his father yet.

But he would, soon.

For a moment she rested her forehead on the smooth, cool porcelain of the tub. She should be glad Miguel wanted to be a part of Tommy's life. She should be glad that he'd come here to Cambridge, rather than asking her to consider moving to Seville.

Yet, she couldn't help wishing that they would have

time alone, to explore the passion that simmered between them. She knew Miguel wanted her, but she didn't know if there was any way he'd ever come to love her. She felt confused and exhausted.

She had her sister to care for, and Tommy too. And soon she'd have to go back to work. There wouldn't be time for her and Miguel to renew their relationship. But there would be plenty of time for him to establish a relationship with his son.

She lifted her head, instantly ashamed of herself for being selfish. Her son was what mattered, not her own ridiculous feelings. Giving her head a shake to clear the troublesome thoughts, she quickly washed Tommy's hair and then pulled him out of the water, engulfing his slippery body in a thick, fluffy towel.

After getting Tommy dressed in clean clothes, and straightening out her own disheveled appearance, she went back out to the kitchen, half-afraid Miguel would still be there. He wasn't, but she was pleasantly surprised to find her kitchen was spotless, every bit of mess cleaned up, including the floor around Tommy's booster chair.

His kind thoughtfulness only made her feel more miserable for her earlier abruptness. Was it too late to catch up to him? She almost headed for the door when she heard thumping noises coming from Juliet's room. Juliet was up, trying to navigate with her crutches, leaving her no choice but to hurry down to help her sister.

Forcing her to push thoughts of Miguel firmly out of her mind.

An entire twenty-four hours went by without any word or visit from Miguel. Kat should have been relieved to have one less thing to deal with, but instead she was on edge. Had something happened to him? Had he decided she was too much of a witch to deal with? Had he decided to return to Spain after all?

She still didn't know his phone number, or if his cellphone from Spain would even work here in the U.S. She felt much better after getting a good night's sleep and was pleased to note that Juliet was also doing better every day.

Getting her sister to therapy wasn't too bad, especially as Juliet insisted on doing things for herself. There was a truce between them, a closeness that hadn't been there before Juliet had left to study abroad. Kat hoped that this terrible accident would bring them closer together.

"Where's that Spanish doctor?" Juliet asked, when they'd returned from therapy.

Kat shrugged. "I'm not sure. Why?"

"Come on, sis, you're not fooling me. He's obviously Tommy's father. And you love him, don't you?"

She wanted to protest, but really what was the point? "My feelings don't matter as he doesn't feel the same way."

Juliet stared at her for a long moment. "You never asked me what happened. I mean, how I ended up getting hit by a car."

Kat pulled up a chair to sit beside her sister's bed. "Jules, you were in the I.C.U. on a ventilator when I came to visit. And by the time you'd recovered, you were confused and told me you couldn't remember. Has that changed? Do you remember what happened?"

Juliet took a deep breath and let it out slowly. "I fell in love with a guy named Enrique. He was much older and so mature. I never told him how I felt, but I thought we had this great connection. Until I found him with another woman."

Kat sucked in a harsh breath. After having both of their fathers leave their mother, she knew that would be the worst betrayal of all. "Oh, Jules…"

"I was so upset I started crying and ran into the road." Juliet shrugged. "Thankfully, I don't remember much after that."

"I'm so sorry." Kat reached out and took her sister's hand. "I'm sure that was really difficult for you to see him with someone else."

"Yes, it was. After the way my dad left, I spend half my time waiting for the guy I'm dating to show his true colors. But now I wonder if I just liked Enrique because he was safe. I think I've been avoiding relationships, Kat. Because of our fathers."

Kat tried to follow her sister's logic. "But you just said you fell for Enrique. Wasn't that a relationship?"

"Not really. He was older and friendly with me. But it wasn't like we even kissed or anything. There was another guy who liked me, who was closer to my age, but I avoided him. I told myself it was because I liked Enrique, but the truth of the matter was that I was avoiding being hurt." Juliet tightened her grip around Kat's fingers. "Don't do that, Kat. Don't avoid Miguel because you don't want to get hurt."

Juliet's words struck a chord deep inside. For someone so much younger, Juliet had great insight. "It's more complicated than that, Jules. He's Tommy's father. We have to get along, for his sake."

"Tell him how you feel," Juliet insisted. "Don't let your pride or fear get in the way."

Was her sister right? Had she avoided talking on a personal level with Miguel because she was afraid of being hurt? They'd never really talked about their joint custody arrangement because she'd avoided the topic. The realization made her wince.

Maybe her sister was right. "Get some rest Jules, okay?" she said, changing the subject. "We'll eat around six o'clock. I have a pot roast in the slow cooker for dinner."

"Okay," Juliet murmured, closing her eyes.

Kat left her sister's room to head for the kitchen. She was surprised to hear the sound of voices.

"Meegl," Tommy shouted and it took her a minute to figure out that it was a mangled version of Miguel.

"Tomas!" Miguel responded, and she entered the kitchen in time to see her son launch himself at his father. Miguel laughed and clasped Tommy close, looking dangerously attractive wearing casual clothes, jeans and a long-sleeved denim shirt. "I've missed you," he said, nuzzling Tommy's neck.

"Me too," her son said, hugging him.

For a moment, seeing the two of them together, father and son, made her want to cry. But then Miguel lifted his head and caught her gaze, with such intensity she could barely breathe. "Hi, Miguel," she said inanely.

"Katerina," he murmured, and for a moment she thought she saw frank desire in his gaze, before he bent over to set Tommy back on his feet. "Would you allow me to take you out for dinner this evening?"

"I'm sorry, I would but I don't have a babysitter," she said, tearing her gaze from his. She figured that he wanted to finalize their co-custody agreement and was determined not to continue avoiding the topic.

Thankfully, she felt better prepared now after a good night's sleep. She forced a smile. "I have a pot roast in the slow cooker if you want to stay."

"Diana said she'd come over to babysit. And she's more than capable of watching over Juliet as well." He took a step toward her, holding out his hand. "Please?"

He'd called Diana? She could hardly hide her surprise. And now that he'd taken that excuse away, she couldn't think of a reason to refuse. "All right," she agreed. "But I need some time to change."

"I'll wait," he said.

The next few hours flew by as she showered, changed and then greeted Diana, who seemed glad to be back on American soil. As Miguel held the door of his rental car open for her, she felt a bit like a girl going out on her first date.

"Are you sure you know how to drive?" she asked, as he slid behind the wheel. "Maybe you should have brought Fernando here with you."

His teeth flashed in a broad smile. "Fernando is taking over the Vasquez olive farm. Believe it or not, my brother Luis has decided he wants to build things, instead of being a farmer."

"So he's okay, then?" she asked. "You found him all right?"

"He's fine. He was afraid to tell me how much he hated the farm." For a moment a dark shadow crossed his face, but then it was gone. "I'm convinced he's going to be fine now that he's following his dream."

Dread knotted her stomach, and she had the most insane feeling he was about to tell her he was going to follow his own dream. His dream of joining Doctors Without Borders. "I'm glad," she said in a choked tone.

He slanted a glance in her direction as he pulled into the driveway of a well-known hotel located mere blocks from her house. "I hope you don't mind if we have a quiet dinner here?"

"Of course not."

He led the way inside to the fancy restaurant located just off the hotel lobby. There weren't too many people dining, but it didn't matter as they were led to a small quiet table in the back.

Miguel treated her courteously, holding her chair for her and then asking what she'd like to drink. They started with a light appetizer and a bottle of Shiraz.

"Katerina," he said, reaching over to take her hand. "I have something very important to ask you."

She felt surprisingly calm, despite knowing they were about to settle their future joint custody arrangement once and for all. Her sister's advice echoed in her mind.

"Yes, Miguel?" She took a sip of her wine and carefully set it down.

In a flash he was out of his seat and kneeling in front of her chair. She stared at him in shock when he flipped open a small black velvet ring box, revealing a large diamond ring. "Katerina, will you marry me?"

For a moment her heart soared and she wanted to shout yes at the top of her lungs.

Except he hadn't said anything about love.

"Miguel, we don't have to get married," she said, tearing her gaze away and wishing she'd ordered something stronger than wine. "We'll work something out so that we'll both be actively involved in Tommy's life. I'll even consider moving to Seville, after Juliet is better, if that's what you want. You don't have to do this."

He never moved, still kneeling before her, his gaze steadily holding hers. "Katerina, I love you. I was foolish to leave you four and a half years ago. I let my mother's bitterness affect my outlook on life. It's true that I want to be a part of my son's life, but that's not why I'm asking you to marry me. I'm asking because I can't imagine my life without you."

She felt her jaw drop open in shocked surprise. She wanted so badly to believe him. Trusting men wasn't easy for her, but wasn't this what she'd secretly wanted? She couldn't allow her mother's tragic life to affect her ability to find happiness.

"Miguel, are you sure? Because there's no rush. Besides, I thought you always wanted to work with Doctors Without Borders? I don't want you resent us at some future point because you didn't get to follow your dream."

"My dream isn't to join Doctors Without Borders any more," he said. "It pains me to say this, but I realize now I've been partly using that dream to avoid getting close to anyone. Until I met you. I've fallen in love with you, Katerina. And I don't care where we live, here or Seville, it doesn't matter. Nothing matters except you and our son. And any other children we decide to have."

He loved her? She wanted so badly to believe him. Her small sliver of doubt faded when she saw the pure emotion shining from his dark eyes. And somehow she managed to find the courage to open her heart to him. "Yes, Miguel," she murmured huskily. "I will marry you. Because I love you, too. And I can't imagine my life without you either." She felt wonderful saying the words, knowing deep in her heart that they were true.

"*Te amo,* Katerina," he murmured, taking out the

ring and slowly sliding the band over the fourth finger of her left hand. She barely had time to enjoy the sparkle when he stood and then drew her to her feet before pulling her gently into his arms. He kissed her, gently at first and then with such passion she almost forgot they weren't alone.

He gently pulled back, simply staring down at her for a long moment. "I love you, so much, Katerina," he whispered. "I promise to show you just how much I love you every day for the rest of our lives."

"I love you, too, Miguel." She lifted up on tiptoe to kiss him again, ignoring the waiters and waitresses clapping in the background. "And I want Tommy to have at least one brother and one sister."

He laughed. "Anything you say," he agreed huskily, before kissing her again.

As she clung to his shoulders, reveling in the kiss, she realized that with a little faith and love…dreams really could come true.

EPILOGUE

MIGUEL was pleased and humbled that Katerina had wanted to be married in Seville. He stood at the front of the church, amazed at how crowded it was. Apparently everyone in Seville wanted to be there to share in their wedding. Juliet was there too, standing as Katerina's maid of honor. She was fully recovered now from her accident and was determined to finish her semester abroad. His brother Luis hadn't touched a drop of alcohol since selling the farm, and he stood straight and tall next to Miguel as his best man.

There were many friends and family in the church, some even having come all the way from the U.S. to be there. And he couldn't help smiling when he saw Pedro sitting near the front, wearing his Sunday best, craning his neck to get a glimpse of the bride.

When the music began, the first one to walk down the aisle was Tomas. Miguel grinned when his son walked slowly as if afraid he might drop the small satin pillow holding their wedding bands. When Tomas reached the front of the church, Luis stepped forward and took the rings. Miguel put a hand on his son's shoulder, keeping him at his side.

"Hi, Daddy," Tomas said in a loud whisper. "I didn't drop them."

"Good boy," he whispered back.

Juliet was next, walking with only the slightest bit of a limp, hardly noticeable to anyone except him.

And then Katerina stepped forward, so beautiful his chest ached. The entire church went silent with awe, but when she caught his gaze and smiled, the love shining from her eyes made him catch his breath. He forced himself to stay right where he was when he wanted very badly to rush forward to greet her.

They had two priests, one who spoke English for Katerina, even though she was already broadening her knowledge of the Spanish language.

"Mama's beautiful, isn't she?" Tomas said again, in a loud whisper.

"Very beautiful," Miguel agreed. "Be quiet now, Tomas, okay?"

"Okay," he agreed, nodding vigorously. When Katerina reached his side, he took her hand in his and together they turned to face the two priests.

As anxious he was to have Katerina become his wife, he planned to enjoy every moment of this day, the first day of their new life, together.

* * * * *

& *A sneaky peek at next month...*

Medical Romance

CAPTIVATING MEDICAL DRAMA—WITH HEART

My wish list for next month's titles...

In stores from 4th January 2013:

☐ The Surgeon's Doorstep Baby – Marion Lennox

& Dare She Dream of Forever? – Lucy Clark

☐ Craving Her Soldier's Touch – Wendy S. Marcus

& Secrets of a Shy Socialite – Wendy S. Marcus

☐ Breaking the Playboy's Rules – Emily Forbes

& Hot-Shot Doc Comes to Town – Susan Carlisle

Available at WHSmith, Tesco, Asda, Eason, Amazon and Apple

Just can't wait?

Visit us Online

You can buy our books online a month before they hit the shops! **www.millsandboon.co.uk**

1212/03